DREAMS
OF A
DRAGON GIRL

DREAMS OF A DRAGON GIRL

DRAGON DESCENDANTS OF DRAKKOIA
BOOK 1

BONNIE JACOBY

COSMICDRAGON PRESS

Dreams of a Dragon Girl
Dragon Descendants of Drakkoia – Book 1

Copyright © 2023 by Bonnie Jacoby

Published by CosmicDragon Press
Cover design by MoorBooks Design

This is a work of fiction. All the characters, organizations, places, and events are a product of the author's imagination and any resemblance to actual persons (living or deceased), places, or events is coincidental.

1st Paperback edition: March 2023

eBook ISBN: 978-1-7387974-1-7
Paperback ISBN: 978-1-7387974-0-0

To the dreamers.
Anything is possible if you
believe in yourself.

DRAKKOIA
The Source
Jason's Keep
Sanctuary
Dragon Mountain Range
Valley Keep
Chartsend
Klaw Keep
gon Treasury
Nightwood Hollow
Thoran Sea
Plague Bog
Deepwater Cove
Buling Coast
Dragon Library
Cromwell
N
W
E
S

EXPECTATIONS
BECCA

Becca loved dragons. Not the plague-riddled beasts of history who were exterminated long ago. No. Her heart belonged to the heroes from her grandfather's stories. Intelligent creatures with complex relationships who explored the world and helped those in need.

She bit her lip as she finished scribing Zanthor's amusing first flight into her journal. One day, sooner than she could bear, these stories would be all she'd have left of Grandfa. With a sigh, she closed the journal and tucked it into her satchel, unwilling to dwell on a future without her grandfather.

After grabbing her cloak from the hook by the front door, Becca left the house as silently as possible. If her mother caught her, she'd have to get her siblings up, and she'd be late. Master Frederick needed her help at the schoolhouse before the other students arrived. He'd barely made it through the lessons the day before.

Sunlight reflected off the rivulets of melting snow as she strode along the cobbled streets of Chartsend. A strange heat wave settled in two days ago, and by noon, it would be hotter than a midsummer day. The unseasonable weather during what should've been the coldest part of winter put everyone on edge. The more superstitious villagers claimed it was a bad omen.

As she approached the Randal farm, Becca's heart lifted. For once, the dirt road was empty. No one to heckle her about her height or her red hair. Now there was a good omen. Something more tangible than a little sunlight.

Heat blasted her face as she entered the single-room schoolhouse. Master Frederick shuffled between the wooden desks, placing a single sheet of lined paper and a sharpened pencil on each one, preparing for the day.

"Healer's blessings."

Even though pain filled his tired eyes, he managed a smile. For her.

"Here. Let me finish. You sit." The winter had not been kind to the eldest member of their village. At fifty-five, he'd held the position of Elder for five years, longer than anyone in the past. He'd been healthy, despite his age, but in the past two days, migraines had stolen his vigor.

His frail body shook as she helped him to his chair in front of the fire he'd insisted on lighting, despite the hot weather.

"Thank the Healer you've come early, Becca. I thought I was better today. But ..." He flapped his hand, then let it fall on his knee.

Her heart ached for him. Teaching was his life.

"You have to take over. I just can't do this anymore." His words wrapped a chain around her neck.

Everyone wanted her to be something. A lady. A dutiful daughter. And now a teacher. No one had offered to help in the classroom. The task had fallen on her. She didn't mind teaching once in a while, but taking his place wasn't an option. She was only fifteen. There was a whole world to explore, and her isolated village was stuck in the past.

"I'll take over today. But I'm sure the weather will let up and things will go back to how they should be." They had to. If she became the village teacher, her life would stop. But she couldn't tell him that.

He patted her hand. "Nothing ever goes back. Life and time move forward. Always."

After she set up the math test, Becca helped him to his cottage behind the schoolhouse and closed his shutters so the light wouldn't exacerbate his pain. His snores filled the tiny room before she closed the door.

She returned to the schoolhouse, smothered the fire, opened the windows, and looked over the lesson book. The little ones would be easy. But the older students wouldn't like her telling them what to do. Especially Nathan Randal. Just a few months older than her, he could do no wrong, at least in her mother's eyes.

Becca pushed her shoulders back. It wasn't as if Nathan ever offered to help. If she stuck to the lesson plan, he couldn't object. But that was a foolish dream. She may as well wish for dragons to return.

SOURCE LAKE
GREGOR

DAY 1 AFTER THE LONG SLEEP

Dragons don't dream.

But Gregor was trapped in a world that couldn't be real. He flapped his wings, catching a warm thermal, and flew through an impossibly brilliant blue sky. Cirrus clouds lurked in the distance, black instead of white. Faint rainbows rippled through the wisps, making them appear more fluid than mist.

It must be a magical vision.

He was no Seer, but he lay within the Source, a lake filled with the world's magic, so anything was possible. He reached out to the minds of the hundred and twenty-eight dragons that made up his coven. They all slept at the bottom of the long lake. But no one was awake to give him an answer.

He couldn't sense the water he knew surrounded him. Instead, the smooth glide of wind over his wings felt all too real. Magic wanted to show him something.

Nutmeg, a human spice, filled his nostrils, his power trying to tell him something important. He tilted his left wing and followed the scent.

Ever since his power had manifested a year ago, shortly after he turned sixteen, his sense of smell guided him. Magical scents warned him of danger, and other times they led him to safety.

When a magical plague infected his coven, a powerful scent warned him, and he fled and survived. His new coven had imposed a strict quarantine to keep them safe. But when Seri, another youngling like him, had learned about the Source lake, she'd convinced the leader that magic was the only way to protect them.

Gregor had followed the tantalizing odor of lilac to the lake. The coven had followed him, the youngest dragon at seventeen, despite the elder dragons' protests. He hoped he'd done the right thing and hadn't led them all to their deaths.

Maybe that's what this was.

Death.

Not a vision.

The scent of nutmeg filled his mind, replacing his fear and pulling him through the sky. He had no control over his path.

The scent was all that mattered.

Below him, a village huddled against the southern slope of the Dragon Mountain Range. Humans scurried about, busy with whatever it was they did. Their clothing was different, not the familiar shades of brown and green. Bold colors mixed with flashes of crisp white, weaving in and out in chaotic patterns.

A young girl with a crown of flames looked up and radiated waves of joy. The intensity of her emotion knocked him back a wingspan.

No human could send thoughts over such a great distance.

Gregor flew closer.

Nutmeg, sweet and enticing.

What did it mean? If he were a Seer, the vision would provide answers. But he wasn't, and his own power caused him more frustration than certainty.

The scent dissipated in the wind, done with him. Ominous clouds consumed the village and spread across the sky, black tendrils reaching for him in the last remaining patch of blue. Clouds couldn't hurt him, but he couldn't shake the dread that filled his chest.

His wing strokes were sluggish, as if encased in water.

He snorted, and bubbles rose from his snout. The sky bulged, and a loud plop resounded through the world. Ripples spread from the distortion. Clouds crashed together, turning the sky pitch-black.

Fear crashed through his heart. He couldn't breathe. He couldn't move.

A tangle of oily threads coiled around him, and death dove through his nostrils.

Gregor choked on water. The vision was gone, and he was back in reality, at the bottom of the lake. Even though dragons could breathe underwater for days, his lungs screamed for air as water pressure held him captive.

He was drowning.

With a powerful thrust of his legs, he pushed off the ground. Exhaustion pulled him down, his wings unable to open and aid his ascent. He kicked frantically, parting the water with his talons, and swam toward the light above.

He burst through the lake's surface and coughed out the water in his lungs.

Gregor gulped in a huge breath, releasing the pain in his chest. His gasp echoed. He swam to shore, his muscles shaking, until he collapsed onto the ice-covered bank. The water in his nostrils froze as his eyes adjusted to the brightness, but he couldn't move. Not yet. He hadn't felt this weak since the morning he hatched.

Blinding light bounced off towering walls of ice. Stalactites glittered above him, dripping into the lake. Plop. The sound echoed through the cavern, bringing back those last moments of the vision. Before he couldn't breathe.

Gregor sat, confused by the lake's transformation. Black water rippled, hiding the depths, and rainbows danced along the surface.

Some of the vision had been real. But it wasn't the sky he'd seen. It was the lake.

The other dragons' heartbeats pulsed through his mind, steadying him. They slept. Alive.

Which meant they'd done it. They'd absorbed the Source's magic and could return to their keep, protected from the plague. They could save the other dragons. At least that was Seri's theory. One year older than him, she'd spent her entire life studying magic. But even she didn't know how magic would protect them.

The strange water and the cavern of ice encasing the lake mocked him. The glow of magic was gone, and it would've taken many years for snow and ice to form the cavern. When they'd arrived, the lake had been open to the sky, magic keeping it from freezing in the icy north. The coven had slept much longer than the week or two they'd expected.

Doubt throbbed through his skull, clamping his jaw shut. He'd been wrong to follow the scent of lilac. Wrong to lead the coven here, possibly trapped in visions and unable to break free.

Gregor shook his head. The Source had messed with his mind, but it hadn't killed him. And it wouldn't kill the other dragons. He pushed himself upright and stood.

He wobbled with his first step, stretching his tail for balance. His wings quivered, as if he'd flown through a tornado. Folding them tightly along his back, he stumbled to the cavern wall and gouged the ice with his talons. It took more effort than it should to create an angled path to the surface, as if the Source had stolen his strength.

No. He'd slept longer than planned, and he'd almost drowned. Even a dragon was allowed to be weak for a moment. It had nothing to do with him being the youngest and the smallest.

Gregor finally broke free of the cavern and roared, the snow-covered mountains echoing his cry of success. He was alone. No one would reprimand him for his youngling ways.

He climbed on top of the ice enclosing the eerie lake. The air was crisp. No taint of the plague that had sent them there. The wind blew cool against his skin, but not freezing.

With a deep breath, he tapped into his power and stretched his sense of smell beyond any normal dragon ability, searching for a scent, a sign they were safe.

Nothing.

Shock reverberated through his body like a lightning strike. He couldn't smell the lilac scent that had drawn him there. But even worse, he couldn't smell the forests surrounding him.

Gregor shoved away his panic. His time in the Source lake had weakened him. That was all.

He sniffed again, freeing his mind of concern.

The wind carried a chill and a warmth, a hint of grass and leaves. Relief strengthened his spine.

He could sense small animals hiding in their dens. Wind brushed over his hide. All his dragon senses tingled as they returned, just like the strength in his legs and wings. Satisfied, he concentrated. The energies were clear of the stink of death.

But something was missing. A scent that had always been there. A comforting spicy odor every dragon knew as well as their mind. The spicy-sweet scent of magic.

Panic stole three beats from his heart. Impossible. For the briefest moment, Gregor wanted to crawl back into the lake and sleep. If he woke again, the world would return to normal. Maybe this was another vision. Because this couldn't happen.

He dove through the hole and stood next to the lake. This was the source of magic. He'd even experienced a vision. Magic must still exist. Seri would know. It was time to wake his family. Together, they could face anything.

Gregor spoke to every dragon mind. *"Wake, my brothers and sisters. It's time to return home."*

Dragons burst from the lake, filling the cavern with roars that pulsed through the ice ceiling and echoed through the mountains like thunder.

Anger. Fear. Grief.

Dragon energy released into the world.

THUNDER
BECCA

It was almost four o'clock by the time Becca closed the schoolhouse door. The sky was clear of any clouds, which surprised her, as thunder had rumbled from the mountains all day.

Her steps faltered as she looked down the road. Nathan lounged against the wooden fence enclosing the Randal farm, along with three younger boys. His band of sheep. From the sneer on his lips, she knew he wanted revenge.

It wasn't her fault he'd gotten the easiest question on the math test wrong. The other students had giggled when she corrected him, and for once, she'd felt like she had the power in the room. She hadn't meant to explain his error so loudly, and she realized her mistake as soon as his face turned red.

"Dragon girl. Dragon girl." Nathan's annoying baritone colored the insult with contempt.

And there it was. The taunt that had grown old years ago. Earned after her five-year-old self had proudly told her classmates she would be a dragon rider when she grew up. It was then that she'd learned about real dragons and how they'd been exterminated to stop the Dragon Plague.

She clutched her dragon journal against her chest. If Nathan read it, he'd never leave her alone. She'd kept her love of dragons a secret, pretending his nickname didn't bother her.

"Dragon girl, fetch some water," Nathan commanded. The other boys chuckled, encouraging him. He thought he was so clever, but he needed to grow up and move on.

A choked laugh made her look up. Marcus? He'd never mock her about dragons. But it was him.

Marcus blushed when their eyes met. "Leave her be." His gruff, half-hearted attempt only made her feel worse. He used to be her best friend, before last summer. Before everything changed. Ever since Nathan's pretty cousin, Isobel, came to visit, Marcus had acted as if they barely knew each other, tossing away the friendship they'd started as toddlers.

Thunder crashed through her skull, not the usual rock-tumble, but more like the roars she imagined dragons would make when they fought. The air crackled with suppressed energy, and Becca's lips tingled.

"Come on, dragon girl. Clean up the shit." Nathan's voice broke as he tried to contain his mirth. He lacked imagination. What made him think a dragon rider would be a drudge to command? They'd probably had judgmental people like Nathan to muck out stalls.

The barrow full of chicken manure lay on its side, spilling its putrid contents across the road. But he wasn't as clever as he thought. She slipped easily between the mess and the fence, treading carefully around the open gate.

Something wet and hard smacked into the back of her head, and her journal flew from her grasp. Mud and snow dripped down her curly red hair and trickled under the collar of her coat. The journal pages immediately soaked up the runoff. Becca blinked away tears as she bent to retrieve it. The boys howled like wolves.

Marcus ran up and took the book from her trembling fingers.

"Aw, Becks." He wiped the leather cover with a handful of snow.

She couldn't handle his fake sympathy. "Leave it. Go back to being one of Nathan's sheep." The journal was ruined, her head hurt, and she hoped it was only mud in her hair.

She snatched her precious book from his hands and lost her balance, slipping on a patch of ice.

Marcus reached for her, but it was too late. She crashed into the gate, scratching her cheek on an exposed nail. Pain brought more tears to her eyes as she landed with a pathetic squeak.

Nathan hooted with uncontrolled laughter.

Heat infused Becca's face as she struggled to stand up. Marcus offered his hand, but she smacked it away. His hurt look was almost enough to change her mind. But she could stand by herself.

Becca swallowed her futile tears as she brushed furiously at the mud soaking through her skirt. The last thing she wanted was for Nathan to see he'd succeeded.

"Oh crap, Becca. You're bleeding." Marcus touched her face.

She jerked away. "Leave me alone. I don't need your help."

Thunder rolled overhead, loud enough to rattle her teeth, but Marcus didn't seem to hear anything.

"That's right. Don't help her, Marcus. You'll end up as crazy as her grandfather." Nathan's mocking laugh rang out. "He's a drunk, spewing nonsense about heroic dragons. They were monsters who deserved to die. We should treat him like a rabid dog and put him down before he becomes an Elder and infects the whole village."

Somehow, Becca knew it was more than taunts and strange weather. Nathan despised her grandfather.

A beastly roar reverberated through her mind, no longer resembling thunder at all.

Anger. Fear. Grief.

Emotions flew at her, tossing her mind like a sparrow in a windstorm. She covered her ears and squeezed her eyes shut. But they kept coming, drowning out her sense of self. She couldn't tell where they came from, only that hundreds of hearts felt them.

She swayed and reached for the fence, anything to center herself in the real world. Her hand encountered the solidness of a hard chest, and her eyes flew open.

Nathan loomed over her and grabbed her shoulders. When had he reached her, and where was Marcus?

"Are you a dog, too, Red?" he taunted in her ear.

His words made no sense, but fear clutched her heart. She lurched sideways, trying to break free of his grasp.

With a possessive chuckle, Nathan stroked the cut on her cheek. "I can cure you."

His desire filled her mind, and dread pooled in her stomach. This was worse than his taunts. So much worse.

With a shudder, Becca tried again to pull away, but his fingers dug into her arm. Claiming her.

Guilt emanated from Marcus. What was happening to her? How could she know what he felt?

A choked sob escaped from her throat.

With a low growl, Nathan yanked her against his chest.

"Let her go." Marcus's voice held a warning, and his protectiveness washed over her. A raft in the storm.

Nathan glared at Marcus. "Go away. This is between Red and me."

Hope filled Becca's heart ... and then died at the sheepish look in Marcus's eyes. He turned away, and pain lanced through her. He was abandoning her. She didn't need his shame, but the emotion bored into her brain.

Becca couldn't take anymore. Not Marcus and his guilt, or Nathan and his twisted possessiveness. Not her own pain. Not anything.

It had to stop. Rage filled her, overruling her thoughts. Her focus narrowed on Nathan. If he'd left her alone, none of this would've happened.

She slammed her hands against Nathan's chest.

He stumbled back, a look of surprise on his face, and slipped on the ice. He fell face-first into the manure. Before he could recover, she leapt on his back and pounded it, over and over, releasing all the unwanted emotions with each hit.

It was hours. It was seconds. Becca lost track of time. Until a strident, feminine voice broke through her anger.

"What in the world, Rebecca Kinsley!" Nathan's mother dug her fingernails into the soft flesh of Becca's upper arm and yanked her upright.

Every single unwanted emotion drained from Becca.

Alice Randal shook Becca so hard her teeth crashed together. "Brawling in the mud. That's no way for a young lady of fifteen to behave."

Humiliation surged through Becca, and tears blurred her vision. She freed her arm and muttered, "Sorry," desperate to escape before a single tear could fall.

What had possessed her? She'd never hit anyone in her life.

The stupid boys bleated like sheep as she fled. Nathan's smirk seared into her brain. Her attack hadn't even hurt him.

Marcus stepped into her path, but she brushed past him, refusing to meet his gaze. Nothing he said would make her forgive him.

Tears poured down her cheeks as she darted past the blacksmith to the lane behind the shops. How could she lose control like that? She bit her lip as she ran, but a sob broke free. And another one.

She shouldn't be able to sense other people's emotions. It was impossible.

COMFORT
BECCA

Thunder chased Becca as she ran into the gray river-stone house behind the town hall and slammed the door. She leaned against the solid wood and gulped in deep breaths. What had she done?

A deep sigh from Grandfa's bedroom made her lurch away from the door.

"Late again?" Resignation colored Grandfa's voice. The wooden chair creaked as he pushed his solid frame up and walked into the hall. He frowned as he took in the cut on her cheek and the mud on her skirt. "What happened this time?"

Becca flung herself into his comforting embrace. She leaned her head against his neck and absorbed his warmth and strength for a few minutes before she pulled away.

Love rolled through her, washing away the rage, but not her guilt. Her lips quivered. He wouldn't feel the same once he heard what happened. She still couldn't believe it. She'd never hit anyone. Ever. But Nathan's taunts still rang in her ears, and his spite still haunted her.

"Come now. Let's get you cleaned up before your mother sees you. She'll have a fit."

Becca sighed. Her mother was always disappointed with her.

Grandfa's room was at the end of the hall, too small for such a tall man. Just a narrow wooden bed, covered with a green log-cabin quilt, a leather stool in the corner, and a row of wooden shelves. The scent of whiskey and old cigars infused the room.

She sat on the lumpy mattress as he pulled out his traveler's healer kit. Grandfa didn't travel with the hunters anymore, but he maintained his kit. His calmness settled over her, insulating her from the emotional turmoil still shuddering through her body.

Grandfa held her face in his work-roughened hand and dabbed her cheek, his touch gentle. She wrinkled her nose against the astringent smell of the healer paste. If Mama were tending to her, she'd be scrubbing the injury away while admonishing Becca loudly and at length about how a lady should behave.

Once Grandfa finished, he reached for her hands. "How did this happen?" His cheeks puffed out as he examined the swollen edges of her palms. "It looks like you hit something."

Becca tugged free. She'd lost control. It was too hard to explain about the onslaught of emotions. She felt nothing now, except her own shame.

"Wash up, then come tell me what happened."

She slid off the bed and washed her hands in the small metal basin. She loved the scent of his soap, like freshly cut wood. Her mother's soap was supposed to smell like some foreign flower from the southern deserts, but it always stung and made her hands red.

After she climbed back onto the bed, Grandfa looped his left foot efficiently under the bottom rung of his stool and sat.

"You're lucky that cut doesn't need stitching. The paste will do."

Becca winced as Grandfa rubbed cream into her hands. Bruises were already forming along the edges.

Grandfa lifted her chin and captured her gaze. She tried to look away, but the slight pressure of his fingers warned her he wouldn't put up with her avoidance.

"All better?"

"Yes," she whispered, but it wasn't. Something was wrong with her, and a little cream couldn't fix it.

"What happened? Were the boys teasing Mutt? Or picking on Lizzy?"

Becca shook her head. Mutt was the blacksmith's old blind dog. Some younger kids thought it was fun to tie branches to his tail. They usually ran off when she scolded them, but they'd thrown a rock or two over the years. And Lizzy was an innocent twenty-two-year-old lady stuck with the mind of a four-year-old. The villagers thought she was a witch who'd been normal until she'd cast a spell and lost her mind. At least once a week, Becca disabled the traps set on Lizzy's front door, not always without injury.

With a sigh, Becca hid her hands in her lap. Her mother was certain to hear about it from Mrs. Randal. And then Grandfa would blame himself. He always did.

"Becca. You can tell me. You're a warrior, a defender of the innocent. It's in your blood. You care about others, and it's your strength, but it gets you into trouble. Despite your height, you're still a sapling, and you'll get hurt."

Grandfa saw her differently from everyone else.

Her lips wobbled, and a deceitful tear escaped. She scrubbed it away before more could follow.

"I was the bully this time."

He frowned. "You hurt someone?"

"Yes. No. I didn't actually hurt him." She searched for a way to explain how she'd known exactly what Nathan felt. How that drove her to react. Grandfa wouldn't understand. "I hit Nathan."

"You. Hit. Nathan?" He frowned as he tried to process her statement. "No. You wouldn't attack a Randal." His hands shook as he grabbed hers. His fear slipped into her mind like a shadow.

She couldn't stop it from happening. Her tears fell unheeded now.

Nathan had taunted her for years. If she hadn't felt his emotions, she'd never have reacted. The Randals were the most powerful family in the village. Mama would be furious. It didn't matter what Nathan said or did. Becca was at fault, and she hadn't even hurt him.

"We have to make this right. Your mother will know what to do." Grandfa stood and carefully put all his supplies back into the healer kit. "What happened, exactly?"

She didn't have an answer. Not one he'd understand. Thunder and rage, and Nathan's feelings. Becca clenched her fingers together.

"He said the council should shoot you. Like a rabid dog. Because of dragons." It all came out backward, but she grasped at what did make sense.

He snorted. "Shot? For telling the truth? People in this village have always blindly followed the Healer way. But I went to university. I've seen the world. Besides, stories don't hurt anyone."

"I know." He didn't understand. He never did. The village rumors had never bothered him. Not as much as they irritated Mama. But it didn't matter. His stories weren't the real problem. Nathan's disgust for her grandfather still made her stomach burn. But sensing emotions was even more improbable than believing that dragons would return.

Grandfa brushed her hair off her cheek. "Never fight because of me. Maybe your mother is right. You're getting too old for dragon stories. It's time to focus on your future."

Becca grasped his hand. He couldn't take away his stories. They gave her a glimpse of a different world. A better life. "No. I love your stories, and I want to see all those marvelous places. The ocean, the desert, the forest of trees as high as a mountain. There's got to be more to life than settling down and having babies."

He shook his head sadly. "The world is changing. People see bad omens in a simple change in weather. Folk will always fear something they can't explain. Today, it's dragon stories, and tomorrow, it'll be talking chickens. My stories are hurting you."

His hand trembled as he touched Becca's face. "It's all right if no one believes. But you need a better life, a safe life."

Becca nodded, but her heart broke. She'd counted on him to support her against her mother's plans. And now he thought Mama was right. Control over her future was slipping from her grasp. Her mother's plan would be the only way soon.

He tapped her nose. "Tomorrow, I'll teach you how to fight properly. No granddaughter of mine will bruise her hands hitting a brute again."

Maybe he was right, and the weather was to blame for everything. All the emotions had been her own, amplified by the thunderstorm. She didn't feel anything unusual now.

Becca slipped off the bed and tilted her head to one side. The house was suspiciously quiet. Not that she minded having Grandfa to herself, but he was supposed to be watching her sister and brothers.

She put her hands on her hips and frowned. "Where are the twins and Kevin?"

He avoided her eyes and cleared his throat. "Well, ah, let's just say you weren't the only one to lose your head today." He rubbed the back of his neck, then looked up with a wry grin. "I sent them to the wood to gather blackberries for dessert."

Becca giggled. "Blackberries aren't in season for another three months." She waggled her finger at him but couldn't resist the teasing glint in his eye.

"I just needed them to stop squabbling for a spell. They'll be back soon. Kevin will give up when the twins lose themselves in their own world."

With a chuckle, Becca ran to the room she shared with her thirteen-year-old brother and the eight-year-old twins. Brandon and Trish shared the bunk bed along the short wall. She undressed, tossing her clothes on the chair, and automatically nudged Kevin's mattress farther under her bed. He never put it away properly. She pulled on a pair of brown britches, modified from her stepfather's castoffs, and a pale green top.

In the garden, Becca shook her mud-covered skirt with a satisfying snap, then beat it with the paddle. With a sigh of resignation, she poured a thimble measure of soap flakes into the washtub. Using soap midweek would upset Mama. But her mother would be more upset if she wore britches to school because she didn't have a clean skirt, even if it was too short. With her Grandfa's height and her father's narrow bones, Becca was the tallest girl in the village, but Mama seemed to think she could shrink Becca into a proper-sized lady with the right clothes.

The mud fell away, but the hem needed to soak for an hour. She brushed the mud from her hair and shook out her cloak.

Kevin sauntered into the garden, pulling the twins behind him. They were strapped into the leather toddler harnesses they'd outgrown ages ago. Kevin glared, daring her to reprimand him, while the twins babbled in their secret language.

Becca snapped her mouth shut. She didn't need another fight today, and the twins didn't seem to mind. A zing of guilt tingled the tip of her tongue. She shook her head to clear the unwanted sensation.

With a "do whatever you want" shrug, she went to the kitchen. Mama would be in a better mood if dinner was ready.

Grandfa grinned as he passed her on the way to the backyard. "Kevin, get that harness off. Great Healer, they're not horses."

Becca lit the cooking stove and chopped the rabbit into bite-size chunks. She stirred the rabbit into the pot on the stove, tossing in a handful of herbs, carrots, and potatoes. While the stew boiled, she spread flour on the thick wood counter, grabbed the risen dough, and pounded it into two small loaves. Between the sounds of Grandfa and her siblings outside and the mealtime routine, her worry about sensing other people's emotions faded.

When Becca returned to the garden, Kevin and Grandfa had disappeared. In the greenhouse, Brandon held a tomato, juice dripping down his chin. Trish stood beside him, her arms full of green onions and carrots with suspicious bites in them.

"We're making new vegetables, Becca." Pride shone from her face.

Becca snorted. Trish was a good girl, but Brandon could convince her that dragons lived under their bed. His look of innocence didn't fool anyone.

Becca gathered the tomatoes and carrots and pushed the twins toward the water pump next to the washtub. "You two better get cleaned up before Mama sees you. And dump your shirt into the tub, Brandon." At least Mama couldn't complain about the extravagant use of soap if there were two items in the tub.

The twins scurried off babbling about "carro-toes" and "toma-rots." They had even more imagination than Becca. So far, Mama tolerated their "development issues," too proud of having the only twins in the village. It was Becca who required fixing.

MAGIC LOST
GREGOR

The younger dragons recovered quickly while others lay on the shore, gathering their strength. The Source had affected them all differently. Gregor led a group to the tunnel, and they dug out a ramp to the surface. He was careful to keep his mental shields up. Everyone had questions, and he didn't have any answers.

The lake's turquoise waters were so dark, it hurt to look at them against the crystal-white cavern. Disturbing evidence that something had gone wrong, and they'd obviously slept for a long time.

On top of the cavern, Gregor stretched his emerald wings, tilting them in the setting sun, pleased at the strength in each tendon. Other than the initial weakness when he swam from the lake and a gnawing hunger in his belly, he was strong and healthy.

"You did well." Zanthor's pride slipped into Gregor's private thoughts.

Warmth eased Gregor's heart. His friend was always there for him. He sent back an embarrassed cough. All he'd done was wake up first.

Zanthor spoke to all the dragon minds. *"I've no idea how long we slept, but we're weak and hungry. We won't make it back to Jason's Keep unless we fortify our strength. Volunteers?"*

Two groups of four dragons quickly assembled. Gregor moved to join them, but to his surprise, Zanthor sent him a quick negative.

Zanthor bowed his acceptance of the volunteers. *"Fly swift and strong. We'll follow once you've found enough game for us. We might eat lean tonight, but we only need to regain our strength for the flight home."*

After the hunting parties left, Zanthor spoke privately with the older dragons recovering along the shore.

It would take time to organize the coven into supported flight groups. The older dragons would need to fly in the higher air currents with a bracket of three strong fliers to keep them aloft.

Twenty dragons still lay under the water. Unease fluttered in Gregor's stomach as he remembered his inability to escape from the vision.

"They might not wake." Seri slid up beside Gregor and butted her head affectionately against his. *"They were so tired when we got here. Not everyone has the stamina of youth to carry them through."*

Gregor grunted. It wasn't youth that kept the older ones going. It was sheer obstinance. He wasn't nearly as surprised as Seri by their survival. It had taken all of Zanthor's powers of persuasion to convince the coven leader, Sarcruze, to pursue this quest for magical immunity. *"Sarcruze will emerge soon, and things will go back to the way they've always been. Zanthor will no longer be in charge."*

Tradition made the eldest dragon the coven leader, and Sarcruze had led the coven long before Gregor, Zanthor, and Seri joined them. At least the 110-year-old dragon had enough vision, despite his love of tradition, to gather as many healthy dragons as he could and isolate them deep in the Dragon Mountain Range, far from the plague. Of course, he conveniently glossed over the fact it was Jason who'd warned him. No way he would credit a human with saving them.

Zanthor sighed. *"It'll be a relief, as long as we've absorbed enough magic to survive this crisis. I'm too young for leadership."* At only thirty-five, it would be a long time before Zanthor would lead, even if most of the coven looked to him for guidance and reassurance.

"Tradition." Gregor couldn't hide his frustration. If they'd stuck with tradition, they'd be dead. Dragons like Zanthor and Seri were their future, and one day, the oldsters would realize it.

Zanthor sent an image of Sarcruze tripping over his infernal pile of rules.

Gregor chuckled. No, Zanthor had fought too hard to let him use tradition as an excuse. They both wanted the coven to thrive, and they'd need to work together.

Seri raised her eye ridge at Gregor. *"What mischief are you and Zanthor planning? We just woke up. Can't you be serious for half a day?"*

Her scolding widened his grin. She'd pushed harder than both of them to fly the great distance to the Source. If they were now immune, all three would have much to celebrate.

At that moment, Sarcruze strode unsteadily up to them, his mahogany hide almost pink with distress. He poked Gregor's chest with his talon, a distinct lack of protocol considering the older dragon was five times the size of Gregor.

"What did you do to us? I haven't felt this weak since I was a youngling." Sarcruze emitted enough anger to fuel a forest fire.

Pain stabbed through Gregor's skull. His shields couldn't protect him from Sarcruze's rage. Gregor swallowed his indignation. At least he'd tried to save them, instead of hiding in the mountains until someone else stopped the plague.

Before Gregor could respond, Zanthor bowed deeply, transmitting calm and caution. *"Sarcruze. I'm delighted you've emerged. We have much to discuss. Perhaps we should leave these younglings to their tasks?"*

Gregor held his breath, hoping Zanthor's distraction worked. But it didn't. Anger washed through him, making his legs wobble.

It took all his willpower to stop his head from bowing in subservience.

Sarcruze scraped his talon over Gregor's shoulder, a warning, then turned to Zanthor and bowed slightly. *"Yes. I can see there is MUCH to discuss. But once we do, I want to know exactly what these younglings did to us."*

The two dragons walked away, continuing their discussion in private. Gregor breathed out. Seri wilted beside him.

"It took all my strength to stay upright." Her voice shook. Neither of them had ever felt a leader exert his power over them. But after the plague killed their covens, they'd joined Sarcruze. A dragon needed a coven to survive.

"See if you two can find answers. We need to know if the plague is still a risk. I'll distract him with our immediate survival needs, but I'll need answers, and soon." Zanthor soothed them privately.

Gregor grimaced. Beside him, Seri groaned. *"How are we supposed to know any more than they know?"*

Three more dragons flopped onto the lakeshore, sending ripples of color over the surface. That reminded Gregor of his dream. He recounted it to Seri.

She frowned. *"Torin's breath. I had a vision too. It was horrible. Only a Seer could interpret what I experienced."*

And that was the end of that. Seri didn't want to talk about her vision. She'd relegated it to a magical anomaly. He wanted to push her. The Source was trying to warn them about the future through their visions. But she could be stubborn, and right now, Gregor was more concerned with the loss of his power.

"I don't want to alarm anyone, and I'm not certain I'm reading things right, but ..." He clasped his talons together. *"Seri. I can't smell magic."* He hoped she'd laugh at his concern and assure him he was wrong, but she didn't.

Shuffles and groans filled the cavern as dragons conversed privately, a muted rumble in the background. Seri's disbelief shot through his mind, before a wave of panic made his talons curl. Magic mattered to her more than anything.

It took Seri longer than usual to raise her mental shields. She'd always had problems with shielding. For most dragons it was automatic, as easy as breathing. Gregor figured it was because of her power. But it embarrassed her. Fortunately, no one was paying attention to them, and she wasn't transmitting publicly. He stepped sideways, physically shielding her from the coven.

After a lungful of air, her turquoise body stilled. Seri's eyes widened, and her cobalt irises whirled.

A faint hint of mint tickled his nose. He kept his own surprise hidden behind his shields. He didn't want to distract her, but it pleased him to know his power had returned.

After a long ten minutes, Seri closed her eyes and groaned. When she opened them, they crossed.

Gregor snorted.

She walloped his snout as embarrassment flooded her thoughts. Pain exploded through the tender channels. His nose had always been sensitive, but after his ability appeared, it was even more so.

Seri's apology was brief, a quick whisper of affection. Her emotions rolled, settling finally on distress. *"Be serious, Gregor. This is very unsettling. When we came here, magic was everywhere. I could see it shimmering over the lake and rising into the sky. It's the source of magic for the entire world."*

She pointed at the lake. *"It's different. But it still exists. Wisps of colors swirling on the surface. Some even rise over the lake. I can see strings of color droplets on you and me. The roof glows a little. Yellow, with wisps of pink. I can't quite discern it. It's like a memory of magic."*

"But that's not possible, right? We can't survive without magic. Do you think we used it all up?"

Seri shook her head, her frown etched deeply into her forehead. *"I don't know. I've always assumed we needed magic. My studies focused on how the wars changed magic, resulting in those of us with powers. But magic exists, like air and water. It can't disappear."*

Her final words held desperation. Gregor's heart clenched for her. Seri's powers had manifested the moment she hatched. Her world was magic. He knew what this meant to her.

Before he could console her, she clapped her talons together. *"We have a new quest, my friend. Investigate magic."* For once her shields held, and all he got from her was excitement.

Gregor sighed. Seri and her grand quests. From the first day of their friendship, she'd dragged him from one quest to another, always to study magic. But it was her research that had guided them to the Source. She'd been certain it would protect them from the plague. His power had led them to the exact location, since Seri's research had only revealed its existence. If Zanthor hadn't believed her, they'd probably be dead now.

Unfortunately, Gregor had no way of knowing if it had worked. Maybe all they'd accomplished was using up the Source and messing with the world's magic.

"If you're done determining the world's fate, get back here and help me organize this lot before the light completely disappears." Zanthor's words admonished them, but he'd speak with them privately later.

Gregor shot back an image of shoving Zanthor into the lake. Once they returned to Jason's Keep, they would find their answers. No point worrying now.

ANGER
BECCA

Long before dinner was ready, the front door slammed open.

"Becca!"

A shiver ran up Becca's neck at Mama's tone. No escape. Her hand shook as she put the knife in the sink. Excuses rushed through her head, but she knew better. It didn't matter what really happened. She was to blame.

"In the kitchen," Becca replied with as much servitude as she could muster. She quickly threw the risen loaves into the oven, next to the flame, then stood, clasping her hands behind her back.

Mama strode into the kitchen and dropped her satchel onto the sideboard. She wasn't a small woman, shorter than Becca, but rounded and tough. Her carefully controlled features twisted with anger.

"Fighting. With Nathan Randal. What has gotten into you? You know how important Alice is to me. How dare you ruin that?" She gripped Becca's chin, forcing her head up.

Becca knew better than to pull away. "I'm sorry, Mama. I won't do it again." She kept her gaze on Mama's heaving chest. Eye contact meant defiance in her mother's world.

"You better not. Thank the Healer, Alice believed me when I said you'd been having terrible headaches. Half the village is suffering. But it doesn't completely excuse your behavior. How could you be so reckless? Tomorrow, you'll repair the damage you've done. You're fifteen. It's time you behave appropriately."

Disgust settled in Becca's mind. The emotional onslaught was back. She'd so hoped it had gone away. But she knew how her mother felt, and it didn't make sense. Becca's lips trembled, and she bit into the soft flesh, trapping her protests. Mama didn't care what Nathan had said. All she cared about was the family reputation. But it was better to let her mother rant. The punishment was always worse if Becca defended herself.

"Yes, Mama."

Pain shot through Becca's jaw as her mother squeezed her chin, as if sensing insincerity. Then she let go.

A wave of annoyance hit Becca, causing her to sway from the intensity and overwhelming her own sense of self. Her mother's emotions were so strong. Sensing them only made things worse. She closed her eyes, trying to block out this strange power.

The kitchen door slammed behind Mama as she stomped outside to wash for dinner. Becca rubbed her sore chin, certain there would be crescent bruises in the morning. She blinked away the tears of pain and finished cleaning the knife and cutting board.

She was placing the hot loaves of bread on the sideboard when Mama stormed back in with Becca's skirt in her hand.

"What did you do to your skirt?"

Anger pulsed through her blood. This time she didn't know if it was her own or Mama's, but it didn't matter.

"I have a cut on my face and stains on my skirt. Proof I was hurt. But you don't care about me!" She tried to stop the words, but the echo of the beastly roar took over her mouth, and her bitterness flew out. "All you care about is what Mrs. Randal thinks, what everyone else thinks."

The seconds of silence slowed to an eternity. Mama's face contorted and fury flashed in her eyes, filling Becca's mind and making her small.

"That's no way to talk to me. I'm your mother." She shook the offending skirt. "You will learn to behave like a proper girl. You spend far too much time dreaming in the woods when you should be working. I've obviously been too lenient. That stops now."

Mama had never been lenient a day in her life. Becca did everything she could to avoid her mother's spite. Every chore, even ones Mama hadn't asked her to do. She tried so hard to make her mother happy. She had to leave before she said something she'd regret. Becca pushed past her mother.

Something wet hit Becca's back.

"Since you've ruined your clothes, you'll sew two skirts this week and convert that one for Trish. And you'll do the laundry for the next month. No help from Kevin or Grandfa. Starting tomorrow, you'll attend Alice Randal's etiquette lessons every day after school."

Becca turned, ready to fling a denial, but Mama wasn't done.

She dug her fingernails into Becca's forearm, just like Mrs. Randal had. "You'll apologize to Nathan for your rude behavior. And ..." She shook Becca hard enough to make her neck snap. "You'll accompany him to school for a week until you appreciate the boy."

Becca sobbed. The roar in her ears pounded at her to defend herself. Her body tensed. But she pushed it all to the back of her mind and nodded. Mentally, she built a wall between herself and the world.

Mama let go of her arm and turned to the stove, as if everything was normal. "Well, at least you made the stew. Wash that skirt and return promptly. There's still much to do."

Becca fled to the washing tub and furiously scrubbed a hole into the hem of her horrible, mangled skirt. It wouldn't matter, anyway, since she had to cut it up for Trish.

After an eternity, Grandfa laid a comforting hand on her shoulder. "She loves you, in her own way."

Her next breath caught in her throat. Did she? Becca wasn't sure anymore. She didn't know how she could sense emotions, but she did know one thing for certain. Her mother was too angry to feel anything resembling Grandfa's love for Becca.

She wrung out her skirt, then hung it next to Brandon's shirt. She'd thought that if she just tried hard enough, her mother would love her the same way she loved the twins. When Becca was little, she remembered laughter filling the house. But then Father died when she was five, and Mama married Uncle Peter, Father's twin, a couple years later.

Over time, the family reputation became the most important value in their family. The twins helped. They were the only twins in the village and made Mama special. It should've made life better, but Becca kept disappointing her mother. Even her brother, Kevin, elicited praise once in a while.

"Becca! You must be done by now. Get back in here."

Knowing things didn't change anything. An echo of thunder rumbled an agreement. She would have to do whatever her mother wanted, and then everything would go back to normal. But just in case, Becca imagined a rock wall behind her eyes, protecting her brain. She had to stop the emotions from attacking her mind.

Jason's Keep
Gregor

The sun was low on the horizon by the time the last group was ready to leave. Gregor followed Zanthor through the cavern tunnel to the lake edge, sensing a great sadness in his friend.

"We'll return what we've borrowed." Zanthor bowed in a deep sign of respect. *"Thank you for your energy."*

Gregor stopped him as he moved away.

"What do you mean?"

"The Source expended a lot of magic to protect us. It is our duty to replenish it."

Gregor didn't understand what Zanthor meant. *"How?"*

"Instead of flying to the Thoran Sea for our final sleep, we'll return here and lie within the waters one final time. The Source has given us this gift. We must restore balance."

The faintest whiff of moonflower tickled Gregor's senses. This was right, somehow. Five dragons still slept. Their minds were fragile echoes within the coven consciousness. Even though Gregor hoped they'd wake, he knew they wouldn't. This is where they would die and become part of the Source.

Zanthor chuckled. *"I'm right, aren't I? I can tell when your power flares. Your mind leaves for a moment. It's like you don't exist, yet I can still see you."*

Gregor looked up, surprised. He barely understood his power, and now his friend could tell when it flared. That was new.

Zanthor grunted and rubbed Gregor behind his wing blades. *"The world has changed. We absorbed magic from the Source. Is it such a surprise that our powers may have transformed as well?"*

Zanthor's conviction became Gregor's. But then, that was his power. If Zanthor believed it, so did anyone he influenced. Gregor shook off the sensation. He didn't need convincing. He already believed.

The last survivors leapt for the sky and followed Zanthor. Everyone kept their thoughts to themselves, but the hunger crept through. By the time they reached the first stop set up by the scouts, Gregor could've eaten an entire herd of cattle.

"Ha. A few stringy goats will have to do. The first group's already claimed the sheep and cows." Seri's voice lightened Gregor's fatigue. She left with her group as soon as Gregor landed.

They ate quickly and flew on through the night. By the time they reached Jason's Keep, he could barely fly straight. His wings ached and his belly still growled. The oldsters were in worse shape. Their bodies were so much larger than his own youngling frame. Some dropped to the caldera floor and fell asleep immediately, while others gnawed on what was left of the goats.

The coven barely made a dent in a keep designed for twice their number. Sarcruze had hoped it would protect hundreds of dragons from the plague. But they had to depend on the humans, Jason and his brother Charlie, to let the other covens know of their refuge. The only way to protect the coven from the plague was to block mind-speech, since that was how the disease spread from one dragon to another. Until they could physically check the other keeps, they were still in quarantine.

Jason's Keep was bleaker than Gregor remembered.

Timeworn.

Yet another indication more time had passed than they'd expected.

"Do we know how long we slept?" Gregor wasn't the only one asking this question.

"No. But it was a long time. Now we're all here, I'll check the stars." Zanthor's response didn't ease Gregor's fear.

He clung to the fact that dragons couldn't breathe underwater for years, but deep down, he knew magic changed everything.

Seri leaned her head against his and sent a soothing hum. She teased him about being the youngest, even though she was only a year older, but she also had an uncanny knack of knowing when he needed comfort. It was one of the reasons he felt a strong bond to her. He'd been a loner, even in his first coven, but Seri and Zanthor believed in him and his unusual power of scent. He couldn't imagine his life without them.

Seri and Gregor walked through the tunnels to the archive stone. Many dragons stood in the circular cavern with their talons against the massive pillar in the center. Marks etched into the surface from their talons spiraled around the surface, making it appear to spin.

He waited patiently to add his experience to the archive while Seri mentally chatted with the dragons leaving, easing their worries too. Her shields were nonexistent, and he experienced her compassion for each dragon as if she bestowed it on him. She cared deeply about everyone in the coven. He shook his head. He'd never felt like he belonged, but she made everyone feel like they were special.

When a spot cleared, Gregor stepped forward and pressed his palm into the stone. It pulsed. His talons scratched the surface, marking his thoughts. It took only a moment.

Outside, dragons stared up at the stars, hoping for an answer. It was Zanthor's right as leader to hold a group mind-link. He flew high above the winter clouds and settled on a nearby peak. Everyone was silent as their minds filled with his sight.

Zanthor's gaze settled on the dragon star. All Gregor's life, it floated above the eastern horizon. Now it sat halfway between the horizon and the apex. Shock and disbelief flashed through the link, magnified by so many minds. For the star to move that much, a lot of time had passed.

More than a few years.

More than a century.

It was impossible. They couldn't survive underwater for that long. But they had. The stars proved it.

Outrage rippled from Sarcruze. *"We may as well have died."*

Gregor's legs trembled as fear echoed from every dragon. He slapped up his shields, trying to reduce the onslaught.

Zanthor sent a powerful wave of calmness. *"Don't be alarmed. We are alive. My coven, we've slept within the Source for one hundred and fifty years. Over the next few days, we'll assess exactly what the Source did for us. But for now, rejoice in your existence. Rest. We are dragons. Centuries are normal for our lifespans. We'll survive."* He followed this with a burst of conviction.

Gregor almost fell over. He'd never felt Zanthor extend his power so deeply into a mind-link. His chest filled with optimism. He'd worried the lack of magic would affect their powers, but Zanthor's was strong. They would survive. Sarcruze sent a weak wave of support, his anger muted.

The mind-link dissolved, and fear, anger, worry, and denial erupted in the caldera. Gregor turned to comfort Fiona, one of the older females, but she brushed away his thoughts.

"You're young. You haven't lost anything."

Which was unfair. He'd lost as much as every other dragon. He'd lost his coven, over three hundred dragons. The plague had killed thousands of dragons before they fled to the Source. Youth didn't lessen his pain. Gregor put up his mental shields and retreated to the caldera's far side.

There would be much discussion as everyone tried to make sense out of what had happened. No wonder the lake waters had been black. The amount of magic required to keep them in stasis for a century and a half must've drained the Source. Because that's what happened. He wasn't the size of a 167-year-old dragon.

He was still a youngling of seventeen.

Had the world changed while they slept? They would need to discover if they were immune to the plague or if it had merely run its course. And what if the other covens had survived? They would be much older.

He fell into a warm sleeping hollow. They could do nothing now. It was time to regain his strength. Tomorrow would bring a new set of problems. Tomorrow always did.

AMENDS
BECCA

The morning light barely illuminated the room as Becca stepped between Kevin's mattress and the dresser. Trish had flung the blanket onto Brandon's head and was curled up against his legs. Becca pulled the blanket off her own bed and covered them up. All three would sleep another hour.

The cold kitchen floor froze her feet as she stoked the fire. She danced around the table, humming one of Grandfa's silly dragon songs. Her mother wouldn't approve of her method of warming herself. But it filled Becca with hope and made her happy.

One day she'd leave all this behind and explore the world. She'd no desire to settle down yet. Girls these days didn't have to marry so young. Grandfa told her to follow her heart. Well, her heart wanted to fly, like a dragon. Everything about Chartsend bound her to the ground. But there had to be more for her, something better.

A murmur from Mama and Peter's room halted her daydream. She'd better hurry. The Randals owned the largest farm in Chartsend, and they were probably already up. Her mother would roast her if she missed Mrs. Randal this morning. Her apology to Nathan wasn't as important as mollifying Mrs. Randal.

Becca cut four slices of nightberry cake and wrapped them in waxed paper. Mama walked into the kitchen and nodded her approval. The recipe had been handed down from her great-great-grandmother, and Mama claimed it could soothe an angry bear.

"Bye, Mama. I'll tell Mrs. Randal you wish her Healer's fortune." The Healer phrase came automatically to her lips, a ward against death. Before her mother could assign additional chores, Becca fled through the front door.

Without her mother's gaze judging her every move, a weight lifted from her neck. The morning light painted the sky orange, hinting at a crisp day, but ominous black clouds shrouded the mountaintops. Sheets of rain blurred the outline of distant trees as the clouds moved over the forest. A sense of foreboding tingled along Becca's shoulders, and she shivered under her leather cloak.

When she stepped onto the dirt road between the fields, wind whipped her hair across her face. She looked up. Faster than seemed possible, black clouds scuttled across the sky, extinguishing the orange and pinks in seconds.

She clutched the cake against her chest and ran. But she wasn't fast enough.

A wall of rain pelted through the fields and drenched her. Water ran into her eyes and dripped off her nose. She licked the rain off her lips, the water oddly salty, like tears.

She ran through the Randals' gate and slipped. She caught the gate, saving her clothing from another encounter with mud, but the cake didn't fare so well. Fiddlesticks. Mama would be mortified when she heard how Becca arrived dripping and disheveled, with a squished cake. A proper lady never slips on ice or rumples her clothing.

Becca knocked on the door and attempted to wring out her hair with one hand.

Thunder crashed through the valley as Mrs. Randal opened the door. Her eyes widened, and she yanked Becca through the doorway. "Healer's grace. It's pouring. Why would you go out in such weather?"

"It wasn't raining when I left." From the look on Mrs. Randal's face, Becca's explanation didn't help her at all.

Mrs. Randal pursed her lips. "Never have I seen weather like this. It's a bad omen. Mark my words." She took Becca's cloak and hung it to dry on the hook beside the entryway. "Come in. I'll grab a towel for your hair and make us tea. You're here to see Nathan, I expect."

Becca cringed as she settled her muddy boots next to her cloak. Then she followed Mrs. Randal into the warm kitchen and placed the crumpled cake in the center of the table. Hopefully, its flavor would make up for its pathetic appearance. She pushed in the sides, trying to make it square.

Mrs. Randal handed Becca a towel, then leaned into the stairwell. "Nathan!"

He raced down the stairs with his socks in one hand and his shirt unbuttoned. As Becca's startled gaze met his, Nathan's cheeks turned beet red. "Oh. Mama. You shoulda said we had company."

Mrs. Randal sniffed loudly. He immediately turned around and buttoned his shirt.

Seemed Nathan disappointed his mother too. Becca held in her glee as she folded the towel and attempted to appear ladylike and calm.

With his clothes sorted, Nathan turned and glared, as if it were her fault he'd arrived in disarray. He was infuriating. But responding to his taunts got her into this mess, and ladies didn't stick out their tongues. Though he totally deserved it.

She stood up as proper as she could and took a deep breath. "Nathan. I am sorry for reacting in an unladylike manner yesterday afternoon. I apologize for hitting you. Please accept this nightberry cake as a sign of my atonement." She clasped her hands behind her back to prevent herself from slapping the smug look off his face.

His mother cleared her throat and raised an eyebrow at Nathan.

He quickly cleared all expression and intoned, equally wooden, "Thank you for your apology, Becca. I was not harmed by your actions, and I, too, apologize for saying anything you may have found offensive."

His mother beamed and gestured for them to sit at the kitchen table. She served tea, then left the room to wake up Nathan's younger brother Max.

As soon as his mother left, Nathan grabbed a slice of cake. "Even if everything I said was true," he taunted with his mouth full.

Becca clenched her hands in her skirt. She was already in enough trouble. Sitting stiffly in the chair, she sipped at the hot tea as quickly as possible. It was proper for a lady to take her time and converse with the gentleman across the table. Becca snorted, then covered her mouth. Nathan was no gentleman.

Thunder rolled through the room. Startled, she splashed tea on the tablecloth.

Nathan smirked. "Scared of thunder?"

Becca curled both hands around the cup and pressed her lips together. She wouldn't react.

Lightning lit the room with an odd blue light. At the edge of her vision, red, gold, and blue swirled in the darkness that followed. She blinked, but nothing was there. A wave of sadness feathered along her senses, too distant to affect her. Becca reached for the sensation, but it was gone. As if she'd blasted a hole in her mental protection, Nathan's smugness filled her mind.

She didn't want to know what he felt, so she focused on the items in the bookshelf behind his head. Maybe if her mind was preoccupied, the emotions would leave her alone.

Mrs. Randal hurried in and smiled. "Nathan, you'll have to wait for the storm to pass before you accompany Becca to school."

His mouth fell open. Becca swallowed to contain her laughter at his stunned expression. He would be punished too. Of course, it was proper for a gentleman to walk a lady, not the other way around. It was fortunate his amends matched her own. Mama would be consoled.

Becca sat quietly at the kitchen table as the Randals prepared for their day. Mrs. Randal chatted about the farm. Because they supplied the entire village and two neighboring villages, they were taking advantage of the warm spell to plant crops earlier. As long as the temperatures didn't drop below freezing, they expected a bumper crop in the spring.

Nobody yelled or dawdled at the table. Mrs. Randal kept Nathan and Max in check with frowns and mild reminders as they ate.

At home, Mama rushed about, yelling at Kevin and Becca to do things they were already doing. The twins had to be badgered to finish breakfast on time, while they babbled in their secret language. Grandfa usually slept until noon to recover from his evening at the bar. On the mornings he joined them, he and Mama argued about his drinking, his age, and how he didn't help enough.

The storm passed as quickly as it had appeared. Nathan escorted Becca from the house and through the gate. As soon as they were out of sight of his mother's spying eyes, he gripped Becca's arm.

"Listen up, Red. I have to escort you for a week because you lost your temper. So, you'll tell your mother that I behaved like a gentleman. Understand?" He shook Becca at the last question.

Becca gritted her teeth and nodded. Nothing but annoyance emanated from him now.

Nathan let her go, and they completed the journey in silence. At the schoolhouse, he left her at the door and sauntered over to the younger boys who adored him.

She could hear them talking as she pulled out the lesson book and readied the classroom for Elder Frederick.

"You have to walk Becca to school every day, huh?"

"Yes. She needs her exercise." Nathan's voice hinted at something else entirely. The boys brayed.

Becca wrapped her arms around herself. She didn't know how to handle him without insulting the Randal family.

Marcus slipped into the room and wiped the blackboard. "Ignore them. They're not worth it."

He didn't understand. It wasn't just teasing. She took a deep breath so her voice wouldn't give her away. "So, you're not a sheep today?"

With nothing left to do at the front of the room, she turned away and moved to the tables for the beginner grades near the mudroom. She put pencils and paper on each table. There was no sign of Elder Frederick yet. But she could start the younger ones on their letters, while the older students worked on math.

Marcus pulled her into his arms. "I'm sorry about yesterday. I've never seen you blow up like that. I should've done something."

For a moment she rested her head against his chest and breathed in. Marcus was so solid and steady. He'd always been there for her. Except yesterday. Pain shot through her heart, and she stepped out of his comforting embrace.

He was like everyone else, bowing to the Randals. They were the richest family in the village with their huge farm, and Alice Randal's cousin was a powerful Adviser in the city. Mama would sell the moon for an invitation to the city for the spring festival.

But Marcus had been different. At least, until last summer, when Nathan's cousin Isobel had shown up. Her country retreat, she'd said, with her golden hair and princess-like accent. And that's all it took for Marcus to fall in love. He'd spent the entire summer catering to her every whim. But a hunter's son had little status in the city. Nathan was his ticket to romance.

Becca could be patient. Marcus couldn't really love Isobel. He needed a practical woman. One who loved the woods and craved adventure like he did. Not one who was too fragile to do anything. Ever since they'd kissed when Becca was twelve, she'd waited for him to realize they were perfect for each other.

But his behavior yesterday changed her mind. Heat rushed to her cheeks.

"You laughed, when Nathan said those horrible things."

"I'm sorry, Becks." He didn't even have an excuse.

"How could you stand there when he ...?" Pain caught in her throat. "I thought we were friends."

"I'm sorry. I've been a donkey." He looped his finger through one of her curls and grinned his crooked smile.

Her heart skipped a beat, and she forgave him. "Why don't we take Kevin and the twins to Amethyst Lake on Saturday? It's probably not frozen anymore. Might be a good chance to catch some fish."

His grin disappeared, he dropped his hand, and his gaze shifted to her toes.

She swallowed her stupid hope. They'd been friends since they were four years old, but he couldn't risk Isobel finding out they spent time together. Isobel had taken an instant dislike to Becca, pointing out her boyish walk and unladylike hairstyle.

Before he could come up with some lame excuse, Becca twisted her lips into a fake smile and pushed him out the door. "Never mind. With this rain we probably can't go, anyway. Now leave. You're distracting me."

He left without a backward glance.

Becca rubbed at the tightness in her chest. Time for a new best friend, but she and Marcus had been together for so long, she wasn't sure anyone could fill the hole.

Tired of pining for something she had no control over, Becca grabbed the container of colored chalk. Marcus would come to his senses or not. She copied the day's lesson onto the chalkboard. Alone in the classroom with the voices of children playing outside, Becca did what she always did when she was upset.

She imagined she was a dragon rider. In the corner of the chalkboard, she sketched a dragon flying over a mountain peak, then drew a fort carved into the mountainside. How she wished dragons were alive. A dragon could take her away to adventure and freedom. No more duties. No more expectations. No more stupid boys and their messed-up feelings.

She'd soar through the sky and explore the world. Grandfa's stories were full of brave dragon riders, defending the countries and saving villagers during storms. There were others, not so grand, about the Great Wars where hundreds of dragons and their riders died fighting. She drew an army tent, then added flames. During the war, dragons carried archers who shot flaming arrows at the enemy. It must've been a terrifying sight.

With a sigh, Becca erased the drawings. She was too fragile for any more of Nathan's goading. Yesterday had been hard enough when she still thought Marcus was on her side. Now she had to face her future alone.

Survival

Gregor

Day 7 After the Long Sleep

Sunlight burst through the clouds above him as Gregor tilted his right wing down, effortlessly shifting into a roll. Warmth encased his body and dried his wings after the relentless week of snow and rain.

Seri laughed as she dropped to join him on the lower wind current. *"Feels good."*

Her joy reflected his own. For just a moment he wanted to savor life, to dwell on being alive in this calmer world, with no taint of human wars or distorted magic. A light caress of understanding brushed his mind, and he grinned as Seri twisted into a spiral, gurgling her pleasure. Aerial games were so much better in clear skies.

Soon they'd be back at Jason's Keep and would have a hundred more duties. He sighed.

For the past three days, he and Seri had scouted the mountains to the west for herds and human settlements. They'd noted tracks in the snow and let the coven know where the animals roamed, but there'd been no sign of human encroachment this far north.

Seri dove through the next cloud formation, probably searching for seeds of magic. She had a theory that rain clouds transported magic from the Dragon Mountains, south to the human lands.

"Nothing. The rain clouds past the mountain range are empty. But the ones pouring on these mountains have hints here and there. It's so frustrating. I can see the colors sprinkled through the clouds, but only if I don't look directly at them."

Gregor skimmed the surface of a lake, envious of Seri's ability to use her power at will. Plenty of fish and plant life. He made a note of the location. No unusual scents at all. His power was aggravatingly dormant.

Seri flew ahead, dipping occasionally as the current shifted. *"I'm more concerned with the lack of magic."* She groaned. *"If only Sarcruze would let me return to the Source."*

Gregor understood her frustration. *"Until Zanthor has checked all the keeps, he won't allow us to travel farther. We would need supplies. I'm amazed we made it back to Jason's Keep after such a long time in stasis in the pool."*

"I know. I know. But we don't know enough about how our hibernation affected the Source. Maybe there's only a tiny bit of magic left, or it will take a while to replenish. I need to know how humans used magic while we slept. They've always had a strange relationship with magic. Ever since our ancestors taught them how to access it." Her head dipped, and she glided a long time before speaking again. *"And if magic is growing now that we've left the Source, it should take longer for humans to control it. We can guide them this time."*

They flew over Jason's Keep in silence. It was a wonderful wish, but he wasn't sure it was possible to influence humans. They wanted to control everything in the world.

With a beat of his wings, Gregor rose over the caldera's edge and glided down to the meeting area.

Fiona's talons were entwined with Sarcruze's as she spoke privately with him. Gregor could feel the intensity of their connection, and a sweet odor tickled the insides of his nostrils. He veered away from Seri and landed beside the two elder dragons. The scent intensified, forcing him to stumble toward them.

Nightberry.

Gregor was so focused on the scent, the blast of outrage through his mind was a shock. He blinked, unsure how he'd gotten there.

"What are you doing? This is a private matter."

Gregor immediately bent one knee and bowed his head deeply. *"My apologies."* He waited, hoping they wouldn't make him grovel long enough for the entire coven to notice his horrible slip in protocol. A dragon didn't interrupt an intensely private conversation ever. Humiliation bent his head lower. His power had finally manifested, and he was in trouble again.

Fiona rested her talon gently on Gregor's head. *"You've never been so insensitive. Is something wrong?"*

Keeping his head down, as Sarcruze hadn't released him, Gregor transmitted the nightberry scent to Fiona. It wrapped around her, and she gasped. An image of her belly, bloated with eggs, flashed between them.

Seri had landed a few feet back, and she sent a wave of support and a quick private encouragement. *"You've already made the mistake. Be strong."*

"Fine. I assume it's that blasted power of yours. What now?" Sarcruze mentally released Gregor from his uncomfortable bow.

Gregor lifted his head and saw Zanthor flying in to mediate. His friend knew him so well.

Fiona turned to Sarcruze and tapped him lightly on his nose. *"I was right. It's time to start rebuilding our numbers. This youngling has confirmed it with his meddlesome magic. Which you were quite willing to follow when it suited you."*

The scent disappeared. Released from the scent's compulsion, Gregor felt his entire face burn. His power had dragged him into the middle of a discussion about breeding. As the youngest in the coven, he had no right to interfere. *Torin's breath.* What had happened to him? Scents usually led him. They'd never taken over like that.

Zanthor interrupted Gregor's fear. *"Don't worry. We'll figure it out. I'm glad to see your power is returning. It certainly makes sense that to ensure our survival your magic would tell us we should procreate, especially since we can find no sign of other survivors."* His laugh was ironic and vibrated within Gregor's mind, doing little to banish his embarrassment or the continued pressure of Sarcruze's displeasure. *"Now go, while I handle the details with these two. I'm not sure how we should proceed with so little magic."*

Seri pulled Gregor away, and they hid in the bathing caverns. A dip in the hot springs and a rest in the geothermal sleeping caves would settle their nerves, while the oldsters determined the future of dragonkind.

He couldn't help the envy that seeped into his thoughts as he watched Seri slip into the hot spring. She'd be twenty in less than a year and would be eligible for breeding. He needed three more years. Dragons rarely formed bond pairs, and she'd have many mates eager to earn her favor, but he wished she'd wait for him. Hastily, Gregor shoved the desire behind his deepest shields. It was not the dragon way.

The nightberry scent had disappeared after Fiona had identified its purpose, but it returned now laced with pepper. Gregor turned away from the pool of steaming water. What could that mean? A shift?

The scent trickled down to his last thought. Something about Seri and waiting.

The scent faded. No.

Choosing?

The pepper made him sneeze, rattling his brain. Wait. Traditionally, male dragons chose their mates. Great aerial contests determined the strongest. He'd never seen one. Thirty-five years of war had stifled the intermingling and breeding of many keeps. He was the last hatchling to join his coven.

Seri shifted in the water. *"Aren't you coming in?"* The water rippled over her wings as she spread them to allow the warmth to penetrate deeply into the membrane.

"In a minute. I'm working something out." He strode from the cavern, unable to stop himself, and found Fiona at the entrance, alone.

Fiona raised her eye ridge at him. *"You have more to say, Gregor?"*

He looped his tail protectively around his belly, but knew the compulsion wouldn't leave until he said the words. *"I think there needs to be a change."*

She snorted. *"Of course there does. This world has changed, and so has magic. We have no idea what effect it will have on our rituals."*

He shook his head. *"No. I mean, maybe. But my power ... it's indicating something else."* He never quite knew how to explain the way the scent picked out an idea and pushed him toward it or sent him physically toward an answer. Many dragons thought his magic told him the answers. It was rarer still to get an image like he had with Fiona. This was purely a guess on his part.

"I think the females have to choose. It's important not to have the contests and ..." He shook his head, attempting to rattle the idea out. He could almost feel it. The pepper overpowered the nightberry now. He sneezed, and the idea popped loose. *"You have to choose your mates. Quantity is more important than ..."* He hesitated to say quality. He didn't want to offend.

"No. You don't have to say it, youngling. The males won't like it, but a long time ago ... longer now that an additional hundred and fifty years have passed, when I was younger than you, there was a time when the females had to make an important choice. It appears that time has come again. Don't hurt yourself trying to figure out what your power is telling you. I know what to do."

Gregor sighed, and the overpowering scent faded. Fiona could handle it.

With any luck, his power would leave him alone for a while, instead of pushing him to do anything else embarrassing. Gregor groaned as he hurried away. His power had saved them, and it would do it again, but not if he couldn't regain control.

He returned to Seri and slipped into the waters beside her. They could enjoy being young and play for a bit before any more important decisions about their survival had to be made.

REQUEST
SERI

Fiona's private request sent a flutter of unease through Seri. She frowned at Gregor as he dove under the hot water. He seemed calmer now. As if his power released him once he did what it wanted.

Seri was grateful her power was passive, simply enhanced vision. Instead of identifying every nuance of gray within a cloud, or every shade of green in a thicket of trees, she could see the magic that wove through the cloud and trickled through the leaves. But her magic didn't compel her, and she could access her sight at will.

Gregor's ability used to be similar, an enhanced sense of smell, but it had changed. Since they'd left the Source, he reacted without thinking, as if he had no choice. The hot water didn't ease the chill that settled at the base of her skull. This new magic was dangerous, and she had to understand it before it hurt Gregor, or he made a fatal mistake.

Seri stepped over the stones enclosing the bathing pool and shook water from her hide. She must focus on the summons and not on her worries.

Gregor's mind was suspiciously blank when he surfaced. *"It's not my fault. You'll see."*

Fiona strode past them and through a wide tunnel behind the bathing pools, her tail straight behind her, indicating her confidence. *"Leave him be. He only confirmed what I'd already suspected. Now come along. Your unique power is needed."*

Seri followed, attempting to straighten her own tail, but it drooped at the end. A visible sign of her uncertainty and yet another dragon ability she had trouble mastering. If it weren't for her power, no coven would want her.

As Fiona traveled deeper into the caverns where the other dragons waited, Seri's concern mounted. They could just as easily speak in a meeting area outside.

"We need the privacy, and I know you'll be tempted to speak with Gregor if we discuss this outside." Renalia's sharp tone cut through Seri's mental shield as if they were made of clouds.

Pain shot through Seri's brain, and she tightened her shields again. Renalia had more mental reach than anyone, but she shouldn't be able to read Seri's private thoughts so easily. Seri ground her teeth and pushed her fears deep into her private mind. The Source had affected her too. She'd have to concentrate on her shields from now on.

Besides, Renalia's assumption was unfair. Seri didn't tell Gregor everything. And Sarcruze was the one who kept sending them off together while he and Zanthor discussed the coven's gloomy fate. Some days she felt more Gregor's keeper than his friend.

She hadn't even checked in on her friend, Garianna.

Garianna was the last survivor from her home coven. Pain pulsed through Seri's heart, and she took a moment to absorb her loss. It was never healthy to push away grief. She missed her mentor Crysta the most. Seri could see the connections between dragons as a colored strand of magic. Crysta had hoped they could uncover a genetic cure for the plague, but to test it, they needed a parent-offspring or a sibling pair of dragons. And Seri had secretly hoped finding her biological parent would help her understand her diminished draconic abilities.

But the strand of magic had led her far from the lands she knew. When Gregor found her, she'd all but given up hope. So many covens had perished to the plague, she was certain her parents were dead. But then Gregor's power led them to Sarcruze's coven.

Seri's biological strand of magic led to the most powerful, self-assured, and respected dragon she'd ever met. Renalia. As if that wasn't intimidating enough, it meant Seri's lack of skill and her magical ability didn't come from her parent. Biology hadn't been the answer to surviving the plague either.

She had more in common with Crysta. She could still hear her melodious voice swirl through her skull, soothing and supporting. Since the day Seri hatched, she could see magic. She followed it to her coven, the only one that had a prophecy of the Oracle, and Crysta had taken over her training immediately. Every day of her eighteen years, she'd studied history and magic. But still she knew so little.

Despite tons of research, they hadn't been able to determine why dragons developed powers. Throughout history, only Seers possessed powers. But young dragons, hatched during the Great Wars, had enhancements. Some were active, like Gregor's sense of smell. He caught scents that shouldn't be there. They pulled him toward what he needed or pushed him away from danger. It was amazing, or it would be if he weren't so rash.

But she had to admit, he was more of a savior than she'd ever be. He didn't let the weight of responsibilities subdue his personality. The coven expected a lot from him, even more than they expected from her. He believed in his power. It would lead them to the best way to survive the plague.

Seeing magic meant nothing. There was no guidance. No direction. Only colors, and those were gone now.

Fiona nudged Seri's shoulder to push her into the final cavern. Seri stumbled, something no normal dragon would do, and concentrated on her flimsy shields. The last thing she needed was to prove Renalia right about Seri's connection to Gregor during this formal meeting.

The cavern walls mocked her lapse. It seemed only a month ago when she'd walked these same tunnels, enthralled at the strands of magic flowing across the walls, weaving through the cracks, seeping with history. She adjusted her vision and accessed her power, hoping magic had survived deep inside the mountain's protection.

Nothing. Not even a shimmer in the volcanic rock. Her wings drooped and her tail curled protectively around her feet. There should be magic. Without magic, she was nothing. Not the Oracle. Not even a proper dragon.

Seri took a position along the far wall next to the other youngsters. The walls were worn smooth, and alcoves held torches. Firelight flickered across the floor, casting dragon shadows that danced with each breath. Unlike most keeps, the floors were bare. There'd been no time to decorate before they'd fled to the Source.

Renalia stood in the center, next to the archive stone, which would record the meeting. She wouldn't need the ceiling's natural formation to direct her thoughts to everyone at once, but it forced them to be still as it amplified every movement.

The black veining on Renalia's deep red hide rippled as she coughed, a reverse image of the magic that used to spiral through the cavern.

"Now is the time to ensure our future. This world has changed. We have changed."

Silence filled the room like a fog, reminding everyone that their existence was tenuous. Seri held her breath, wondering what her role would be in their future survival.

"It's not surprising that we must breed, frequently and quickly. We will need numbers to survive the humans that have had one hundred and fifty years to multiply. We need to ensure more hatchlings will survive."

A few dragons shifted their weight as tails curled protectively around them. Seri wasn't sure why they were so disturbed.

"In the Treasury archives, not only did the bearer of eggs choose their mates but each coupling was regulated."

Gasps and denial bounced around the cavern.

"There is precedence. Long ago, before my time, before humans came into being, females were tasked with building our race. And dragons didn't disintegrate into chaos. We are the best equipped to make this decision. Even during the wars, we instinctively bred for survival, even as we bred less frequently. Dragons like Seri and Gregor were the result, and we're still not entirely sure of the extent of their abilities. But you must admit, the magic in these younglings has served us well."

Flashes of gratitude swept through Seri. Warmth flooded her chest. Humans lacked the ability to feel the mind-link of validation for their choices. It's why they questioned themselves and others so much. With dragons, you knew where you stood, always.

Renalia sent a wave of faith to everyone. Seri had never felt so much strength and determination and wondered if she'd be as confident as she aged. Fiona placed her talon on Seri's shoulder and privately said, *"No one has suffered as much as Renalia. You'll have your own confidence as you grow based on your own experiences. Do not envy her, but admire. And tighten your shields."*

Heat suffused Seri's cheeks. Her shields had slipped yet again. She'd probably been leaking every single thought since she checked the walls.

Renalia's faith in their task washed over Seri. *"We must increase our population, without overtaxing ourselves. And we don't want an entire clutch of hatchlings all at once. Traditionally, we selected the males based on their prowess in the games. We do not have the luxury or time for games. Suggestions?"*

Seri leaned back as the ideas flew around the cavern. She was both terrified and excited, but she was careful to project only acceptance. Usually, dragons had to reach twenty years of age before they were permitted to mate. With so few of them now, she might be called on early. There were so many stories, good and bad, about the experience. But at least there used to be thousands of potential mates. Now there were fewer than a hundred.

Fiona sent an image of herself as a young dragon, a smirk on her face. *"You'll love it. Don't worry. You won't be unprepared, and I doubt you'll go first."*

Seri held back a snort. Fiona's smugness was one of the worst-kept secrets. Seri replied with an image of Sarcruze on the floor begging for Fiona's favor. Those two had a love-hate relationship spanning over sixty years. Fiona would make him squirm before deciding, even though they had an unusual mating bond. She had him completely wrapped around her talon. One day Seri planned on finding out how, but first she wanted to explore relationships on her own.

Fiona responded with an image of Sarcruze surrounded by hundreds of chubby rabbits and desire in his eyes.

Seri snorted, drawing the attention of those standing beside her. Her tail curled in response. She quickly reset her tail, hoping no one had noticed. *"Stop it, Fiona. This is a serious matter. But bunnies? Is that the way to your heart?"*

Fiona's strong mind pulled away from Seri's with a last impression of heat and something else Seri couldn't quite define.

A silence settled over the females. The older ones nodded. A shiver of excitement tingled from Seri's spine to her tail. Somehow, she'd missed the conversation while Fiona had distracted her, which might have been the point. Seri frowned at Fiona, who shrugged innocently.

"Good. We have a plan. Garianna and Hazley will breed first, as they're strong and have a history of large clutches. Then two others will mate a month later. If we need to, more will breed."

Relief flowed through Seri. She wasn't ready, anyway, and Garianna was thrilled. Seri sent her friend a supportive wave of pride.

"This world differs from the one we left. Until we know if the plague is gone, we must be cautious. We can't lay our eggs near any human settlements, and Sarcruze doesn't want us traveling far from the keep. Once the eggs hatch, we must collect the hatchlings and bring them here."

A startled gasp echoed through the cavern. Of the hundreds of eggs in each clutch, only ten percent hatched. Hatchlings made their way to a coven after they broke free of their eggs. Many never made it. This ensured the strongest survived.

Covens raised all hatchlings as their own. Unlike humans, there were no parents and young. In a single mating flight, a female could breed with three different males, if she wanted, and produce three clutches of eggs. This change meant they would all know the parents of each hatchling.

Anger flew around the room. Seri cringed, worried they knew of her search for parents. Her fear leaked past her shield, and she squashed it with confusion to reflect the rest of the room. Renalia wouldn't expose her secret.

"That's not the way it's done." Surprisingly, it was a middle-aged dragon who voiced what many were thinking.

A thick silence fell as Renalia stood tall, the light flickering off her glowing red hide. Patterns of black flowed from her wings, along the scales on her back, and around her body. Patterns that marked her age. Slowly, every dragon bowed their heads in respect.

"I know." Deep sadness accompanied her words. *"I don't want to change our ways. I've known them for all of my long life. After everything we've done to survive, we must ensure the survival of our hatchlings. We need strong younglings, and that means monitoring the results of our pairings."*

Her words moved Seri deeply. She often forgot how much life the elder dragons had seen, how much they had lost. Renalia's resolve overrode all the concerns in the cavern. They must do everything they could to ensure their survival.

"This can be an important change to our customs, instead of a trial." Glee infused Fiona's words with anticipation. *"Our males will have to show us they're worthy. We have the power. Let's enjoy it and make our coven stronger than ever."*

The females roared with excitement. Seri's heart leapt at the sound.

As the others left, Renalia pulled Seri aside. *"Seri. Your ability is essential to our survival. Monitor the eggs for any adverse effects from our long sleep, and check the lines of parental connections. The others don't know about that aspect of your powers, or that you already know the results of matings within our coven."*

Seri bowed deeply in respect, relieved her secret was safe, and hid her fears behind her tightly controlled shields. She mustn't slip now. *"The magic has changed. I can't see it in the keep's walls. I'll transfer every connection I discovered before we slept to the archive, but I can't see the threads connecting sire to youngling anymore."*

Renalia's eyes whirled her distress. *"I'll speak with Sarcruze. I, too, have noticed differences. It's imperative we know everything about magic and how it has changed over the years we were in the Source. This affects all of us and our future."*

Her legs trembled as Renalia turned her attention to Garianna and Hazley. Seri didn't know how Sarcruze could deny Renalia's request with so much power behind it. Excitement beat her heart a little faster. She couldn't wait to tell Gregor about their new impending quest, certain Zanthor would include Gregor in any hunt for magic.

Fiona rocked on her feet and clasped her talons across her chest. *"Sarcruze will have to convince me he is worthy. It will be a fight worth winning."*

Her confidence in her sexuality made Seri laugh. She wondered how many others had already picked out their mate and planned on torturing them before letting them know. Maybe she should start on Gregor now.

Power tingled deep inside her heart. In three years, he'd beg her for attention.

DRAGON STORIES
BECCA

By the time her week of punishment was over, Becca was too drained to feel anything other than exhaustion. Nathan hadn't been as churlish as she'd expected. They'd mostly hurried to the schoolhouse in silence. He mocked her and tossed out insinuations only when his friends were around. But this was the last time.

"Thank you for walking me home." Becca forced out the words as politely as she could, in case Mama still had neighbors reporting back to her. Becca wasn't about to risk another week of torture.

Nathan grabbed her shoulders and yanked her close, his breath hot on her face. "You did good, Red. Obedience suits you. As long as you control your temper, I won't get in trouble again." He branded her cheek with his hard lips. "See you later." His whisper held a promise that crawled up the back of her neck as he ran away. He'd behaved because people were watching, but that ended today.

Becca carefully closed the door behind her, resisting the urge to slam it over and over again. It was difficult enough keeping her mother mollified. Now she'd have to avoid Nathan without getting in trouble. The only thing good about the past week was that she could no longer sense emotions. It was a relief, but she felt oddly lost too.

A bark of laughter snapped her head up, and she encountered Grandfa's mischievous grin.

"You did a grand job, Becca. Your mother can't complain. Looks like Nathan's sweet on you too. She'll be pleased."

Her heart fell to her stomach. That was the last thing she needed. If Mama heard, Becca would be trapped forever, taking care of the twins, working at the Healing Center, always at her mother's beck and call.

"Now, hurry up and change. The twins are at Hannah's, and Kevin's with his friends. Your mother's going to the town meeting straight from the Healing Center, so we have the afternoon to ourselves."

Having Grandfa to herself was a rare treat. They both needed a break from bending to the village's disapproval. He'd vowed no more stories, but he'd change his mind once they escaped. She needed a story. She needed hope.

The hike to Grandfa's isolated cabin at Mountain Lake took an hour. Long enough for the forest to calm the turmoil in Becca's soul. They ran the last stretch through the rain, and Becca laughed as Grandfa shook, covering the entryway with water droplets that sparkled like crystals in the fading sunlight. It was magical when it rained while the sun still shone, as if the clouds poured only on them while the rest of the world was light. As Grandfa stacked logs in the fireplace, Becca hung their wet things over the mantel.

The plinking on the tin roof wrapped Becca in memories of comfort. She loved staying at the cabin. Grandfa built it shortly after his wife died. To get away and think, he said. To drink himself to oblivion alone, Mama said. She never went to the cabin. It was a place where Grandfa became the curious adventurer he must've been in his youth.

With the hearth lit and a pot of water boiling over the fire, Becca snuggled into the deep cushions of the oversized couch. A story would do them both good.

His eyes twinkled. "No foraging today. If only I had a story you hadn't heard."

"Grandfa!" She grabbed his hand and stroked the leathery smoothness. "How about the one about Jason and Zanthor?" Becca tilted her head, and her hair fell across her eyes.

Grandfa moved the red strands away, his touch gentle. "Hmm. I think you'd be tired of that one. You don't enjoy hearing about the devastation from the Great Wars."

"No. After that, when they set off on a quest. What did they do? Where did they go?"

"Ah. Well, we don't really know. I used to ask my grandfather for the stories about the time before the wars, much like you. So, I only know a little. Let's see ... I remember one. It doesn't have a proper ending, though." He frowned, as if pulling the memory from deep inside his head.

She squeezed his hand. "Whatever you can remember is fine. I can make up the rest."

Grandfa chuckled. "Yes. You create better stories than I do. Maybe you can figure out a good ending and tell it to Trish. She loves dragons almost as much as you. The boys want to hear about my travels with the hunters."

Curling her legs under herself and wrapping a quilt over her shoulders, Becca blew on her tea and waited for Grandfa to settle beside her.

"Here goes: One time, after the Great Wars but before the Age of No Dragons, there lived a heroic boy, Jason, who rode the smartest dragon in the world, Zanthor.

"The dragons were dying from a plague. Nowhere was safe. So, the two heroes flew deep into the Dragon Mountains searching for a place where the dragons could quarantine, just like the human villages had done to survive. It took many searches, but finally, they found a special forest, surrounded by huge, ancient trees.

"As they flew over, they discovered a caldera from an extinct volcano. They landed, and the air was crisp, clear of the stench of disease. Jason and Zanthor searched the world for healthy dragons and sent them to Jason's Keep. But only a few dragons believed isolating was necessary.

"An old dragon, Sarcruze. Remember him from the story of Fiona? He gathered his entire coven, and they flew to Jason's Keep, even though the journey was long and treacherous. But he wanted to protect the dragons more than anything. So, after he built a home, he sent Jason away. He sent all the dragon riders away.

"There are more stories about Jason, his brother Charles, and their valiant efforts to save as many dragons as they could. But there are no more stories about Zanthor or Sarcruze. The dragons slowly died off, but no one knows what happened to the dragons of Jason's Keep."

Becca frowned. "What do you think happened? Didn't Jason go back to find Zanthor?"

The fire snapped as a log shifted, and Grandfa stroked his chin.

"Well now, I think maybe he did. But I couldn't find any record of it. Years later, long after dragons became extinct, a brave knight searched for Jason's Keep. He'd found an old history book with stories of a caldera surrounded by snow-covered trees. He rode for weeks on his horse and found an ancient forest. He built a cabin and spent two years hacking a trail through the massive trees. But all he found was a dormant volcano with no way to climb to the summit. He didn't find any sign of dragons, alive or dead. He returned home, finally convinced the dragons were gone forever."

After a long silence, Becca blinked, breaking her trance. "That's it?"

A frown wrinkled Grandfa's forehead as he twisted his lip in concentration. "Yes. It's a mystery. But I bet you can solve it. Did Jason's Keep exist? If it did, what happened to the dragons? Perhaps the knight lied. Or he actually found them but kept it a secret."

Something was wrong with Grandfa's story, other than being too short. "Wait. The knight found a *history* book with dragons like the ones in your stories? Not monsters."

"Could be. Or I've mixed up the story from all my time in the university archives. I spent hours searching for proof that noble dragons existed. But I never found anything. Maybe there wasn't a book. Maybe he'd grown up with the same stories I did." Sadness clung to Grandfa's face.

"Or it did exist and then it was lost or destroyed. Why else would people not believe now?"

Grandfa slapped his knee. "Ah, Becca. There are no dragons now, and people don't believe what they can't see. Any evidence disappeared a long time ago. After the plague, entire villages were burnt to the ground to stop the disease from spreading. People were terrified it would come back. So anything to do with dragons would've been destroyed too. It is called the Dragon Plague, after all."

Becca shivered and tucked the quilt around her knees. "That's depressing. Tell me the one about Renalia and her famous lady rider, Diane. That's my favorite. Start with the song."

Together they sang, "There once was a rider so bold, who never did what she was told …"

Valley Keep

GREGOR

Day 14 After the Long Sleep

Gregor dove for the deer below, snagging it as the creature leapt over a rock. His strength and agility were returning, though slower than he liked. He couldn't figure out why the Source would keep them in stasis for a hundred and fifty years. The plague would've run its course long ago.

Seri streaked past, diving for a sprinting buck. She snatched it up and broke its neck in one smooth motion. A perfect kill, until she dropped the beast in the middle of the herd. Her embarrassment shot through him.

"Sorry. Now the best ones have scattered." Seri bit into the flesh, shrugging away Gregor's instinctive pulse of comfort.

"I caught mine before you landed." He snapped the neck of his own meal to stop its bleating. Seri was too hard on herself. Her magical power more than made up for her delayed physical prowess.

Ronin swooped over the stampeding herd and located the largest buck. He landed beside them with a dismissive grunt.

Showoff. Twice the size of Gregor, Ronin towered over them. Ridges along his supple blue hide hinted at the scales that appeared as dragons aged. But it was Ronin's wingspan and powerful legs that Gregor envied. His own limbs were narrow and long, and his wings were only a little longer than his torso. Compared to Ronin, he was gangly and clumsy.

"You need to stop thinking and trust your body to do the work." Ronin's advice to Seri wasn't new. They'd traveled together before joining the coven. Ronin didn't talk about his coven much, but he hadn't been happy there. He supported Seri, and he protected the powered dragons from the older traditional dragons. He was large for a thirty-year-old and spoke with authority, so he had earned their respect.

Still, it rankled that Sarcruze had sent Ronin to supervise their small hunt. As more scouts came back with news of empty keeps, Sarcruze was imposing more restrictions.

As if his annoyance at being corralled had knocked something loose, a whiff of pepper tingled along Gregor's nostrils, barely there, but foreign.

"You have something?" Seri leapt to the sky, sunlight shimmering off her turquoise wings.

He shrugged. *"I think so. From the other side of that range."* It could be nothing. After trying so hard to invoke his power since the day he'd smelled nightberry and interrupted Sarcruze and Fiona, he could be imagining the scent.

Ronin's chuckle rumbled through Gregor's skull. *"Careful, Sniffer. We don't want to wind up trapped in a cave-in because we followed your snout."*

Gregor rolled his eyes. One time. And Ronin wouldn't let him forget.

As he joined Seri in the clouds, the scent intensified, tugging him across the sky and over the ridge. Ronin followed with a lazy stroke of his wings, while Seri darted up and down, assessing the magic in the air.

A snow-covered valley lay below, nestled between the Dragon Mountain Range and the Coastal Mountain Range. A road followed the river through the valley and turned into a fort.

"Careful. It might be inhabited." With a single fluid stroke of her wings, Seri hid within the clouds.

The scent of pepper was overwhelming now. *"I think we need something there. I'll fly closer and see if I can identify what my power is trying to tell me."*

Ronin gasped. *"No. Wait. I sense humans."* Every dragon could sense life forces, but Ronin's power enhanced this ability, allowing him to sense energy at great distances and identify it. He veered to the northern range, caution in his thoughts.

But Gregor's power urged him closer.

"Turn away, Gregor. We need to report this settlement." Seri's voice seemed far away.

Gregor ignored her. This was important. For him. For the coven. Humans had never settled this deep within the mountains. He flew lower, below the protective clouds.

Within a large inner courtyard, humans scurried about, disappearing under fabric awnings along the walls of the sprawling fort. Gregor stretched his other senses. He was close enough to feel their energy. At least a few hundred humans and animals. He couldn't sense any fear.

"I need to land. Maybe they can tell us about this world." Oddly, the scent diminished. *"Or there's someone I must meet?"* The scent intensified. He followed it to the enclosure's east side. *"I'm not sure what it means."* His power led him, but he had to figure out whether it was a warning or a clue.

"Stop! We don't know if they've ever seen a dragon. We don't know how they'll react."

He understood Seri's concern, but he knew this was right.

"Too late." Ronin pointed at the humans running into the courtyard. Their gasps echoed through the valley.

Gregor landed as gently as he could on a platform against one wall and folded his wings along his back, attempting to look as small as possible. Humans were so easily frightened. The wooden beams creaked alarmingly beneath his weight. It would've collapsed under Ronin.

A man ran out from the nearest guard tower and halted as soon as he looked up. Gregor caught glimpses of his thoughts. He was supposed to keep the platform clear of snow, and the sound had reminded him he'd forgotten the day before. The man squeaked.

Before Gregor could communicate, the man stuttered, "You … Stay right there. I …" Then he ran off. An image of a tall, dark-skinned woman flashed into Gregor's mind. The man must be on his way to get the leader.

Gregor lightly touched the minds around him. Farmers, most of them. Families, craftsmen, cooks, all the usual members of a community. About a hundred humans surrounded the courtyard, examining him, some with fear, but most with curiosity and awe. They'd never seen a dragon, but a sense of vindication flavored their thoughts.

Ronin and Seri remained out of sight, their worry making him uneasy. Gregor had to do this. His power existed to help them.

A tall woman strode out, and the villagers' adulation for her reverberated through Gregor's mind. Elizabeth. Something was off about their reverence for their leader. He tightened his mental shields, his faith in his power wavering.

Elizabeth climbed the platform, despite the creaking and groaning of the timbers. She bowed slowly, keeping her eyes locked onto his. "It is an honor to meet you. I am Elizabeth, the Dragon Prophet of Valley Keep."

A shimmer surrounded her. He tilted his head to see it better. Like the clouds in his dreams, a sheen of oiliness swirled and slipped through her energy. The only prophets he'd heard of had died out during the Great Wars. After thirty years of wars, even the most devout of believers will stop listening.

"Will you not speak to me, dragon lord? Have you come to take us to our destiny?"

Seri snorted.

"Don't distract me," Gregor responded privately.

Ronin sent a warning. *"Her energy is unusual and strong. Be careful."*

Gently, Gregor whispered into Elizabeth's mind. *"I'm Gregor. I've come seeking information."*

Humans were generally flattered when offered a trade, but shock shot through her body, and he could feel her revulsion to his mind-speech.

"Can you not speak out loud?"

"No. I can only speak this way." Gregor tried to transmit calmness to ease her fears.

"This won't do." Her thoughts were muddled, but he caught a glimpse of terror before she slammed up a mental shield worthy of a dragon mind. He could no longer sense her thoughts.

Elizabeth turned to the courtyard and raised her palms to the sky. "People of Valley Keep, your belief in me has been rewarded. The dragon lord has come to tell us it is our time to rise, as has been foretold."

Disbelief held Gregor still. She'd lied.

Humans dropped to the ground, bowing their heads. But not everyone believed her. The pepper scent intensified, along with a wave of anger. Gregor caught sight of a boy glaring at the back of Elizabeth's head.

"This is an omen. Our time to rule has come."

Suddenly, energy pulsed from Elizabeth, and everyone started chanting, "Prophet. Prophet. Prophet."

"She's using magic, but it's slippery. I can't quite see … it oozes?" Seri's startled thought confirmed what Gregor suspected.

This woman was a Manipulator. They'd held positions of power throughout human governments. He'd never met one. He'd never wanted to.

"Are you real? Please tell me this isn't a dream," a voice whispered in Gregor's mind, hesitant, but filled with awe.

It was the boy. Chaotic images of books filled his mind, wrapped in a yearning for the stories to come to life. The boy didn't know how to organize his thoughts for proper speech, but at least he wasn't caught in the Manipulator's thrall.

"Who are you?" The pepper scent tickled Gregor's snout, and it took all his effort to hold in the sneeze.

"You're real. I'm Trey." Then his mind filled with images and colors too chaotic to understand.

Gregor frowned. Between Elizabeth's fear and the fragments from the boy's mind, it was obvious these humans had never seen a dragon. Elizabeth knew the protocol, but she hadn't expected a response and had now closed her mind to him. Maybe this boy was the key.

Gregor returned to Elizabeth's mind and encountered blankness. She had amazing mental control for a human who'd never encountered mind-speech. Unfortunately, he wouldn't get any answers from her.

Elizabeth strode away, gesturing to a large bald man at the platform's base. "Speak to the steward."

The man trembled on the steps. "I'll have the platform reinforced for your next visit. We hope you're satisfied with our offering, Oh Great One."

Gregor cringed. Sarcruze was going to blast him for exposing them. Finding a boy wasn't enough of a reason, no matter what his power indicated. He wouldn't be allowed to return to Valley Keep.

They had to leave before he made things worse. Images of offerings of gold and jewelry flashed through the steward's head. Useless to a dragon.

"Just leave." Ronin's laugh rumbled through Gregor's skull. But he wouldn't be the one who had to explain this infraction to Sarcruze.

Gregor's power was frustrating. The whiff of pepper was gone. He was sure it had led him to Valley Keep for a reason, but he couldn't figure it out. If he could convince Sarcruze to let him scout the village, his power might guide him.

As Gregor leapt for the sky, the boy's longing caught him.

"Can I see you again?"

Gregor wanted to say yes. But no scent appeared to guide him. He didn't know if he'd flown there to meet the villagers or this boy. He turned in the sky, away from the fort. Seri and Ronin flew ahead, too far for the humans to see them.

A final image of a lake, nestled in a nearby mountain, flashed through the boy's mind. Gregor could find it easily, and he sensed the boy wanted to meet him there at dawn. But he couldn't respond. He didn't want to make a promise he couldn't keep, even if a whiff of pepper encouraged him to try.

FOREST TREASURE
BECCA

The rains continued relentlessly through the rest of winter and into the first days of spring. On Saturday, Becca woke to silence, the roar of nature subdued. Hope forced her from her bed.

Teaching at the school had worn her out. Elder Frederick had suffered from migraines since that horrible day her power came to life. Becca needed time alone in the forest, away from everyone's expectations. Even if rain threatened overhead, she had to escape.

Quietly, Becca tugged on her oldest britches and a worn plaid shirt. She stepped over Kevin on the floor, and past the twins. For once, they didn't need to be covered. She grinned. A good omen for the day.

The kitchen was bathed in the muted glow that comes from the sun trying to burn off the fog. Becca danced across the kitchen, light with happiness. Through the window above the sink, fog blanketed the yard. The laundry line disappeared into the haze.

This was even better than no rain.

Mama hated fog. She'd insist on trapping everyone in the house while poor Kevin ran back and forth to the woodpile to keep the fire blazing, making the house as hot as the village drying room. It was a time to bake. The twins were old enough to help, and they'd have fun. As long as Becca left before Mama woke, no one would follow her.

Grandfa needed a break too. He and Mama had fought constantly over the last week. It was a perfect day to search for treasure in Oldwood Forest.

Becca stretched her fingers, easing the ache from running wet clothes through the wringer the day before. She'd worked hard, but her mother had only grunted at her efforts. She could never get past Mama's disapproval.

It would get worse once she heard the rumors. Ever since Nathan had escorted her to school for that week of punishment, he'd found innovative ways to corner her alone. She'd thought he lacked imagination, but all he needed was determination. She'd fought off more than one slobbery kiss over the past two weeks. It didn't help that all his friends thought they'd rolled in the Randal barn. So far, Mama hadn't heard, but it was only a matter of time.

Grandfa said his interest would pass when he moved on to the next girl. But Becca had no intention of giving Nathan the slightest encouragement, especially after that strange day when she attacked him. His possessiveness still made her shudder, even though she hadn't had that horrible sensation since the storm. And she dared not complain to Mama. She'd only tell Becca she was ungrateful, and how lucky she was to have caught Nathan Randal's eye. Mama wouldn't understand her revulsion at all. Becca shivered.

Too bad Mama wasn't Mrs. Randal. Becca really didn't see the point of which fork went where and why she needed to bow and keep her eyes down at certain times. Mrs. Randal was kind, and Becca actually enjoyed her etiquette lessons. Mama wasn't going to change, and there was no point wishing otherwise.

Becca whirled around. She ached for the peace she could find only in the woods, and if she didn't get moving, she'd lose her chance.

Avoiding the squeaky board outside the kitchen entry, she crept down the hall and pushed on Grandfa's door.

He woke mid snore, as if aware she was there, then rolled out of bed. He tilted his head, listening to the world.

"Time for a treasure hunt?" A conspiratorial grin spread across his face.

She loved that he needed no explanation.

"It's foggy." She couldn't contain her glee.

His eyes lit with shared delight as he thrust his healer's kit into her waiting hands. "Go, I'll grab the gathering pouch and be right there."

She barely remembered to avoid the board as she rushed to the kitchen, grabbed her green forest cloak, travel boots, and a walking stick, then slipped through the kitchen door. Grandfa was already behind her. He shut the door, and they dove into the mystical world transformed by the fog.

Silence everywhere. No birdcalls. No wind rustled through newly budding leaves.

Becca inhaled, and tension floated away as she exhaled. The air smelled crisp, wet, earthy, and so very green. Mist clung to her face, a delightful change after the constant drip of rain. She squinted at the muted, morning light trapped inside each tiny droplet. The sun was a blurry glow low in the sky, a faint beacon in a world of gray.

With a contented sigh, Becca slung the healer kit's strap over her head and settled the pouch against her hip. Grandfa grabbed the walking stick from her, and they strode past the wash line, along the narrow path through the soggy spring grass toward the forest behind their home. They didn't speak. Only their steps punctuated the silence.

Oldwood Forest was merely a dark smudge in the mist. As they walked closer, branches appeared, deep green in the muted haze. Becca loved how the fog made even the ordinary mysterious.

Becca stepped between the trees and silence enfolded her. The fog played tricks. New pathways appeared randomly, begging to be explored, but she stayed on the trail.

After only half an hour, the sound of cascading water broke the stillness. A small bird scolded her from a branch overhead. Becca laughed, too delighted to feel sorry for startling the sleepy bird.

The fog cleared once they reached the waterfall, the spray of water carving a path through the mist. The waterwheels farther down the river splashed as they turned, providing power to the village. Everything smelled so fresh and alive. Even the water's energy had a scent, which tickled at Becca's mind as she tried to find a way to describe it. Crisp. Metallic.

A flutter of fear whispered in her mind. Becca pushed it away. She was happy, and as long as she ignored the occasional unwanted emotion, she didn't have to deal with it.

"Do you hear that?" Grandfa stopped and peered at the rocks beside the waterfall.

The fear pulsed, tiny and delicate. Becca frowned. The emotion refused to be ignored, and she couldn't hear anything over the water's roar.

Her grandfather squatted near the falls' edge, next to a large rock jutting from the mountainside.

Becca cautiously kneeled beside him.

Grandfa slowly pushed away the branches of a shrub protecting a small pool of water. Resting on the rocks around the pool were three tiny creatures, no bigger than Becca's longest finger. Their deep gray lizard skin, a perfect match to the rock on which they lay, shimmered with flashes of red, gold, and green.

Becca sucked in her breath. "What are they?" She didn't want to frighten them.

"Drakelings. I saw a dead one when I was a boy. When I went to university, I researched them. They're timid and can blend in with their environment, but I don't remember anything about them having such beautiful wings. Look at those colors."

As if the creatures understood his awe, their fear shifted to curiosity. Their eyes glowed with moonlight and intelligence.

"Why do you think they're here now?"

"I don't know. Strange weather. Maybe they needed the right conditions." He shrugged, and the branch shifted.

One drakeling blinked. And disappeared.

Becca gasped. "Where did it go?"

Grandfa pointed to the bottom of the pool.

She stared without blinking while the forest stilled around her. Finally, the drakeling shifted, revealing itself.

The other two drakelings lifted their heads. Becca stretched out her senses, feeling safe here to explore. She sensed only curiosity. The drakelings were as curious about her as she was about them.

They unfolded tiny translucent wings, and a rainbow flashed along them.

"Be still," Grandfa warned as he slowly lowered his hand. A tiny silver tongue reached out and licked the tip of his finger. After a long moment of stillness, the creature climbed onto the offered perch.

It had two sets of wings, one longer than the other. Its skin changed color to match Grandfa's finger. As the drakeling folded its wings against its back, it rose on its hind legs to investigate Becca.

What did it think of her? She smiled. "I won't hurt you. I'm just admiring your beautiful wings."

It tilted its head, as if listening to her, then unfolded its wings and fluttered them. Pride slipped into her mind. She laughed, and it disappeared.

A ripple was the only indication of where it had gone. The other drakeling squeaked at them and dove into the water too. Her laughter had startled the poor thing.

Anger, followed by relief.

At this moment, Becca was glad she could sense their tiny emotions. They helped her understand the drakelings. She was connected to them. It wasn't at all like the invasive feelings bursting from people.

Grandfa sighed and released the branch that covered their hiding spot.

"That was incredible." Becca flopped onto her back and closed her eyes, trying to store the image in her brain forever.

Grandfa grunted. "I've never seen wings like that." He shook his head and chuckled. "Wasn't too sure that little fella would let me hold him. He was brave."

"How did you hear them?"

Grandfa shrugged. "Don't really know. Been able to see better and hear better lately. Not a bad thing for someone my age."

Embarrassment colored his words. She wondered what else had changed.

"Are they tiny dragons?"

He shook his head. "Dragons aren't truly lizards with wings, or birds, or even drakelings. They're something else. Their hide is like a lizard, only stronger. They have bones like birds, so they can fly. They can be any color. Everything you can imagine. There was even one who could change color at will, like the drakeling did."

"Great-Great Jason's dragon, Zanthor? Right?"

"Yes, Becca." Grandfa sighed, his eyes wistful. "I wish I could've seen them. I wish we lived in that time, and I could share them with you."

Becca hated it when Grandfa was sad. "But you do share them with me." She hugged him tightly.

He rubbed her hair. "Ah, Becca. You would've loved that time. I'm sure of it. Your strength and passion are made for dragons. You're stifled here. Your mother ... Well, our lives changed when my dear Rebecca died. Your mother worked hard to raise her brothers when I couldn't, and now she wants you to have a better life."

Becca grimaced. Mama's idea of a better life was the source of their arguments. She didn't want Becca to travel and explore the world. She didn't want Becca to be like Grandfa.

"I know." Grandfa moved to collect the herbs that grew at the waterfall base. "You crave adventure. You don't have the temperament for a small village like this, but that's what you have. You'll adapt. Once you find yourself a young man and settle down, your mother will be satisfied and let you be. Things will get easier. She was happy you handled the Randal situation so well."

Becca shrugged, disappointed her grandfather no longer encouraged her to leave. She was trying to handle Nathan, and she was certain her mother would blame her for every lie. Mama would never take Becca's side or even listen to reason. But she'd always thought her grandfather would have her back. He was tired. That's all. She pushed away the tiny feeling that he was more than tired.

While Grandfa climbed up the trail beside the waterfall to collect mushrooms, Becca waded into the shallows, searching for her treasures. There were bound to be a couple of unusual rocks after the miserable month of rain. The swollen river flowed from the mountaintop, carrying many types of crystals, from quartz to the more elusive sapphires. Sometimes she could find fragments of jade. The village jeweler was happy to give her trader coins for whatever she brought him.

As she searched, Grandfa's words rang in her head, along with a sense of loss. Becca scanned the path for her grandfather. He was still far away. She thought he'd meant she'd adapt to life in the village, but with the emotion whispering through her heart, she wondered if he really meant she had to plan for life without him.

She swallowed.

No. He was strong and healthy. He would reach fifty next month and become an Elder like Frederick. Never mind that no

Elder survived long, and Frederick was declining rapidly with his constant migraines.

If she didn't think about Grandfa's death, it wouldn't happen.

FRIENDSHIP
GREGOR

Day 17 After the Long Sleep

All the nearby dragon keeps had been searched and found barren, with no signs of survivors. Sarcruze had lifted the restrictions on the younger dragons, and they could hunt without supervision now. Gregor flew through the blue sky, wishing Seri were with him. But she was occupied with the other female dragons.

He spun slowly, enjoying the wind caressing the edges of his wings and flowing along his body. Everyone had a task, even Ronin. But Gregor was in the way.

He sighed. Though he wasn't the only survivor of the plague who'd fled to Jason's Keep long ago, the majority of dragons came from Sarcruze's coven. The rest, only twenty of them, were not only refugees, but they were also powered dragons, with abilities that made the oldsters nervous.

So, he'd been sent to explore the southern caves. Fine with him. Gregor enjoyed his new freedom. And he wasn't old enough to participate in the sudden flurry to be chosen to mate. He hoped Seri wasn't involved. She was only eighteen, and there were plenty of older females. Bile worked its way up his throat at the thought of an oldster taking an interest in Seri. He swallowed and shook away his unease. He had time.

With a twist of his tail, he altered the current over his body and forced himself down. Another twist sent him spiraling up through the darkened bottom of a dense cumulus cloud. He burst out the top and spun into the next cloud formation, his movements reflecting his thoughts.

Pepper tickled the tip of his snout, a memory of the last time he'd flown this way with Seri and Ronin. They'd returned and informed Sarcruze of the humans at Valley Keep. Sarcruze had forbidden any further contact with them, but there had to be a reason Gregor's power had led him there.

The boy.

His desire to speak with Gregor had been so powerful. And technically, Trey didn't want to meet at Valley Keep. He'd sent an image of Meadow Lake. There was no reason for Gregor to avoid a lake, and he could use a swim. He tilted his wings and caught the wind vector heading south. If the boy happened to be there, that wouldn't be Gregor's fault.

Oddly, the pepper scent didn't return. But maybe he'd already found what he needed. It was difficult to know for sure, but he'd felt a connection to the boy, and Trey had been immune to the Manipulator. That could be important for the coven.

Gregor flew low within the cloud cover. A dip down revealed fallow fields and a lake. He aimed for the other side where a dense forest led up the next mountainside. His dragon senses indicated at least one human and a dog walking beside the water. Excitement bubbled in his stomach. But then Seri's cautions echoed in his mind. He couldn't assume it was the boy. He inhaled deeply and concentrated. His power didn't flare, but the human smelled familiar.

Fortunately, humans couldn't see far. Gregor swooped low in the skyline, certain his emerald hide would blend with the pine forest.

It *was* Trey.

Gregor's heart thumped. If Sarcruze found out, Gregor's freedom would be stifled. But he wasn't exposing the dragons any further. Trey already knew about him.

With a sweep of his wings to orient his legs beneath him, Gregor landed inside the tree line. Snow flurried away, leaving a bare patch of frozen dirt to dig his talons into. He tucked his wings along his back and waited.

Trey ran up and halted twenty feet away. He gulped in breaths as he bowed slightly, maintaining eye contact. His mind was a jumble of pictures—Gregor, Elizabeth, hallways, a kitchen, and the trail to the lake. The dog crawled up, its belly rubbing on the snow, a proper reaction of submission. It quivered with terror, but stuck to the boy. Impressive loyalty in a beast who knew it was prey. Not that Gregor had ever eaten a dog, but he did enjoy wolves.

He sent the dog a soothing thought, and it rose and leaned against the boy. Trey absentmindedly rubbed the dog's head, initiating a tail wag.

"You came. I've come every day since you left, hoping you'd return."

Excitement, guilt, and a little fear blasted Gregor. Not as much fear as there should be for a human who'd never seen a dragon. This boy had guts. Seri's grin flashed through his mind. She'd see the similarity.

Gregor tilted his head. He didn't want to mind-speak yet. Trey had spoken out loud and seemed to need to ground himself. Plus, these human minds seemed more disorganized than those he'd encountered in the past.

With one last inhale, Trey's emotions settled and his mind calmed. *"Can you hear me if I think like this?"*

His mind-speech was clear, no longer muddled with conflicting images.

"Yes," Gregor whispered, wondering if Trey would shut him out the way Elizabeth had.

Trey grimaced and clenched the dog's fur.

"But you can understand me if I speak normally?"

"Certainly."

Trey closed his eyes and rubbed his temples.

"Mind-speech hurts your head," Gregor mind-spoke at a range lower than a whisper. The boy was obviously in distress. A hundred and fifty years ago, humans had no problem communicating mentally. Many of the mages preferred it among themselves as a sign of intelligence. He wondered if the change in magic had affected human development. It would be difficult to communicate if he couldn't even whisper to the boy without causing pain.

Trey grimaced. "A bit. I need to get used to it, that's all. It echoes inside my skull and leaves no room for my own thoughts. And thinking at you takes a lot of concentration."

"Perhaps you're trying too hard to project your thought. You don't need to yell. Just let it rest on the surface of your mind, as if I were sitting beside you." Gregor had never analyzed mind-speech from a human perspective, but Jason never had to work at it. Gregor could feel the strain in the boy's mind. Careful to keep his own tone as low as possible, he sent a wave of soothing comfort, uncertain if the boy could even sense it.

Trey ran his hand through his hair, causing it to stick up. "I'll get the hang of it, but it's easier to speak right now. Your voice isn't echoing so much either."

Gregor examined the boy as he fiddled with the buttons on his dark green travel cloak. His brown hide boots shone in the sunlight, completely different from those Gregor remembered from the soldiers. Everything had been muddy shades of brown and beige. But this boy wore bright green britches and a multicolored scarf. He suspected more than clothing styles had changed.

Gregor wasn't sure what to say. Concern for the coven's safety halted each of his attempts. Finally, he settled on something innocuous.

"Tell me about your life." Gregor settled into the snow, trying to put the boy at ease.

Oddly, Trey's mind fogged. It was a weird sensation for Gregor. These humans were more mentally cautious than the ones from his time before the long sleep.

"There's not much to tell. I've lived here all my life. My grandmother, Elizabeth, is my only family." Trey sucked in a huge breath. His excitement battered at Gregor's mind, stronger than his mind-speech.

Gregor smiled in encouragement.

Trey squeaked, all the air escaping, and fear blasted Gregor. Whoops. Gregor covered his teeth with his lips. Dragons didn't usually smile at one another. It was a custom he'd adopted while traveling with Jason.

Trey's desire to know about dragons overrode his fear, and he grinned sheepishly. "Sorry. You startled me. You're not going to eat me, are you?"

Gregor snorted. *"No. I don't eat friends."* There was no way he could explain he'd never wanted to eat humans, but not all dragons were opposed.

Trey visibly relaxed, and it was like another part of his mind clicked open. Gregor was fascinated. This human was complex. The coven needed to know about this unusual development.

"That's good. But don't tell anyone else. Especially my grandmother. She's already planning on capturing one of you to see if you're trainable." His disgust with the concept distracted Gregor from his words. The boy could project his feelings more strongly than his thoughts.

"You're magnificent and don't belong in a cage."

Gregor was about to scoff at the boy's concerns when Seri's cautions about thinking before he acted echoed in his memory. A human shouldn't be able to capture him, but he'd be foolish to ignore the risk. These humans were different, and not nearly as respectful as they should be. He stretched out his senses, checking his surroundings.

The dog had wandered off and was exploring the ice at the lakeshore. Gregor inwardly chuckled at his own sense of unease. The boy could be a distraction, but his sincerity was too intense. If it was a trap, the boy didn't know about it. Gregor scanned the forest one more time but sensed nothing unusual.

He relaxed his shoulders, aware his wings had automatically stretched in preparation for a hasty flight. He tucked them back against his body. The sight of a dragon's outstretched wings often intimidated humans.

"I'll let the others know to be wary of Elizabeth's plans. And I'll be careful."

Trey nodded, satisfied, then his thoughts dove in a new direction.

"What's it like? To be a dragon. To fly above the trees. Do you have the same senses as a bird or a dog? Where do you live? Do you feel the cold?" Trey vibrated with energy, his eyes as bright as the sun reflecting off the water.

Gregor chuckled. *"What's it like to be a human?"*

The boy's laughter was a shock. Ripples of joy spread from him and washed against Gregor's soul. It was as if Trey's entire body was involved in the emotion.

Gregor allowed his own happiness to flow to the boy.

Images of Trey's life flashed through Gregor's mind. Leaning over piles of books, writing carefully on lined paper, Elizabeth scolding him, meeting villagers, riding horses, and eating soup alone late at night. Woven through them all was an ache Gregor recognized. Trey's life had been as lonely as Gregor's.

Over the next hour, Gregor learned about life in Valley Keep. Daily sermons and a focus on crop production that was almost obsessive. The boy loved his grandmother, the Manipulator, but there was an overwhelming sense of disappointment. Gregor wasn't sure if it came from Trey or from Elizabeth. Human emotions attached inconsistently to their thoughts.

Gregor told Trey about his life before the plague, and Trey's wonder filled a hole in his heart he hadn't known was there. He'd been the youngest in a coven. No one had ever looked up to him or admired him.

"Would you like to fly?" Gregor interrupted Trey's monologue about breeding animals for specific traits.

Trey stopped midsentence and held his breath so long, Gregor feared he'd pass out. No reaction flew from the boy. It was as if he'd shut them off.

"Really?" The question released an ocean of longing.

"Climb on my back, behind my wings, and I can fly you up to the top of this mountain." At least Gregor hoped it would be that simple. He'd never felt the weight of a human. And usually, dragons wore riding straps for humans to hold on to. He would have to be very careful not to drop the boy.

Gregor was prepared for the intense emotion this time. Exultation, hope, and a whisper of sorrow.

Trey's smile turned down. "I'm not dressed for it. Ice covers the peak, and I'll freeze. And how would I stay on your back? You're bigger than a Clydesdale horse. My legs couldn't span your girth."

He was right. Gregor didn't want to kill his new friend. He paused as warmth washed through him. Yes. Trey was a friend. Pepper tickled his nose, as if his power agreed and approved.

He sent Trey the image of riding straps Jason had used when he rode Zanthor.

Trey slapped his hand against his thigh. "I can make those. It will take more than a day or two. Wow. That dragon looks bigger than you. How big do you grow?"

Gregor sucked in a breath. He'd slipped up. Now Trey knew about Zanthor.

But Sarcruze was wrong to distrust humans. Trey had given Gregor tons of important information, even though Gregor hadn't shared anything important. He bet Trey could tell them more about this world.

"I'm young. As I age, I'll get bigger. The largest dragons are the oldest." It wouldn't hurt to tell Trey a little, and Sarcruze couldn't stop him. *"I can return in a week. I'm sorry I can't tell you exactly when. Will that give you enough time?"*

A huge grin crossed Trey's face. "Yes. I'd like that. Is there anything you need? I can gather it for when you return."

Angry at his own restrictions, Gregor shifted his weight and his tail whipped into a tree. It didn't hurt, but it startled Trey. Gregor stilled. He didn't want to ruin this new relationship by frightening the boy.

But Trey wasn't frightened. He was embarrassed.

Eager to make the boy feel appreciated, Gregor's mind flashed to what the coven needed to survive. *"What happened after the Great Wars? How many humans are in the world now?"* It was a risk letting the boy know that dragons didn't know these things.

Although confused, Trey was too excited about riding Gregor to dwell on it. "I'll bring a history book, but most of that stuff is boring. We have great inventions and better homes now."

It was getting late. Someone was bound to notice Gregor's extended absence and look for him. *"I must leave now. But I look forward to meeting you again."* He couldn't keep his own longing from his voice.

Trey held his hand to his heart. "It would be my honor."

Warmth flowed from dragon to boy and back. Not even fear of Sarcruze would keep Gregor from seeing Trey again. This is what his power wanted him to find. A part of his soul.

TURMOIL
BECCA

The afternoon sun had burned away the fog by the time Becca returned home. White clouds flew across a gray sky. The warmth wouldn't last long, and the relentless rain would return.

The twins babbled in the garden, something about "carro-toes" again.

"Becca, come see!" Trish's enthusiasm made Becca smile.

She handed the full gathering sack to Grandfa and kneeled to see what mischief Brandon had concocted. The smell of nightberry squares and apple pie wafted out the kitchen door as Grandfa went inside.

Trish plunked a bright red carrot into Becca's outstretched hand.

"What?" It was a carrot, but it was soft. Like the tomato in Brandon's sticky grasp.

The twins chortled. Brandon thumped his chest, leaving a splat of tomato seeds and juice. "We made it."

His pride fluttered against her mental shields, trying to get in. First the drakelings, then Grandfa's hearing, and now impossible vegetables. She couldn't ignore it anymore. Something unusual was happening. And maybe she could sense feelings.

Becca stood in a daze, the carrot-tomato mashup still in her hand. Grandfa would know. He went to university and was the smartest person she knew.

She ran through the kitchen door, and a wave of annoyance blasted through her mind.

Mama's strident voice echoed loudly from Grandfa's room. "Stop encouraging her. She already romps the forest like an animal, instead of perfecting her stitching and cooking."

Becca dropped the carrot and slammed her hands over her ears, hoping that would stop the wave of emotions. It didn't.

Grandfa harrumphed. "You didn't think it was nonsense when you were little, Gennifer. Just because you've become hard and unyielding doesn't mean everyone else has to be. Besides, you're too hard on her."

"I have to. She's too much like you! You disappeared for days, searching for proof of your stupid dragons. I don't want that for her. Look at what it did to you. You couldn't handle reality when Mama died. I had to take care of my brothers. Of you. I was ten, Father!"

Grandfa's guilt overrode his own anger. Becca imagined a ball of light, a wall, a blanket, anything to stop knowing how they felt.

Her mother's tone changed to a plea. "I don't want her to waste her life yearning for things she can't have. I worked too hard to earn the villagers' respect. You're filling her head with impossible dreams. She needs to be practical and plan for her future before there's nothing left for her."

Silence followed, and Becca exhaled a sigh of relief as the onslaught halted. But it didn't last long. Grandfa's grief buckled her knees and stabbed her heart.

"She's a good girl, Gennifer. She tries so hard to please you. Can't you let her dream a little?"

"What good will that do? How do you expect her to earn a beneficial marriage? Gallivanting about, climbing trees, and fighting. Don't think I've forgiven her for attacking Nathan. She's rougher than her brothers, for Healer's sake. You ... You fill all their heads with stories and nonsense. Dreaming never got anyone anywhere. Look at you."

Mama's scorn and disgust drilled holes in Becca's world. Pain shot through her chest, making it hard to breathe. Pleasing her mother wasn't going to change anything. The room spun. She was nothing more than a nuisance. Becca thought she just had to try harder, and her mother would love her. But she was like her grandfather. And Mama had no love for him.

"Me? I've lived a full life. I've seen more of this world than you can imagine. You're the one who grew into bitterness. I pity you, with your narrow view and lack of imagination, my dear," he replied with quiet dignity.

But Becca sensed his guilt too. He'd done what he could to make up for his past mistakes, but it wasn't good enough.

Silence followed. A deep, hopeless wave of sorrow knocked Becca back a step. Grandfa. What could make him so sad?

She had to interrupt, even if it angered Mama. But her mother spoke again, and a vortex of grief and anger struck her. It took all she had to stay upright.

"I'll never forgive you for giving up after Mama died. You should've been a stronger man. I took care of everything while you drank your way through life. You should've taken the burden on your shoulders. You owe me, Father. No more of your stories. Understand?"

Her emotions settled on a simmering rage. Becca clutched the door frame, unsure if her body could take any more shifts.

"Or I'll kick you out of this house. Becca can care for her brothers and sister. We don't need you. I let you live here out of *pity*."

Waves of hurt engulfed Becca. She sank to the floor, covering her ears. With every part of her head pulsing in agony, she built a wall in her mind. She couldn't take anymore. She wanted whatever was happening to her to go away, forever.

Grandfa emitted a choked laugh. "You think you don't need me? You can't even see the wonder in your own children. They're more than pawns in your quest for status. They'll grow to hate you as much as you hate me, and you'll be alone. Then, you'll know real pain." He stomped into the hall, almost tripping over Becca over in his haste.

His face was contorted with pain.

"Don't leave." Becca scrambled up and hugged him tightly. "I love you. Please stay. We need you." Tears poured down her cheeks, her heart shattering into a thousand pieces.

She needed to make it better. His grief was so strong.

Mama scowled in the doorway.

"Don't coddle him, Becca."

Grandfa gently pushed Becca away and wiped her cheek. Then he shook his head, glared at Mama, and strode out the front door, slamming it behind him as he left.

"Stop sniveling and get to work. I suppose you heard all that?"

Never had Becca wanted to lash out at her mother so badly. But that would only make things worse. It was all she could do to keep her lips pressed together. At least her anger stopped anything else from attacking her. Or maybe her imaginary wall was finally strong enough. She nodded while clenching her fists behind her back.

"Don't give me that look. Your grandfather will be back tonight. Probably drunker than usual. He always comes back. The arrogant fool. He deserves the headache in the morning."

It was difficult for Becca to maintain an obedient expression while blinking to stop from crying.

"For Healer's sake, I didn't mean it. He can stay. But there'll be no more of his foolishness. You too. Alice Randal says you've done well with your lessons. It's time you start behaving like a proper lady."

Her mother continued to mutter to herself as she slammed pots on the stove and ran water over the vegetables, preparing for the evening meal. The twins had been silent during the entire exchange, their eyes wide, tomato juice smeared across their lips. Becca grabbed their hands and pulled them outside, certain Mama wouldn't have any patience for red carrots and Brandon's imagination.

Grandfa didn't return for dinner.

It was almost bedtime when someone pounded on the door. Mama looked up from her needlework, alarmed. Becca opened the door.

Sam swayed on the step, his face bright red. "You must come." His slurred speech made it obvious he was drunk. He grabbed the door frame for support. "Stephen ... your grandfather is in trouble. Gonna make him fly with his dragons." He fumbled the anti-hex sign for the Dragon Plague with his left hand across his chest.

"Who's going to do what?" Becca didn't need to sense emotions to hear Mama's exasperation. Though she wasn't sure how her mother expected Sam to be coherent in his state.

Sam swayed. "Everyone. No dragon lovers allowed." Then he slowly slid down the door to the steps, unconscious at their feet.

Mama turned around, annoyance in her eyes. "Run. Get Peter. It's probably nothing, but those drunken sots at the bar won't listen to me. Be quick about it. Just in case."

Becca ran to the meeting room where her uncle was conversing with Mr. Randal. As she flew through the door, a look of reprimand crossed Peter's face.

"Father," she said, knowing he'd be more likely to listen if she called him that instead of Uncle. "There's trouble at the bar with Grandfa."

Peter frowned and waved her away.

"It's urgent." She was willing to risk a reprimand for interrupting the meeting. Sam had been worried enough to come, despite being drunk.

Peter addressed the men Becca hadn't noticed. "Excuse me. I'll be back in a few minutes."

He gripped Becca's arm. "You know better than to trouble me with family issues."

Thankfully, her mother rushed up with Peter's coat. "Sam said they're going to make him fly. It could be nothing. He's probably spouting one of his dragon stories. But he might do something stupid. Please."

Peter shook his head, but he put on the jacket, anyway. "Did you two fight again?"

They walked away, bickering about what Mama might have done. Becca followed, hoping her mother wouldn't notice, and concentrated on the wall she'd built to keep Mama's feelings out. She couldn't survive another emotional battle, but she had to make sure Grandfa was safe.

Men's shouts filled the air long before they reached the bar. It wasn't a big building. The bar occupied the main floor, with two rooms for travelers above it. Five men stood on the roof, staring and pointing at the ground on the other side.

Becca's stomach lurched up to her throat as they ran around the bar.

Mama grabbed Peter's arm and gasped.

"Get the Healer, now." Peter's shout sent the barkeep scuttling to the Healing Center. Peter ran to a crumpled form a few feet from the back of the building.

Becca forced herself to follow, her mouth dry. It felt as if a horse sat on her chest. Each breath rasped in her ears.

Grandfa lay on the ground, his eyes wide open, staring at the stars. His leg was bent, obviously broken. Her mother sank to the ground beside him.

"It's too late." Her voice held sorrow, but Becca wasn't certain it was real. Not anymore.

Peter closed Grandfa's eyes and stood.

Agony filled Becca, destroying her fragile wall of protection. It didn't matter. No one else's emotions could get through. There was no room for anything else.

She was an ocean of pain crashing against a shore of emptiness that stretched out forever.

Grandfa couldn't be gone.

One drunk shouted, "Did the dragon man fly? He had wings." The others shushed him, dragging him away from the roof's edge.

The Healer, Mathew, arrived and examined Grandfa. He shook his head. "I'm sorry. He's dead."

Mama waved her hand helplessly toward Grandfa's leg.

"The broken leg didn't kill him. The fall was too much for a man of his age." Mathew stood and peered at the bar's roof. "I'm sorry, Gennifer."

Mother glared at the people gawking. They muttered as they slunk into the bar.

"Do we know who threw him?" Mathew asked. "He's too far from the roof to have tripped. It would've taken two men, at least, to heave him this far out."

Peter pulled Mama into his arms and held her. "No. And likely they won't remember in the morning. The barmaids might've saw something."

It didn't matter. Didn't they understand? Grandfa was dead.

Certain she would drown in her grief, Becca fled. Tears streamed down her face, and her sobs filled the air. There could be no end. Becca swerved around the house. She couldn't go inside where his last moments had been so terrible. Mama's angry words still rang in her ears. If Mama hadn't argued with Grandfa, hadn't belittled him and made him feel unloved, he'd still be alive.

Becca plunged down the forest path. She ran as fast as she'd ever run. She kept going until she reached the waterfall, and there she collapsed.

He was gone.

Killed by a bunch of stupid drunk men who hated his dragon stories. What was wrong with everyone? What was wrong with dragon stories? Why? Why had they thrown him off a roof? The pain kept rolling up, a bottomless well. There was no way to stop it from flooding into the world.

QUEST
GREGOR

Day 21 After the Long Sleep

Gregor hurried through his early-morning meal, gulping down the deer without even chewing. The dawn sun lit the clouds in shades of brilliant pinks and oranges. Seri had a quest, and it was a fantastic day for flying.

He'd snuck off to visit Trey a few times and was looking forward to flying with him once the riding straps were completed. Mind-speech continued to cause headaches for the boy, so Gregor spent their time together absorbing human history.

Seri would love the stories. Each day he struggled to keep his mental shields up, worried his excitement would leak, and she would discover his rebellion. But she'd been so busy, leaking her own thoughts of breeding rosters. Her shielding had been unusually inconsistent. Gregor suspected that's why Fiona kept her in the meeting cavern so much.

"Ready?" There was more to Seri's question than the anticipation in her mind. She'd been asking to return to the Source for a while, but what really drove her was concern over her connection to magic.

Zanthor's farewell was laced with worry. *"Fly swiftly, you two, and don't get into trouble. I can't hear you if anything happens. Maybe I should send Ronin, after all."*

"No. We'll be fine." Gregor was quick with his own assurance. Seri had waited long enough, and Ronin was away from the keep. Zanthor couldn't change his mind now. Besides, Gregor needed uninterrupted time with Seri. He'd missed her.

His longing must've slipped through, since Zanthor chuckled. *"Fine. Have fun. But I'll send Ronin if you don't return by noon tomorrow."*

Anticipation filled Seri's mind, and she leapt for the sky. Gregor followed, keeping his shields tight on his emotions.

They flew above the cirrus clouds for an hour. It should've been comfortable, but it wasn't. Seri was unusually silent, and Gregor struggled with what to say. She'd always been easy to talk to. He curled his talons. He had secrets to keep. Maybe she did too.

Finally, Gregor couldn't stand it. *"What do you think we'll find at the Source?"*

Seri turned her head, and he was startled to see her eyes whirling.

"Are you using your power?"

She shook her head, settling her eyes. *"Yes. I can see shimmers of red and green in the corner of my eye. But every time I try to examine it with my power, it's gone. There are hints of gold in the clouds. It could mean magic is returning."*

Gregor was stunned, but not by the possible return of magic. Seri used to have to stand still to access her power.

She grinned. *"I've been practicing. My power has changed too. You've noticed I can't keep my shields up?"*

He looked away. *"It's not that bad."*

"It's frustrating. But I think my shields and my ability to see magic are linked to the amount of magic that exists in the world. I'm struggling with the skills I had before we slept. But some things, like accessing my power while I fly, have become easier." She waved at the clouds below them. *"These clouds contain hints of gold. But not every one. It's as if only some contain magic."*

He'd never thought about how magic flowed through the world. Seri had explained about the world's water cycle. Her coven had maintained the learning stones of the Dragon Library, so she knew the source of magic existed in a lake. But his power was the key to find the actual location.

"Does that mean we consumed specific types of magic or that it will take time for it to move through the water system?" He'd only had his power flare a few times. In the days before they escaped the plague, it had been constant. He sniffed now. The scent of magic was a little stronger than yesterday, but still faint.

He tried to invoke his power, but all he did was sneeze.

Seri's laughter made his heart stumble, and he tightened his shields. *"Given how much effort that took, I'd say yes. Some magic may take longer to appear. But I've never seen magic in single blocks of color. It's always been all colors woven together. And our powers have changed, either from our time in the Source, or because there's so little range of magic. I'm not sure. It has probably changed for humans, as well."*

He yearned to tell her what Trey had told him. How humans didn't even believe magic existed. To them it was a trick performed for entertainment.

"What if magic didn't exist for them, because we depleted it?"

Seri dipped her head. *"I don't know. Magic is part of the world. Everything has magic. I don't think the world can exist without it. But it's possible."*

She twisted her tail and spread her wings, spinning slowly through the current. Her turquoise body rippled with sunlight, like ocean waves breaking.

"But when we woke, there was no magic." Gregor had to concentrate to continue their conversation. Seri was magnificent.

"I worried about that, too, but there must've been some. We couldn't have survived that long under water without magic. But it's changed now. Maybe because we used so much. I don't know if it will

ever be the same as it was. It's so fragmented. I must investigate the Source, so I can figure out why."

Her understanding of magic defied logic, and he was tired of trying to make sense of it. They would adapt. If the plague was gone, they had all the time in the world to figure it out.

He spiraled around her, enjoying her laughter. Being with Trey soothed his loneliness, but Seri made his whole being lighter, happier. And yet there were things she needed to know.

"Seri." He hesitated, worried she wouldn't understand his relationship with Trey. Defying Sarcruze was easy, but Seri had always treated him with respect. She'd made it clear she agreed dragons should keep their return a secret. But Trey already knew they existed. He wasn't exposing them to anyone new. She'd realize Gregor had done the right thing. *"What if I know what happened while we slept in the Source?"*

She dropped a dragon length, skimming the cloud, her distress stabbing his heart. She was silent as she flapped to regain height. Resignation colored her thoughts when she finally spoke. *"You went to see that boy, didn't you?"*

"Sarcruze is wrong." He couldn't restrain his outburst. She worried too much about appeasing Sarcruze, even though it was obvious he was too cautious. He clung to the old ways, refusing to gather the information the coven needed to survive. Sarcruze and his rules would kill them all.

Seri's shock hit him in the middle of his head, and Gregor closed his eyes for a moment. He took a calming breath and opened his eyes.

"He is. We need humans, or at least we should know more about the ones who exist now."

Seri shook her head. *"Gregor. You can't. He's our leader."*

She was afraid. For him. But once she heard the stories, she'd understand. And Sarcruze would listen to her, the Oracle.

"I'm not saying he's completely wrong, and I was careful, but I found out so much about what happened after we left. Humans blame dragons for the plague during the Great Wars! They've even renamed it the Dragon Plague."

For once, her shields worked. He couldn't tell what she thought. He'd expected shock, not silence. Gregor had to convince her he'd been thinking of the coven first.

"My power led me to him. That's the reason I had to see him. He just wants to help. Seri? Say something."

"Talking to that boy was wrong. You don't even know if he's telling you the truth. When Sarcruze finds out…" She sighed and lifted her gaze back to his. *"What's done is done. As long as it was only the boy?"*

"Just Trey. That's it. He's keeping our meetings secret. I believe him. He wants to help."

"Fine. You obviously can't wait to tell me what you've learned, and we have a long flight. Start at the beginning."

Relief flooded his chest. Seri wasn't mad at him, and once he told her about the things humans had invented to replace magic, she'd understand. The villagers at Valley Keep weren't normal. They respected dragons, even though Elizabeth had unpalatable plans. The rest of the world wanted dragons to remain extinct.

MAGIC RETURNS
SERI

Trey's information surprised Seri. She really hadn't considered how much humans would change, which was silly. Of course they'd adapt, especially if they lost their dependence on magic. Gregor was right. The coven needed to know human history to survive this new world.

"They built walls around their cities and villages to keep out the plague. They revere the Great Healer as if he was one of their gods."

Seri snorted. Humans and their beliefs. They had to create something bigger than themselves to explain things, rather than using their own senses. Dragons had been worshipped as gods at one time too.

"Dragons fell from the sky, and entire villages were burned to keep the plague from spreading. He didn't seem to understand that humans gave the plague to dragons. Not the other way around."

A dragon would have to be desperate to fly while in the agony of the plague. It must've been terrible. Seri's heart ached for them.

Gregor's chuckle broke the mood. *"He even had a story about dragons breathing fire and killing villages full of people. I told him we can't breathe fire."*

He shouldn't have done that. They might need to protect themselves from superstitious humans. If they believed dragons could burn them to death, they might leave them alone.

Seri shook her head. Since the day dragons helped humans with magic, they'd cared for the fragile species. Dragons existed thousands of years before humans crawled from their caves. Now humans thought of dragons as infected beasts? Years of coexisting wiped away as if it didn't happen. She couldn't imagine how their history together could disappear. And magic. The world was magic. How could humans lose that knowledge?

Trey's information came from books, and it wouldn't surprise Seri if Elizabeth controlled what information her followers had of the outside world. Other villages might have different stories.

Seri's strength lay in her knowledge of dragon history, not in her ability to see magic. Even their quest for the Source came from her research. But the coven followed her because of the prophecy, not her knowledge. Zanthor used her to convince an entire coven on the brink of extinction to fly the great distance into the coldest part of the Dragon Mountains. All because she was seen as the Oracle. A figurehead.

Gregor had obviously bonded with the boy. There was no way Sarcruze would allow that. Human interaction was supposed to be formal and based on mutual respect. Given the state of things now, it would be a long time before dragons interacted enough with humans to bond. Dragons were on their own to survive.

Another problem for another time.

As they neared the Source, colors wove through the clouds, more vibrant and easily discernible. Even the air felt heavy. Seri's heart raced. Magic wasn't gone. She forced her wings up, then down, judging the change in resistance. Definitely thicker. She glided beside Gregor. His emerald wings glimmered with reflected light, and the gold and brown spun in his eyes as he tried to access his power again. She wasn't sure why he kept trying. He sneezed every time.

The clouds opened ahead of them, exposing the mountain peaks surrounding the lake. Seri flew over the first range and gasped. Below her, the lake wove through the towering mountains, no longer encased in ice.

Even though it was a little before midday, the sky was midnight indigo. A green shimmer glowed above the lake, and columns of sapphire blue and pale emerald reached for the stars. Every color imaginable swirled through the water below them. She'd never seen so much magic, even when they'd arrived at the Source so long ago.

"Guess we didn't consume all the magic from the Source, after all."

Seri realized she hadn't adjusted her vision to use her power. *"You can see this?"*

"Yes. It's amazing. Is this what you see when you use your power?" Gregor's awe mixed with her own and floated down to the deeper recesses of her mind. There'd been no way to show him what she saw before. Now, he shared her joy and wonder.

Her heart skipped.

She wanted to grab his talons and spin in the currents. Heat rushed to her cheeks. She'd been spending far too much time with the mating dragons.

Now wasn't appropriate.

Forcing away her joy at Gregor's pride, she dove to the lake's edge. Much had changed in only twenty days. Magic flowed over her, overloading her senses. She inhaled deeply.

Pure magic.

More than she'd ever experienced. Her vision spun, and every part of her body felt lighter than a cloud. Everything was heightened and full of potential. Excitement bubbled through her veins, and she laughed into the swirls of colors.

The world wanted her to know something dreadfully important, if she could just stand still enough to absorb it. But she couldn't. Magic coursed through her entire being, making her tingle with electric shocks. She wove and danced, every part of her wanting to move. Her sinuous tail took on a life of its own and tangled with Gregor's.

He chuckled but seemed unaffected. Gregor kneeled beside the lake and dipped his talon in the water. He caught a swirling pool of magic as it released vapor to join the streaks in the sky. *"It's warm. Just like when we first came. But it's different, the texture. Thicker?"*

Seri was almost afraid to access her power. Her teeth ached from clamping her jaw shut. But Gregor was calm. What was happening to her? Seeing magic had never affected her before.

Jolts of fire and ice shot through her toes. There was so much energy.

Gregor closed his eyes and lay his head against hers. He knew when she needed support. His calmness flowed through her mind, deep into the private parts, an oasis in the chaos.

For just a moment, she wanted him to try his power first, but this was her task. She knew he sensed her doubt, but she didn't want to project false bravado. He was her friend. He'd be there if she needed him.

She leaned against Gregor's head and clutched his talons, needing to absorb his solidness, the part of him that believed in his power and took risks. The part of him that dove into danger without considering the repercussions. She cautioned him all the time, because she didn't want him to get hurt, but she admired his strength of conviction, even when it was wrong. His hold was steady, a rock of assurance.

With a shift in her breath, Seri stepped away and opened her mind to her power.

Magic was everywhere.

It pulsed from the lake's deepest part in an ancient rhythm up through the water. Ripples of color, invisible to her naked eye. Magic swirled on the surface, blending and separating, then rose in a mist over the lake. The columns of color were ten times brighter than what she'd seen with her dragon eyes. There was no way to describe the depth and range. It flowed around her and through her.

She was made entirely of energy. She could feel herself expand and solidify all at once. Seri dug her talons into the earth, grounding herself so she wouldn't dissipate into pure magic. She could do this.

As Gregor swooshed his talon in the water, blue magic flowed through him and settled in his nostrils, enhancing his power.

Beyond the mist of magic, waves stretched into the atmosphere, forming columns of visible color. Magic fell from the columns like rain, landing in the clouds huddled against the mountain ranges enclosing the valley.

Magic flowed over her wings, and Seri felt a sense of rightness. The magic hadn't changed. It was stronger here, merely faint whispers back at the keep. But it was the same as before, just compressed into a small space, instead of spreading throughout the world.

Gregor sniffed loudly. *"I can smell everything. It's like every scent I've ever experienced and more exists here."* His words held reverence.

Relief filled her soul, banishing the fear they'd used up all the magic in the world to save themselves from the plague. The black waters had disturbed her more than she'd allowed herself to admit. It must've taken a tremendous amount of magic to hold the dragons in stasis. No wonder walls of ice had formed around them. The Source needed to concentrate the magic in one place. But the cavern had prevented the magic from interacting with the world.

A world without magic. Seri could believe it now, after seeing what true magic looked like. The lake they woke in had been barren.

Now, it was life itself.

Still, the lake drained through underground waterways to the rivers. So, magic must've trickled to a few villages close to the mountain ranges, where the magic would've evaporated and seeded the clouds. Like Valley Keep. Enough to enhance natural abilities, like Elizabeth's manipulation. But the rest of the world would be barren of magic.

The things Trey had told Gregor made more sense. They would've invented things to replace the magic they lost. Over time, the knowledge of where the ideas came from had disappeared. Humans had such short lifespans, few living past their fifties.

Now, the ice had melted, even though the mountain peaks and nearby ice fields were still frozen, and magic once again flowed through the waterways. Between seeded rain clouds and rivers, the world was about to get a lot more magic.

Sarcruze wouldn't be happy with her news. Magic hadn't simply changed. It was now flooding a world that hadn't had magic in over a century. Dragons would need to prepare. Historically, humans hadn't handled magic with respect. The Great Wars and the horrible plague, which had chased dragons from their keeps, had been the result. Maybe with dragon guidance, humans wouldn't abuse the power this time.

A flutter of fear interrupted her awe. It was too much power to contain. The coven expected so much from her as their Oracle. But this was overwhelming. This was more than the ability to see magic. She could feel it.

Magic coursed through her talons, changing her.

She stumbled away from the lake, but it didn't help. Magic flowed through her veins, pulsed in her heart, and flooded her mind. She was nothing more than magic's pawn.

Missing
Gregor

It had been a perfect day. Spending time with Seri had made Gregor happier than he thought possible. And their trip had relieved his deep-seated worry that dragons had used up all the magic and destroyed the world.

Seri was certain the Source had enhanced both of their abilities. He tried to activate his power as they flew home, but nothing happened.

The sun eased its way over the horizon as they approached Jason's Keep. Gregor inhaled deeply, and Seri giggled.

"What makes you think it will work this time?" She swooped under him, a frown marring her beautiful forehead, as she checked another cloud for magic. She'd confirmed the concentration diminished the farther they flew from the Source, but, like him, she kept checking her power.

The faintest odor of kelp slid into one nostril. He turned his head and focused all his senses on the scent.

An ocean filled his mind, rotting kelp lining the shore, with flies buzzing over the drying tangles. Despair hung in the air. He shook the image free, dropping below the clouds.

"Gregor?" Seri's question came from far away.

He couldn't shake the emotion. His vision of Fiona hadn't felt so involving. A shiver of unease settled at the base of his skull. His power had changed.

"Wait." He needed to figure this out. Usually, there was a force pulling him toward what he needed or pushing him away. He shoved down the guilt that haunted him from the first time his power had flared. If he'd understood his power then ... He knew what to do now.

The scent tugged at him, but the sense of loss made him want to turn away.

"Something's wrong." His power had never tugged him in two directions before.

Seri radiated concern. *"Great Torin, Gregor. I've been trying to get you to react for a while. Magic completely engulfed your snout, but your mind went blank. I could sense your emotions. Otherwise, I was going to smack your sensitive nose to get you back."*

"I'm fine. But there's something going on at Jason's Keep. I don't know if we should go faster or proceed with caution." His power was frustrating.

She sent a mental shrug. *"Might as well get there and see. But we should keep within the cloud cover."*

Urgency propelled his flight toward the keep.

As soon as they were within range, Zanthor sent relief. *"Good. You're back. We can't afford to lose you too. Fly swiftly."*

His cryptic message increased the scent of rot. Gregor blew out, hoping to clear the odor from his senses, but it refused to leave him.

"Stop doing that." Seri's tone had an uneasy edge to it.

"I can't stop my ability, and the smell is getting stronger." Every part of him wanted to turn around and flee as fast as he could, to listen to his power. *"We need to turn away."*

A tiny part of him was thrilled his power was working correctly. But he was terrified it meant that the plague had returned.

Seri grabbed his talon when he turned. *"No. Zanthor would've warned us of any danger. We need to let them know about the Source. Is it bad? The smell?"*

Seri was right. The scent was strong, but the need for escape wasn't as strong as when his first coven died. A warning? Something personal. His heartbeat thumped in his skull.

What if Sarcruze had found out about Trey? Fear crawled along Gregor's spine.

By the time they landed, anguish had settled in the caldera like a fog.

Garianna ran up to Seri and clasped her hands. *"You must help me. Find them. Please, dear heart."*

Possibly because they'd spent hours speaking privately, Gregor felt Seri's shock at her friend's words. A personal cry for a miracle.

"What's happened? Why are you so upset?" Seri's voice was barely a whisper.

It had to be the plague to evoke such fear. The Source hadn't saved them. Gregor's knees buckled. It had all been for nothing. They were going to die.

"My eggs. They're gone."

Relief flooded Gregor, and he almost laughed. Nothing was as bad as the plague. But then the implications became clear. If their eggs couldn't survive, then they were the last dragons. There wouldn't be any more. Dragons had no future.

At that moment, Sarcruze bellowed, dropping Gregor to the ground with the force of his rage.

Waves of blame and outrage assaulted Gregor's mind. He whimpered and curled up into a ball, as if that could protect him.

"Stop it!" Fiona sent soothing mint into Gregor's mind, attempting to alleviate Sarcruze's attack.

"Sarcruze. It's not his fault. None of this has anything to do with him." Zanthor was exerting all his power of conviction. Even Gregor could feel it through his trauma.

"We followed him. And you. All because of that ridiculous ability. Everything is because of him." Waves of frustration and anger rolled through Gregor. Sarcruze wasn't holding back.

"One hundred fifty years, lost. Our way of life, lost. Now our future is lost. Being in that lake has destroyed our fertility. With no eggs, we'll go extinct. We should've stayed in quarantine until the plague had run its course. We would've survived, if it wasn't for him."

"NO!" Fiona's roar rivaled that of the Great Torin and overpowered Sarcruze's rant. *"Enough. You ridicule and put down Gregor because of his unique ability, and you know what? That's your fault. You're his biological father. He got his power from us."*

Stunned silence blanketed the cavern. The onslaught stopped. Gregor grabbed his aching head and rose to his knees. No one dared speak. Parentage was never discussed. Covens claimed all younglings as their own.

"Not anymore," Seri whispered gently as she helped Gregor to his feet. *"I meant to tell you. About Fiona and ... We're monitoring the matings. To increase the chances for survival."*

Fiona and Zanthor pulled Sarcruze away, speaking intently to him as he shook his head.

"This isn't finished." Menace and confusion laced Sarcruze's very private message to Gregor.

Gregor shook. The change in his power. The sense of loss. The vision of rot, just like when his own coven perished. It was too much to bear. Sarcruze hated him. Seri had kept something important from him. And Zanthor. His friends should've warned him to stay away until Sarcruze had calmed down.

Anger filled the holes left by their betrayal and pulled together the frayed edges of his pain. Gregor flexed his shaking legs and leapt for the sky. He had to get away. His body had known all along.

As he flew, he shielded his mind from everyone. He didn't want to hear their blame or their consolations. The mountains called to him, cold and lonely. All he'd ever wanted to do was belong and prove his worth. He'd never considered both were impossible with Sarcruze as the coven leader.

With each beat of his wings, the scent of decaying kelp lessened, replaced with the tang of salt water. Or maybe that was his tears.

STRATEGY

GREGOR

Fury drove Gregor's wings like the beat of a war drum. Sarcruze was wrong.

Gregor wished he could go back to the days before Sarcruze and his coven had arrived. When it was just Zanthor, Seri, Ronin, Garianna, and himself. And Jason's group of humans.

No one was better than anyone else. Not human or dragon. They'd supported each other and found a solution.

But Sarcruze believed he was the dragon to save all dragons. That all the answers lay in adhering to tradition. He couldn't accept that quarantining at Jason's Keep wouldn't have been enough. Otherwise, there'd be other dragons alive.

When Gregor joined Sarcruze's coven, there'd been nothing else they could do. But his group had still searched for a cure. They'd found other survivors and brought them to Jason's Keep. And Seri had learned about the Source of magic. When Gregor's power flared, he'd been so certain it was the answer. The scent had pulled him through the vast Dragon Mountains to the Source. They wouldn't have found it without him.

If they hadn't slept in the lake, they would've died, just like every other dragon from their time.

He settled into a smooth flight pattern, circling the keep, hoping his power could tell him what to do now. It had been so strong before. He wanted that strength back. He wanted that certainty.

But there was nothing. No scent to guide him.

Seri begged him to return, but he shut out her pleas.

She could've told him about Sarcruze being his sire during their day together, but she hadn't.

Pain needled him at the deepest level of his private mind, as if fraying an image. It didn't matter who his parents were, obviously, since he'd inherited nothing from them.

He wasn't like Sarcruze in any way.

His mind shied away from comparing himself to Fiona. He admired her, and it wouldn't be the worst thing to be related. But what did that matter to a dragon? Other than Seri's belief in passing on traits, there was no reason to know.

The coven was family. They weren't humans.

Although, most humans would die for their progeny. He admired that in them. But he'd seen more orphans than families. The Great Wars killed so many. Even Trey spoke only of his grandmother. Humans still had short lifespans.

Being with Trey made Gregor feel special.

A warmth spread across the back of his neck, easing his tension. Trey might even die for Gregor. Human emotions were so single-minded and uncomplicated.

Gregor flew into the shimmer of the full moon, toward Valley Keep.

Trey would soothe his soul.

DAY 22 AFTER THE LONG SLEEP

Gregor spent a miserable night alone next to Trey's lake.

As soon as the weak rays of sun broke through the trees, he shook and stretched his wings. The silence in his head was a welcome relief. At the keep, there was a background of public conversations and a constant thrum of emotions. Being connected mentally left no room to think. But it also meant he was never alone.

He could still feel the others, especially Seri and Zanthor, since he hadn't traveled far enough to lose contact.

Birds twittered, and a rabbit hopped over his toe. With a quick snap, Gregor gobbled the easy meal. It eased his hunger moderately. In the aftermath of Sarcruze's anger, Gregor had forgotten to eat. After a night alone, he wasn't sure he wanted to see the boy today, but it was a safe place with plenty of food.

Gregor dove into the lake, sucking back fish, and swimming until he felt the last of his anxiety fade. He floated, spreading his wings on the surface to catch the sunlight. Someone would find him soon. Zanthor never let him brood for long.

He'd smelled kelp before he reached the keep. It had to mean something.

Sarcruze's unjust accusations burned through Gregor's mind. The eldest dragon didn't approve of the younger dragons' abilities. But it wasn't as if they had a choice. Shortly after the wars started, younglings and new hatchlings developed powers. Not all of them, but most. It baffled the elder dragons. Zanthor was eighteen when his power manifested.

Gregor had been barely sixteen, and it was the worst day of his life.

He shied away from the memory, even as the smell of burning dragon flesh filled his nose. He blew out and sneezed twice. A light breeze blew the calming scents of pine and grass against his face, replacing the terrifying past.

It was the future he must focus on. The eggs were the key. Without them, dragons would perish over time until none were left. The egg casings were tough enough no animal could've eaten them. Animals might collect one or two, hoping they'd soften over time, but not hundreds of eggs.

When he'd hatched, small, hard, dead eggs had surrounded him. Maybe his power was indicating that the hatchlings had died in their shells. Only ten percent of eggs hatched, and then those hatchlings had to survive their journey to a coven. Fear and hunger had driven him from the river to the sky. He was the last hatchling to join his coven.

It was too early for the eggs to lose their outer casing. If the hatchlings were dead inside the eggs, there was nothing they could do, and Sarcruze was right. The long sleep had made dragons infertile.

But Gregor couldn't believe they'd survived the plague to be faced with another form of extinction. His power must be warning him. Maybe the eggs were dormant because they needed magic to develop. The scent of kelp could indicate life. It was related to the ocean, which was a lot of water. Magic transferred through the water system. But the vision of decay was a warning. He could be running out of time to find them.

Gregor shook his head, and ripples of water flowed over his outstretched wings. He'd never thought about eggs so much. Gregor snorted and bubbles popped in the water.

Sarcruze would blame humans. But humans didn't even know dragons existed. They wouldn't search for eggs. They wouldn't even recognize them.

No. It had something to do with magic.

Nightberry tickled his nose. Gregor sniffed to capture the scent, but it disappeared.

That's what he'd do. Search the waterways for the missing eggs. Nightberry would guide him. He would prove to Sarcruze that his power was useful. And he'd be the one to save them.

Gregor swam to shore. Seri would help. He'd already forgiven her. She probably hadn't told him about Sarcruze because it wasn't important. He didn't care who his sire was. No other dragon would care either. That wasn't their way.

Another whiff of nightberry sealed his intent. Once he found the eggs, even Sarcruze couldn't cast him from the coven.

It was full morning now, and Gregor hoped Trey would show up soon. He needed the boy's help, just in case any villager had discovered colorful orbs. But he could only wait for a short time.

He couldn't risk the coven looking for him and finding out he'd befriended a human.

QUESTIONS
SERI

The way Sarcruze had dominated Gregor terrified Seri. She couldn't shake the image from her mind. No dragon should humiliate anyone that much. It certainly wasn't Gregor's fault the eggs were missing.

She'd tried to contact Gregor all night. He ignored her, but she knew he was at the lake where he met the boy. She wanted to go to him so badly she felt physically ill at having to stay in the keep. But leaving right now would make things worse.

The coven was at a tipping point. Sarcruze had overstepped, and there were concerns his mind had been damaged from his time in the Source. He was the eldest.

"He's a danger to us all. We need you to lead us, Zanthor." Ronin usually kept to the sidelines, but the fear in his voice reflected that of all the powered dragons. There weren't that many of them. Twenty, maybe. Seri had never actually checked, and now she would have to wait for her power to return.

Zanthor held up three talons, the signal for silence. More than half the coven circled him in the caldera's center. Fortunately, Fiona had given Sarcruze belladonna mixed with valerian to help him sleep.

"Sarcruze is the rightful leader of his coven, and by right of age, he is the leader of our joined coven. We decided long ago." Zanthor made it sound like a peaceful decision. But many dragons had argued about who should lead when they fled to Jason's Keep. Seri

remembered how much it had pained Zanthor to step aside. He'd refused to use his power to convince the coven. Though Sarcruze had been smart enough to put Zanthor in charge of their journey to the Source.

"But he detests those of us with powers. We can't help what we are." The dragons bobbed their heads in agreement.

Seri hoped her shields held through this meeting. She still hadn't told them about magic pouring back into the world. Dragons who feared magic abilities would be even more afraid of them if they knew powered dragons might change.

Garianna clasped Seri's talons. *"Do something. You're the Oracle. Speak up."* Her private demand made Seri's heart stutter. She didn't want anyone to remember her destiny right now.

"It's not time. Please, Garianna, don't say anything."

But Garianna was in too much pain over the loss of her eggs, and she'd believed for so long. *"We already have a savior. Seri will know what to do."*

Seri cringed as every eye turned to her. Defensively, she projected calmness, despite the expectation stabbing at her shields.

"Seri has a special role in our future. But I don't believe leading the coven is the best use of her abilities." Seri sighed as Zanthor's conviction drew their attention back to him.

He was right. That would be a complete disaster. And it would expose her for sure. She was no leader.

"I'll speak with Sarcruze and voice your concerns. We don't need a new leader and more chaos. But I agree he needs help. At least until we deal with this latest crisis. More importantly, I think all of you should come up with solutions and present it at the meeting tonight."

Zanthor held private conversations with the more vocal dissenters while Seri waited silently at the edge of the crowd. Reinforcing Sarcruze's leadership was wise of him, but their concern was valid. Dominating a dragon was a punishment for a crime that endangered the entire coven. Gregor didn't deserve it. No one did.

It had been easier when there'd just been their small group searching for a cure. Seri yearned for that time. Since they'd awoken, everyone had been busy with their own concerns. She missed their focus. Hopefully, solving the egg crisis would bring everyone together.

Seri sent Gregor a wave of sympathy when he finally returned. After the morning meeting, most believed they weren't doomed, but Zanthor would need a solution soon.

Seri searched the archive stone for answers. It stored all their memories, from before their long sleep and after. But she found nothing she didn't already know. The Treasury and its repository of archive stones since the beginning of time would have answers. This must've happened before in the thousands of years of dragon history.

"Seri, I have a quest." Gregor's voice was quiet, not wanting to interrupt, but she sensed his resolve.

"Are you all right?" Her concern overrode everything else.

Gregor waved her question away. *"It's over. We have more important issues right now than Sarcruze and his bias against magic abilities."*

Seri vowed to protect Gregor from Sarcruze. Others would help. No one believed Gregor was to blame for anything.

She exited the cavern in time to witness Gregor striding past, his tail straight, confident, and determined. Fiona placed a talon on Sarcruze's forearm. Seri was pleased to see Zanthor, Ronin, and

Garianna waiting for them, a sign of support for Gregor, their original quest group together again.

Sarcruze was strangely silent, his powerful shields hiding his reaction.

Gregor laid out his plan logically. Powered dragons needed to search the clutching sites. They could find clues that weren't visible to normal dragon abilities.

"This affects everyone in the coven. Let them help." Fiona's passion shone through her voice. She believed in them, all of them. Their survival depended on procreating.

"We have abilities our ancestors didn't. Using them in this time of uncertainty makes sense." Zanthor's tone held only respect.

"But we need protection. I can't have half the coven disappear." Sarcruze stood taller, towering over them all, a reminder he was the leader and the eldest. He glared at Zanthor, ignoring Gregor as if he had nothing to do with it.

Seri held back a snort. If half the coven had powers, there wouldn't be any issues.

"Agreed. A group of five with abilities should be sufficient, and a scout. We still need to keep our existence a secret from humans." Zanthor soothed Sarcruze with waves of conviction.

While they gathered supplies, Sarcruze spoke with each member of the party and carefully avoided Gregor.

Fiona came to send Gregor off. *"I've known since Seri joined us, and I've always been proud of you and your ability. He'll come around, in time. Especially if he wants my affection again. He's stubborn and sticks to the old ways. But he also wants us to survive and to thrive. He'll adapt."*

She turned and leaned her head on Seri's. *"You take care. The desire to fix everything fills your heart. Concentrate on your magic. Depend on the others. I'm sure you'll find a solution by combining your abilities. You don't have to do it alone, dear heart."*

The endearment stunned Seri. She dipped her head and sent her appreciation, knowing she'd dropped her shield again.

Fiona laughed. *"Don't worry. Your shields will grow as you age. You're still a youngling. Now fly strong and swift. And come back safely. The plague may still be out there."*

Seri had forgotten about the plague. It couldn't still be waiting for them. But the image of the magic pouring from the Source filled her mind. Magic created the plague. The world lost magic while the dragons slept. Now it was back, so it was possible for the plague to return.

"Eggs first. Then we'll figure out how to deal with the plague." Gregor's confidence wrapped around Seri's heart, soothing her fear. Then he leapt into the sky, and she followed.

GRIEF
BECCA

A week of miserable rain had kept Becca inside since the day Grandfa's body burned to ash on the funeral pyre. Pain had filled her soul, keeping everything else out. But it hadn't lasted.

Many villagers offered their condolences, but she felt every one of their true feelings and heard their whispers. "He was a drunk who rambled on about things best left in the past." "Good thing he died before he became an Elder. He would've sent the council into the dark ages of the wars." Each criticism drove the stake deeper into her heart.

They didn't know him. He was a compassionate man who drank to drown his pain over losing her grandmother.

Only a few people remembered him fondly. But even their emotions had been too difficult. Desperate to protect herself from the onslaught, Becca built more layers on her mental wall between the world and herself.

But she couldn't muffle her own grief. It rolled through her soul, crashing waves of conflict. First pain and sadness, then anger so strong she thought she'd burst into flames. How could he leave her?

Everyone was angry. Kevin stomped around the house, breaking things. Finally, Becca had begged Marcus for help. Her heart had fluttered when he'd smiled and kissed her cheek and agreed to take her brother with the hunters. "Whatever you need, Becks."

Kevin needed discipline and activity. She didn't know what she needed.

Mama had left the care of the twins to Becca. At first they'd been quietly obedient, lost in their own grief. But now they wanted to talk about Grandfa, and, more dangerously, they wanted dragon stories. They didn't understand when Becca explained they needed to forget about dragons. Probably because she couldn't believe Grandfa's stories had killed him.

But today was different. The constant patter of rain on the roof was absent, and the morning sun shone through the windows. Silence settled deep into Becca's mind. Uncle Peter had no meetings and would help Mama with the twins.

It was time to bury her grandfather.

She knew exactly where to go, but first she needed to convince her mother.

Becca's heart beat unsteadily as she clutched the plain wooden box containing Grandfa's ashes tightly against her chest. The dishes clattered as Uncle Peter helped Mama at the sink. Kevin had left at dawn with Marcus, and the twins were still asleep.

She had to do it now, before Mama recalled it was Becca's fault Grandfa had died. The fight had been about her. With a deep breath, Becca sucked in her courage and stepped into the kitchen.

Mama's gaze locked onto the box, and she gripped the back of the kitchen chair. "No. We'll bury him in the garden when we plant the summer gold blooms."

Mama's feelings tumbled through Becca's mental wall as if it were no more than an unsteady stack of firewood.

Denial. Pain. Guilt.

Becca clutched the box harder, ready to give up. But for once, this cursed ability might help. She could use Mama's guilt. If she hadn't kicked Grandfa out, he'd still be alive.

"Mama, please. You know he loved the waterfall. He went every day, even in the middle of winter. It was home for him. You owe him that comfort." Never mind he went there to escape their arguments. He went to the bar, too, but Becca didn't want to bury him at the place where he'd been killed.

Mama shook her head, her gaze on the table.

Uncle Peter put his hand on Mama's shoulder and whispered in her ear. A sob burst from Mama, and tears flowed down her cheeks as she turned into Peter's arms.

A new emotion slapped Becca in the face. Mama's grief was real, but it was insignificant compared to her satisfaction. She was using the situation to manipulate Peter. She didn't care what Becca did with the ashes.

Peter met Becca's gaze over her mother's head. "This is too difficult for your mother. The waterfall is perfect."

Before Mama could say anything to stop her, Becca grabbed the gathering satchel and dashed through the kitchen door. She didn't want to know how little her mother cared for Grandfa.

As she walked along the trail to the river, the twitter of birds and a light breeze eased the ache in her soul. The climb up the rocky, overgrown path to the plateau above the waterfall was familiar and poignant. She hadn't been back since that magical morning of fog and drakelings.

A lifetime ago.

At the top of the falls, Becca sat on the bench Grandfa crafted before she was born. Here, no emotions could beat at her mind. The roar of water, the rustle of branches moving in the breeze, and the tiny chitters of small animals wrapped her in a cocoon of peace. She smiled at a squirrel's angry tirade, before it ran up the nearest pine tree.

Becca rubbed her hand along the worn armrest, comforted by the smoothness of the rounded logs.

"Grandfa." His name slipped from her lips, a whisper of loss. "I miss you so much."

The past week had felt like a year.

Becca closed her eyes and took five deep breaths. There was nothing to hurt her here, and she could imagine Grandfa sitting beside her, like he had so many times before. She wished she'd told him so many things when she had the chance.

"Don't worry about Kevin. Marcus is teaching him to be a hunter. I think Kevin wanted to be like you, but he never had the patience for herbs. Brandon and Trish will be OK. Although, something is happening to them, just like me. You know how you could see and hear better? Well, I can sense emotions. It's not as great as it sounds. It's a curse. I hate it, and I can't control it. And the twins ... they've always been in their own little world, but somehow their imagination is becoming real. Or I'm seeing things. I wanted to tell you. I wasn't sure you'd believe me."

The wind shifted, blowing Becca's hair across her mouth. She sighed and turned her face up to the sky, blinking at the brightness.

"I wish Mama were more like Mrs. Randal. She never yells, and she says I'm a natural lady. At least Mama can't complain about that. Not that I have any desire to act so proper and pompous. Why can't I just be me? Mama wants me to change, and I just can't."

She almost heard his snort of disagreement. Grandfa had never liked Alice Randal, said she was a busybody, poking her nose into other people's lives.

"Nathan's a problem. He's being a donkey, making up stories about what happened when we had to escort each other to and from the schoolhouse. Jenny snickers every time she sees me. I don't know what will happen when Mama hears."

Grandfa didn't answer. He couldn't. But she knew he'd tell her she could figure it out. He believed she could do anything.

"I wish you were here."

But he wasn't, and he never would be again. Becca let the tears roll down her cheeks. She caught one with her tongue, salty and sad. She rubbed a few pine needles between her fingers. The scent would always remind her of Grandfa and his soap. She missed his hugs most of all.

He wouldn't want her to cry. He loved her laugh. It was hard to laugh now.

Shaking her head and banishing the tears, Becca stood. Water rushed over the outlook's edge and plummeted into the pool below. A breeze blew her hair into her eyes as the spray misted her face.

The moment, the space, felt right.

After removing the lid, she tilted the box upside down. Ash tumbled above the water, a gray column of life extinguished. Three drakelings darted from the falls and flew through Grandfa's ashes, forming the image of a dragon. Becca gasped.

The nebulous gray shape spun in the spray and then spread out to the edges of the falls. Becca's heart stilled, and she exhaled.

Wings, translucent and barely visible.

A faint hum vibrated deep within Becca's ears, and the drakelings dove through the center of the ash dragon as it fell to the rocks below. A hazy tail flickered before the rushing water swallowed the last of the ash.

A sense of rightness settled deep into her soul. Grandfa had found his dragons. He'd certainly had the soul of one.

A light wind swirled through the leaves, hinting at change. "I'll find joy, Grandfa. I'll be strong. For both of us. And I won't forget your stories."

Her heart was lighter as she strode deeper into the woods, searching for drakelings and secret places where a girl could dream of adventures and dragons.

After three wonderful hours of exploring, Becca had filled the gathering satchel with herbs. It was time to return home, before Mama decided Becca was at fault for something else. At least she had something to show for her time in the forest. Their supply of herbs had run low.

A whimper, soft and mournful, halted Becca's steps on the trail back to the falls. Thinking an animal might be caught in a trap, she tilted her head, trying to figure out where the sound had come from. But she heard nothing.

Loneliness, tiny and nebulous, an echo of her own yearning. It came again, tugging her off the path. Her mind flew to the drakelings. One might be hurt.

Before Becca's father died, he had shown her how to feel the life in the trees and plants. Every person and animal had a vibration. He used it when he healed, claiming he could sense what was wrong with his patient. She wished, for the first time in a long time, that her father was still alive. He could tell her if sensing emotions was part of the healing power.

Mama claimed none of her children had the healing power, but Becca remembered sensing energy as a child. Somehow, it felt right to try it now. It differed from the onslaught of emotions from people. Gentle. Subtle. A rightness with the world.

She carefully stretched her awareness outward, searching for the vibrations that signaled different energies. Her own energy pulsed in her ears.

The forest came alive. Tiny pockets of life hid in the trees. Unseen birds flew above her. Even the fish in the river had a vibration. She couldn't identify much. It wasn't the same sensation as when she was five.

The sense of longing was stronger now, and she followed it to a small landslide of rocks and trees. The sensation disappeared, snuffed out like a candle. She couldn't sense anything unusual. But it had to have come from somewhere.

On the other side of the rubble, Becca discovered a narrow cave. Grasping a broken branch, she poked cautiously into the opening.

A flutter, like a tiny beating heart, settled against her throat, and a yearning filled her mind. She grabbed her head, suddenly afraid she'd changed her power and made it worse. She tried to rebuild her shield, but it was impossible. Tiny beats of longing vibrated through her entire body. She turned away, ready to flee, but it stopped.

And the absence almost broke her heart.

She couldn't leave.

Turning sideways, she slipped into the cave entrance, peering through the darkness. She could make out a faint light. She placed one hand against the side and proceeded carefully. Trickling water echoed, pulling her forward until she found the source.

Sunlight poured through a hole in the ceiling above her. Colors danced, a moving rainbow. She steadied herself against the wall. Water from an underground stream trickled down the walls into a small pool. Sunlight bounced off the ripples. Becca sighed, entranced.

Her senses flooded with the flow of energy. She could almost see it swirling through the cave, trapped in the beams of light. Becca kneeled on the hard rock floor and peered into the pool.

Shimmering stones lay along the bottom, vibrant greens, blues, and pinks. She plunged her hand into the freezing water and grabbed a turquoise stone. Her palm throbbed from the cold. She rolled the stone in her fingers. The colors swirled as the water flowed around the perfect sphere in her hand.

Treasure. Memories of her last hunt with Grandfa brought tears to her eyes. But they had never found anything like these. Perfect orbs of vibrant reds, blues, greens, and yellows.

Her heart clenched. What if it was one of the rare dragonstones? Healers used to hand them out to ward off diseases. Mama even had a pendant with a slice of dragonstone, passed down from her grandmother. But Mama never allowed her to touch it. Of course, Nathan insisted his cousin had a fist-size dragonstone on display in her home. His stories were taller than Grandfa's.

As soon as Becca lifted the orb from the water, it transformed into an ordinary rock, misshapen and gray. She frowned and rolled it over in her hand. She could still feel its smoothness.

The twins' invention of a carrot that tasted like a tomato flashed through her mind. Maybe it was an illusion. A stone couldn't actually transform.

She lowered it back into the water. Once it was completely submerged, the stone shimmered, and a lumpy gray translucent layer surrounded the turquoise orb. As she pushed the stone deeper, the surface smoothed out, and the color shone through.

It didn't make sense. Unless? It must be a dragonstone, and that's why none had been found for hundreds of years. They changed when exposed to air. Or the storms had made them reappear, like the drakelings and their colorful wings.

She closed her eyes and felt for the energy that had enticed her into the cave, but it was gone. She laughed at her own imagination. Rocks didn't have energy. They weren't alive.

She pulled out a green stone, half the size of the others, and felt a single pulse. Startled, she dropped it. She waited, but there was nothing. No emotional tug. No energy vibration. The frigid waters must have caused her hand to throb. That was all.

With a shrug, Becca gave up. Finding the stones was reward enough for following her senses. Maybe they gave off a different energy, or it was the water. It didn't matter.

Becca tucked the small green stone into Grandfa's box. Hopefully, the jeweler could identify it. If she was lucky, and it was a dragonstone, then she could sell it for trader coins.

The walk through the forest had helped. Her mind felt clearer. With Grandfa gone, she didn't have to stay anymore. Kevin was taken care of, and the twins were old enough to do things themselves.

She could leave and explore the world as she'd dreamed. Her heart filled with hope and fear. It was one thing to wish a dragon could sweep her away, and another to head out on an adventure all alone.

Mama wouldn't like it, so she'd have to be careful, collecting travel clothing and earning trader coin without her mother finding out.

Becca turned from the pool of colorful stones. She'd miss Grandfa, but his death had given her a gift. There was nothing keeping her from a future of adventure and exploration anymore.

DREAD
BECCA

The sun was directly overhead when Becca strode through the village square on her way to Lyle's shop. Two older boys looked up from their conversation and smirked. As she passed them, one muttered, "Nathan's mutt."

Becca blushed and scurried to the other side of the square. Wolf howls dogged her steps. Mama was certain to hear the rumors, and Becca had no idea how to stop them.

"Hey, Red."

Becca faltered. She'd been so focused on the boys, she'd forgotten to scan for Nathan.

He grinned as he wrapped his arm around her shoulders.

"Back from the woods?" He plucked a twig from her hair, then brushed her cheek with the back of his hand. "Find anything interesting?"

She clutched the straps of her satchel and swallowed, frantically trying to think of something to say to make him go away.

"Just rocks and herbs." She avoided his gaze and attempted to dislodge his heavy arm.

Nathan turned her back to the square, where his friends watched. "Come to the lake for a swim."

She lifted her head. The water would be freezing. The look in his eyes indicated he didn't mean swimming. "I have chores."

He squeezed her shoulders.

Smugness. Excitement. Anticipation.

The emotions were quick and intense, then gone. He leaned in and whispered, "You can't run forever. But I can wait."

Then he forced his slobbery tongue between her startled lips.

Becca tried to pull away, but he gripped the back of her head, and she couldn't move. His lips mashed into hers, and his tongue explored every inch of her mouth, ensuring she knew he was in complete control. Becca whimpered. His chuckle thumped against her chest. He wrapped his other arm around her waist, clamping her against his body. The assault lasted forever. And when he was done, he let her go.

She stumbled, wiping his spit from her lips with her forearm.

"Don't." It was all she could manage. When he reached for her, she jerked away and fled.

"Go ahead, run away. More fun for me when I catch you." Nathan's smug laugh sent ripples of dread through her stomach.

Becca ran to Lyle's shop. She leaned against the wall, her heart pounding in her ears, and gulped air. Her hand shook as she brushed her hair out of her face.

A sob burst from her chest, reliving the moment he'd forced his tongue into her mouth. Waves of helplessness threatened to overwhelm her.

She should've bitten him. Why didn't she fight? She could've hit him or screamed.

But his hand on her head had felt like a vise, and his kiss had shocked her. It was so unlike Marcus's gentle exploration, or even the quick pecks when they'd played spin the milk bottle as kids. There was no curiosity. She felt branded.

She shivered and rubbed her arms. The two boys had seen. Everyone would know within an hour. The intent in Nathan's eyes looped through her mind.

It was only a matter of time before he caught her. No one would help. Grandfa was gone, and Mama adored the Randals. She thought she had until the summer to prepare, but she had to leave as soon as the first trader caravan came to town. She'd need trader coin to book passage to the next town. From there, she'd find another town and get as far away from Nathan as she could. Mama couldn't stop her.

With a final bracing breath and a plan, Becca's heart settled, though her stomach still clenched. She opened the door to the jeweler's shop. The bell tinkled, but Lyle didn't appear. Protective cloths still covered the displays, so she slipped behind the counter into the dark workshop at the back. Lyle stood in front of the kiln.

Becca coughed to get his attention, careful not to startle him.

He poured metal into the mold, tapped it to release the air bubbles, and placed the mold into a stand.

"One second, Becca." He picked up long tongs and moved the mold from the stand into the kiln and closed the door. After removing his gloves and rubbing his hands on his apron, he turned back to her with a twinkle in his eyes. "What treasure have you got for me today? I haven't seen you in a while."

Since she was three, she'd brought stones to Lyle, certain she'd found a wonderful treasure. He enjoyed her appreciation for gems and rocks, and he assessed her finds with great care. She hadn't been to the shop since that wonderful day with Grandfa and the drakelings, when she'd brought quartz and jade pieces.

She brushed aside the sadness that stole into her heart whenever she thought of her grandfather and plucked the stone from the box.

"First day of sunshine. Had to go exploring. I found this."

Lyle plucked the stone from her hand and rolled it around in his fingers. He hummed, then tapped it lightly with a small hammer.

"Sorry to disappoint you, but it's just a piece of granite. Not your usual find." He tilted his head. His curiosity gently feathered her mind, releasing the tension in her shoulders from Nathan's attack.

"Put it under water." Becca rocked on her feet, eager to see his reaction when it changed.

Lyle pursed his lips, then filled a basin with water and dropped the stone into it. Immediately, the color changed to a vibrant green with blue marbling, the stone once again a perfect orb.

"Hmm. What am I supposed to see?" He tilted the basin, and the orb rolled around the bowl, catching the light from the window and splashing green sparks around the workshop.

Becca looked from the colorful shimmering orb to Lyle's face. Though he'd always been kind, she was suddenly unsure how he'd react if she told him about a transformation he obviously couldn't see. Grandfa had been called strange all his life because of dragon stories. She wasn't about to add fodder to the rumors about her.

"A hint of green quartz?"

With a shrug, Lyle lowered a magnifying lens over his eye and held the stone up to the light, then back into the water. After a few times, he sighed and rubbed his chin.

"I don't see anything. Doesn't mean nothing's there. People have been seeing unusual things lately. Probably a bit of quartz reflected the sunlight. Let's take a closer look."

He selected a cutting tool and lightly pushed it against the surface of the stone. The tool slipped off. He grunted. "Harder than it should be."

Ice zipped up the back of Becca's neck, and the room tilted. Cutting the stone wasn't a good idea. But how else could she see if it was a dragonstone? Most of the jewelry she'd seen with the stone had thin slices, so it should be easy to cut. She shook her doubts away. It was just a rock.

Lyle put the stone in a vise on the workbench, tightened the clamps, then tried cutting the surface again. Smoke curled up and a thin line appeared. He hummed as he put down the tool and switched to a small hammer and chisel. Slowly and carefully, he pried and hit until he'd removed a chip about the size of his thumbnail.

Becca picked up the piece while Lyle examined the rock again. An oval of green was clearly visible, even though the stone had turned gray again. Bile rose in her throat, and she swayed.

"You all right?" Lyle grabbed Becca's arm.

She shook her head. "Just hungry. Had a long hike in the woods today."

Lyle peered at her, concern transmitting through his hand. "You're as translucent as moonstone."

He lifted the rock out of the vise and handed it back to her. "Sorry. It's just granite. What did you think it was?"

"Could it be a dragonstone?" There must be a reason he couldn't see it while she could.

He laughed. "That would be a real treasure. No one's found one of those in my lifetime. Follow me." He strode to the front of the shop.

Becca tucked the stone into her satchel and followed him.

He pulled an old leather-bound book from a shelf behind the counter and flipped through the pages. He handed it to her. "There. A dragonstone in its natural state. Nothing at all like your rock."

The first page had a column of spheres with dimensions, starting as small as a fingernail up to the size of a pumpkin. Beside that was a rainbow chart with arrows under various colors and notes on rarity. Deep green was the most common dragonstone color. The next page had images of the stone cut into slices, with a dark outer rim and concentric circles of colors inside. A sample pendant setting with the slice of dragonstone above it showed how the stone could be cut and mounted to allow light to filter through. A final image showed a shape, like a curled-up drakeling, illuminated through the stone.

Lyle tapped the page. "I'm not sure why they're called dragonstones. Looks more like a chicken to me. Those rings of colors made them special."

As Becca stared at the last drawing, her vision blurred. A heavy weight pressed on her chest, and a roar filled her ears. This was wrong. The room shifted, and the book dropped from her limp hands.

Lyle snatched the book before it hit the ground and held it tightly against his chest. "Becca! Be careful with that." His shock barely made a dent in her mind.

She closed her eyes and steadied herself against the bookshelf. Colors swirled behind her lids. Each breath took all her concentration. She ran from the shop.

When she reached the blacksmith's, she stopped and inhaled deep breaths of crisp air. Mutt nudged her hand, his tail wagging. Petting him calmed her down.

Maybe she was ill. Her reactions were all over the place. She touched the stone in her satchel. It felt like an ordinary lumpy rock. But it wasn't. She didn't know why Lyle couldn't see it, but the pictures had confirmed her suspicions. It was a dragonstone.

But if no one else could see it, she couldn't sell it. She'd have to find another way to earn trader coin.

CONTROL

BECCA

As soon as Becca stepped through the door, Mama called out, "Becca, is that you?"

Of course it was her. Who else would it be? She strode into the kitchen where her mother was carefully placing apple cake into a wooden box. Cinnamon and nutmeg tickled Becca's nose.

"About time. Where have you been?" Mama didn't bother looking up as she put the lid on the box. "Never mind. I need you to take this to Alice while it's still warm."

Mama pulled the leather straps up and fastened them. Her head lifted, a sly smile on her face, then she gasped. "Great Healer! You're filthy."

Heat flooded Becca's cheeks. She swiped at the line of dirt on her britches, probably from leaning on Lyle's workbench, and curled her fingers to hide her dirty nails. If Mama had given her a chance to clean up before demanding her presence, her hands wouldn't still be dirty from her time gathering herbs. Not that it would help to have clean fingers.

"Rebecca Kinsley, you're turning sixteen in a few days. You could at least *try* to look your age."

It was never a good sign when Mama used her full name. Becca sighed and held out her hand for the straps.

"No! You'll wash. Quickly. You mustn't make Alice Randal wait. And wear that pink dress. The one with the white underlay."

Becca's mouth fell open. That dress made her look eight, which is why she'd stuffed it in the bottom of the closet. It was more suitable for Trish. Besides, the road was muddy from all the rain. By the time she arrived, her dress would be splattered, and she'd have to do a second round of laundry for the week.

"Why should I wear a dress to deliver cake?" It wasn't like her mother to suggest such an impractical outfit.

Glee danced in her mother's eyes. "The Randals have graciously agreed to consider you as a wife for Nathan."

The blood drained from Becca's face, and her stomach sank to her knees. Nathan's possessive kiss. He'd known all along.

Mama held up her hand. "Before you say anything, I worked extremely hard to get you this opportunity. Every girl in this village wants to become Mrs. Randal, and Nathan's a handsome fellow. Don't you ruin this."

Revulsion rolled through her chest. Not Nathan. She'd rather die. Her mother couldn't do this to her.

"But Mama. You were eighteen before you married Papa."

Mama scowled. "It's your own fault. Don't think I haven't heard the rumors. At least you had the good sense to pick Nathan. But I taught you better than that. Never give away anything for free.

"Be thankful I stepped in. If only you'd been discreet. But Alice agreed you'd be a good fit. She thinks you have potential." Mama's snort stabbed through Becca's heart.

"You have no control. No discipline. Just like your grandfather. A dreamer with no concept of consequences. That ends now. I'll not have you mooning about town, gallivanting with every boy, and ruining the reputation I had to build after your grandfather drowned in drink."

Her disgust for Grandfa had grown stronger since his death. It wound through Becca's mind, tearing down her carefully constructed shields. She didn't want her mother's emotions.

Becca furiously tried to come up with something reasonable that would change her mother's mind about Nathan. "What about Marcus?"

"Oh, goose poop. Marcus isn't worthy. He'll be a hunter like his father. Nothing wrong with that, but Nathan will open opportunities for us. You should be pleased. You obviously like him."

"Pleased? I don't want to marry Nathan. He's ..."

Mama wouldn't listen to all the real reasons. He's arrogant, mean-spirited, and stupid. And the worst kisser in the world. No. She'd believe everyone else over her own daughter. Becca settled on the one thing that should matter the most.

"I don't love him."

Mama sniffed. "What's love got to do with it? No one marries for love. You marry for a better life. That's it."

Shock snapped Becca's mouth shut. Mama hadn't loved Papa? But they'd been happy, she was sure of it. Her mother used to twirl Becca around their old kitchen as they sang and danced, Kevin in Papa's arms. She'd thought it was Mama's grief that made her so hard and unhappy with Becca.

"I'm not unreasonable. Alice agreed to wait until a month after your birthday, so we could have a proper spring wedding. No one will think it odd if you're pregnant." Mama offered it up as if it were a gracious sacrifice, even though it was the family reputation she really cared about.

Before Becca could voice another protest, her mother continued, her voice high and excited, "The Randals have property allocated to build a house! It'll be grand, and when Peter finishes his term as village leader and rejoins the steam-work mechanics, we'll move in with you!"

Mama didn't care what Becca wanted. All she cared about was status. It didn't matter how much Becca tried to please her. It would never work. Becca's unwanted ability had revealed the truth.

Her mother would never be proud of her. Even marrying Nathan would change nothing. It was impossible. Her mother wanted someone else. Not Becca.

Rage swirled with disbelief. Her own emotions rolled and twisted, unable to settle on one.

"I won't marry Nathan. He's horrible. You'll have to find another way to be as good as Alice Randal." Becca stomped past her mother and slammed the kitchen door as she left the house.

Tears burned her eyes, and she swiped them away angrily. Grandfa would help. He could talk to Mama, convince her that Becca was too young to marry. Pain shot through her chest. He couldn't help because he was dead.

A sob burst from the hole in her heart. She ran along the path behind the house, dove into the forest, and kept running until she reached the waterfall. She collapsed, wrapping her arms around her knees, nestling her head into the protection of her arms. Free of Mama's expectations, and of her own hopes, Becca gave up on stifling her emotions.

Why did Mama have to control everything? Why didn't she love her? Grandfa was wrong. He'd said Becca could be anything, do anything. But she couldn't.

It was a long time before the steady splash of water soothed her rolling thoughts. Her chest ached, and her throat was raw.

Her mother was right about one thing. There weren't a lot of marriage prospects in the village. Nathan's sheep were all younger. Marcus had been her choice since their first kiss when she was twelve. But he was sweet on Isobel, and it looked like he wasn't about to give up on her.

Nathan wasn't an option. No matter what.

She had to leave, much sooner than she'd planned. In twelve days she would turn sixteen, and Mama would plan the wedding of her own dreams. That meant Becca had less than three months to gather supplies, trader coin, and escape.

She took the dragonstone out of her satchel and plunged it into the river. It immediately turned bright green. She rolled the pretty orb in her fingers. Selling dragonstones wouldn't work, not if Lyle couldn't even see them. She lifted it from the water and watched it transform into a lumpy rock.

She couldn't travel without trader coin. Another sob escaped. It was hopeless. If she had a dragon, she could fly away. But she didn't. Grandfa's stories couldn't help her now.

The first trader caravan was due in two weeks. She'd have to figure it out before then. At least she'd be old enough to travel without any awkward questions. The caravan would take her down the river to the next village, or she could convince the trader to let her stay on a little longer by performing chores. Eventually, she'd find a place to stay.

She could trade herbs for passage. Grandfa had taught her where to gather the herbs the Healers needed the most. There was a spot, beyond the cave with the dragonstones, where belladonna grew. She could collect jade and quartz for Lyle too. He didn't pay much, but every bit would help.

Until then, she'd have to go along with Mama's plans. Nathan was the real issue. He already thought he owned her. She ground her teeth together, then let out a frustrated groan. The only way to avoid Nathan was to be too busy planning a wedding with their mothers. She'd have to try on impractical dresses and gush over colors and flowers.

Becca splashed water against her swollen eyes. Even if she couldn't get enough coin to book passage on the caravan, she knew enough about the woods to run away. All she had to do was collect the right supplies without her mother noticing. Either way, she'd escape.

It was time to control her own life.

SEARCH

SERI

DAY 24 AFTER THE LONG SLEEP

The river where Garianna laid her eggs was the closest to the Keep, so Seri, Ronin, and Gregor flew there first. Water cascaded under snow-covered branches, tunneling through snowbanks, and flowed to the valley below.

It reminded Seri of her home, before she and Garianna had left to search for a cure. She missed her coven. Life had been difficult, being the chosen one so young, but she'd always felt safe.

Seri shrugged off her nostalgia. There was no returning to the past, and humans had probably destroyed her home long ago. Her focus had to be on the future.

With no effort at all, she shifted her vision and scanned the river. Blue and yellow threads wove through the water, pooling between rocks before moving on. Magic hung like a mist over the river and clung to the trees as wispy clouds.

A flicker drew her attention to a cluster of rocks where green magic swirled, trapped by something. Seri dug between the rocks, but found nothing. As she pulled her talon free, a green thread caught for a moment before slipping back into the river.

That was different. She snagged a strand of yellow. It had no weight, like trying to hold a wisp of smoke.

This world was so strange. She'd never been able to interact with the magic she could see. Tingles shot up her arm as magic strands twined around her talons.

Gregor sent a wave of curiosity. *"Did you find something?"*

"Nothing yet."

Gregor was bound to jump to conclusions. Just because she could touch the strands now didn't mean they would find the eggs. But he must've sensed her doubt, because he leaned down beside her and inhaled deeply, checking with his own power.

"Lilac." He sounded unsure.

"Wasn't that the scent that led you to the Source?"

"Yes. But it's weak." He grunted. *"I don't know what it means."*

The scent of nightberry had pushed him to inform Fiona it was time to mate. But he rarely had such a clear motive. His power was still too new, but she suspected each scent had a meaning and he'd figure it out over time. They already knew that lilac meant the Source, so this magic came from there. Nothing she didn't already know.

But something had been bothering her ever since they saw the magic pouring into the sky. *"Did you ever wonder how the Source hid our existence?"*

"I figured we were too far from anyone, and the ice cavern grew around us." Ronin frowned, letting slip that he wasn't certain of his conclusion.

Gregor sneezed. *"It's more than that. The scent gets stronger when I think of hiding."*

A memory whispered at the back of Seri's mind. The first magic used by humans. Illusion. Changing the appearance of an object, but not the structure. *"What if the Source hid us? An illusion that eventually became reality as years of snow enclosed us in a cavern."*

"Yes!" Gregor sniffed deeply. *"The scent is stronger."*

So, the Source could be hiding the eggs too. But why? And how come her ability couldn't pierce through the illusion? She shook her head, feeling as though something was missing in her logic.

Magic was rebuilding itself after protecting dragons in the lake. Possibly their time in the Source had changed dragons' interaction with magic. Still, they should be able to see their own eggs.

"Maybe the eggs are hidden with an illusion?"

Ronin shrugged. *"I should still be able to find them. Eggs are a different density than rocks."* His ability allowed him to see through solid objects.

Seri tugged a green strand of magic. It resisted and broke. The strand fell and rejoined the eddy in the rocks. Something kept it from disappearing in the current.

For once she sympathized with Gregor's inability to understand his power. This new ability with magical strands didn't tell her anything. Only that magic had changed. And she already knew that.

Seri slapped the water. *"The eggs aren't here. Let's search farther down the river."* But she couldn't help feeling they wouldn't find anything.

DRAGONSTONES
BECCA

After four days Becca was no closer to her goal. Storms had prevented her from heading to the forest and gathering herbs. Instead, she'd spent the days teaching and the evenings trapped in the house with Mama and her plans. Elder Frederick's migraines prevented him from creating lesson plans, so even that task had fallen to her.

Fortunately, Nathan and his flock weren't at school. The rains had flooded the Randal barns, and the boys were busy moving the animals to high ground and sandbagging the fence line to prevent more damage.

At least the twins enjoyed school. Their antics and imagination kept the little ones entertained. Mama would've been outraged, but she was busy too.

The Healing Center was overrun with patients suffering from hallucinations. Many feared it was fever brain—the first stage of the plague. So, everyone wanted a protective dragonstone in case. Even Mama wore one around her neck.

The slices of dragonstone didn't bother Becca, not like the stone she'd shown the jeweler. But the constant onslaught of fear and worry gave her a headache. It didn't help that with each flash of lightning, a rainbow shimmered at the edge of her vision. When two students jerked their heads to look out the window, she suspected they saw it too. They couldn't all be hallucinating the same thing.

Fortunately, the twins hadn't *created* anything new. Although, the carrots and tomatoes had returned to normal the next day, Becca could still taste the sweet burst of tomato whenever she ate a carrot.

They could hear better too. Just like herself and Kevin. She remembered Grandfa mentioning changes with his hearing and eyesight. But no one ever complained about that, so she didn't know if everyone had changed.

Becca climbed over the fallen branches beside the waterfall. The rain had stopped, and early morning was the best time to hunt for herbs and stones. Her stack of trader coin was woefully small.

Water dripped from leaves and trickled down newly formed streams, creating a soothing melody. Becca sucked in the crisp air, clearing the stuffiness from being cooped up inside. The twitters and creaks of the forest wrapped around her soul. She missed Grandfa the most here, but she also felt more alive. Free.

A whisper of joy fluttered in Becca's mind. She turned, trying to identify the source, and dropped her mental shield.

A faint tug pulled her toward the cave with the dragonstones.

Becca set off with a determined stride, hoping no one else had found the stones. These should not be cut up to make jewelry.

She reached the cave and crawled inside.

Water flowed down the walls, through the pool, and out the cave entrance, but the glowing dragonstones tumbled at the bottom of the natural basin. Safe.

Becca pulled out a white crystal orb, surprised at its warmth, despite the glacier waters. She rubbed her thumb along the dragonstone's smooth surface.

Her mother's judgment faded away. The ever-present grief for Grandfa eased. Becca closed her eyes and stretched her senses outward.

The plop of water dripping from the cave ceiling matched her heartbeat. Wind rustled the branches over the hole above her.

Pungent pine tickled her nose. The air felt heavy, yet comforting, like a hug.

A warmth spread through her fingers, up her arm, and to her chest.

Love.

Becca sighed, her mind open.

Acceptance flickered like a gentle stroke through her hair, tentative, shy, with a hint of fear.

Was it the spirit of Grandfa? Some villagers believed the dead stayed to guide their loved ones to a new life without them. Of course, Mama thought it nonsense.

A giggle tickled her ears.

Becca whipped her head up, worried that someone was watching her from the hole in the ceiling, but there was no one. Only the branches, the water, and the cool cave.

The presence was too small to be a person. Maybe an animal.

She stroked the dragonstone, drawing strength from its warmth. There was no threat, only curiosity.

The stone flared with an intense heat, and Becca gasped, dropping it. She caught it before it crashed to the ground.

The presence came from the dragonstone.

Rolling the misshapen rock in her palm, Becca remembered the yearning that had pulled her to the cave the first time.

Tentatively, and feeling a bit silly, she said, "Are you in there?"

It was one thing to imagine Grandfa's spirit, and quite another to expect a life within a rock.

The dragonstone was silent.

Becca chuckled at her whimsy, and a shadow moved across a large red dragonstone at the bottom of the basin. She held it up to the dim light, but despite staring at it for a long time, she saw nothing. Then it transformed back into a rock. Frustrated, she plunged it into the water. It would be easier if they didn't change as soon as the water dried.

As she lifted the red dragonstone, a shadow scuttled around the edge. She grabbed the smaller white stone. Bits of embedded crystal sparkled as she turned it, and then a golden light flickered between the specks.

Becca held the stone against her chest. Something was inside it.

A wave of encouragement swept through her mind.

In one of Grandfa's stories, dragon riders had searched for dragonstones, but what if the story had changed over the years, because no one knew what they really were? What if they'd been searching for dragon eggs?

Holding the orb with both hands, she searched for a presence, hoping she was right.

A flicker and a faint throb, like a heartbeat.

Tiny intermittent pulses came from more than one. She picked through the stones, finding the ones that vibrated with energy, with life. She knew what these were.

Dragon eggs.

The craggy stone appearance protected them from being discovered. Excitement bubbled through her, and she laughed, her heart so full of joy she felt as though she would burst.

After examining every egg, she discovered that the smallest stones didn't have any energy. In Lyle's book, the image of a dragon had been centered in the dragonstone. She swallowed, scooping a handful of water to cleanse her mouth. Dragonstones must be dragon eggs that hadn't developed.

But some had been larger than these lifeless eggs. A shudder went through her. Those eggs must've had partially developed baby dragons. The nausea she'd felt when Lyle had cut off a piece of the green stone wasn't because she'd been sick. Somehow, she'd known the stone contained life.

Gently, she returned the gray rock to the pool, relieved when it transformed into a green orb, with only a shallow scar on the surface. A tiny pulse reassured her that the dragon inside was still alive.

She couldn't sell any of these. They were dragon eggs, not dragonstones to be hacked up. "I won't let that happen to you."

The crystal egg flickered gold, and Becca's heart swelled.

Tiny dragons.

She sent a mental hug to all the eggs. "I love you."

They had to be protected from discovery. She gathered fallen branches and covered the cave entrance, ensuring the water could flow out, but the eggs would remain inside. They were safe, for now. But when she left, she'd have to take them with her. There was no way she'd leave dragon eggs anywhere near her village with their fears of the Dragon Plague.

Nutmeg
Gregor

Day 30 After the Long Sleep

Gregor was bored. There'd been a few days of excitement searching for eggs, but they hadn't found them. He hoped Seri was right, and the Source was hiding them. Sarcruze didn't agree, but Renalia halted all breeding activities until they knew more.

Gregor had been certain he'd find the eggs. Nightberry tickled his nostrils, taunting him. He'd been so certain it was time to procreate, and now the coven's future was uncertain. He'd been wrong. It made him wonder if he was wrong to believe the eggs weren't dead.

He flew down to Meadow Lake by Valley Keep, hoping to see Trey. He wasn't there, so Gregor swam through the underwater grass, chomping up tiny fish. He was alone again. At least he was unsupervised now, as long as he stayed within mind-speech range. The coven had bigger problems to deal with.

He hadn't seen Trey since the day before he traveled to the Source. So much had changed since then. He swam to shore and shook, spraying water droplets.

Trey's laughter lifted the weight from Gregor's chest. He was here.

Trey sat on a rock, munching on bread and cheese. "I came every day. Where did you go?" The wistfulness in Trey's voice shot through Gregor. The boy was as lonely as him. He wondered if Trey had someone like Seri to confide in.

"Had to make a long-distance trip." He kept his voice light, determined not to get into any more trouble with Sarcruze. The Source was a dragon matter.

"Oh." Trey bit into his bread. He didn't transmit much, a flash of pleasure at the cheese, curiosity as he gazed at Gregor. It was disquieting, since Trey's thoughts had spilled out when they first met.

Doubt made Gregor hesitate to say any more. The boy could be guarded because he'd told Elizabeth about their meetings.

"You could've let me know when you'd be back." Trey's words dropped into the silence, full of hurt and anger.

Relief surged through Gregor. The boy had kept their secret. *"I'm sorry."* He knew what it was like to want to spend time with someone who wasn't there. *"I didn't know I'd be gone so long. I missed you."* If Trey had been a dragon, Gregor wouldn't have to spell out all his emotions. He let Trey feel his own loneliness.

Doubt still clouded Trey's thoughts. "You did? I figured you were too busy doing dragon things and forgot all about me."

Gregor wanted to bring back the joy that usually bubbled from Trey. *"Want to go for a ride?"* They didn't have riding straps, but Trey could balance between his wings for a brief low flight.

Trey's excitement filled the air, and all his doubts and hurt disappeared. He stuffed the remainder of his lunch into his satchel and jumped to his feet. "I have the harness, just like you showed me."

He tugged a tangle of leather straps out of a sack. "It was hard to get the leather without my grandmother noticing, but I combined five broken horse harnesses." A baffled expression crossed Trey's face. "How do I put it on you?"

Gregor laughed. *"You don't. I'm not a horse."*

Then he plucked the harness from the boy's tight grip and looped it over his shoulders. The strap in front of his wings and around his torso was a little snug, but it would do for a short flight. Trey could lengthen it for next time. He hoped Trey enjoyed flying. Some humans were terrified of heights and actually became ill.

Gregor crouched, bending one knee for the boy to climb on and placing his talons on the ground for support. Riders usually leapt onto their dragons. But since Gregor had never had a rider, he wasn't certain how to explain the maneuver to Trey. He felt like prey on all fours, but he could sense that Trey was more comfortable thinking of him as a horse for their riding adventure.

"Now get up."

Trey gingerly placed his foot on Gregor's thigh.

"You won't hurt me." Gregor chuckled at the concern.

With a grunt, Trey threw his leg over Gregor's back and grabbed at the straps. He almost slid off the other side in his enthusiasm, but Gregor caught him. The boy weighed nothing, his body heat the only indication he even sat on Gregor's shoulders.

"Hold tight to the straps and let your body move naturally. I don't move like a horse. If you lean forward, you'll get a bloody nose." Or a concussion. But he didn't want to frighten the boy.

Gregor slowly stood, attempting to keep Trey upright. Trey gasped. Terror and excitement spilled from his mind. The straps around Gregor's chest tightened uncomfortably.

A short glide over the lake should be safe enough for their first flight. If the boy fell, the water would cushion his landing.

"I'll be all right." Trey's mind-speech was much easier to understand. He was afraid, but he was way too excited to care. Tingles shot through the membranes of Gregor's wings.

"Here we go." Gregor jumped and pumped his wings. Trey's insubstantial weight didn't affect his balance in any way, but he did have to be careful to fly at an angle instead of straight up.

"This is amazing!" Trey's wonder was everything Gregor had hoped for. Gone was the hurt and loneliness. They were together.

Gregor flew low over the lake and turned to fly the length again. By the third time, Trey had loosened his grip, and the straps eased across Gregor's chest.

"Can we go higher? I won't fall."

With two mighty strokes, Gregor flew up to the clouds. Trey was silent, but awe filled his mind. The straps didn't tighten at all. Confident Trey wouldn't fall, Gregor flew toward the mountain peak, connected to Trey in a way he'd never felt before. They thought as one. Gregor hummed his appreciation.

Nutmeg swept through Gregor's nostrils. His power was trying to tell him something. Turning his head, he caught the scent and pumped his wings, rising through the clouds. The scent intensified. He must find it.

The tightening of the straps broke Gregor's concentration. Trey. He'd forgotten him.

"Where are we going?" Trey's question was loaded with anticipation. Gregor winced at the headache building in Trey's mind. The boy couldn't handle mind-speech for too long.

They'd flown too far. Gregor should return Trey to the lake.

Nutmeg blew into his snout, filling his head. Remembering what Seri had said about losing mental contact, he concentrated and flung a call to her. *"Nutmeg. Must follow."*

Then he gave into his power, casting his head back and forth, his nose so full of the scent he couldn't tell which direction to fly. It was stronger to the south. The scent was the one he'd encountered in his vision when he woke in the Source.

Nutmeg swirled deep into a part of his mind he'd never accessed, interlacing reality with the dream. He flew swiftly; no heavy water hampered his wings this time. There would be a village at the base of the Dragon Mountain Range, one that hadn't existed over a hundred years ago. They wouldn't look up. They wouldn't notice him at all. But the girl with the hair of flames lived there.

She was important.

Seri said he needed to think before he acted. Gregor tried to shake the magic free from his mind. It was like trying to clear fog. He had something to do first, but his power beat away his thoughts.

Fly. Faster. Fly.

So he followed the scent as fast as he could. A tightness around his chest increased the urgency. There was no time. He didn't hear the screams of the boy on his back, or feel the tiny fists pounding on his neck.

DRAGON

BECCA

After dropping the twins off at Lizzie's, Becca jogged to the far end of Amethyst Lake. With five new cases of fever brain that morning, the Healer needed more supplies. Becca picked through the lake grasses, searching for the distinctive purple stalks of fever weed. Once it was steeped for a day in water, it was added to the healer paste and applied to the scalp, soothing the patient so they could rest. The fever affected their senses, making them see or hear things that weren't there. If it weren't for the fear that this was a precursor to the plague, it would be hilarious. Alice Randal had come in complaining that her chickens wore suits.

It was working out for Becca. Selling herbs to the Healing Center was getting her the trader coin she needed. Once the caravan arrived, she'd have enough to leave. She hummed to herself as she cut the stalk and tucked it into her herb-collecting satchel. The sun peeked through the clouds, glinting off the lake and hinting at a break from the rains for a while.

Energy tingled along Becca's neck as she reached for the next stalk. She slowly lifted her head and searched the forest behind her. She couldn't tell where it came from, but she sensed something large, like a bear. Becca gathered her things and moved closer to the trees. If a bear needed the lake, it was best she left it alone.

She felt a flutter at the base of her throat, like a slow, steady heartbeat. As it grew stronger, she fought the urge to run. As long as she stayed calm, she'd be all right. Any animal would be as wary of her as she was of it.

A shadow drew her gaze upward. Over the past few days, there'd been more lightning storms, flashing with unusual colors. But, unlike the superstitious villagers, she didn't believe it was a result of fever brain.

Dark rain clouds obscured the Dragon Mountains, and long gray clouds whipped overhead. A sign the sunlight wouldn't last long. A dark speck appeared.

Too big to be a bird.

Becca's entire body tingled. The energy, the heartbeat, the sense of danger. They all came from the sky, not the forest.

Her fear of an animal encounter dissipated, and her focus shifted to the sky. Energy tightened her throat, a warning of something more than flashes of color in the rain.

She grabbed the lowest branch on the tree next to the path and climbed as far as she could, hoping to identify the creature. The wind whipped her hair around her head, and she clung to the trunk for support.

The dark shape moved steadily through the sky, cutting through the clouds, single-minded in its trajectory. Then it tilted and revealed two huge wings and a long narrow tail. Becca gasped, her brain trying to tell her something that shouldn't be possible.

The creature flew through a gap in the clouds, and sunlight glimmered off a bright emerald body before it disappeared.

Becca clutched the tree as her heart thundered in her ears. Her scalp itched, and it felt as if her hair vibrated around her head. The air stilled, and the world held its breath. There was no wind, no sound. Her eyes stung from trying to see farther than was humanly possible, but she couldn't blink. She couldn't breathe. She wished so hard for it to be true.

And finally, it popped through the cloud. If Becca hadn't been holding on so tightly, she would've fallen. Spots danced in her eyes, and she sucked in a breath of mind-clearing air. The world rushed back into focus.

A dragon. A magnificent, wonderful green dragon.

"Dragons are real." She whispered it, reverently, as if saying it would make it disappear.

Her mind was pulled to the dragon as if drawn by an invisible force. Without trying, she could feel its energy. His energy. Becca grinned. She knew it was a male. She felt a connection, deep in her soul. She was meant to see him. Grandfa would've loved this. A real dragon.

And it was flying straight toward her.

Becca inhaled deeply, trying to calm her heart and body. Now wasn't the time to panic. She focused on the dragon's energy.

Becca's world tilted and spun. She sensed the dragon, warmth and sunshine. She could feel the power in his legs, the blood pumping through his veins, and his mind. A power that called to her, a vast potential. Questions and answers, time and distance, magic and science, future and past. She gasped, suddenly afraid of disappearing into a swirling vortex of thought.

Abruptly, she couldn't sense anything, not even the tree she gripped so tightly. She tried to center herself with the solid feel of the world around her. Within a few breaths, the branch cut into her palms, calming her with its roughness.

The dragon was close enough she could make out more details. His head was huge, much bigger than she'd expected, and his body was about the size of the biggest horse in the world. Beautiful wings spread out, twice as long as his body, and his tail acted like a rudder, turning and tilting to control his direction. He flew faster than she thought possible.

Excitement made her giddy. This was much better than her imagination. No longer just a story. First, she'd found the eggs. Now, there was a dragon in the sky.

Tears rolled down her cheeks, and she wished her grandfather were still alive to see it.

As the dragon flew from the next cloud, there was no mistaking him for a bird anymore. Fear stole Becca's joy in a single beat.

If she could see him, so could others.

ATTACK
BECCA

Angry shouts confirmed Becca's fear as four men ran down the path to the lake. She froze, her pulse racing. Should she hide or climb down and explain? But she wasn't sure they would listen. They wouldn't see the beautiful creature from her grandfather's stories. They'd only see a dragon to be feared. A plague-bringer.

The men stopped under Becca's tree.

"It's definitely a dragon. That explains the fever brain." Becca didn't need her power to sense Roger's gloating. He constantly opposed Peter's decisions and had been warning the village that the weather and the fever meant something worse was coming. His emotion churned in her stomach, filling her with dread.

Peter grabbed Roger's shoulder. "Hold on. Even if it is a dragon, that doesn't mean it carries the plague. We've had a bout of fever brain, but no one is actually sick."

Roger shoved him against the tree trunk. "You never did have the stomach for tough decisions."

The other men, Dave and Frank, stepped back, their unease swirling in Becca's mind. She didn't know them well, but Peter was calm, controlling his own emotions.

"Go back to the village and protect them while I rationally assess the danger. The council will decide what to do. Not you." Fury rose from him, and she knew it wouldn't take much to break Peter's control. He didn't like being questioned.

Frank pointed to the trees on the other side of the lake. "It's here."

The dragon swooped low over the treetops, as if preparing to land. Becca's heart beat so fast she missed Roger's response. She was finally going to see a real dragon up close.

A shot rang out, and the acrid smell of smoke rose through the branches hiding Becca. The dragon flapped his wings and reared, knocking the top off a tree.

Thunder filled Becca's mind. Outrage, shock, fear. Every emotion crystal clear, like the day she'd attacked Nathan. A beastly roar followed. But she didn't hear it with her ears. The dragon's scream filled her head, overwhelming her own thoughts. His emotions became hers.

The dragon dropped low, skimming the trees. *"Humans and their guns."*

The voice, deep and rumbly, was unlike any she'd ever heard. Becca whipped her head down, terrified the men below had found her. But Roger still had a rifle pointed at the dragon.

The dragon had spoken in her mind, just like Grandfa's stories. For a moment, joy filled her heart, but the dragon was in danger. Becca's throat ached as she resisted shouting. Maybe she could warn the dragon with her thoughts.

"Leave. Please leave. It's not safe." She felt the dragon's presence in her mind. A whisper of hope confused her.

Peter shoved the barrel of the gun down. "By the Healer, what are you doing? Trying to enrage the beast?"

"Kill it, and we're safe. What are you going to do? Talk to it?" Roger pulled the trigger.

The sharp sound released Becca's connection to the dragon's mind, as pain ripped through him. With an impossible twist of his body and a mighty flap of his wings, the dragon abruptly changed directions, dropping something into the trees.

"Damn it. You made me miss. Now it will return and destroy our village. What kind of leader are you?" Roger swung the gun from the sky.

Peter jabbed Roger's chest. "Shooting was a mistake. You're the monster."

Becca had never heard him so angry. Joy soared in her heart. He would make them see reason. He was their leader. They had to listen to him.

"Monster?" With a growl of rage, Roger slammed the rifle butt into the side of Peter's head.

Peter crumpled to the ground.

Dave yanked the rifle from Roger's grasp. "Are you mad?" Then he yelled at Frank, "Don't just stand there. Get the Healer." He pulled on Peter's arm, trying to get him to sit. Peter groaned as he collapsed again. Blood flowed down his face. Dave didn't notice that Frank hadn't left.

Roger's disgust made Becca's stomach churn as he kicked Peter's foot. "Leave him. He deserves to die. He put our families at risk."

Dave stood, the rifle wavering between them. Fear and honor battled within each man as they stared at Peter. Dave wanted to help, but he was afraid of Roger. Peter gripped his head, emitting pain and confusion. Becca gripped the tree tighter, her own fear holding her still. Tension filled the air.

"Dave, you know I'm right. If that beast had landed, the Dragon Plague would destroy us. Peter was going to let that happen. We must protect our families. That dragon will return, and we have to be ready."

"You don't know that." Peter's voice was strangled, as if speaking hurt.

Roger kicked him in the gut. "Shut it. You were going to talk to the beast. Old Man Stephen infected you. Tame dragons? You saw it. There's no controlling that. We have to kill them before they kill us."

Frank shook his head. He didn't speak much, but most people listened. "Once Peter's healed, the villagers will listen to him, and they'll lock you up, Roger. You can't attack the leader."

"You're right. I don't need anyone questioning my leadership."

Their emotions shifted. Revenge drove Roger, but fear drove the others. Becca pushed down her own fear. Peter needed help, now.

Once she leapt from the tree, she would run as fast as she could back to the village. Her heart tried to beat its way out of her chest, and she sucked in a bracing breath. She could do it. They wouldn't catch her.

"No," Peter gasped, shaking his head. His eyes locked with hers, and his concern held her still.

Roger's chuckle drained the blood from Becca's limbs. He'd won. She slammed up her mental shields, terrified his feelings would undo her.

"Move." He pulled out a knife and pushed Dave aside.

Becca stifled her protest. The world went black, and her fingers went numb. Everything happened in slow motion. Roger stabbed Peter's heart, then slashed his chest and stomach, shredding his shirt and his flesh.

Peter screamed. Becca couldn't block his torment. Her power was a curse. Feeling his emotions didn't enable her to save him. All it did was make everything worse.

Peter's outstretched hand fell to the ground, blood pulsed, pouring across his body, forming bright red puddles in the dirt. It looked as if huge claws had ripped him open. He stared past Becca to the sky.

Roger wiped the blade on a cleaning cloth and neatly tucked it into the holster at his waist. Smugness in every movement. He felt no remorse.

"The dragon attacked our leader, and we ran for help." He defied the others to disagree. They didn't. Roger gave Peter's leg a final kick, and the men ran to the village, leaving Peter lying in his blood.

It was more than a desire to protect the village that drove Roger. Vengeance. But knowing his emotions didn't help. Peter was dying, and Roger had no intention of getting the Healer in time.

Becca dropped to the ground and crawled to Peter's head, tears pouring down her face. Pain filled her soul. He was her uncle and her stepfather. Family.

She held his gaze until hope faded. She couldn't save him. Becca sobbed as she held his hand. He gasped a last rattling breath as blood filled his lungs, and the light disappeared from his eyes. He was dead.

She stood on legs that wobbled under the weight of her grief, her heart weeping. Who would believe her? No one. They'd believe Roger's story. And her mother would want the villagers to hunt down the dragon that killed Peter. She'd never believed in Grandfa's version of dragons. This would only confirm everything she'd always said.

Becca would have to return home and pretend she believed Roger's truth. He could never know she'd been there. She hoped the dragon survived and stayed far away. His pain from being shot still echoed in her chest.

Then she remembered that he'd dropped something when he flew away. Whatever it was, she couldn't let anyone else find it.

DRAGON RIDER
BECCA

Becca ran around the lake and searched the underbrush. The ominous clouds decided to dump their load. Rain poured down, slapping the leaves and causing the forest to twitch.

Someone groaned and swore. Becca's heart raced. Her hands shook as she pushed aside a large branch. A young man lay on the ground, his right arm at an awkward angle. Not anyone she knew. He struggled upright, then fell back with another groan.

Becca kneeled beside him. "Don't get up yet. You're hurt."

Confusion glazed his eyes as he blinked at her. He must've hit his head.

"Hi. I'm Becca. Let me help you."

At his nod, she quickly assessed his legs, neck, and back. He cried out when she moved his right arm. Angry purple bruises covered his shoulder. Hopefully, it was a sprain. Her hands stilled when she noticed the broken branches surrounding them.

The dragon hadn't dropped something. He'd dropped someone.

A dragon rider.

A thousand questions rushed to her lips, but there was no time. The villagers would show up soon to witness Roger's display of dragon violence. A sob caught in her throat. Everyone already believed dragons were dangerous. Roger didn't have to kill Peter to prove anything.

She helped the young man sit, realizing he was younger than she'd first thought. Only a little older than herself.

He grabbed his head and moaned.

"I thought we were friends." His distress brought tears to her eyes.

The dragon had betrayed him, dropped him, and left without him. Everything was in that one beat against her mind.

Becca concentrated on her mental shield. Sensing emotions would only get in the way.

"Get up. We have to leave, now." Water ran off her face. The storm would make it easier to hide, but she couldn't take him to the Healing Center. Everyone knew everyone. They would regard a stranger with suspicion, especially after a dragon attack.

"Where am I?" He was too calm, almost polite. He stood with an inarticulate gasp, his useless right arm clutched against his chest.

"Chartsend. What's your name?" They couldn't travel quickly with his injury. She unwrapped her hair and tied the leather strap around his wrist and neck to support his arm.

"Trey." He sounded uncertain, then he tilted his head back as if searching the sky for his dragon. When he dropped his gaze, his shoulders drooped, and her heart ached for him.

Shouts stabbed through the rain. The villagers had discovered Peter.

"We have to go now." Grabbing Trey's good hand, Becca dragged him deeper into the forest. They could hide in Grandfa's cabin. It would be a long miserable hike through the rain, but it was stocked with healing herbs, clothes, and food. They'd be safe there for a little while. At least until the storm passed.

The dragon had spoken to her. Trey was a dragon rider. Everything Grandfa had told her was true. She couldn't send Trey into the forest on his own. Not with his injury. He wouldn't travel far before one of the villagers found him. Roger would use him to get the dragon. She couldn't let that happen.

Everything had changed in an instant. All her supplies and trader coin lay in her dresser, her plans useless. She didn't know what would happen next, but she couldn't go home. Not now.

EXPOSURE
GREGOR

Storm clouds protected Gregor from any humans below. He couldn't believe he'd dropped Trey. Nutmeg had consumed his mind so much he'd forgotten about the boy on his shoulders.

Remorse slowed his wing beat, and his tail drooped. Gregor's trajectory faltered, and he slipped below the concealing cloud cover. It took more effort than it should to rise.

He'd done everything wrong.

The thrill of flying with Trey had intoxicated him. He'd felt invincible, but he shouldn't have followed the scent. Not with Trey. Not on their first flight together. And not with a faulty harness. Now Trey was gone, and he'd exposed the dragons' existence to volatile humans. All for a girl from a dream.

His certainty of her importance had shattered with the first gunshot. Jolted from his entrancement, he was too shocked to consider the fragile human clinging to his back. When the second shot ripped through his wing, he smashed into a tree and felt the harness loosen. He remembered Trey then, but it was too late. He'd twisted to grab the boy, but the effort almost cost him his aerial advantage, so he'd fled to the sky, to freedom.

He'd landed on the nearest mountaintop, waiting for the villagers to leave. He prayed to the great dragon Torin that Trey still lived, and that he'd hidden from the villagers.

As Gregor flew back to the lake where he'd dropped the boy, the storm broke from the clouds. He struggled to maintain his altitude in the winds and rain. His wing tore, ripping closer to the tendon, agony shooting through the membrane.

"Trey!" Projecting through his pain made his head spin.

But there was no answer. No sense of Trey or any human. Even the animals had fled the lakeside. Then he smelled it. What he'd been dreading all along.

Blood.

A lot of it, even with the rain washing it away. He shuddered. That was it.

Trey was dead. No human could survive that much blood loss.

Gregor turned away. There was nothing he could do here. He must warn his coven about the guns that shot farther than those in the past, of the humans who knew about them now and would look for them. Sarcruze had been right, and his wrath would be fierce. Gregor was dragon enough to accept it.

Rotting kelp filled his nose. He sneezed it away. He didn't need his power to tell him there was death ahead. His power had betrayed him. Maybe, he'd interpreted the smells incorrectly all along, and traveling to the Source had been a huge mistake that would cost them everything.

The flight back to Jason's Keep took longer than it should. Wind currents pulled at the rip in Gregor's wing. Soon, he'd be unable to fly at all.

Every flap jolted excruciating pain through his wing and shoulder. He soared the last length to the keep, resisting the temptation to call Zanthor for support. This was his fault. He deserved this agony. No one should ease his burden.

"Fiona, I need a repair." He kept it brief, hoping she'd tend to his injury before they cast him out. Sarcruze would already sense Gregor's pain.

Her response was quick and pragmatic. *"Land in the northern bay. The supplies are there."* His heart lifted for a moment at the brief flutter of concern she sent before severing the connection.

"Gregor, what have you done?" Seri's distress brought tears to his eyes. She couldn't save him from his foolishness this time.

A gust of wind lifted his good wing and tumbled him like an exhausted youngling. He landed snout first in the dirt, unable to back-wing properly. Immediately, Fiona lifted him to his feet while Seri ran her fingertips delicately along his injured wing, testing the structure.

Sarcruze stomped up, his eyes whirling with anger. *"Who did this to you?"*

Gregor's breath caught. He'd been so focused on what he'd done, he hadn't considered their reaction to his injury. They would assume he'd been attacked.

Fiona tugged the broken harness free. *"Why do you have riding straps?"* Her disappointment shifted Sarcruze's anger. It was obvious Gregor had broken the rules.

He lay on the ground, his eyes level with Sarcruze's feet. *"I've endangered us all."*

Seri gasped. *"No. You wouldn't."* Her belief in him only added to his guilt. She was wrong.

His desire to prove himself had put them all at risk.

While Fiona stitched his wing and slathered it with a numbing mud, Gregor told his story. Everyone in the coven listened. He was careful to keep his emotions clear. They needed to know the facts. How he defied the rules and spent time with a human. How he'd taken Trey for a ride. Then how his power controlled him. That was the most difficult. Most dragons didn't have powers and didn't trust those who did. This would confirm their suspicions.

Zanthor sent a private wave of support. *"We'll deal with your powers later. Keep going."*

Sarcruze paced, his mind closed. By the time Gregor recounted the villagers shooting him, and how he'd killed the boy, rage exploded from Sarcruze.

Gregor couldn't lower himself any further, but he tried as he gasped out his fears. *"Their guns are more powerful now. We must leave Jason's Keep before they find us."*

"I'll decide what we must do. You've done more than enough. I knew these powers would be the death of us, and I was right." At Sarcruze's words, every dragon with power flinched.

Zanthor laid a talon on Sarcruze's arm. *"Let's not go making broad statements that rip our coven apart. Now, more than ever, we need to work together."*

Sarcruze huffed but dipped his head in assent. He turned his back on Gregor, an obvious and brutal indication of his refusal to accept Gregor's offer of submission.

Disparagement would've been better. At least that would mean he stood a chance. This was worse. Sarcruze wouldn't waste energy on punishing a dragon who didn't belong in the coven. He didn't exert any force on Gregor at all.

It was inevitable, but still a shock, when Gregor's connection to the coven was severed. They were gone from his mind. He couldn't hear anything. He couldn't even sense Seri's emotions, after being so sure their connection went deeper than family. The coven surrounded him, deciding his fate.

"Please don't banish me." His plea fell into a void. There was no response, and if they banished him forever, there never would be.

His knees shook. He wouldn't survive. The loneliness he'd felt all his life was nothing compared to this.

The other powered dragons moved together protectively, and Gregor realized his actions had affected them. Sarcruze barely tolerated powers. He wouldn't trust any dragon with power to maintain control now.

Fiona's talon on his shoulder startled him. She strapped his injured wing to his side and guided him to a resting alcove. Her motions were jerky, indicating her anger, though he didn't know if it was directed at him or Sarcruze. As if she sensed his worry, she took a moment to lean her head against his in a show of sympathy. Then she left, and all he had was a memory of her warmth, fleeting compared to being able to sense her emotions.

As the argument continued around him, Gregor had a long time to reflect. He hated admitting Sarcruze might know what he was doing with all his rules and precautions. But Gregor was discovering that decisions had unexpected consequences, and the things he'd been so sure of before didn't seem so right anymore. His neck ached from keeping his head up as he lay on the resting stone. He'd traveled far. His wing trembled with pain. But he couldn't show any more weakness.

Sorrow tightened his chest, reminding him of the riding straps. He'd lost his human friend. His power had cost the life of the boy he'd been certain he'd never harm. Had he been wrong all this time? Did his power make him less of a dragon?

There was no answering scent. He'd expected something. A protest from his power. But the only scents around him were of his coven. He inhaled, taking comfort in their odors. Sarcruze couldn't take his sense of smell away from him.

Gregor shook his head. He wasn't one to dwell on things he had no control over. If Sarcruze lifted the mental block, Gregor would follow the rules and learn to control his magic. If the villagers hadn't attacked, Trey would still be alive. His power wasn't to blame.

He'd learned his lesson the hard way.

Sarcruze was their leader. Seri was right. Gregor needed to trust him to lead.

But he still couldn't help wishing, in the most private part of his mind, that Sarcruze would leave the villagers alone. Even though he'd been shot, the girl's warning filled him with hope. Her mental voice had been desperate for his safety.

A shiver ran up the back of his neck. She'd sent her mind-speech way beyond the reach of a normal human.

He didn't doubt anymore. She was special, and not everyone would fear dragons. Some humans might help them survive. If his coven gave them a chance.

DESTINY
SERI

Gregor's mind disappeared. Shock ricocheted through Seri.

Sarcruze had banished him.

Gregor lay there, completely submissive, but he was gone from her mind. She'd never realized how much comfort and strength she drew from his mental presence. Loneliness filled the spots where he'd been inside her mind.

"No!" Her anguished cry echoed through the coven. No dragon had been banished in their lifetimes.

Fiona tended to Gregor's injury, defying the tenet of full banishment. Her steadiness stopped Seri from falling to the ground and begging Sarcruze to return Gregor to her. Seri wanted to clutch Gregor's talons to reassure herself and him that he was still a part of their coven, a part of her.

Instead, she stood tall, stiffened her tail, and resisted the minds pushing her to speak.

"It's time. You're the Savior," Garianna whispered along their private bond.

But Seri wasn't ready. She'd never be ready.

Sarcruze filled the shocked silence. *"He has endangered the coven for the last time. I knew these powers couldn't be trusted. Magic is unpredictable. It can't be controlled. Magic created the plague. The Source stole our lives. And now it's taking over the minds of those afflicted by the magic of the human wars."*

Every dragon under the age of forty took a physical step back and shielded their minds. Seri felt it rather than saw it as they all joined her mind.

They should stand behind Zanthor. He'd led them before. He knew what to do.

Zanthor sent a wave of support. *"They've always looked to you, Seri. Your power IS magic."*

But he gave her time to gather her thoughts. *"Sarcruze, you can't banish the youngling. What he did was impetuous, but we're safe here. No villager could find us. And we can learn about the world from Gregor's friendship with the human."* The power in Zanthor's voice rang out with conviction.

This wasn't the disaster Sarcruze was making it to be. Heads lowered. Not all the dragons agreed with Sarcruze.

"I must protect us from every threat." Sarcruze held the fortitude of his years as a leader. He had the power of experience and age, even if it wasn't magical. He would do everything necessary to keep them alive and well.

Seri's mind rang with his strength, and she bowed in acceptance.

"We know that. You've proved it over and over. We're alive. We're safe. But Gregor's not a threat. He saved us when all hope was lost. We survived the plague. He deserves leniency for that alone." Zanthor's response served as a reminder that they owed Gregor's powers a lifelong debt.

Fiona was done with Gregor. Her straightened tail quivered as she strode over to Sarcruze. She stretched her neck to its limit and caught his gaze. *"Release him now."*

Her demand hissed through all their minds, shocking Seri. *"Their powers are not their fault. They were born with them. And to blame them for something that's as much a part of them as their skin is ridiculous."*

Everyone gasped. Seri clenched her teeth, hoping Fiona wasn't challenging Sarcruze for leadership.

Sarcruze shook his head, his posture softening. *"No. It isn't their fault. But these powers are putting the coven in danger."*

"Stifling powers is more to blame than the powers themselves. You can't expect a dragon to swim underwater for weeks the first time. It's the same with magic. They need time, and a place to practice and make mistakes. They must learn what they can do." Fiona's neck softened. She'd made her point.

"I agree."

Seri wondered how much private conversation had occurred to make him change his position so quickly.

He laid his head against Fiona's for a brief caress, then straightened.

Fury emanated from him with his next words. *"Humans attacked one of us. That can't go unpunished. Because of Gregor, two villages know of our existence. With the boy dead, Valley Keep will retaliate. We've all seen how humans start wars for their families. Both villages must be destroyed. Tonight."*

A force pushed Seri forward. Magic swirled through the air, yet she hadn't shifted her vision. She felt the strength of all the powered dragons as if it were her own.

"That's not the path to survival." The words flew from her mind, loud and strong.

Shock clamped her jaw shut. What had she done? Is this what Gregor meant when he had no control? Fiona was more right than she knew.

Garianna's next words only made it worse. *"The Oracle has spoken."* The reverence in her tone made Seri want to throw up.

Zanthor sent another wave of assurance. Seri resisted. She couldn't become what Garianna wanted.

"And why not, youngling?" Sarcruze's insult was slight, pointing out her youth, but his voice still held respect. He may distrust powers, but he treated Seri a little differently, which only made

her feel more of a fraud. He didn't fear her power like he feared Gregor's.

Now wasn't the time to hesitate.

Seri scanned the magic swirling around them. It settled on Zanthor, Gregor, and Ronin. That was no help. The silence stretched, anticipation in every mind. She sucked in a breath of courage.

"Attacking the villages will make things worse. Trey told Gregor stories of humans hunting dragons until there weren't any left. We can't let that happen.

"Magic is showing me three dragons with powers and a path to the north. Our solution lies within the coven. Not destroying humans."

Trying to project certainty while every part of her wanted to flee took the last of Seri's energy. She collapsed. Ronin and Zanthor were there, supporting her between them.

Her proclamation shifted the coven. While they discussed both options, expectation crashed against Seri like waves on a beach. Others, like Garianna, sent more, her reverence a shackle around Seri's throat.

Seri leaned into Zanthor's shoulder, his solidness comforting.

"You did well and stopped the coven from doing something rash. We don't have to know what your powers mean. It's enough to have a direction." Zanthor's whisper did much to ease her fears.

"For now, we won't attack the villages. But we must monitor them, and if they assemble armies, we'll stop them." Sarcruze no longer had thunder in his voice.

It was a good compromise.

"And Gregor? He's important, and he's one of us. Banishing him is more dangerous than training him," Zanthor said, more eloquently than Seri could've.

Sarcruze growled. *"He lacks discipline."*

It would take time for Sarcruze to forgive Gregor. A lot of time.

Sarcruze bowed slightly. *"Fine. But he will be monitored. He can travel north with Seri and use his powers to help the coven instead of making things worse. At least he won't find any humans."*

Everyone sighed a breath of relief and bowed their acceptance of his decision. But Seri had no time to dwell on her own relief.

As each dragon left, they touched her and thanked her for her wisdom. Most simply whispered, *"Oracle,"* until their belief bound her to them more than any physical chain.

She could never be what they needed.

At that moment, Gregor's mind returned to the coven, and Seri latched on to his essence, a raft in the sea of expectation threatening to destroy her.

She wouldn't lose him again.

Grandfa's Secrets

Becca

The trek to Grandfa's cabin took longer than expected. With the heavy rains, the narrow path up the mountain had deteriorated into slippery runnels of mud. Becca fell often, and Trey hadn't done much better. They'd traveled without speaking.

Several times Becca felt a shift in energy, and Trey would frown. At first she'd thought his head was causing him pain, but then she remembered the dragon's voice in her mind. Trey was communicating with the dragon. But as his footsteps slowed and his shoulders slumped, she suspected his calls went unanswered.

Becca pushed open the door and stumbled into the cabin. After wrenching off her mud-caked boots and socks, she strode barefoot across the wooden floorboards to the fireplace.

An icy chill from the rain had seeped into her bones. Her hands shook as she assembled the kindling and wood, then lit the fire. Fortunately, the firewood was stacked inside, ready for Grandfa's next visit. Sadness clenched her throat, but she shook it away. Grandfa was helping her, even though he was gone.

Trey shivered in the doorway, dripping on the mat.

"Come in." She guided him to the wooden chair at the table.

The large room acted as both a kitchen and living space. Becca grabbed a towel for herself and tossed another one to Trey. While he dried himself, she searched for warm clothing in the single bedroom. Fortunately, Grandfa had been a tall man. She set aside the longest britches for Trey and stripped off her wet things.

Grandfa's clothes still smelled of pine soap. After dressing, she wrapped herself in the quilt from the bed to stop the shivers that shook her body.

Trey had dried his brown hair and his face, but a puddle had formed under the chair, and mud marked his path from the door.

"Sorry. I made a mess." His grin was sheepish, but she was happy to see a light in his hazel eyes. His depression over his dragon's desertion didn't sink into her head anymore.

Becca untied his laces, and he kicked off his boots with a heartfelt groan.

"We're safe? From the people who shot Gregor?" He grabbed her hand, his worry washing over her.

"Gregor is your dragon?" She had so many questions about him and his dragon.

Trey dropped her hand, wariness in his expression, even after everything she'd done.

"This is my grandfather's place. Eventually, someone will come looking for me. But with this storm, we're safe for the night." She wanted his trust but wasn't sure how to reassure him.

If Grandfa were alive, he'd know what to say. But he wasn't. It was up to her.

"Where did you come from? Why are you here? Are you really a dragon rider? What's it like?" Becca couldn't help it. The questions rushed out of her.

Trey frowned and took a while to answer. "It's a long story."

They had time.

But then a shiver shook his body, and he swayed. His answers could wait.

"You need food. You're still in shock." Becca rummaged through the pantry for the snacks she used to eat when she'd sneak away with Grandfa for his dragon stories. She missed those quiet moments with him most of all.

While Trey told her about his home, she assembled a meager meal of walnuts and dried nightberries. Bread and cheese would be better, but a quick glance in the cooler proved they hadn't kept well.

He ate quietly, lost in his thoughts.

She ground up a stalk of fever weed and added it to Grandfa's healer paste. She rubbed it into Trey's shoulder. It would help ease Trey's pain and heal the bruising. Color had returned to his face, but his silence concerned her.

"I'm so sorry the villagers shot at you. Please, tell me about your dragon. I'm not like them." She smiled to let him know she wouldn't hurt him or the dragon.

He looked into her eyes, and she felt the shift. His pain had lessened, both physically and emotionally. He trusted her.

"Gregor. He's not mine. He's ... He was my friend."

Becca leaned across the table, eager for more.

"Dragons hibernated for over a hundred years in the northern Dragon Mountains. I don't know how many there are. I've only met Gregor. He uses mind-speech. Sometimes it hurts. And he's teaching me to ride." Pride in this honor flowed from Trey. Then his eyes clouded.

His distress was a discordant note, but Becca didn't block it. She wanted to feel his wonder. But thinking about flying hurt him. She shook her head, unable to imagine anything more wonderful than riding a dragon.

"At first it was amazing. We swooped over the lake and then above the forest. The trees were so tiny. But then something happened. We flew high into the clouds. It was freezing and hard to breathe, but he didn't respond, no matter how much I yelled. And he flew incredibly fast."

Trey stroked his injured arm. "When that man shot us, Gregor reared, and the strap broke. I held on for as long as I could. But when I fell, he didn't even notice. He left me."

She'd been wrong. He didn't feel betrayed. He felt abandoned. Her throat ached. Snaps from the fire filled the silence. Becca put the food and dishes away, leaving him to his thoughts.

"I want to go home." Trey's longing for home was so intense, it made her realize she'd never felt that way, even when Grandfa was alive. Home was simply a place of obligations and restrictions. Even her siblings were work.

"Where's that?" As soon as she asked, she knew she wanted to go with him.

Trey sighed, letting go of his fear. "Valley Keep. I don't know how to get back, or how far I flew."

"That's easy." Becca yanked a map from the chest against the bedroom wall. "We're here, up the hill from Chartsend, at the base of the Dragon Mountain Range. That's Amethyst Lake, where I found you."

He took the map and traced his fingers along a trail north into the mountains. "It's not on the map, but this trail might go there. Valley Keep is between the third and fourth range, right in the middle of Dragon Valley."

Becca's mouth dropped open. As far as she knew, her village was the farthest north. But Trey's sincerity convinced her. She peered at Grandfa's notes.

"Pilgrim's Trail. I wonder what that means."

Trey leaned back, his lips compressed, as if regretting his openness.

"If that's the way we have to go, it'll take at least a week to get there, and we need supplies."

But where else could they go? She'd planned on joining the trader caravan and journeying to the sea. He could come with her, but then she'd have to hide him until the caravan showed up.

She growled in frustration and stuffed the map back into the storage trunk. Grandfa's journals were stacked inside. She pulled one out and held it against her chest, feeling a little better. These were part of him.

"What's that?"

"My grandfather's journals. He would've been so excited. He told me so many stories about dragons, and their riders, and all their heroic quests." Becca stopped, half expecting Trey to scoff and ridicule her like everyone else.

Trey tilted his head. "They went on quests? Amazing. I've read about dragons and the protocols for interacting with them, but nothing about what happened in the past. I've suspected there were more. My grandmother says the rest of the world only knows about the plague. Guess she was wrong."

His excitement lifted a weight from Becca's shoulders. He believed. Her heart wanted to fly around the room. She had so many stories to share. There might even be stories Grandfa hadn't told her.

Becca sank into the couch and opened the journal. Diagrams covered every page. Tiny scribbles everywhere.

Trey sat beside her. "Wait. Jason's Keep. Gregor mentioned that."

Question marks surrounded a diagram of a dormant volcano, followed by a travel log, noting dates and distance traveled. Grandfa had marked the coordinates of medicinal herbs. His note on the last page made her head spin.

I finally found it. Abandoned. Like all the others. No dragons. No remains. Nothing.

It was all for nothing.

He'd been to Jason's Keep. The story he'd told her about the knight who searched for dragons had been about him. About his search. And his loss.

Searching the chest for more clues, she discovered an old map with five large *X*s. One journal was filled with images of eggs and dragonstones. He'd known the stones were actually dragon eggs. He'd known so much more than he ever told her.

Becca sighed. He'd gathered proof, but he let everyone call him crazy. She could picture him as a young man, eager to find dragons. His disappointment must've been overwhelming. So he'd shared only the good parts. With dragons extinct, there was no reason to dwell on what people had done to them.

But now dragons were back.

A knock on the cabin door startled them both. Trey bolted upright, the blanket falling to the floor. Becca shoved him toward the bedroom.

The fire glowed, filling the cabin with flickering light, a beacon announcing her presence. She'd made a fatal mistake.

Stuffing Trey's boots under her satchel, Becca cautiously opened the door.

Marcus stood, water dripping off his hood. Becca clung to the door, unsure if she should let him in or tell him to go away.

He pushed past her, hanging his cloak and kicking off his boots. Then he turned and enveloped her in a tight hug. "I've been looking everywhere for you, Becks."

Becca rested her head against his chest. Listening to his steady heart made everything all right with the world. She could forget everything in his arms, his concern soothing her soul.

After a few minutes, he loosened his hold. "I have bad news. Peter's been attacked."

She left his embrace, the fantasy gone. Of course, Marcus searched for her to tell her. A dozen scenarios rushed through her mind. She should pretend she was devastated, and he'd be there for her.

He was her friend. It would be so easy to dump all her worries on him.

Trey's fear reminded her that she couldn't. Marcus wouldn't trust a stranger.

A flutter of anxiety from her satchel sent tingles through her mind. The dragon egg was reacting too. She had to keep them both safe, so she could protect the dragon.

"Are you in shock or something?" Annoyance swirled through a flash of lust. Obviously, she wasn't reacting the way she was supposed to. Frail and needy, like Isobel. And finally she understood why he couldn't love her the way she wanted. He needed her to be helpless so he could be the hero. She was too independent.

"No. I already knew. Roger killed him." She was done pretending.

"You saw the dragon attack?" His shock warned her to be careful.

"The dragon didn't even land. Roger shot it, and then he stabbed Peter. He made it look like a dragon attack to cover up what he'd done." Her voice broke as horror washed through her.

"You must be in shock. This isn't one of your grandfather's stories. You can't rewrite reality."

Of course, he didn't believe her. Another piece of her fantasy shattered. They'd done everything together since they were little. Went on imaginary quests, learned to hunt together, and listened to Grandfa's stories in this very cabin. He'd always been a part of her life. How could he think she'd make this up?

Marcus grabbed her hand. "Come home. Everyone is worried about you."

It was late. Between the darkness and the rain, it was impossible to travel back to the village. He would've known that when he headed out. Suddenly, Becca knew he'd come for more than comfort. Her heart broke a little more. Nathan's rumors had gotten to him too.

A thump from the bedroom echoed through the cabin.

"Is Nathan here?" Marcus's eyes narrowed, confirming her suspicions.

"No. I was reading Grandfa's journals. One must've fallen off the bed." Becca edged over to the closed door and blocked it with her body.

"Don't lie. I've heard all about you and Nathan."

His scorn stabbed her chest. He'd been there the day she'd hit Nathan. He knew she detested him. How could he believe Nathan's lies after all the years they'd been friends?

Marcus shoved Becca aside and opened the door. The bed was empty, but the room was small. There was only one place for Trey to hide. Marcus found him behind the bed.

"Healer's wrath, Becca. You really have changed."

Pain at his accusation lanced through her.

Marcus stormed past her and retrieved his boots and cloak. He turned and glared at Trey standing in front of the bedroom. Then he grabbed Becca's head and ground his mouth against hers, bruising her lips.

Just like Nathan.

Her heart shattered into a million pieces. Marcus would never love her. He wanted to control her, just like everyone else.

She pounded his chest, and he let go, shock reflected in his eyes.

"Aw, shit. Sorry, Becks." He fled into the stormy blackness, leaving behind his own sense of betrayal.

Becca's hands shook as she latched the door behind him. Maybe the pain she'd felt had been his and not hers. No. Her pain was real. Even if he'd been hurt, that was no excuse for how he'd reacted. Unfortunately, Marcus wouldn't be the only one to remember her fondness for Grandfa's cabin.

She looked up and caught Trey rubbing his hand through his hair. "Sorry."

His apology didn't fix anything. As soon as the sun rose in the morning, she had to leave.

ESCAPE
BECCA

The next morning Becca woke before dawn. Trey had been so exhausted, he fell asleep on the bed while Becca pored over Grandfa's research. She'd tossed and turned on the couch for the rest of the night, upset about Marcus and worried he would tell her mother she was spending the night with a stranger.

Any hope of marrying Marcus, instead of Nathan, had been obliterated. Despite all her preparations, she hadn't even realized she'd hoped he'd leave with her. She'd been foolish.

It was time to give up on impossible dreams. Time to leave for good. Even if she sent Trey off by himself, she couldn't go back home. Roger had killed Peter. Drunk villagers had tossed Grandfa off the pub roof. Everyone was terrified of dragons, and she was the dragon girl. Whatever happened, it wouldn't be good.

The best she could hope for would be that Mama would lock her up and discredit anything she said. Mama had probably already leveraged Peter's death to increase her status in the village. Becca wondered if her mother had ever felt anything for him.

Grief squeezed her heart for the twins. Losing a father left a scar deep in one's soul. Kevin would be devastated. Peter was the only father he remembered. She wished she could hug them one last time, but she couldn't.

Trey needed her help. She'd spent all night searching the map. His village lay deep within the mountain pass, at least a week of traveling on foot, probably more. They needed supplies.

Becca strode through the drizzle to the woodshed behind the cabin and twisted the door's wooden latch. Firewood was stacked up to the low ceiling along one wall and shelves lined the other wall. Becca grinned. Grandfa was an organized man.

She rummaged through a stack of leathers and discovered a large camping pack tucked on the top shelf, complete with bedroll and cooking supplies. Grandfa's secret stash of Healer paste was stuffed behind the door. She tossed it next to a bar of pine soap and two small animal snares. That would do.

Back inside the cabin, Trey sauntered from the bedroom. He rubbed his head and yawned. "Sorry to hog the bed."

His sheepish grin sent flutters through her stomach. He reminded her of Marcus when they'd been younger. Before he became a heartbreaker. Becca pressed her lips together, resisting his tousled hair and sleepy eyes. She was done with boys.

"We need to get going, and soon. Marcus will tell someone you're here. And that won't be good for either of us. My village is already wary of strangers, and the fake dragon attack will make it worse." Becca handed Trey the pine soap and a face cloth.

Her stomach growled loudly, and Trey's responded in the cabin's silence.

He cleared his throat, his cheeks as red as Becca's felt. "We should eat."

Becca dipped her head, too embarrassed to speak, and grabbed all the deer jerky from the cupboard. Trey went outside to the water pump to wash. She stuffed two blankets and two sets of Grandfa's clothes into the travel pack, along with a rope, cleats, a small skinning knife, and an ax for kindling. The pack was heavier than she liked for such a long trip.

Two journals and the map fit easily into her collection bag. She held the rest of Grandfa's evidence and stared at the remnants of the fire in the hearth. Her chest constricted, making it hard to breathe. She couldn't destroy his notes, but she couldn't take them with her, and she didn't want anyone else to find them and follow.

Trey took the journal from her hand. "Don't burn them. Is there somewhere we could hide all this? A cave?"

His question reminded her of the dragon eggs. "Maybe. It's too damp with all this rain. I'd need something airtight." She spun around the room, searching for a container to keep the weather from destroying the papers.

Anticipation. Gloating.

Becca straightened, her heart racing. She'd recognize that emotional resonance anywhere.

Nathan was coming.

"We have to leave. Now." She didn't know how far away he was, but for once, her curse was helping, warning her.

Trey stuffed Grandfa's journals and maps into the bulging collection pack and slung the strap over his shoulder and across his chest. He winced as his arm moved, but he didn't make a sound.

Slinging the travel pack and her collection bag over her own shoulders, Becca clutched Grandfa's winter jacket and ran out the door. She dove between the trees, away from the trail. Trey couldn't sense Nathan's presence, but he followed her without hesitation.

She'd spent so much time with her grandfather, she knew the surrounding woods better than any hunter. She located the narrow animal trail leading to the top of the waterfall, and followed it. Hopefully, when Nathan found the cabin empty, he'd assume she was on her way home. By the time anyone figured it out, their footprints would be covered by the animal tracks.

Nathan's voice reached her through the bushes. "Red." His glee felt too close.

Even though she was far enough away he couldn't possibly see her, she jumped when he knocked on the cabin door.

"Come on. Don't be coy. Marcus told me you were here. You can't grieve alone. I can help."

She froze, holding her breath, afraid any sound would give away her position. It was clear Marcus hadn't mentioned Trey. Boys and their games. Maybe he wanted to punish her. Or he thought Nathan would confront Trey. She shuddered, certain Nathan would've taken his anger out on her.

"Becca? Come on." His voice needled into her brain as the door opened with a forbidding groan.

Her heart thudded in her ears as she waited for him to discover she was gone.

Trey put his hand on her shoulder and tilted his head in inquiry. He obviously couldn't hear Nathan. Yet, it sounded as if Nathan stood beside her. She put her finger to her lips, warning Trey to be quiet.

The cabin door slammed, and she jumped.

"Damn you, Marcus." Nathan's anger was half-hearted. He whistled as he left, his emotions shifting to anticipation.

Becca wilted, then forced herself down the path, away from the safety and comfort of the Grandfa's cabin.

As feeling returned to her limbs, she sucked in a shuddering breath. They had to travel fast, before anyone else searched for her. But first, she had to get the dragon eggs.

Trey stumbled, crying out when his shoulder hit a tree. His pain throbbed in her skull.

Guilt slowed her steps, but his worry pushed her forward. She couldn't block his emotions. Not now. Her cursed ability could warn her if anyone was on their path. Especially since everyone knew about Grandfa's bench at the top of the falls.

DRAGON EGGS
BECCA

Halfway to the waterfall, the storm hit, soaking Becca. The patter of raindrops shut out the rest of the world. At least the rain would wash away any evidence of their journey, and delay a search. Probably not. But so far, only Nathan and Marcus cared about finding her.

Becca wiped the water from her face and winced. Marcus's angry kiss had left more than a bruise on her tender lips. She'd been so sure he was the one for her. But he wasn't the shy, intense boy she'd kissed when she was twelve. He was still a good man. He'd taken care of Kevin after Grandfa's death. But now she couldn't deny the truth. He didn't see her, didn't trust her, and certainly didn't respect her.

She was a person, not a possession.

As she clambered over a log, she vowed to stop pining for something that didn't exist. She didn't need a man, not when they wanted her to be someone she wasn't. It was time to give up foolish dreams of romance. Mama was right. Love didn't exist.

Other than the occasional grunt from Trey whenever he moved his shoulder too much, the hike was quiet. Soothing.

When they reached Grandfa's bench above the waterfall, the smooth wood under her palm comforted her. The roar of the falls was muffled, and silence hung in the air as if the forest was taking a breath.

She stretched out her senses, searching for any sign of energy, but she found nothing. Even the tiniest animals hid from the downpour. She wished she had her rain cloak, hanging behind the kitchen door. But there was no way she could return home to fetch it. Someone was bound to see her. It was risky enough being this close.

"Why are we stopping?" Trey's lips next to her ear sent her heart into an erratic beat. Focused outward, she hadn't realized she'd stopped.

A gentle nudge inside her head pushed her forward a step.

"We're not." Her words came out more breathless than she'd intended. She turned her head, and the sensation disappeared. "Come on. We're almost there, and then you can rest."

Her powers were frustrating, but she dared not shield herself from them. The villagers were probably at the community center figuring out how to kill the dragon. She wished she could convince them to talk to the dragon before attacking. If they could see that he was healthy, they wouldn't be so terrified of the plague.

She hoped Gregor never returned. Then he'd be safe, and Trey could see him again. But for now, the only thing she could do was collect the eggs and keep moving. They'd find shelter once they were a safe distance from the village.

As she strode toward the cave, curious tugs pulled at her chest. The tiny dragons knew she was coming. Hope grew from their connection. Maybe Trey would see the eggs too.

She stopped outside of the crevice hiding the cave entrance. Trey dropped the packs with a groan and stretched. Guilt kept her gaze from his. He'd carried the heaviest of their packs, and she'd never once offered to switch the load.

"You rest. I'm going to get the dragon eggs." She removed the branch concealing the cave.

"They're in there? How'd you find them?" Curiosity and admiration flowed from him, but she wasn't sure he'd believe her connection to the eggs.

"I was searching for herbs when I found the cave." She waited for his disbelief. It didn't come. He sat with another groan and cradled his arm.

Becca pushed into the cave. Rain poured through the hole in the ceiling, flooding the ground. The pool of water extended to the walls now, but the eggs rolled in the depression, transmitting contentment.

Red, yellow, green, brown. Ten perfect orbs. But they'd grown. She cradled a white egg the size of two fists and as heavy as Mama's stock pot. The egg shifted, and joy filled her mind, bubbling through her entire body. Becca could sense flutters coming from inside the egg.

It was a tiny dragon.

The egg shifted in her grasp again, so she clutched it against her chest. This dragon needed her.

Becca shook her head at her foolishness. Why would a baby dragon need her?

She stood and carried the egg to Trey. Her hands glowed as the crystal orb pulsed. It didn't transform into a rock. Probably because of the rain. She held the egg out to Trey.

He raised an eyebrow. "What's this?"

"What do you see?" She held her breath.

He shrugged. "A rock. Granite, with some flecks of quartz. Is the egg inside?"

Her hope withered. He couldn't see it.

"Yes and no. It only looks like a rock. Water transforms it into a perfect sphere. An egg. I think it's like a magician's illusion." She started to bite her lip but stopped as soon as her teeth grazed her bruise.

He wouldn't believe her. How could he? But the emotions coming from him were not disbelief.

Curiosity. A desire to help.

Becca's world spun. He didn't think she was making things up.

Trey frowned. "People come to my village, seeking answers. They claim to have unusual abilities, or they know and see things others can't."

She could see that familiar look in his eyes. At least he wanted to understand. "Something's happening to our world. First the heat wave in winter, then these weird storms. The dragons. Science and logic can't explain any of it."

He nodded, and hope made her bold.

"It's magic. I've changed. I bet you have too."

His emotions dissipated as if blown away by the wind. "I don't see anything, but that doesn't mean it's not real. Dragon eggs disguised as rocks. Why not?"

His attention had shifted. He didn't care about eggs or rocks. He wanted to go home. She didn't need to convince him of anything because it didn't matter.

The egg pulsed against her chest. The tiny dragon mattered.

She dug through her satchel, searching for something to leave behind, so she'd have room for the egg. Grandfa's journals and map had to go with her. She couldn't leave them. It would be like losing him all over again.

It would be like leaving Kevin, Brandon, and Trish. She was leaving her home forever. For a boy she barely knew and an impossible hope that a dragon would talk to her. What was she doing?

Becca flopped beside the tree. She couldn't save anyone. She couldn't save her brothers and sister, and she certainly couldn't save a dragon.

It had taken all her energy to help Trey escape. It wasn't like Grandfa's stories at all. There was no heroic choice, only loss. Her heart shattered, and no matter how hard she tried, she couldn't get all the pieces back together.

Becca buried her head in her knees and sobbed.

Trey's hand rested on her shoulder at the same moment her tiny dragon sent acceptance. She would carry as many eggs as she could. Since Trey couldn't see them, maybe no one else could, and they were safe in the cave.

She scrubbed her face and pulled wet strands of hair out of her mouth.

"I want to take all ten eggs, but they're too heavy. I'll carry this one. Do you think you can find room to carry one or two more?"

His hesitation was expected, but he nodded, anyway.

A yearning came from the cave. One tiny dragon didn't want to be left behind.

She dove back into the cave and grabbed a smaller green orb.

An image of rolling in the water came to her. The tiny dragons were letting her know what they needed.

"Thank you. I'll be sure to keep them safe." It felt a little silly talking to eggs, but their satisfaction made it worthwhile.

When she handed the green egg to Trey to put in his pack, it pulsed with joy. This was his dragon.

She grinned. Of course, Trey was tied to dragons as much as she was. The tiny dragons would let her know what they needed, and one day she'd return for the others. Hopefully, before they hatched and risked being found by the villagers, but for now, she had to focus on their journey to Valley Keep.

One problem at a time.

CONNECTION

BECCA

The first night, Becca huddled under the branches of a huge redwood tree with Trey, too exhausted to do more than mumble good night. The second night, they stumbled upon a cave, but they didn't sleep at all on the freezing ground. They followed the river so she could let the eggs tumble in an eddy whenever they stopped to eat.

Trey helped. His emotions didn't stab at her. They existed, and she felt them, but that was all, which made Becca wonder how her power actually worked. Maybe she felt the emotions from the people in her village because she'd known them all her life, and it wouldn't be as strong elsewhere. Or possibly Trey was different. She had plenty of time to experiment as they traveled.

According to Grandfa's map, as long as they stuck to the stream, they'd reach Pilgrim's Trail. There were a lot of locations on the map with no names. She wondered how her grandfather had obtained the map. It was old, and Chartsend was marked in his handwriting. Many of the peaks in the Dragon Mountain Range had obscure symbols over them.

On the third day, the sun finally broke through the clouds. Steam rose from the ground as if the rain wanted to return to the sky.

Dry clothes improved Becca's mood. No one was chasing them. The day was beautiful, and she was on an adventure. She'd left her village. Not the way she'd planned, but now she couldn't remember why it had been so hard to leave.

She spread her arms as she walked, soaking up the warmth from morning sunlight.

Trey laughed behind her, a rich timbre of joy.

He'd been an easy companion, working just as hard as she did, anticipating her needs at each stop.

She'd miss him when she left.

Becca stumbled. She could do anything she wanted now. Go anywhere.

Search for the dragons.

But she had nothing. No supplies. Only a handful of Grandfa's clothes. Even her trader coins were gone, buried under her clothes in the chest at home. She couldn't hike into the mountains by herself.

All her obstacles didn't matter. Wonder spread through her chest, filling the dents and bruises from the past few days, as if waiting for her to feel safe before she could absorb her new reality.

Dragons existed.

"Tell me more about Gregor." She loved the dragon's name. It suited his voice, rumbling and strong. Brave. Trey had already told her about Gregor's visit to his village, and how he'd begged to meet the dragon later.

"I traveled to our meeting place every day, hoping he'd remember. But it wasn't easy. I couldn't let my grandmother find out. She wants to capture him."

Becca could feel his hesitation. He wanted to tell her more, but he also had to protect the dragon. Her heart melted at his loyalty. She'd thought Marcus was loyal, but he'd hurt her when she'd thought he never could.

"Please. I promise I don't want to hurt him. I'll keep your secret. You already know most of mine." She couldn't help the suggestive hint at the end. She wanted to see his smile.

Trey touched her shoulder, and his emotions tumbled through her.

Admiration. Fear. Worry. Sexual interest.

Becca slammed up her shields. She'd been so certain his emotions couldn't hurt her. But she was wrong. One touch, and she knew more than she wanted. Was this her life from now on? Avoiding people and making sure no one touched her?

Becca jerked away and increased her pace.

After a few moments of silence, Trey sighed.

"He speaks inside my head. I try to send my thoughts to him, but it takes a lot of concentration, and it hurts. So I speak out loud, and he answers in my mind. He says human thoughts are noisy and messy, so I try to focus on only one thing. I'm certain he whispers.

"He doesn't tell me much. He's mostly interested in our history."

It was hard not to prod him for more. But Becca had suffered sneering questions about dragons and their supposedly heroic deeds throughout her childhood. She'd give him time to trust her.

"He's asked me about magic." Trey shook his head as if this confused him more than the dragon's lack of information.

"Dragons can use magic?" Nothing in Grandfa's stories ever mentioned magic. There were other stories of witches and spells. But they were cautionary tales about what would happen if children lied. No one actually believed they were true. Even when the villagers called Lizzie a witch, it was no more dangerous than being called crazy. Or at least it hadn't been. Until fever brain spooked everyone, and drunk men killed Grandfa. But the eggs looked like rocks to everyone but her, so it had to be magic.

Trey laughed. "That would be unfair. They're already powerful. Why would they need magic?"

Becca grimaced. He made sense.

"Anyway, I told him all about the people who come to our village claiming to have magic. He said their abilities weren't magic. But my grandmother has found ways to use them."

Since her shields were up, Becca had to rely on her usual senses, but the disgust in his voice when he talked about his grandmother's actions was clear.

Becca held a branch while Trey walked past. His frown disappeared as he looked down at her. The sky tilted as she gazed back.

"You don't have any parents?" Her breathless question steadied the world around her.

Anger flickered in his eyes. Or fear. It was gone before she could figure it out. She lowered her shields, wanting to understand him more.

He stepped aside, and she let the branch fall behind them.

"No. My grandmother's all the family I have." His love for his grandmother wasn't what she'd thought. There was respect and a familiar desire to please.

Grandfa's love still warmed her heart. But Trey's unsettled emotions reminded her of her attempts to earn her mother's love. Until her power showed her how impossible that was.

Trey sighed and ran his fingers through his damp hair, causing it to stick up at odd angles.

Drakelings fluttered in Becca's chest, stuttering her next breath. Her fingers twitched as she imagined running them through his hair.

He stopped and grinned. "Are we taking a break?"

Becca's stomach flipped at the shift in conversation. His brown eyes had tiny gold flecks that sparkled. It was like seeing his soul, mischievous and craving adventure. Becca blinked, and the trees spun around them.

Great Healer. What was wrong with her?

Heat rushed to her cheeks, and she dropped her head. "Not yet. We should cover as much ground as we can, but for lunch we can sit in the sun and dry out properly."

He chuckled, his appreciation slipping through her shields.

Or maybe she let them in. Sensing emotions didn't have to be a curse.

TROUBLE
GREGOR

DAY 34 AFTER THE LONG SLEEP

Nothing had changed for Gregor, yet everything felt different. He hunted and collected bark, leaves, and plants to replenish the medical supplies. But he always had company, usually Seri or Ronin.

The coven needed every dragon to survive. Zanthor had ensured Gregor wouldn't do anything rash. It hurt that he didn't think Gregor knew how much he'd messed up.

Over the next four days, the shift was subtle. Seri had confirmed that all dragons under forty had powers, even if it hadn't manifested. Their magical aura was different from the older dragons. This fragmented the coven even more.

Many older dragons feared those with abilities had no control and would destroy them all, while the powered dragons feared banishment for something they couldn't change.

Seri spoke with every dragon, alleviating their worries. Gregor watched as she grew into the Oracle with each conversation. Her powers made her special, but her logic is what swayed them. His power would never do that.

Her claim that their species was adapting, that magical abilities were their future, hit a stalemate. Most believed the Great Wars had imbued the younger dragons with magic and given them abilities.

They clung to the hope that their hatchlings would be normal, which meant those under forty might never mate.

Gregor sighed. Until there were hatchlings, there was no way of knowing who was right. They should focus on finding the eggs, and not on why they had abilities. But he couldn't say anything. His search for eggs had already caused enough problems.

"Gregor, Ronin, Seri." Excitement wove through Zanthor's call. *"I have a quest for you."*

Finally. Gregor snatched the thought and hid it deep within his private mind. He couldn't reveal his true emotions. Not yet. Maybe not for months.

Seri bounded up to Gregor and squeezed his talons before she shot into the sky. She could project excitement and anxiety all she wanted. Her abilities didn't hurt anyone.

Gregor grimaced as he stretched his healing wing before leaping after her. That wasn't fair. She had the worst shields and constantly leaked emotions she didn't want anyone to know. She'd understand his desire to conceal his feelings. He brushed his wing against hers in the briefest show of appreciation.

They landed next to Ronin in the field below Jason's Keep.

Zanthor wasted no time. *"We have several problems. Sarcruze and I agree that the best solution, for now, is to build a new home, deep within the mountain range, where no humans can travel. Jason's Keep is too close to Valley Keep. We don't know when Elizabeth will discover her grandson's death and react. So those of you with talents will search for places we can settle."*

He was sending them away to ease tension. It was Gregor's fault. His banishment lay at the front of Zanthor's thoughts. But Gregor didn't blame Sarcruze. A leader maintained order within a coven. And Gregor had defied the rules to meet with Trey.

He was surprised by the number of older dragons who supported his choice. They missed their bond with their riders and didn't blame him for seeking a connection just as fulfilling as the coven bond.

"I wish I could go with you, but there are other tasks to do."

The wistfulness in Zanthor's voice tugged at Gregor's heart. They'd spent so much time together before they found Sarcruze and his coven, and then they'd been the ones to discover the Source. Since they woke, Zanthor hadn't left Jason's Keep. The weight of his responsibility to the coven sank Gregor's shoulders in sympathy.

Sarcruze led according to tradition and adapted reluctantly, but Zanthor listened to every dragon and provided stability. He was the one who convinced Sarcruze to adapt, which meant a lot of talking and no time to do anything. These last few days had stifled Gregor, but Zanthor had been shackled since he'd passed the leadership back to Sarcruze. While Gregor had been trying to prove his power could save them, Zanthor had ensured everyone had a voice.

Gregor dropped his head. *"I'm sorry for the trouble I've caused."*

Zanthor nodded. *"I know. Do not concern yourself about me. Youngling chafe at restrictions. And your heart is in the right place. We have to adapt to this new world, but give us time."*

His chuckle filled Gregor's mind with hints of Zanthor's past rashness, easing his shame. *"I still struggle with time. I'm young enough to want things to happen right away. But the older dragons have experienced so much more than we have, and they resist change."*

Zanthor sent a wave of encouragement. *"Trust your power. The Source gave it to you for a reason. Just try to think before you follow your nose. And lean on the coven. We all want to succeed, together. You don't have to figure it out alone."*

He bowed and then turned away to let the other dragons know their tasks privately.

It might have been Zanthor's power or his words, or his friend's belief in him, but Gregor felt renewed with purpose. He would be more cautious. Not just for the coven, but for his friend. Together, the powered dragons would save all the dragons. But deep in his mind, where no one could sense, Gregor promised himself that humans were part of the solution.

SURVIVAL QUEST
SERI

DAY 35 AFTER THE LONG SLEEP

As Seri flew away from Jason's Keep, the weight in her chest eased. Gregor's banishment had shocked everyone, but the division between powered and traditional dragons had worsened. Human history was filled with fractures and war, but dragons had always worked things out. This time she wasn't sure.

Magic gathered in storm clouds, dark and swirling, over clusters of dragons speaking privately. Coven discontent was changing magic. It shouldn't be possible. Magic was a natural resource, as much a part of the world as air and water. Humans had polluted the water and filled the air with smoke, but nature restored itself. Humans cast spells and performed rituals, shaping magic to their own ends, but even during the Great Wars they hadn't changed it. Or maybe she'd never seen as clearly as she did now.

Her ability had transformed. Before the long sleep, she'd seen auras and connecting threads. But now she could see the movement of magic as clearly as she could see water flow over rocks. Each thread was distinct, no longer a haze of color.

Seri dipped in the wind, enjoying the caress of air over her wings as she flew between Brin and Ronin. Gregor and Drekan flew below them. She could do nothing about the change in magic, the tension in the coven, or Garianna's missing eggs. For now, she could simply enjoy flying with her friends.

"Another adventure for us." Gregor's forced joy broke her moment of serenity.

He was trying so hard to pretend everything was normal. But it wasn't. He'd been humiliated and banished. Every dragon felt the wound as if it had happened to them. The coven needed time to recover.

"Absolutely. We'll find so many places to settle, dragons will thrive and rule the world." She laughed at her own attempt to make their quest sound grand.

Ronin grunted. *"You and your quests. We're flying into the freezing cold to search for even colder homes, when we should fly out to the old keeps and restore them."* Ronin had enjoyed the southern climates. Of course he was grumpy.

Seri sent him an image of waves crashing against a cliff, with all the dragons lying in the warm sun.

He snorted. *"That's exactly what we need."*

Brin chuckled. *"Wouldn't that be lovely? But we're headed north. Nothing but snow and ice."* She sent a montage of hunting and fires, imbuing them with comfort and camaraderie.

This wouldn't be a hardship for her. Twenty-five-year-old Brin had lived in the Dragon Mountain Range all her life and loved it. She'd teach them how to be snow dragons.

The last member of their party kept to himself. Drekan's power enabled him to hunt better. Since they'd left the Source, he'd spent every day hunting for the coven. Seri was surprised he'd agreed to join them.

A tingle at the back of her skull drew her gaze down to his eyes, and suddenly she could see herself. Seri blinked and her vision returned to normal.

Drekan raised an eye ridge and chuckled.

She dipped her head in respect. Lately, dragons were sharing their power with her. She suspected Garianna and her whispers of Seri's destiny had something to do with it.

Drekan's ability was stronger than those she'd experienced so far. It was more than transferring sight. They'd been connected, as if they were one dragon, tethered to the world. She was left with an afterimage of knowing something just beyond her reach. They'd connected heart to heart, soul to soul.

His aloofness made sense, a way of controlling his ability. Connecting randomly to the coven would terrify a lot of dragons. Their shields afforded them privacy, but Drekan's ability let him feel everything. Her thoughts stuttered. He must feel his prey when he hunted. She shuddered. It would be like killing yourself.

His ability was more powerful than seeing magic. She didn't understand why she was the savior when other dragons could do so much more. She shook her head free of the lingering connection to Drekan and flapped her wings to fly higher.

All of their abilities were more than they appeared. Gregor's sense of smell didn't guide him to solutions. It was more complicated. He followed the scent to a location, and he had to figure out why it was important. Often, things took time to reveal their purpose. Like Valley Keep. His power had led him there, and he believed it was to find Trey. But Seri wondered if it wasn't more. If the village was linked to their future.

Gregor had followed a scent to the girl from his Source vision, but he'd never figured out what she meant. Instead, he'd been shot, and Trey had died. His power led him to what he or the coven needed.

Seri shuddered as she recalled her vision from the Source. Fires had consumed every dragon around her as she stood helpless and alone. Other dragons had also had visions of doom. But Gregor's had filled him with hope.

"There's a depression ahead that looks promising. A series of tunnels and fresh water." Ronin sounded uncertain, but it wasn't about his power. Rather, he didn't believe they'd find any place worth settling.

Seri mentally nudged him with an image of him tumbling through the snow and turning into a giant snowball.

The others chuckled. They could shift Ronin's pessimism with humor, but it took effort. Most dragons gave up. But Seri and Gregor had spent months with him and knew his truth. He cared too much, and his power was more than it appeared. He could see through anything. Avoiding other dragons was his way of coping. No dragon wanted their digestion exposed.

They landed in a field of ice. Seri's feet tingled as the freezing cold seeped into the pads.

Ronin projected an overlay of the cavern system below them. Tunnels stretched deep into the mountain, some dead-ending and others leading to interconnected caverns.

Brin hummed. The sound vibrated deep inside Seri's skull. She'd heard of echolocation but had never seen it used above water.

"This has potential, but the system is deep under the ice. It would take a great deal of heat to expose the caves and to keep the snow from overtaking the site again. We need a place closer to the surface." Brin's assessment confirmed Ronin's image.

They flew onward.

Awe filled Gregor's mind before he spoke. *"I smell ... spring. There's no other way to describe it. Grass and saplings, dew and warmth, all wrapped into a bouquet of scents."*

Purple, green, and gold wisps of magic puffed from his nostrils.

He turned his head east, his mind far away, only his words connecting him to Seri. *"This way."*

"Wait. Gregor. Focus." Seri tried to pull him from his trance before he lost himself to his magic. Zanthor had called it a blankness, but a dense fog hid his essence from her.

Gregor shook his head and snorted. *"How? I can feel it taking over my mind. This power wasn't so overwhelming before."*

"That's why we're here. Our powers are changing. We have to learn to control them before something bad happens." Maybe that was the real reason Zanthor had sent them on this quest. Their group had the strongest abilities of the powered dragons.

Tension vibrated through Gregor as he tried to resist the pull.

"What happens if you don't follow the scent?" Genuine curiosity reinforced Brin's question.

Gregor tilted his wing and tried to fly back to Jason's Keep. The fog in his mind solidified, forming a hazy wall. He grunted, and they all felt the physical pain in his head. He reversed course and flew up to them.

Gregor's eyes clouded as Drekan used his power. Seri gasped. Threads of blue magic wound between them, connecting their minds and hearts. The threads twined around each other, strengthening the bond.

"He's fighting the pull as hard as he can. It's different from my power. I can disconnect. He has no choice. I could feel it. Wow. Gregor." Tears shone in Drekan's eyes and understanding flowed through them all, making Gregor's banishment seem more hopeless and wrong. They were all at risk.

"There must be a way." Seri's frustration wanted to burst through Gregor's mind and blast the wall of fog between them.

"Follow it, Gregor. We'll stay with you and keep you safe." Ronin's encouragement eased Seri's fear. Gregor couldn't turn his power on and off like the others. The scents came, and he reacted. But this time, the four of them were with him.

"Most of them aren't this strong. But this is as powerful as the one that sent me for the girl. It will ease when I get to where the scent originated. I don't think it's tragic." Gregor laughed, a hollow sound. No dragon wanted to be helpless to their own power. But he wasn't afraid.

"The scent is more intense when I think of home and safety. There is no scent of danger." With that last assurance, his mind closed, but Seri could still sense his essence, compassion, and excitement.

Until he learned how to control his magic, she'd help him with the repercussions.

He flew fast and straight. He didn't use the currents. He *was* the current. Drekan linked them to Gregor's body, and they flew as one.

Magic completely shrouded his head, rolling into his nostrils and permeating his brain. Even his eyes changed colors, pulsing and whirling as they flew toward their destination.

Seri smelled the ocean before they could see it. The scents of salt and fish flowing in the wind over the mountains covered in ice and snow.

"I know where we're going. You won't believe what I can see." Ronin's voice had never been filled with so much wonder, even when they found the Source. *"It's perfect, Gregor. Don't fight it."*

Gregor dove toward a huge ice field and landed. The magic thinned around his head, and his mind returned to Seri. Snow stretched between four mountain peaks, filling the bowl between them.

"There's nothing here." Gregor's disappointment showed how frustrated he was with his power.

But Seri could see magic over the snow, almost as much as over the Source. It didn't stretch up to the sky, but it covered the field.

"It's an illusion, hiding what's really there." Tingles raced through Seri's tail.

Ronin leaned his neck into hers. *"Go ahead. Look properly."*

If Drekan could link them, so could Seri. She opened her mind completely, dropping all her shields, and shifted her vision.

Blue, pink, red, yellow, and green swirled in front of them, forming a wall to the sky. At first it was overwhelming, but then she realized a bubble covered the entire ice field.

Ronin grabbed her talon and added his power to their collective view.

Under the bubble was a caldera of life. Birds and small animals capered through grass and trees. Three magnificent waterfalls flowed from the mountain peaks into a river that circled the entire valley.

It was perfect.

Seri shifted her vision back to normal, and the beautiful oasis disappeared.

"Can we fly through it?" Brin's grin was infectious. Excitement bounced through their collective mind.

"Gregor led us here. I think the Source wants us to find out." With an exuberant roar, Seri dove into the snow.

DISCOVERY

GREGOR

Snow filled Gregor's nose and obscured his vision. He held his breath and resisted the urge to change course and escape. Each beat of his wings was a struggle against the weight. Pain shot through his healing wing. If he didn't break through, his injury could incapacitate him. Fear reminded him of his breathless escape from the Source lake not that long ago.

The crisp scent of grass engulfed his mind, easing his fear and drawing him downward. A promise of freedom. His power rarely let him know if something was dangerous or welcome, but this time it did. The holes in his confidence since his fatal error with Trey shrank, and he forgave himself, accepting his power.

He burst through the dense bubble of snow to a land shrouded in clouds. Seri still led the charge, her excitement pulsing through his mind in waves. She had no doubt. No fear. A shiver of unease twitched between his shoulders at her unusual display of certainty.

Below him stretched an oasis surrounded by mountains of ice. He exhaled, and his entire body felt more alive than he thought possible. Whispers of energy flowed over his wings and wrapped his chest in comfort. The air was warm, heavy with dampness after a recent rainfall, which should be impossible. There had to be magic in this place.

While Seri landed, her thoughts leaping untethered from one joy to the next, Gregor flew around the perimeter. Thermal hot springs dotted the floor, keeping the ground from freezing.

Heat from the springs melted the snowpack into three waterfalls cascading down cliffs gouged from the enclosing mountains. The water flowed around the edge of the caldera forming a circular river. More magnificent than Ronin's hazy overlay.

Birds, drakelings, and small animals flitted among the vibrant grass and trees. A huge sprawling Nightwood tree sat majestically in the center of the caldera. Its skeletal branches ended in long, talon-shaped leaves drooping to the ground. Long before Gregor hatched, humans had all but destroyed the rare trees, but some survived in remote locations no human could reach.

Gregor relished the power coursing through his tendons with each stroke of his wings. With a jolt, he realized his injury was gone. Shock ruined his landing.

Ronin's laughter as Seri rushed to help Gregor to his feet was humiliating. Only hatchlings fell on their snouts, and he'd done it twice.

There was only awe in Ronin's voice as he examined Gregor's wing. *"All healed. Let me take off the splint."*

"I've never felt better." Seri twisted and stretched.

Every scrape and ache had disappeared. Gregor's gaze was drawn to the base of the tree. The mound's shape made him uneasy, though he couldn't say why.

He wasn't the only one.

"I can show you." Ronin's somber tone brought tears to Gregor's eyes, and then Ronin's vision connected them.

A young male dragon, about Gregor's size, lay beneath the mound, his body curled with his tail clutched in his talons. Roots grew from the dragon's chest and wrapped around his torso, cradling him, before combining to form the tree trunk. More roots stretched out in a circle, tapping into the river flowing around the valley.

"He's surrounded by green magic." Seri rose into the air and twirled, suspended by her wonder. *"Magic infuses the entire caldera. Every color. And the Nightwood…"*

Her awe sent a flush through his body. Seri restrained her emotions around others, but this broke through her reserve. Their powers connected them on a different level than their bond with the coven.

"A ball of gold magic pulses in the branches of the tree, breathing life into this place. It draws magic from the dragon buried within the roots, even though he's dead."

Through Seri's vision, Gregor watched the golden ball spin slowly in place. He sensed there was more than he could see. As if third mind connected to her magic in a way he couldn't. She was amazing.

"So, this is it? Our sanctuary?" Ronin voiced their hope.

Gregor felt it was, but he'd made mistakes in interpreting his ability. The sensation of peace lessened, as if his doubt reduced his power.

Nightberry wound up his nostrils and stabbed his head.

"Partially. This is for the eggs." The thought burst free before he could analyze it, and the smell faded.

Brin grabbed Seri's talons and pulled her to the river. *"Yes! It's perfect. The river has enough friction to wear the outer casing on the eggs. Renalia will be pleased. Dragons can lay their eggs at the top of the waterfalls, and I can monitor them. We won't lose them."*

They'd found a solution for their future eggs, but they'd been looking for a home.

"It can still be our home too." Seri cut through Gregor's disappointment.

Ronin flew up to the rim. *"The ocean is on the other side of this ridge. Food and water. Everything we need is here."*

His pleasure wrapped around Gregor's chest. Everything was heightened. Ronin's emotions. Seri's magic. Even his own strength and energy. But the dragon trapped in the mound concerned him. Was this really a place for them to live or a place to die?

Waves crashed against the cliff's outer walls, a reminder of the violence of nature. Snow, ice, and freezing ocean waters awaited them. They could live here, in isolation, leaving only to hunt and fly. But dragons were meant to roam the world. They shouldn't be contained.

Seri laid her talon on Gregor's shoulder. *"I don't think the Source provided this for us to stay forever. It's ideal as a nursery. Magic is everywhere, giving life where there should be death."*

Gregor leaned his head against Seri's, working through his worry. *"The dragon. He's a youngling, like us, which means he had a magical ability. What if the Source didn't create this? What if he did, and it killed him? I know you believe the Source has a plan for us. I'm just not so sure it's to protect us."*

He sighed, knowing she wouldn't understand. If he hadn't ruined everything with his overconfidence, he wouldn't be questioning anything. He wished they could return to the time before the plague when life had been about hunting the largest bear or traveling farther than before.

Seri stroked his face. *"You're doubting yourself because you were banished. This is a victory. Sanctuary will give us what we need to survive. Let me worry about the Source."*

Sanctuary would keep them safe from humans and their guns. But dragons couldn't hide forever. Gregor still believed dragons would be better off if they found a way to work with humans.

Nutmeg wafted through his mind, reinforcing his desire. He'd find a way.

PILGRIM'S TRAIL
BECCA

By the time Becca and Trey reached Pilgrim's Trail, they were hungry and tired. Each morning it had rained. By noon the sun would chase the clouds away, but never enough to dry their clothing.

Becca had been debating whether they should set up camp for a couple days so they could fish and set a snare. They needed more than berries and jerky to survive the long trip.

"We need to stay in one place for a bit."

Trey kicked at the packed dirt road and scowled. "No weeds."

She wasn't sure he'd heard. He seemed lost in his thoughts, so she reviewed what he'd told her about his home. Even though his village was more isolated than hers, trader caravans showed up three times a year. They brought more than supplies. People flocked to his village during the summer months from all over the world to seek answers from the Dragon Prophet. Talented craftsmen, disgruntled apprentices, and even Healers went to Valley Keep when the Great Healer failed them. Many stayed and became acolytes, serving in whatever capacity Elizabeth chose. Trey's village sounded as prosperous as the city where Nathan's cousin, Isobel, lived.

Trey had cleverly avoided talking about himself. Becca kept her own tales to the safe areas, telling him about the twins' mischief and Kevin's habit of treating them like puppies. She didn't speak about Mama and couldn't think about Peter without tears threatening. So, she shared her favorite dragon stories, warmed by Trey's acceptance and eagerness to hear more.

But Trey's frown remained, and he hadn't responded to her suggestion. She kept her shields up. He'd tell her what was bothering him, eventually. She didn't need to peek.

It didn't take long.

"The road is too packed. No weeds at all. See the ruts here? A caravan has been here recently. They usually don't show up for at least three months. Always with her secret projects."

Becca wasn't sure who he was meant. "So, you don't want to stop?"

He shook his head. Hunger gnawed at her belly, but she could wait a little longer.

They hiked in silence until the sun was high in the sky. She shed her coat, looking forward to stopping by the river to bathe her eggs and learn more about dragons. Grandfa's journals were filled with notes on their biology, eating habits, and the responsibilities of dragon riders. One contained the locations of tall standing stones that marked dragon keeps.

Voices cut through the peaceful silence, followed by the distinct whinny of a horse. Becca's heart stumbled a beat. She'd gotten careless, and Nathan had found her. They should've stayed off the road.

She scanned the shrubs for a hiding spot. All those days alone with Trey had made her forget the danger. She couldn't go back home to the demands and expectations.

Trey grabbed her hand, breaking through her shields. Calmness flooded her mind, but his emotions couldn't change anything.

"Great Healer, Becca. Your heart is racing." His voice was far away, but he reached out and cradled her cheek.

His hand was warm.

"Probably travelers heading to Valley Keep." His soothing tone calmed her chaotic thoughts, and the world rushed back into focus.

She swayed.

He was right. No one from Chartsend could be ahead of them. Multiple voices, female and male, intermingled with the creak of wagons. She leaned her head into Trey's chest, and he rubbed the back of her neck. His comfort washed away the last of her fear, leaving her weak.

He laughed. "You looked like a terrified deer. I thought you were going to bolt into the forest without me."

She choked out a laugh but couldn't do anything about the fire in her cheeks. She buried her face into his chest and took a shuddering breath. His heartbeat, steady and slow, was far too comforting.

The last thing she needed right now was to fall for another boy. She'd been wrong about Marcus. And she certainly wasn't ready for marriage after escaping Nathan.

Trey, with his gentle hands on her neck, must stop, now.

With a determined push, Becca stepped away from the refuge he offered. The tender look in Trey's eyes almost undid her resolve. His emotions held no hint of possessiveness, only appreciation and concern.

She shook her head, denying what her power told her. She knew that look. He'd change eventually. Just like Marcus.

She inhaled resolve. They had no future. She was leaving as soon as she obtained supplies. But she didn't get the chance to warn him away.

She sensed the man's presence moments before he strode from the shrubs.

"Howdy, folks." His voice was cheerful.

She wondered how long he'd watched them before deciding they weren't a threat, and she blushed again. Trey had distracted her.

The man was wary, but there was no sense of aggression. Maybe her power wasn't a curse.

"Hello." Mama insisted politeness could counter any volatile situation. Becca cringed at taking her mother's advice, but after years of being crazy Stephen's daughter, Gennifer had earned the villagers' respect.

"You two look like you've had a rough time." The man's sun-crinkled eyes and statement eased Becca's tension. He wouldn't badger them with uncomfortable questions.

Trey grimaced. "Yes, sir. We didn't pack as well as we should have. You heading to Valley Keep?"

The man chuckled, then swept his hat down in a bow. "Nothing else on the other end. John's the name. Pleasure to meet you. And yours?"

"Becca."

"I'm Trey."

"You look like you could use some food in your bellies. Keep heading up the road, and Maggie will sort you out. You're not the first couple we've rescued." His laugh welcomed them to join in on the joke, though Becca was at a loss as to what he meant.

They must've looked a little battered, with Grandfa's ill-fitting clothes covered in mud. But she didn't have trader coin to pay their way.

John must've read her mind. "We're not your typical caravan. Most folks can't pay for passage. As long as you do your share, you're welcome to join us. It's a long journey, and we have only one rule. Be decent. That's it."

"Thanks for your hospitality. We're happy to help out." Becca grinned her relief. Food and shelter would make the journey easier, and people to insulate her from her growing awareness of Trey would help too. She didn't want to escape from one stifling village to another.

John disappeared into the forest, and another man escorted them to the caravan. The traders who came to her village consisted of a single wagon. Occasionally, there'd be a second wagon with musicians or actors, and on rare occasion a magician. But this was a small village. In a clearing next to the river, five wagons formed a semicircle. Goats, sheep, and chickens roamed freely, while a dozen tethered horses munched on grain next to large water buckets.

"Marie. I found you some help," their guide shouted as they approached the largest wagon Becca had ever seen.

She tightened her shields as his longing to please Marie slipped into her mind. She had enough problems with her own emotions and didn't need this young man's yearnings clouding her judgment.

A young woman with dark skin and straight, raven hair stuck her head past a wooden door. The rest of the wagon was made of Oldwood, but the windows and door were framed with smooth driftwood.

Marie's face lit with delight. "Becca. Finally."

Becca's steps faltered, and she gripped Trey's fingers. "How did you know my name?"

"A dream," Marie said abruptly, her face suddenly shuttered.

Becca recognized Marie's fear of ridicule. As the "dragon girl," she knew exactly how Marie felt.

"You, boy. Follow me. The livestock need tending, easy enough work even with your injury." The man strode away.

Trey squeezed her hand, a promise to find her later, and ran after the man. Her hand tingled. She was already getting too attached.

Determined to focus on something else, she climbed the two metal treads into the wagon. "What kind of dream?"

Marie shrugged. "It's hard to explain. You'll discover everyone here is a little unusual. You'll fit in. But never mind all that. I'm so excited you're here. John didn't believe me. Come meet the kids." Her grin begged Becca to leave the questions for another time.

At least she seemed friendly. Becca focused on her shield. She couldn't handle an attack with so many strangers.

Marie moved to the side, and ten curious faces looked up at Becca, all under five years old.

"Who's that, Marie?" piped a high, defiant voice, so much like Trish that Becca's throat constricted.

The children sat around a huge circular rug, building a tower from colored blocks.

Marie swung her arm. "As you can see, I'm in charge of the wee ones. I keep them fed, entertained, and as clean as I can. They generate messes out of nothing."

She squiggled her nose and crossed her eyes. The kids giggled.

"Some of them need to be watched more than others." She indicated one small boy with solemn eyes and a mischievous grin. "Wee Justin has been lost, oh, about three times. After he joined the caravan, the mothers insisted we corral them somehow. This used to be the storage wagon, but now it's a traveling school. Right, monsters?"

"Yes, Marie," they responded in unison, delighted to be called monsters. Then they giggled and jostled each other, claiming each was the "bestest" monster.

Marie pulled Becca to the side. "Paper, coloring pencils, and here, a few puzzles and books that some families brought with them. Most people don't have much. We've made a lot of toys, though. These wee ones love making things." She chuckled and rubbed her back. "Love destroying things more. I spend more time cleaning than anything else."

Much to Becca's surprise, Marie wrapped her arms around Becca. She fit easily under Becca's chin.

Marie's sadness seeped through. Becca couldn't block the transfer during physical contact.

"I'm so happy to have company over the age of five," Marie whispered. "Excuse me if I babble."

Becca didn't mind Marie's chatter. Marcus had never been much for small talk, and she'd never been friendly with the girls in her village, not with her family's reputation. But Marie touched her without fear, and Becca wondered if the village rumors had affected how people treated her.

The door opened, and the toddlers dropped everything, squealed, and ran for freedom. In seconds, the wagon was empty.

Marie chuckled. "Don't worry. Maggie has them. They behave for her. She feeds them so I can have a break. Bet you're hungry."

Becca's stomach chose that moment to agree loudly. Marie laughed, but there was no malice in it.

Becca stepped into ordered chaos.

Emotions attacked Becca, breaking through her shields as if they were made of mist. She cringed against the wagon steps, closing her eyes as she frantically imagined a solid rock wall between her mind and the world.

Marie touched Becca's shoulder, and her sympathy gave Becca something to cling to in the maelstrom. But then Marie gasped and a vast well of sorrow threatened to drown Becca.

Becca frantically built her mental wall, wilting when the onslaught stopped. She'd never survive anywhere if she couldn't shield herself better.

"I'm sorry, Becca. I didn't realize you'd have any troubles." Marie snatched her hand away and stood still, giving Becca space to collect herself. "Take your time. There's no rush."

Becca sucked in a relieved breath. Marie seemed to understand what Becca needed. She was still reeling from the depth of Marie's sorrow. It hadn't been an immediate emotion. It was distant, as if from the future. A premonition? She frowned, uncertain how she knew.

Love flickered through her mind, healing all the tender parts. Becca's heart swelled. It was her tiny dragon. Reaching into her satchel, she stroked the egg and felt stronger. With her tiny dragon by her side, she would figure out how to control her power.

223

Trader Caravan

Becca

Marie dragged Becca to a table where two girls peeled vegetables. They were chatting, so Becca grabbed a potato and a knife. Preparing a meal centered her. If she concentrated hard enough, they wouldn't even notice she was there.

Trey walked past, tugging a goat who had other ideas about going wherever he was taking it. He shrugged, his grin inviting Becca to share the humor. The girls tittered, and Becca hunched her shoulders, focusing on her potato.

One girl, her dark brown hair tied in a braid that flowed past the bench, leaned across the table. "Please tell me he's your brother."

Her tone was so melodramatic, Becca snorted. She resisted the urge to stake her claim. Trey wasn't hers.

"Don't be ridiculous, Jane." Even through the other girl's heavy accent, Becca could hear her scorn.

Jane shrugged. "Can't blame me for hoping. I'm Jane and that's Shelly." She pointed to herself and Shelly with her paring knife.

Jane was almost as tall as Becca while Shelly was tiny, with the curliest brown hair Becca had ever seen. Both had the sun-touched skin of traders. Becca felt like a wraith in comparison. They hadn't suffered through months of snow and rain.

"I'm Becca." She'd inadvertently peeled the entire potato away. Becca grabbed a bowl of carrots, hoping they wouldn't notice.

"We know. Everyone's curious about you and that tall breath of air. Trey." Jane's sigh was filled with longing.

Shelly rolled her eyes. "He's just a boy, like any other. Silly girl. Doesn't matter how much you wish for it, he won't stay."

Their light banter invited Becca to join in, but she didn't want to ruin it by saying the wrong thing. The girls in her village talked *about* her, not *with* her.

She took a deep breath. It was just a conversation. They didn't know her or her family's history. She could start fresh.

"Where are you from?" she asked.

Jane's paring knife punctuated her speech. "I'm from Cromwell. Shell's from Deepwater Cove, a small village off the coast of the Thoran Sea. Shell's been with the caravan way longer than me. I joined with my mom and dad about two months ago."

Shelly bobbed her head and spoke with her heavy accent. "My family are fishermen, but village is tiny. Not many girls. So, my brother Scott joined traders to find wife. He loved it too much to settle down. And I came too. Life is good. I see world and many peoples." She blushed and stopped.

"How 'bout you, Becks?" Jane interjected before the silence got awkward.

Becca's smile slipped. The nickname reminded her of Marcus. She'd been wrong about their friendship.

"Don't mind Jane and her short names." Shelly frowned at her friend.

"No. It's fine." Becca forced a smile. They'd done nothing wrong. At least her shields were holding. "So, this is a real trader caravan, then? John said something about picking up strays."

Jane's laughter drew smiles from the people walking past. "No. We're transporting questors to the Dragon Prophet. Shell knows more about it, but John was called to make this journey, picking up strangers in isolated towns along the way."

She shrugged. "My mother's been ill, so we joined hoping the Dragon Prophet could cure her. The Healers have given up."

Becca frowned, unsure what to say, but Jane shrugged, forcing her own smile.

"I'm going to stay on with the caravan. John's talking about traveling down the coast. I've never seen the ocean. Shell says it's salty and not that impressive. But she doesn't know what it's like to live in crowded, run-down buildings with no water in sight."

Becca slowly peeled the carrot. Seeing the world had always been her dream. She could join the caravan. But then she wouldn't find the dragon, and she had two dragon eggs. Then there was Trey. She'd planned on leaving, but she wasn't ready yet.

"I like your shirt." Shelly fingered the leather cross-stitching along Becca's sleeve. "We use leather for shoes and satchels. Practical things. But Mother weaves cured kelp into my ceremonial skirt."

Marie plunked two pieces of bread and a bowl of dried fruit in front of Becca and sat down with a weary sigh. "Let's eat before the monsters return."

They talked about clothing and crafts and the differences between their villages, until the toddlers filed past, silent and well behaved.

Marie grabbed Becca's hand. "Come on. It's back to work for us."

A few hours later, the children dispersed back to their families. John led Becca to the wagons beyond the kitchen area, stopping in front of a wooden wagon covered in painted vines and flowers.

"This is where you'll sleep. Maggie'll fix you up with everything you need."

He rapped on the door. It opened, revealing a woman whose face had so many lines, she must be seventy years old.

"That her?" The woman's voice was as rough and weathered as her hand clutching the door. Tufts of gray hair waved on her head as she moved.

Becca tried not to stare, but she couldn't believe this woman was standing. No Elder had ever looked so deathly.

John strode off. "Good luck, Becca."

Maggie peered over Becca's head, as if she couldn't see her. "Can't you talk? Did I get another useless chicken?" Her frown added even more wrinkles.

"Ma'am. I'm Becca, ma'am." Becca couldn't help the nervous warble in her voice. She wasn't at all certain Maggie was human.

"Don't you 'ma'am' me. I'm Maggie, plain and simple. Well, don't stand there growing roots. Come inside and let me have a look at you."

Becca climbed into a room filled with beds. She blinked. Sunlight poured through a long window in the roof. Six beds were mounted three high on each side of a narrow passage, enough for twelve people to sleep at once. A blue velvet curtain covered the far end of the wagon where she assumed Maggie lived.

"Hope you're not afraid of heights. You'll sleep in the top bunk. And that young man of yours will sleep across the way. I'm a light sleeper, so no shenanigans."

She spun Becca around, her gnarled hands digging into Becca's waist. "You're tall for a girl. I'll have Jack pull something from the stores, but you'll have to wear men's clothing."

She tutted. "You got no meat on your hips to hold anything up. We'll fix that while you travel with us. Show me your feet."

She didn't give Becca any time to do anything but obey.

"Goodness. Those boots are worn through. Good thing you're a size eight. We have plenty of those. Most girls don't want to admit their feet aren't dainty, but feet are feet, I say."

She rummaged under the first bunk and pulled out a pair of boots and a shirt. "Put these on. The pants you're wearing will have to do. Unless you want a skirt?" She squinted up at Becca.

"No, that's fine. Or a skirt if it's easier." Deference had worked with Mama, and Becca didn't want to offend this creature.

Maggie smacked the back of Becca's head. "Don't be fake with me. Do you want pants or a skirt?"

Becca clutched her fingers behind her back so she wouldn't rub her head. "Pants."

"Thought so. Know your mind, girl. Now, go. Enjoy dinner. The horses are rested, and we're leaving early tomorrow. So, you better be back here before I get to sleep. I won't tolerate lateness."

"When do you sleep?"

Maggie cackled. "Ha. Never. Finally, a chicken not afraid to ask questions. Pay attention, girlie, and you'll do fine. Now off with you."

Becca left, feeling like she'd passed a test.

Dinner was a wash of voices. People discussed the strange weather occurring all over the world. Becca's village wasn't the only one to encounter a heat wave in winter. There were many theories, but the most popular was that magic explained it all. No one mentioned dragons or the plague. Only her village thought they were afflicted with fever brain.

Some travelers had fled their villages, fearing for their lives. Others had chosen to travel to the Prophet, certain they'd find answers in Valley Keep. Trey was still doing chores, so she couldn't ask him about it.

A tingle of unease whispered at the back of Becca's mind while she washed dishes. And then again when she put the cooking supplies away. She reinforced her mental shields, but the sensation didn't go away. Rubbing her neck, she climbed into the wagon. It had been a long day. She just needed sleep.

She pulled her satchel off the top bed and sat on the bottom mattress. As soon as she stroked her egg, distress throbbed through her skull.

Something was wrong with her tiny dragon.

The last time she'd dunked the eggs in water was before they met the caravan. She rubbed her egg, attempting to soothe it and pulled out the other one. A choking sensation stole her own breath.

Trey's egg was dying.

How could it die? There was no answer. But their urgency transmitted clearly. She stuffed both eggs into her satchel and sprinted to the river not caring if anyone saw her. She must save them.

It took forever to find the right spot. The current was too strong close to the caravan, so she searched upstream for an eddy. With each step, the eggs felt heavier, as if every second brought them closer to death. Their desperation drove her to select the first eddy she found.

Becca kneeled beside the river. Panicking now could lose them forever. She steadied her hand as she dipped her egg into the flowing water, and was rewarded with a tiny flutter inside her head, faint and feeble.

A twig snapped behind her. Becca spun around, clutching her egg against her chest.

It was only Trey.

Relief made her weak. Too weak. And joy at seeing him tipped her emotions into the danger zone.

"Thought you might need help." He held out his hand for his egg and kneeled beside her.

Warmth cradled her soul, easing the fear caused by the eggs' desperation. Trey would help. Between the two of them, they could save the eggs.

"I shouldn't have waited so long. I don't know why they need the river, but I almost lost them." She couldn't help the catch in her throat.

He nodded. "This one feels heavier. Don't worry. I can help when you're busy. I'm tending the animals, so no one will think it odd if I go to the river to collect water."

His calm offer reminded her of Grandfa so much, tears filled her eyes. She blinked them away, not wanting him to see her weakness.

Becca nestled her egg between two rocks and sighed as the pressure in her skull eased. The eggs tumbled in the current, transforming into perfect orbs. She hoped that meant they would recover. The water was freezing, but she kept her hands submerged, blocking the eggs from escaping.

She wished Trey could see them, but he supported her without proof.

Even though she'd wanted to talk to Trey all day, they sat beside the river in comfortable silence. The eggs were content. Becca hadn't harmed them, but she'd have to be more careful.

Her stress melted away. Trey's calm acceptance helped too. That was one of the best things about Trey. He simply let her exist.

Darkness had fallen by the time the eggs glowed, once again a vibrant green and white. Her fingers were numb, and she fumbled the egg as she pulled it from the river.

Trey caught it with a chuckle. He retrieved the green egg and slipped them both into her satchel. Then he grabbed her hands and pulled her up.

"You've frozen yourself." He brushed her hair off her cheek.

She looked up and was instantly captured. Stars swirled in his eyes. Wonder filled her, and she sighed, her lips parting, an invitation she had no intention of giving.

Trey slowly bent his head until his breath brushed her lips. "Becca?"

He was asking permission. Joy bubbled through her, smothering the caution from her brain. He was perfect.

Becca stood on her tiptoes, closing the last bit of distance, and placed her lips against his.

The kiss was tentative and gentle, giving her a chance to change her mind.

Her shields fell away. He thought she was beautiful and strong.

They'd just spent an hour dipping rocks in a river, and he didn't think she was crazy. Her heart raced as she opened her mouth to deepen the kiss.

She needed this.

She needed him.

Tingles spread from her lips, down her neck, to her chest. Trey let her control the kiss. Holding her steady with his hands at her waist when she swayed.

It felt so warm and comforting. Too comforting.

She pulled her head away, a reluctant sigh on her lips. Her plans didn't include falling for Trey, no matter how appealing he was.

She stepped out of his embrace, immediately missing his warmth. Her lips still tingled.

His grin was lopsided, and his disappointment washed through her, but he didn't push it.

"That was nice." He handed her the satchel, emitting acceptance.

She grinned shyly and tucked an errant hair behind her ear. "Yes."

The twinkle returned to his eyes. He might try again, but he'd give her time.

They walked back to the camp. Maybe she didn't have to push him away. Being with Trey was different from what she'd ever expected to feel around any man. He made her feel special.

Trey joined the campfire, and Becca slipped back to the wagon to leave the eggs there. When she returned to the flames, she heard her name.

"Had a little alone time with Becca, huh? Lucky dog."

Her face instantly heated at the insinuation. She braced herself for the inevitable ugliness, hurt that something so magical would become shameful so soon.

Trey's voice carried over the snapping fire. "That's inappropriate. Becca's an amazing person, and she deserves respect. We're friends." His warning was clear. Don't hurt his friend.

Her heart melted. His words stopped any rumor by their simplicity.

"That's a keeper, for sure," Marie whispered in Becca's ear. She patted the bench, an invitation to sit.

Trey glanced up and waved, a frown still on his face. Yes. He was a good man.

Becca groaned. Her life was getting more complicated. The eggs needed tending. Her feelings for Trey were growing. And the need to find the dragons was constantly at the back of her mind. Trey was her best chance at finding them. Instead of feeling free, she had more responsibilities than at home.

Despite everything, she was happy. This band of misfits filled the hole left by Grandfa's death in a way she'd never dreamed. The impossible seemed possible. She'd figure it out, somehow.

It was late when Becca returned to her wagon for the night. Maggie was still singing loudly by the fire. Becca giggled, giddy with fatigue. Maggie was right. Becca would know when the woman retired to bed. There would be silence.

Caravan Magic

BECCA

In the morning the caravan was ready in under an hour. Tables were folded and stored away. Cooking supplies disappeared into compartments on the sides of wagons, and the animals were loaded onto a trailer pulled by two horses.

After a bowl of gruel, Becca cleaned the pots until Maggie sent her to the river to fill waterskins. "Take the wee ones with you. They're getting underfoot."

Marie took the four eldest children downstream, while Becca corralled three toddlers at a shallow bend where the current wouldn't whisk them away.

Justin raced to the river and hopped onto an exposed rock, babbling, "Pish. Pish." Then he squatted, perfectly balanced on the slippery surface. His waterskin fell into the eddy with a plop.

Becca retrieved the waterskin and tousled Justin's hair. "The fish are happy. Leave them be."

He nodded solemnly, his gaze fixed on the tiny fish darting between the rocks.

Upstream, a sparkle of orange caught her eye. Her heart leapt. It might be a dragon egg, but she couldn't leave the children to check.

"Want pish," Justin's high voice announced, before he plunged face-first into the river.

Becca lunged and scooped him into her arms, soaking wet but unharmed. No wonder his mother needed help. Water dripped down her shirt and britches as Justin squirmed free.

"No fishing today, young man," she shouted as he giggled, unconcerned, and ran off to join the others. They'd discovered a beetle under a stone and were poking it. He was incorrigible, but adorable. She couldn't scold him any more than she'd been able to scold the twins.

A cascade of shimmering colors flowed past her.

Becca stood transfixed, the roar of the river blending with the children's voices, a song of glee.

Sunlight flashed on each orb, forming a hazy rainbow over the river. Some eggs caught in the rocks for a moment, swirling, then moved on. Bubbles of happiness burst in her mind. Tiny dragons on an adventure.

"Becca. Are you all right?" Marie's touch was tentative, and a tendril of concern slipped through Becca's shields.

When she didn't concentrate, her shields seemed to disappear. Although she always sensed emotions from the dragon eggs.

She turned from the sight, wishing she could follow them on their wondrous journey.

"Sorry. Lost in thought."

Marie leaned in close. "Did you have a vision?"

"No. Why?"

One of the older children answered, "Because you stared at the river and played statue. Right, Marie?"

Marie bit her lip. Heat rushed to Becca's cheeks. Little eyes were far too observant.

"Yes, Kate. Go help the younger ones put the waterskins in the bucket before they unstopper them all and we have to start over."

Justin was happily flinging water into the air and squealing. His waterskin would have to be refilled.

Maria kept her voice low so the children couldn't overhear. "You looked like you were in a trance. Mama has them often. Sometimes they're hard to break, but you returned as soon as I touched you."

Becca frowned, certain she'd only been staring at the river for a short time. Shielding herself from emotions was bad enough. Now she went into a trance when she saw dragon eggs? How would she stop that from happening?

"You didn't know. Don't worry. I'm still learning to control my visions. These little ones get up to even more mischief when I have one. It's worse when I fall over. Embarrassing. And it's not as if they all come true or even make sense. I had two visions about you, and only one happened. I didn't know when you'd show up, just that you'd join us. In the other vision you were running from angry men, and John had to rescue you."

A pulse of assurance came from the egg in her satchel. Her tiny dragon seemed to know what she needed. Tingles ran through her body, echoes from the eggs down river. Her connection to the eggs was growing stronger. Could she have more than one form of magic? A dragon would know what was happening to her. For now, she needed to protect herself from her own reactions.

"I don't have visions. I sense emotions. If I didn't shield myself from them, I'd know what everyone felt all the time. Maybe you need a shield?"

"Not sure a shield would help."

The confusion on Marie's face struck Becca as hilarious. Happiness burst from her, as if the delight from the eggs had to escape, and she couldn't stop giggling. It was contagious; all the kids joined in.

Finally, she sucked in a breath for control. Emotions hadn't affected her physically before. Yet another thing to worry about.

"No. Not a physical shield." Becca tried to pretend her outburst hadn't happened, despite the twitch in Marie's smile. "A mental shield. An imaginary wall between you and the part of your brain that has the visions."

Marie tilted her head. "I'll try anything. The visions come at the most inconvenient times." Her calm acceptance touched Becca. She didn't think Becca was crazy, even after she'd made a fool of herself.

Becca had never expected acceptance. In her plans to leave her village, she figured she'd have to hide her true self. But somehow the impossible had happened. She'd not only seen a dragon, but she'd also found eggs and met people who believed in magic. Maybe Valley Keep was where she was meant to be all along, and she didn't have to do everything alone. Trey and Marie could be her friends.

Becca stroked her egg, her heart bursting with a new dream. Maybe she could have more. She would find Trey's dragon, Gregor, and when her tiny dragon hatched, they could stay together. She could be a dragon rider too.

STRUGGLE
GREGOR

DAY 37 AFTER THE LONG SLEEP

Gregor enjoyed the healing powers of Sanctuary for two nights, happy to stay away from the coven's turmoil. On the way back to Jason's Keep, Ronin and Brin continued to look for another place that would suit all their needs. They could live in Sanctuary for a while, but it couldn't sustain a full coven of three hundred dragons. They needed other options.

It would be easier if they could investigate the old keeps. Some were isolated enough to satisfy Sarcruze's demand for secrecy. But it was Gregor's fault they had to be so cautious. Any suggestions would have to come from someone else.

The coven would love Sanctuary, especially once they experienced its special healing.

As the sun sank low on the horizon, they were almost at the keep when Seri missed a beat and dropped below the cloud layer.

Gregor was about to tease her when her panic crashed through his mind.

"Something's wrong. Zanthor is blocked from me."

There couldn't be anything seriously amiss. Otherwise, a scent would've warned Gregor. Zanthor must be busy with the elders again. *"Fiona, we have great news. We found ..."*

"It won't make any difference. Zanthor hoped tensions would cool with you five away. But it didn't work. Stay away, Gregor. I don't know what Sarcruze will do," she interrupted, her conflict between her love for Sarcruze and her love for the coven evident.

Whatever was happening, Gregor needed to be there. Determination drove his wings. Icy mint filled his mind, slowing his heart, Fiona's attempt to calm him.

Seri flew past him. *"We need to get to the keep, now. Zanthor needs our support."*

Gregor landed at the far end of the keep. Tension vibrated in the air.

Seri looked at him, her eyes whirling in dismay. *"There's magic everywhere, but it's dark and roiling, like a disease, full of fear and anger. How did this happen?"*

He squeezed her talon. They would face this threat together.

Their group strode together to report to Zanthor. He took their news with little reaction. As they spoke, others clustered around.

"I'll have no secrets in my coven," Sarcruze shouted publicly. *"So, the chosen ones have returned."* The sneer in his tone churned Gregor's stomach.

Something had transpired while they'd been away. The coven felt poised on a cliff.

Seri put her talon on Gregor's shoulder. *"Be very careful, Gregor. He's shrouded in red magic. I think Fiona's right. The Source affected all of us, not just those with powers. Every emotion is amplified right now."*

Zanthor's mental eye roll could've toppled a bear. *"We weren't keeping secrets. My party was reporting back as per protocol. You depend on rules and tradition. I'm following coven procedure."*

"Enough defiance!" Sarcruze enforced his will on the entire coven with a single thought.

Gregor bowed his head under the weight, along with everyone else. He'd already experienced this subjugation, but the others hadn't. Their shock reverberated through him.

Zanthor's pain washed over every dragon as he fought the compulsion. *"I'm not defying you. I admire and respect you as our leader. It's your right. But this is going too far. You can't force us all on your path."*

But Sarcruze didn't let up. Zanthor's protest only fed his rage. He forced Zanthor into a prostrate position of total subservience.

Dismay pulsed through the coven, before shifting to outrage. Sarcruze *had* gone too far. The tension on Gregor's neck eased, and one by one, dragons lifted their heads, still restrained but not obsequious.

Zanthor rose to his feet and straightened to full height. Even though he was only one-third the size of Sarcruze, he commanded attention. Size wasn't everything, nor age.

A shiver of fear shook Gregor. Zanthor wasn't just risking banishment. He could be killed for defying Sarcruze.

"You're frightened of our future. We all are. But falling back on ancient traditions that haven't been practiced since the time of Torin is not the answer. You can't dominate us and determine our fate. We have evolved. We have survived." Zanthor's words shifted the coven's energy.

All the dragons who supported him moved to his side, suddenly free of Sarcruze's control.

Gregor stood slowly, but terror kept his heart from beating in victory. The coven was splitting. The only way to break free of the leader's compulsion was bonding with another leader. Another coven.

A scent tingled in his nostrils. Rotting corpses.

The coven couldn't split.

His concern raced to Zanthor who replied privately, *"I don't want that either."*

"You would challenge me for leadership?" Surprise filled Sarcruze's voice.

"I've led this coven before. To the cure. To the Source. You supported me then. Can't you trust and support me now? It's too hard for you to adapt. We need new solutions. And that means using the resources we have."

More dragons stood. Not just the powered ones, but others too. They agreed with Zanthor.

But Sarcruze was too angry, too afraid. *"I'll fight you, youngling."*

"I don't want to fight you. We need every dragon here to survive. Please, Sarcruze. Relent and pass on the power." Zanthor's influence spread through the coven and all but ten dragons now stood.

Gregor hoped Sarcruze wouldn't fight for leadership. It was his right, but he'd already lost most of the coven.

Sarcruze shook his head. *"I can't."* The pain in his words cut through Gregor, reminding him of how long Sarcruze had led, how much he'd sacrificed. It was more than a position. It was his identity. *"I must ensure our survival. My duty is to the coven. You're young and lack the experience we need to survive."* Truth and certainty rang through every mind.

He was right, but their world had changed, and the old ways were too rigid.

Zanthor gave them a moment to respond emotionally to Sarcruze's claim, then he straightened, his tail lashing, indicating his decision. *"A fight for leadership, then."*

It wasn't what he wanted, but what Sarcruze needed. And it was a sign of Zanthor's respect that he'd offer his life in a battle to follow tradition. The outcome was uncertain. Sarcruze was handicapped. Only ten dragons moved to his side to support him.

Fiona wasn't in the group.

The rest clustered behind Zanthor, lending him their strength. They'd already chosen their leader.

Gregor hoped Zanthor's desire to honor Sarcruze wouldn't kill his friend.

POWER
SERI

Magic twisted and transformed as it spun around the dragons. Seri had to stop this madness. Zanthor and Sarcruze didn't know that magic was affecting them. She ran to Zanthor and grabbed his arm. Mind-speech wouldn't be enough.

"You can't fight him. He's three times your size."

He leaned his head against hers, his voice filled with sadness. *"I must. I respect Sarcruze too much. His code is traditional, and he won't adapt to this world. More than half the coven is no longer bound to him. You felt the shift. We can't hope to survive as two covens. Not yet."*

"No. You don't have to fight. Magic is influencing everyone. I can see it. Talk to him. Get away from the magic and talk somewhere safe." He had to understand. He couldn't die.

Zanthor put his talons on her shoulders. *"It doesn't matter. It's what he needs. Whatever happens, the coven will have a new direction. You can do that. He believes in you. I know you don't want to be the Oracle, but you are. If I don't win, you'll guide the coven. You can see how magic is changing us. They need you. More than they need me. That is why I must fight."*

Seri's wings drooped. She'd failed. He wouldn't listen. What kind of savior was she? She couldn't even save her friend from a suicidal battle.

Zanthor rose to his full height and addressed the dragons who now supported him. *"Do you want me to concede? Will you follow Sarcruze?"*

It was unanimous, which they already knew. Otherwise, they'd still be bowing to Sarcruze. No one wanted to go back to the way things were.

Fiona's eyes whirled her distress, but she supported Zanthor.

Seri's heart broke for her, and she transmitted acceptance and hope. That she could do.

"Then I'll fight for you. For our future." The finality of Zanthor's words made Seri want to scream.

In all the history she'd accessed, only a handful of battles had been fought between younger and older dragons.

The elder dragon always won.

There were rules to a leadership battle. They would fight until one conceded. But their world was different now. There wasn't another coven to monitor the fight and intercede if it became too aggressive. No one to prevent a death.

With the battle declared, the coven split. Seri couldn't hear the dragons who supported Sarcruze. And he wouldn't hear those who supported Zanthor. Fiona clutched Seri's talons, her sorrow and fear for both dragons inconsolable.

The first part of the battle took place in the air.

Zanthor had the advantages of youth, agility, speed, and endurance. But Sarcruze was over seventy-five years older and significantly larger. He'd also fought before and maintained his position against other challenges during the forty years he'd been a leader.

Seri hoped their mutual respect would factor into the battle. Although Sarcruze's harsh treatment of Gregor frightened many dragons, they still respected Sarcruze for all he'd done for them. This was a coven of choice and shared beliefs. So different from the covens they'd lost to the plague.

Sarcruze shot to the sky first, Zanthor tight on his tail. One flap of Sarcruze's wings pushed him farther from Zanthor than Seri thought possible. Rarely did they see the breadth of Sarcruze's power. Zanthor's wings beat furiously as he tried to keep up.

They rose into the higher stratosphere where the air currents wouldn't affect their maneuvers. This was smart. Although Zanthor would expend more energy to fight, Sarcruze would require more oxygen than the smaller dragon, so he couldn't stay there long.

Zanthor darted over Sarcruze, raking his talons across his back. Sarcruze arched, trying to snap at the younger dragon as he flew past. With a sharp turn, Zanthor darted under Sarcruze to attack his belly.

He wasn't fast enough.

Sarcruze caught Zanthor with his powerful foot talons and squeezed.

Zanthor's pain transmitted to Seri's torso, and she gasped along with the other dragons connected to him.

"Release." Zanthor sent a mental command. It didn't matter that he was no longer linked to Sarcruze through the coven bond. His power of conviction could affect anyone.

Sarcruze loosened his hold.

Zanthor dashed away, gulping in huge breaths. Seri inhaled her own relief.

Sarcruze turned, his anger evident as his wing beats slashed through the sky. She'd never seen the huge dragon move so fast.

Zanthor might be small and agile, but Sarcruze could cover so much more distance with his powerful wings. Zanthor darted and twisted, barely keeping ahead.

Then he abruptly changed directions and shot higher.

Sarcruze took a moment to adjust, a moment that cost him energy. He flew up, but the air was thinner, and it affected him. His movements slowed, and he was forced to drop to the cloud layer to recover.

Round one to Zanthor. He'd forced Sarcruze from his more advantaged choice by pushing him beyond it.

Zanthor's voice rang out. *"Sarcruze. I honor you. Do you yield, brother?"*

Sarcruze roared, *"No. Tradition will save us. Not your tricks. Fight like a real dragon."*

The powered dragons gasped. Zanthor was right to use all his abilities. Although he'd won this round, he couldn't possibly win them all. Once Sarcruze caught him, he'd be done. It wasn't like the little birds who banded together to fight off the huge eagle.

Seri's breath skipped. Why not? This wasn't just a battle for leadership. It was a battle for her kind, for those with abilities. They weren't tricks. They were the evolution of dragonkind. That's why Zanthor fought for them.

She opened her mind to Gregor, Ronin, Brin, and Drekan. *"We need to give Zanthor our powers. Our strength. If he's to win the battle for our kind, he must use our abilities. This is new to us. But we already know we're stronger together. I don't think it was being in Sanctuary that made us so. It's our power."* She felt their strength as they melded.

"Zanthor. Open your mind to us. Use our power. Your fight is so much more. You're determining the future of dragons. You must not surrender."

Her interruption distracted him, and Sarcruze raked his talons across Zanthor's tail.

Zanthor tumbled from the sky.

"Now, Zanthor." Seri's panic lent more power to her command.

She could feel his resistance, and he could've used his power to dissuade her, but he searched her mind as he fell.

This was the way. Deep within her, a flame ignited.

Magic was their future. This battle would determine their fate.

They must embrace their evolution.

"Yes, Oracle."

Seri cringed at the title, but now wasn't the time to let her doubts influence the combined strength of their powers.

Zanthor rolled out of his fall and opened his third mind. Magic swirled between them. Each of their powers merged, twisting into a thick rope that pulsed with blazing white energy. Seri swore he grew, at least mentally, as big as Sarcruze.

Using his power, Zanthor enticed Sarcruze lower.

Grass, new and sharp, filled her snout. Gregor's power, adding a scent of growth. It felt right.

Ronin's power showed a path to the ground through the clouds and mountains.

Drekan's power was the most unusual. They linked to Zanthor, felt him breathe, saw Sarcruze through his eyes, but even more. They felt Zanthor's respect protecting his opponent.

His feelings for Sarcruze hindered his drive to win.

They hadn't really explored the full potential of Brin's power, but a hum filled Seri's head, revealing the weakness in Sarcruze's joints and heart. He was older and stronger, but his body was wearing out. His left knee was the weakest. If Zanthor could get the older dragon to the ground, he could pin him.

Zanthor shook his head, denial pushing back.

Seri's heart vibrated with their energy. Zanthor had to win, but she wasn't sure he believed it was important enough to overpower his sense of honor.

More dragons lent their powers to their bond, and the coven became something new, something more than their individual selves.

Sarcruze loomed over Zanthor, intent on driving him to the ground where his size would overpower Zanthor.

Hope flickered through their bond, distant and new. A hatchling adding her strength!

The magic shifted, transforming, as joy spread through the dragons. At least one egg had survived.

Seri shared their joy, but she knew it meant more. Her thought became Zanthor's.

The hatchling had magical power.

Zanthor's resolve grew, strengthening the ties between the powered dragons and pulling the strength from those without powers. Their future was magic.

Their young might be magical. Not all, but certainly this one.

He needed to win this fight for them, for their future. It wasn't about respect. It was about ensuring their kind had an equal chance to survive and find acceptance for who they were.

Zanthor dove to the ground.

Sarcruze hesitated, shocked at this change in strategy, his own respect for Zanthor hindering him from taking the easy win.

Zanthor landed on the edge of the caldera surrounding the keep, apparently unconcerned.

Sarcruze flew in slowly, assessing. His eyes whirled. Instead of attacking, he sat and faced Zanthor. *"Is this it, then? Do you concede?"* With his question, Seri knew he'd calmed down. Sarcruze didn't want to kill Zanthor.

Zanthor blinked, his eyes steady, the gaze of forty powered dragons shining from them, and one tiny heartbeat.

Sarcruze gasped, and his eyes rolled violently.

Zanthor didn't touch him. The powers rolled through him—fire, strength, illusion, and his own conviction. *"No. I can't. But you must, dear friend."*

And he reached into Sarcruze's mind. Zanthor didn't need a coven bond. Not anymore, maybe he never had, since his own power was strong.

"Our survival is more important than tradition." Those who supported Sarcruze gasped as Zanthor's power invaded them too.

Waves of magic rippled through every mind. Zanthor's power, boosted by all theirs. He was bigger. He was stronger. He would ensure they survived.

Sarcruze's head lowered. Still, he resisted.

Zanthor didn't want to do it, but Sarcruze needed to feel the magic. He needed to understand.

Seri sent a wave of support. He could do this.

He mentally applied pressure to Sarcruze's weak leg and his heart. Pain emanated from Sarcruze, but he fought to hide any weakness. Still, he couldn't prevent his collapse when his leg failed to support him. His age betrayed him. His heart slowed, no longer capable of pumping blood through his body. His head fell to the ground as he fought his body for life.

Seri's heart ached in sympathy. She knew Zanthor wouldn't kill him, but it was still terrible to witness. The entire coven held their breath.

"What are you doing?" Sarcruze's voice was strong, despite his obvious agony. Only the quiver at the end gave away his fear.

"Our powers make us stronger. Not weak. They're not tricks. They're our future. They're how dragons will survive this hostile world. We have evolved. We are dragons." Zanthor slowly pulled away from Sarcruze's heart so he wouldn't shock the elder dragon's body.

Everyone roared at his last words.

They were dragons. Powered or traditional didn't matter.

Sarcruze dropped to the ground. *"I concede. For the good of the coven. We'll survive. I put my faith in you, Zanthor."*

At his words, the entire coven joined Seri's mind. There was confusion and fear, but mostly respect.

Fiona rushed to help Sarcruze, but he glared at her. He stood on his own, his powerful heart doing the job it was supposed to. He limped to Zanthor and leaned his head against his.

Their conversation was private, and the coven silently waited.

Their combined magic still swirled around Zanthor. Seri turned to the coven members who'd supported Sarcruze. She'd expected the dark pockets of magic to be near them, but that wasn't the case.

Magic had chosen a side too. There was no magic around the other dragons. Everyone was connected. She could see threads of white pulsing from every dragon's head and flowing to Zanthor. But the magic colors rippled and rebounded among the powered dragons, occasionally touching on the dragons who'd always supported them. She wondered what it meant.

Sarcruze stepped away from Zanthor and stood tall. He didn't need to say anything. He'd shown his acceptance in the traditional way. He would support Zanthor.

Zanthor raised his head and roared, mentally and vocally. All the coven joined in, a celebration of victory.

As the coven surrounded him to offer their congratulations, Zanthor sent Seri a private thought.

"Take Gregor. Find that hatchling. It must be close. And thank you."

ARRIVAL
BECCA

Traveling with the caravan was more work than Becca had expected. John coordinated people, animals, and wagons with an ease she admired. Every day, the caravan set out after breakfast, stopping briefly in the afternoon to eat and rest the horses, then continuing until daylight faded.

Becca spent her mornings teaching the little ones math and reading with Marie, and her afternoons with Maggie, sewing patches and altering clothes. She quickly adapted to the rocking of the wagons. Trey spent his days on a horse, keeping the stragglers from straying too far behind.

After some experimentation, Becca discovered that the best shield was a waterfall. She could still sense emotions, but they didn't affect her. Intense ones could break through and then she'd throw up a stone wall. The children afforded lots of practice. Their feelings jumped from absolute joy over a new color to despair over not getting a piece of cake.

Noise filled the days, but evening was her favorite time. Trey met her every night at the river. They watched the stars while the eggs tumbled contentedly. They would kiss, but it was light. New. He never pushed her to do more than she wanted. She was getting better at bracing herself for the emotional onslaught from his touch. He would talk about Gregor, and she would tell him one of Grandfa's stories. She'd never felt so accepted.

As the caravan neared Valley Keep, Becca tossed and turned each night, a nebulous tension filled her, and she'd awaken with a sense of impending doom.

After five days of travel, they descended the mountain.

"Ho." John's voice carried over the creaking of wagons. They stopped, and the horses blew out noisy breaths in the early-morning mist.

People streamed from their wagons to a vantage point overlooking the valley. Becca wasn't sure what she'd expected. A village like her own, but larger. This wasn't like anything she could've imagined.

A river wound between two towering mountain ranges, and the valley stretched for miles. Large squares of green, yellow, and brown covered the valley from the forest to the river on both sides. Roads separated the blocks of color, with tiny bridges crossing the river to connect them. Barns that made the Randals' look like a backyard shed, perched against the trees, surrounded by storage silos and animal pens. Hundreds of animals grazed in the fields.

Far beyond the farmland, the village stood out, houses packed tightly around more than one central square. And towering over it all was a huge square stronghold. Trey called it a keep. Now she knew why. Three villages could fit inside. Carts and horses moved along the road through an open gate.

Marie clutched Becca's hand, and her fear erased Becca's awe.

"What's wrong?" Becca was careful to keep her voice low as she tightened her shield.

"Danger. You're not safe here." Marie's low voice quivered.

Becca squeezed Marie's hand. "I'll be careful." Trey wasn't around to ask what might have prompted Marie's outburst.

It took hours to traverse the abundant fields of crops, many of which Becca didn't recognize. As they rolled past the houses, people came out and waved. Some smiled. Most quickly went back to their tasks.

The entrance to the keep loomed over the roofs, as tall as four men standing on top of each other. It must've taken years to build. There were no guards. The caravan simply rolled through the gate to a huge central courtyard. A tall platform projected from one wall. A man conferred with John and then people streamed out of obscured doorways to help the caravan unload.

It was too much for Becca. Even her stone shield couldn't keep out so many emotions. She slipped into the school wagon. As soon as she closed the door, the pounding in her head stopped. She rubbed her temples.

Once everyone was settled, she'd find Trey and figure out where she'd stay. Then the real work would begin. She'd need a job, and clothing, and supplies.

Becca reached into her gathering satchel to rub the eggs.

"We've arrived. It's unlike anything I've ever seen. I'll keep you safe."

She spoke to the tiny dragons with her mind, just like Trey had taught her. But this time, there was no flutter of emotion. Actually, her dragon had been silent the night before too. Worry tumbled in her stomach.

She stroked her egg, wishing Trey would show up and show her where to bathe the eggs. There were too many people in the keep, and the river was far away.

The door opened and Marie climbed in, throwing herself on the floor with a heartfelt groan. "Ugh. I keep getting flickers of visions. It's killing my head. You having troubles too?"

Becca shrugged. Her sensible friend seemed overly dramatic.

"John's moving the wagons to Meadow Lake. There's a campsite there where we can fish and swim. It sounds lovely. I'm going with him. My family's staying here, but I can't. Want to join me?"

It was the best news. Becca could tend to her eggs away from the keep. "Yes."

"Trey's disappeared. John's worried about him. But I told him this was Trey's home. Don't think John realized I meant it literally. Why didn't you tell me Trey came from Valley Keep?"

Becca grimaced. She hadn't liked keeping secrets from Marie, not that anyone could for long. Her visions gave her glimpses all the time. Only full visions disconnected her from reality, trapping her in a trance.

"He didn't want anyone to know. I only met him a few days before we joined the caravan."

Marie laughed. "There's a story there, and don't think I haven't noticed you've kept that from me too."

Marie wouldn't push, even though she was curious. Relief rushed through Becca. She'd never met anyone quite like her, so accepting.

Marie's face stilled, and her eyes focused over Becca's head. Then tears fell from Marie's eyes, but she made no sound. It was eerie and beautiful.

She was having a vision. An intense one. Her emotions beat at Becca's shields, but they held strong.

Marie gasped and opened her eyes. "You have a dragon egg."

Becca's heart raced through her limbs, and she stood, clutching the satchel against her chest. She must run. She must hide. Something other than her own instinct drove her.

"No. Don't leave." Marie gasped as she grabbed Becca's hand. "You're safe. You're all safe."

Pride cut through the Becca's shields, oddly for Becca and not for the eggs.

Becca collapsed, no longer controlled by her power, and their hands fell apart.

"I won't hurt them. They're special. But you're something else. Oh, this is so exciting. Dragons!"

Marie paced around the small wagon. "Trey knows about the egg? Of course, he knows. Who else?"

Becca shook her head.

"Good. Keep it secret. And we've got to keep you safe from ..." Marie shuddered, her jaw clenching to stop the words.

"What exactly did you see?"

Marie's protective fierceness confused Becca. Even if she *saw* Becca discovering the eggs. But she kept saying *egg*, as if there were only one.

Marie groaned. "Emotions are the easiest for me. Like your ability. But I see images, too, some as detailed as paintings, and others like looking through a foggy window. I wish mine were clear like Mama's. She gets the whole picture." Marie's frustration furrowed her brow.

"Marie. The vision?"

"Oh. Don't worry. I could never forget this one." In her excitement, she grabbed Becca's hands.

Awe. Excitement. And a little fear for Becca.

Marie's emotions wound their way through Becca's soul, soothing pockets of pain and grief. That anyone could feel awe for her was too amazing to block.

"You found a glowing white egg in a cave. It called to you. I'm not sure how I know that. The vision only showed you holding an orb of light, and I knew it was an egg. Then a dragon flew in the sky." Marie's voice trembled. "It was intimidating, but you weren't afraid. You really love them."

Tears rolled down Marie's cheeks. "Your feelings are so pure. I thought the vision was finished, but then a dark shape swooped from Valley Keep. It covered everything. I figured I was blacking out. But ..."

The radiant expression on Marie's face stunned Becca. "A white glow fought off the darkness, and you stood in the center, a tiny white dragon on your shoulder. I thought at first the glow came from the dragon. But it came from you.

"As the darkness cleared, I saw one final image. Hundreds of dragons surrounded you, honoring you."

Marie's head dropped and her body slumped. "It's gone. Their intensity. But you're the key."

A denial rose through Becca's throat. She loved dragons, but she was nothing to them. Marie's vision left Becca feeling wrung out.

"I'm nothing special. I found the eggs. That might help the dragons. But I don't see how I can save dragons from darkness. Emotions attack me. If anything bad happened, I'd be useless." Becca twisted her hands free from Marie's.

Why did everyone want her to be someone else? Now Marie saw her as a dragon savior.

Marie closed her eyes and clasped her hands. "I'm sorry. I know it's difficult when we touch. I didn't mean to hurt you." Her distress assured Becca that she'd never meant to force her to do anything.

"No. You didn't. I just ... What you saw is impossible. But we'll figure it out." It was difficult for Marie to share her visions. So many of her own emotions were entwined with what she experienced. Becca wanted to hold her friend's hand and reassure her, but she wasn't certain she'd remain calm with Marie's emotions rolling through her mind, so she settled on words.

There was one part of the vision she could share with her friend. "Now you know my secret. Do you want to see my dragon egg?"

Marie's face glowed. "Really? Did it happen like my vision?"

"Almost. I found it in a cave, but no one else can see through its protective illusion. Maybe you can." Becca lifted her egg from the satchel.

Marie laughed. "That's a rock."

"When I hold it under water, it's a perfect crystal-white sphere." Becca wanted Marie to believe her.

Marie grinned. "Dragons use magic to disguise their eggs? That's incredible."

None of Grandfa's stories mentioned dragons having magic. Becca was beginning to believe there was a lot about the past she didn't know. Or it had been hidden for some reason.

The travelers gathered in a huge dining hall. Becca walked around the tables, searching for Trey, when someone grabbed her arm.

"Did you hear, Becca? We get to speak with the Prophet tomorrow. I'm one of the first ones." Justin's mother was young and hadn't lost her youthful excitement.

Becca sat, removing her arm from reach. "That's wonderful news, Emily. I hope she can help you."

Justin wasn't just a curious toddler with the urge to explore. He escaped from everywhere. Emily believed he could teleport. Becca hadn't seen him actually do such a thing, but he had a knack for sneaking away.

Jane leaned over and whispered in Becca's ear. "Nothing a good ol' fashioned harness wouldn't solve."

Becca giggled as the memory of Brandon and Trish in their harnesses obediently following Kevin flashed through her mind. Emily would've thought the twins had powers too. They did—transforming vegetables—but not teleportation. She missed them and their secret twin language.

She'd left her entire life behind to help Trey, and now she couldn't even find him.

Throughout the meal, Becca listened to the excited chatter around her as she watched the villagers. They spoke enthusiastically about Valley Keep and its abundant resources. The village was self-sufficient and needed nothing from traders.

When asked about the Prophet, the conversation twisted. By the end of the meal, every visitor had been questioned about their past and their hopes. Becca revealed as little as possible. She'd run away from her small village to avoid an arranged marriage to a man she disliked. Yes. She'd noticed strange things and thought they might be magic. No. She didn't have any powers.

After dinner, she left, frustrated that Trey hadn't shown up. She wondered if he was hiding from her, or if he had a girl waiting for him that he'd forgotten to mention.

REVELATIONS

GREGOR

Day 42 After the Long Sleep

Despite searching the forests and rivers around Jason's Keep, the dragons couldn't find the hatchling they'd all felt during the leadership battle.

Gregor had tried to capture a scent, something other than the ordinary. But he'd only given himself a massive headache and possibly an infection from sniffing too much. Even his thoughts were stuffy.

Seri hadn't done any better. Using her magic she'd followed the connecting strand from Garianna, but she'd only found two older dragons who were related. Nothing led her outside of the keep. Even Ronin had used his powers, flying a grid pattern around the keep, scanning caves and hollows for any sign of a tiny hatchling.

Their abilities were no help at all.

They searched the rivers they'd already checked for eggs. Even if the hatchling was hiding, they should find it.

Seri dipped her talons in the spray from the waterfall next to Gregor.

"Magic is confused. Or it's changing. I noticed, even before the fight. Pockets of darkness, with colored threads moving through them. The water here is the same. Swirls of colors mixing and changing. But here, there's darkness. Not a void, exactly. More like the colors

combined and blackened. I can't pull the strands apart. They're all clumped together, but there's a difference in the texture. I wonder if magic has a soul, and it's ill."

Gregor shuddered. That was the last thing they needed. If magic could get sick, then the plague might return. Seri was the only dragon who could see magic. Hopefully, she'd know in time to save them.

It was a heavy burden, especially in the aftermath of the battle. Dragons had merged their powers to help Zanthor win, but many had only done so because Seri, the Oracle, had asked them. Gregor knew that responsibility weighed on her, and she questioned if she'd made the right choice. Only her belief in Zanthor prevented her from voicing her doubts. So she received their devotion with a grace he admired, all while sending him thoughts of panic.

He sighed. They wouldn't find the hatchling. Seri would have to find them. He still remembered the fear that had consumed him as he'd searched for his coven. Only the certainty there was food and safety at the end of his journey had kept him moving.

Gregor rubbed his chest. He'd never be able to remember his first coven without feeling guilty. If he'd understood his power then, he could've saved them. He pushed his grief away, into the deep recesses of his memories.

The hatchling could survive.

He had.

Hope for their future balanced on a thin thread. The coven needed to look forward instead of dwelling on the past. They would lay their eggs in Sanctuary, and many hatchlings would thrive without the need to battle nature and predators to reach their coven. Their numbers would grow, and dragonkind would survive because of it.

Ronin circled overhead, transmitting excitement, and then landed.

"Did you find the hatchling?" Seri spread her wings, anticipating a fast flight.

"No." Ronin grabbed Gregor's shoulder, transmitting joy. *"I was searching the caves near Valley Keep and I saw the boy. He's alive."*

Gregor's chest tightened. He hadn't killed Trey. But how? There'd been so much blood. He stifled the questions tumbling through his mind. Ronin couldn't answer them. *"Are you certain? Humans are difficult to distinguish."*

"It's him. The coven is safe, and we can stop worrying about reprisals from Valley Keep, now. You deserved to know first." His anger at Gregor's banishment tinged his thoughts.

Trey was alive. It took every ounce of his self-control not to jump to the sky and race to Valley Keep.

But would the boy want to see him?

Gregor had taken him on a terrifying flight and then dropped him. Maybe Trey was better off without him.

"Be happy, Gregor. You didn't start a war with humans, and Sarcruze was wrong to punish you." Ronin flew into the sky, heading to Jason's Keep.

They needed good news. Any news, really. The entire coven was restless, anticipating the next disaster. But Gregor needed more information. Where had Ronin seen Trey? At the lake, or at the keep?

He bent his legs, preparing to depart, when Seri's voice intruded. *"This is wonderful. But you can't fly to Valley Keep now."*

Gregor dropped his wings, tips resting on the ground, his tail curling slightly. That Seri thought he'd be so impulsive, after all they'd been through, disappointed him. His intent had only been to follow Ronin for more answers. Or at least that's what it would've been after a few flaps of his wings.

"I know. I really do. The boy is special to you. But we don't need anything more to go wrong. Speak with Zanthor. See what he says."

Correcting her assumption didn't matter. The best way to support Zanthor was to show the coven he could follow the rules. He'd made a lot of mistakes with Sarcruze. But Zanthor wouldn't forbid him from following his power. Zanthor's belief in Gregor was unwavering.

Gregor settled his wings on his back. They would finish searching the river above the falls and then fly back to the keep. Zanthor would have a plan by then. The most important thing was that Trey was alive.

Joy and worry twisted through Gregor's chest. He would see Trey again. Hopefully, Trey didn't hate him.

Gregor found Zanthor alone at the archive stone. He grunted when Seri and Gregor joined him. *"Ronin told me the news. I assume you want to see the boy."*

Gregor attempted to contain his excitement and transmit suitable respect. Too many dragons felt Gregor needed controlling, even if they didn't agree with banishment. Frustrating when everything he did was for the coven.

Zanthor sighed and bowed his head, his talons still resting against the stone. *"We need more information. Maybe the boy can help. But you must be cautious. Wait for him at the lake. Don't seek him out. And for the love of Torin, don't let anyone see you."*

Gregor would be careful.

Zanthor stepped away from the stone. *"Seri, how many covens had archive stones older than five hundred years?"*

Seri clutched her talons, hope leaking through her shields. *"Three. The most isolated ones. And the stones of the Treasury."*

Zanthor's eye ridge almost covered his eye as he worked through his private thoughts. *"There must've been other times in dragon history when changes in the environment threatened our existence. Maybe as far back as the ice age. We need to know how they survived and how they rebuilt afterward.*

"Sarcruze was right to isolate us from humans. Unfortunately, with two villages already aware of our existence, eventually the world will know we've returned. We must prepare. The ancient stones may have knowledge we can use. You're the most qualified to obtain that information, but I can't risk anything happening to you.

"On the other talon, we also need to know what happened after we flew to the Source. It's possible dragons found the cure, but too late. Or some survived, and they've hidden from the world with no magic to sustain them. Our initial search revealed no survivors, but we limited it to nearby keeps.

"Trey revealed the human version of things, but we need the dragon truth."

Seri glowed with restrained elation. She'd wanted to access the archive stones ever since she woke in the Source.

Gregor grabbed her talon in support and yelped as pain shot through him. She'd never shocked him before.

"Seri?" His attempt at private conversation met a wall of resistance. Her magic was controlling her the same way his did. He grabbed her talon and held on, despite the startling spikes and zings.

Zanthor shook his head, his tone gentle. *"I can't send you to the Treasury. Not yet. It's not safe, and it's too far. But I think it's time we venture farther, and your knowledge of history will help. We need older stones to guide us."*

Seri frowned, dipping her head, and the shocks disappeared. Then she straightened and clapped her talons, her disappointment over. She had a way of looking at the positive.

Gregor groaned. *"You're sending her on another quest. You know what that means?"*

But he was only teasing. This meant a lot to her, and possibly to her magic too. He wouldn't get in the way, but he'd watch her carefully, now that he knew her magic could take over her mind too.

At least this quest would ease her obsession with the Treasury.

Which reminded him. Gregor sniffed loudly. Nothing. He didn't know if that meant it wasn't important enough to activate his power or something else.

Zanthor turned back to the stone. *"First, help Gregor exercise some restraint with the boy. I can trust you to do this for me, Seri."*

She nodded while sending Gregor a threatening mental glare.

"We'll continue to search for the eggs, but I don't expect we'll find them. That hatchling's joy is the only clue we have that the eggs survived. At least you two found Sanctuary so future hatchlings can be safe. See Renalia. She needs help to coordinate the next attempt at breeding."

Renalia wouldn't need Gregor's help. Seri and the others knew everything there was to know about Sanctuary. He'd check in with her, though, because Zanthor asked him to. But as soon as he could, he'd fly to the lake and discover if Trey was still his friend.

Dragon Prophet

BECCA

The next morning, John knocked on Maggie's wagon door. "Both of you have appointments with the Prophet this morning. Better get a move on. Shelly's waiting with the horses."

Marie pulled her blanket over her head. They'd both had a rough night, her moans keeping Becca from dropping into a deep sleep and Trey's egg transmitting vague feelings of unease. Nightmares of Trey falling from his dragon and shattering into a million pieces hadn't helped.

She must find him today.

"Do we have to?"

John shrugged. "It's required. I'd go early, if I were you. Get it over with."

Discussions at the evening fire had centered on not only the Prophet's meetings but the intense way the villagers elicited information. Most of the traders had felt uncomfortable.

"Come on, Marie. We just have to survive our interviews, then we're free to do what we want." But Becca couldn't shake the sense of dread.

Shelly was quieter than usual as they traveled through the streets to the keep's stable. "I'll stay with the horses."

Becca wondered if she's already had her meeting.

A villager appeared from a hidden alcove and led Becca and Marie through a series of tunnels to a small, empty waiting room. Huge double doors dominated one wall while the early-morning light squeezed through four narrow windows high above her. At least Becca could watch the sky while they waited.

A cloud shifted and sunlight illuminated the carving on the doors. Large dragons flew over a village filled with people in various stages of death, some decomposing, some gasping for breath, all carved into the blackest of wood. Nightwood, the legendary tree of death and disease.

Becca swallowed the lump in her throat. It couldn't really be Nightwood. The Prophet wouldn't have a door that could kill any who touched it.

"Rebecca Kinsley." The attendant's voice was high for a portly man, but his look demanded obedience.

"Good luck." Marie clutched Becca's hand, her fear slipping through which didn't help.

Becca's heart thumped in her ears as the carved doors closed silently behind her.

An elderly woman reclined in a massive dragon chair. A dragon head loomed over her as she sat against a curved back depicting the belly. Dragon arms wrapped around the chair and strong legs encased the seat. The entire thing was as black as the door.

It should've dwarfed the Prophet. But an amber crystal centered on the dragon's chest glowed, enhancing her aura. Even her gray hair shimmered.

This was Trey's grandmother? Becca blinked, but the vision didn't go away.

"Rebecca. So nice to meet you. Trey tells me you healed his shoulder after his accident." Her smile invited Becca to share her secrets, or Trey's secrets.

Becca hoped Trey hadn't told his grandmother what really happened. But she hadn't been able to find him to know for sure.

"Yes ..." Her words trailed off.

"Fascinating. Exactly how did you and my grandson meet?" Elizabeth didn't sound fascinated.

The energy around Becca rippled. Her gaze was drawn to Elizabeth's, and she relaxed. She needed to tell the Prophet everything.

"He fell and injured his arm."

She resisted, trying to unwind her own desires from this new impulse. She had to protect the dragons, but this wasn't the same as sensing emotions. These were her own feelings.

Elizabeth was using magic to influence her.

Becca's hands trembled. She clenched them until her fingers bit into her palm.

"I'm the daughter of a Healer." She had to stick to facts that didn't involve Gregor and Trey. Cautiously, she lowered her shields. If she could discover what the Prophet wanted, maybe she could avoid the truth.

"Tell me about his accident." Again Becca felt a shift in energy. Elizabeth exuded only concern for Trey.

"I'm not sure. You'd have to ask him." She hadn't actually seen him fall through the trees.

Rage. Flickering so fast, Becca wasn't sure she sensed it. Nothing but calmness and warmth radiated from Elizabeth.

Energy shifted again, stronger this time. "He's a handsome lad. You must've spent some time together."

Becca's breath stuck in her throat. Elizabeth was doing something with her voice. Her questions didn't match the answer she wanted. "I ..."

Frustration.

This time Elizabeth didn't try to hide it. But if Becca continued to resist, Elizabeth would exert more force. Becca had to reply with something she would believe.

"Yes. So handsome, and a gentleman. Do you know where he is? I can't find him. We belong together." Becca hoped the last wasn't over the top. She tried to emulate the way Isobel gushed about Marcus.

Satisfaction.

"I'll send you to him. Once you tell me how he traveled so far from home."

Becca scanned the walls, searching for a plausible lie to satisfy Elizabeth. A tapestry with a dragon rider bending before a king, his dragon high in the sky, caught her attention. She turned back to Elizabeth's inviting gaze.

"I don't know. He was on a heroic quest for the king. Isn't he amazing?" Becca cringed at the simpering tone of her own voice, but Elizabeth needed to believe Becca was under her spell.

Elizabeth's eyes narrowed.

Becca clenched her hands and released them. It was too much. She'd made a mistake. If only Trey had warned her.

The next ripple of energy was stronger than any of the others.

"Tell me about the dragon." Elizabeth's voice had changed, slithering inside Becca's skull, whispering of common goals, helping the community, saving the world.

If her shields had been up, Becca would've missed the need for control. She would've fallen under Elizabeth's spell. She fought the desire to please Elizabeth. To tell her everything. She snagged every memory that tried to make its way to her lips. It was getting harder to resist, and the silence had stretched on too long.

"The Dragon Plague killed millions of people before the dragons were destroyed. Civilizations disappeared, and knowledge was lost. The world started over and is better now. But we still watch for the hallucinations that accompany fever brain." She quoted the history lesson to stop the truth from spilling out. The words centered her, protecting her, a shield against Elizabeth's compulsion.

Annoyance.

"Forget that." Elizabeth waved her hand as if the conversation was of no importance, but Becca knew it was the whole reason for the interview.

"Now, about your problem. You will live here, and you won't have to marry the man you dislike from your village."

Relief flooded through Becca. As if the Prophet had given her the answer to her most difficult, unsolvable problem. Gratitude weakened Becca's knees.

It wasn't real.

She threw up her strongest mental shield.

Elizabeth didn't just use her voice. She projected emotions that changed how Becca felt.

Becca pushed away the false feelings, focusing on her shields. They were strong. Nothing could penetrate. Doubt would weaken them. Now was the time to believe in herself. She didn't need to please anyone. Not Mama and certainly not this false prophet. They would never love her. The unwanted gratitude faded, and she exhaled, able to think clearly.

"Oh, thank you, great Prophet. Trey is all I want now." She poured every emotion into convincing the Prophet she was infatuated.

She had to find Trey. His disappearance didn't seem so benign anymore. She'd thought his desire to return home was due to his love for his grandmother. Now she wondered if he was locked in a dungeon. Or worse, if Elizabeth had used her power to influence him, and he'd forgotten all about Becca. No, that couldn't be right. She seemed pleased with Becca's interest.

Elizabeth gestured to the small door behind her where another acolyte waited.

"It was a delight to meet you, Rebecca Kinsley. You'll be happy here."

Marie's nightmares had been a warning. The keep was dangerous, and now Becca had no way to warn her friend about Elizabeth's power.

After traversing a maze of hallways, the acolyte left Becca at the stable.

"The Prophet blesses you." His words brought an instinctive protest to her lips, but she only nodded.

Something sinister was going on in Valley Keep, something more than the Prophet's incredible power. Elizabeth could manipulate what people thought and felt. But she wouldn't be able to maintain that magic over thousands of villagers.

Trey had a lot of explaining to do.

Shelly wasn't around, so Becca rubbed down her horse and leaned into his warm body for comfort.

Trey sauntered through the stables, completely unharmed. The timing was suspicious. Her fears for him changed in an instant.

"Where have you been?" It came out more accusing than she'd intended.

At least he had the decency to look ashamed. He ran his hand through his hair endearingly and he looked more handsome than ever.

Becca clenched her lips, worried her reaction was a lingering effect from her time with the Prophet.

"I didn't want anyone around when I met with my grandmother. I knew she'd be upset. You understand?"

She did, unfortunately. Especially after meeting Elizabeth. Trey's grandmother was a lot like Becca's mother, determined to control their futures.

"But how did you get here?"

He swung his arms wide. "There are tunnels everywhere. I slipped into the mine by the overlook and took a shortcut. I didn't want you to miss the front entrance. It's a grand sight, isn't it? My great-great-grandfather built it."

He hadn't warned her about Elizabeth, and how did he know she hadn't spilled everything about Gregor? But it was more than that. He'd lied to her from the moment they met. There was a simple way to find the truth.

Becca squeezed his hand, accessing his emotions. "I missed you. And your grandmother is intimidating."

Wariness. And a tingle of happiness that she'd touched him.

She looked into his eyes and fell into a vortex of stars.

"Be safe," he whispered as he stroked her cheek.

Becca blinked, and the sensation faded. She wasn't even sure he'd spoken out loud.

His eyes no longer held stars but something else. He wanted to kiss her.

Becca's lips parted and her body flooded with heat. But he didn't bend down.

Energy rippled gently through her mind.

"Did you see the Prophet? Tell me about your interview." The question had levels of meaning, and Becca felt pressure in her mind. She suddenly wanted to tell him every detail.

Shock helped her resist. He was doing the same thing as Elizabeth. Becca dropped his hand and stepped away from their almost embrace. She clutched the horse's saddle for balance.

"You can do what she does!" She should've pretended, but anger at his attempt to manipulate her overrode her caution.

He was just like everyone else. Wanting to control her. Deciding what she should do and feel.

Pain constricted her throat, but her heart begged her to give him a chance. He wasn't the same as all the rest. He'd never made her do anything she hadn't wanted to. Had he?

"Have you been manipulating me all along?"

His reaction wasn't what she expected.

Relief. Joy.

He laughed. "Oh, thank the Healer. I hoped you could see through her. I was so worried."

He wrapped his arms around her. His breath moved the hair by her ear. "No. My sweet Becca. I haven't manipulated you. Not since ... Well, I did, just now, and you resisted. You're amazing."

His emotions matched his sincerity. But she couldn't help the doubt that settled into her soul.

An acolyte walked up, leading a dazed Marie. Becca's questions for Trey could wait, for now.

"The Prophet is very wise." Marie sounded radiant.

"Are you all right?" Becca grabbed Marie's hand, once again depending on her own power to reveal the truth.

Euphoria.

That wasn't what she'd expected. "What happened, Marie?"

"She's magic. Did you see that? I can embrace my visions now and stop fighting them. They are the future. It was so wonderful."

Marie wasn't making any sense. The sooner Becca got her away from this place, the better.

Trey groaned. "She's been influenced." His ripple of energy was gentle, different from Elizabeth's. "Marie, did you tell her about the eggs?"

Becca held her breath. She hadn't considered what Marie might say. Her visions could be a problem. Another worry wormed its way into her soul. How did Trey know that Marie knew about the eggs?

"The Prophet is thrilled. I'm to bring her every egg I find." Marie tugged on Becca's hand. "Give me your egg. She'll be so happy."

Trey grasped Marie's hands and stared intently into her eyes. "Marie, the Prophet desires rare blue goose eggs. Not dragon eggs."

Watching Trey manipulate Marie confused Becca. They needed to protect the eggs and the dragons. But it was wrong to mess with Marie's thoughts. Becca didn't stop him, but she wished he could simply undo whatever Elizabeth had done to Marie.

"Go back to camp. Rest. When you wake, you'll forget about pleasing the Prophet." Trey reinforced his words with another pulse of energy, then he let her go.

"Will that work?" Becca couldn't sense any change in Marie.

Trey shrugged. "I don't know. I've never tried to reverse her compulsions. I've modified them, but it doesn't always work."

There were so many things he hadn't told her.

Shelly strolled up, carrying full saddlebags. When Becca turned to help, Trey slipped away.

Marie sighed dramatically, lost in her own mind.

"What's wrong with her?" Shelly clucked her tongue.

Becca helped the stupidly vacant Marie onto her horse and mounted her own. "She's basking in the glory of the Prophet."

She meant it sarcastically, but Shelly's head bobbed up and down enthusiastically.

"Hopefully, she'll recover by the time we get back to the caravan." Shelly clicked to get the horses moving, and they headed out. Becca wondered if Shelly had been influenced too.

Coven Bonds
Gregor

Day 43 After the Long Sleep

Gregor didn't get to see Trey the next morning. The coven was adjusting to the change in leadership. Even those who had supported Sarcruze were happy. The leaders had fought with respect and honor, according to tradition, and Zanthor had won.

But Fiona had supported Zanthor and lost Sarcruze. Her mind was closed to the coven, and she wasn't hunting.

Renalia begged Gregor to try something. He was stunned. What did he know about heartbreak? But she insisted. So, while Seri and Renalia worked through the breeding schedule, he left to find Fiona.

"Fiona?" He infused his fondness into the call as he searched an empty cavern behind the pools. He could sense her, but it was as if the walls reflected her presence rather than her being there. He sniffed. Not to invoke his power, but because his sense of smell was still the best in the coven. Her distinctive minty scent led him to the darkest part of the cave.

She lay curled in a protective pose, her tail tucked under her snout. She lifted her head. *"Gregor. What are you doing here?"*

He lowered to his belly, giving up any dragon status. She'd been kind to him. Being his mother made no difference, but in case it did, he placed his chin on the floor and captured her gaze. Her eyes swirled slowly, a feeble protest that made his throat ache.

"What are you doing?" He echoed her own question back.

"It hurts too much." Her weak tone didn't match her emotions. Pain, guilt, and a loneliness he knew deep in his soul.

Her mating bond to Sarcruze had been special, rare among dragons. Gregor didn't know what that was like. But he knew what it was like to love his coven, to lose them through his own actions, and to search for that missing bond again. He'd thought he'd die, and the agony returned every time he remembered his family.

"I understand." He leaned his head against hers and closed his eyes so he could concentrate on exposing his feelings. They were more important than the words. He shifted through his fear that he'd never find that special coven bond after his coven died. But he had. The powered dragons accepted him.

"The coven is your bond. We want to help. We love you." It wasn't a dragon sentiment, but it felt right.

She'd lost love, a connection that had no replacement. But she could never lose the coven bond.

"You've been so strong. You've helped us survive the plague, find the Source, and then start over here. You're so much more than his mate."

She shook her head, another weak denial. Everything about her was weak. This wasn't the same dragon who had defied Sarcruze for punishing Gregor. He focused on his memory of that moment and how impressive she'd been. She'd believed in him. She'd stood up for all powered dragons.

He believed in her.

Fiona chuckled, a little of her fire returning. *"I was unstoppable that day."*

He grinned. *"Yes. And we need your ferocity."*

"But I was protecting you. Protecting our future. Powered dragons are how we'll survive. This is different."

She was right. It was different. She needed a new focus, and it occurred to Gregor she might not have felt the emotion from the hatchling. Maybe none of the traditional dragons had. Fiona believed in their future. She had a passion for protecting the young.

"We need your help." He sent her the moment when they'd all felt the flutter of hope.

Her eyes whirled, amber, green, and indigo.

"A hatchling? The eggs are hatching."

"Yes. And powered."

"Of course. All the hatchlings have had power since the mages tampered with magic." Her statement made Gregor realize she knew about magic before the Great Wars. Seri didn't need to risk accessing the archive stones of abandoned keeps. He'd discuss that with Seri later. For now, Fiona's excitement had given him an idea.

"Someone will need to guide the hatchlings, once we find them, and protect them." He sent an image of Sanctuary with growing eggs and new hatchlings stumbling on the grass.

It worked.

Fiona sucked in a breath and though guilt still wound through her thoughts, she rose, no longer filled with despair.

"We need to build training grounds at Sanctuary. This world is unforgiving. These hatchlings will need to control their powers." She tapped him lightly on the nose, mindful of his sensitivity. *"You too. And we must search for them, even if it risks exposure. We can't have any more powered dragons causing havoc."*

Plans rolled through her mind as they left the cavern. She was better. Not whole. That would take more time. But now she had a quest.

Gregor grinned. Fiona was more like Seri than he'd expected. And maybe Fiona would teach the hatchlings how to control their magic before it controlled them.

EXPECTATIONS

SERI

Seri was proud of Gregor. His plan for Fiona was brilliant. He'd handled her pain with consideration and support. She, on the other hand, wasn't handling things well at all.

Renalia sent her away, stating that Fiona could record the matings, and they'd call on Seri when they wanted to research genetic connections. Since her magic hadn't only returned but leveled up, she could see them clearly.

Not that Seri wanted to spend her days tucked in meetings about mating and progeny. She wanted to visit the archive stones and find out what had happened to the rest of the dragons while they slept. Gregor hadn't been the only one disturbed by the dragon buried under the Nightwood in Sanctuary. Sadness had woven through the magic threads of healing and growth.

She needed to find out if magic had changed gradually or disappeared abruptly while the Source kept them in stasis. She could no longer think of it as a long sleep. Protecting them had taken an enormous amount of magic.

Zanthor had given her permission to go to the stones. She wanted to leave right away. But between Renalia and Gregor, she couldn't.

As soon as Seri stepped from the tunnel, she was surrounded. Garianna's glee was all the warning she received.

"What's the magic telling you, Seri?"

"Do the archive stones speak to you?"

"What path should we follow?"

Their questions demanded her to be more than a dragon who saw magic. They wanted the Oracle.

She sent a wave of entreaty to Garianna. She wasn't ready.

Her friend worshipped her and wanted her to become the Oracle of prophecy, but she also knew how to handle Seri's believers. *"I'll send them away, but first you must give them something. You can't avoid it any longer. You brought all the powered dragons together to help Zanthor. We all felt it, powered and traditional. You were the nexus."*

Dismay almost made Seri turn and run to Renalia for advice. But no. She couldn't hide from this. She wasn't what they wanted, but Garianna was right. The coven needed strong leadership, and despite everything she'd done to support Zanthor, many dragons expected her to give them guidance.

She shifted her voice and thoughts to project certainty for their future. That's what they needed.

"The archive has revealed a path. For now we must focus on growing our numbers. Our way of doing so will change. And you must be strong. But we'll thrive, and dragons will fly the skies again."

Her heart constricted. It reminded her so much of her lost mentor, Crysta. Say hopeful things with vague promises that would come true. That was the art of "oracling." Seri wished she could ask her friend's advice now. If only she could convince Zanthor to let her go to the Treasury. Crysta would've recorded a detailed history. She'd been researching a cure for the plague. Her memories could tell Seri more about what had happened than any coven archive stone.

"The Oracle has spoken. Her knowledge will lead us to a wondrous future. But you must be patient and be ready for when she needs you." Garianna sent the others away with a feeling of being blessed.

Seri kept her snort hidden behind her shields. Garianna should be the Oracle. She'd mastered the art of saying inspirational nonsense a long time ago.

One of the traditional dragons, Tayla, stayed behind. Her eyes whirled, even though a white film covered them. Purple threads of magic wound around her mottled beige head as she clutched Seri's talons. *"It's a hard road, youngling. Gather your strength. The Source gave me a vision of two futures. You must embrace yours for us to survive."*

Seri's heart beat in her throat, certain Tayla knew of her doubts.

Tayla's chuckle was kind, comforting. *"There are many of us who have known Seers and Soothsayers. The Great Wars were foretold. There was a reason dragons didn't fight. Even the plague was predicted, but not as it occurred. I wasn't a Seer, but the Source gave us all a little something special, no?"*

Seri bowed her head. She'd researched many of the Seers' predictions stored in the Dragon Library. Some had been amazingly accurate, but many had not. This inconsistency made her reluctant to say anything. She saw magic. She didn't see futures or have more knowledge than anyone else.

Tayla tapped Seri's brow. *"You're more special than you know, youngling."*

Embarrassment flooded Seri. Her damn personal shields might as well be mist. She quickly tightened them. How could she be special when she couldn't even maintain her own shields? Even hatchlings had shields. At least Tayla hadn't heard Seri's deepest fear.

Tayla tilted her head as if listening beyond what Seri was thinking. *"Until you accept your true power, your shields will falter. Don't worry. You're young, but we have less time for you to grow than you need. Just remember that many of us have experience. I, for one, would be happy to help. You don't have to do everything alone."*

But to ask for help was to admit she wasn't what they thought.

Tayla unclasped their talons, setting Seri free. *"When you're ready. We're not going anywhere."* Then she laughed, a chime of subtle tones inside Seri's mind.

Garianna grinned. *"What was that all about?"*

Seri was surprised her conversation hadn't leaked through her pathetic shields. But then she decided Tayla probably kept their conversation private. Garianna would've heard Seri's side of things, which wasn't all that much.

Hope and doubt churned, unable to settle. She knew she didn't have to do anything alone. But she didn't want to be the Oracle. Garianna kept pushing her into that role. And now Tayla said she must embrace it. She couldn't see how.

So, she focused on what she could control. *"Please stop encouraging them."*

Garianna's eyes whirled. *"Being our savior is your destiny. I've known it since the day you arrived at our coven as a hatchling. The Seer's prediction when you were barely four years old confirmed it. You need to use your magic and embrace your potential, and you're running out of time. I can see that. Why can't you?"*

Seri had never seen Garianna so angry. Not since her younger years when two older younglings had disagreed with Seri's uniqueness and trapped her in a hole.

So many dragons believed in her. She didn't know how she could ever be what they expected. But she couldn't simply wish it all away.

"I'm working on understanding my magic. Once I access the archive stones, I'll know more. And Tayla offered to help me understand the ways of a Seer. Satisfied? I'm trying my best. I'm not the only one working on our future. It'll take more than an Oracle to survive."

It was the best she could do. She accepted the responsibility, but Garianna had to realize that one dragon couldn't solve all their problems. It would take the entire coven.

ANSWERS
BECCA

The next morning Becca crouched over her horse as she and Marie rode through the miserable rain. She should be wrapped in a blanket, drinking hot soup. All night she'd tried to convince herself that Trey hadn't manipulated her emotions. But nightmares of Elizabeth and that horrible experience plagued her. The eggs transmitted nebulous emotions, increasing her agitation.

When she'd crawled out of bed, a familiar tugging sensation drew her gaze to the snow-covered mountains behind the keep. She'd left home to escape the demands of others. Now the Prophet, Trey, her eggs, and the mountains wanted something from her.

Becca pulled her cloak tighter, suppressing a yawn. Everything would be fine once she found Trey. His emotions would reveal the truth, and then she could decide what to do about it. Still, his secrets and betrayal hurt.

She'd been so certain of her path. Travel to Valley Keep, get supplies, and search for the dragons. Then Trey had wormed his way into her heart, and she'd dared to hope they could be together. But he'd changed since they'd arrived.

The boy who spoke of dragons and kissed her in the moonlight might never have existed. It had all been an illusion.

Her horse whinnied, slipping in the mud. Becca loosened her grip on the reins, letting the horse pick the safer path.

"I hope Mama can help with my nightmares." Marie slumped over her horse, as drenched as Becca, and probably equally exhausted. Becca had been relieved when the Prophet's influence had left Marie as soon as they returned to the caravan.

"I'm sure she can." Something had to help. Her moans still haunted Becca.

"The visions are relentless and don't make any sense. I know we just got here, but I want to leave so badly, my stomach aches."

"Me too. I hope John isn't planning on staying much longer."

"I feel like the visions would stop if I could just understand what to do." Marie sighed.

Becca hoped Marie didn't believe the Prophet could help her. At least she didn't show any interest in her dragon egg. Trey's modification must've worked.

They rode in silence until they reached the entrance.

"When you find Trey, stake your claim. More than one village girl had her eye on him at dinner."

Becca blushed, the change of topic catching her off guard.

Marie laughed and patted her horse when it shifted at the sound. "He feels the same way, but if you don't let him know, you could lose him. Take my advice."

With Marie's inability to resist the Prophet, Becca couldn't voice her doubts. It was better to let her believe everything was the same between her and Trey.

He was at the stables when they arrived. Becca's heart danced. Despite her worries, she was happy to see him. Unfortunately, he wasn't happy to see her.

"If you had waited an hour, the rain would've let up. It's worse at this time of day."

She wasn't sure how she was supposed to know that.

"Sorry," he mumbled. "Seems everyone's visiting today, and the stable's full." He waved at the stalls and the horses tethered under the eaves.

Becca slid off her horse and grabbed the reins. "Do you have somewhere else for them? I can help."

His smile of gratitude spread through her chest. But the weariness in his shoulders worried her. She was supposed to be grilling him, but all she wanted to do was ease his burden.

"See you later." Marie scurried for the covered hall. She'd be toasty and warm next to a fire soon. Hopefully, her mother could help, so she wouldn't feel compelled to visit Elizabeth again.

Becca grabbed the reins and followed Trey out the main gate to a shelter a short way behind the keep walls. Two young boys tossed fresh hay under a tarp awning. The horses snuffled and snorted, obviously happier under cover than out in the rain. Becca removed the wet saddles and blankets. Heat rose from their bodies.

Trey groaned. "There, that's done. Now I'm off to the wheat silos."

"Can I come?"

His startled look indicated he'd expected her to leave. They needed to talk, and if it meant following him around, then that's what she'd do. He grinned, and they ran through the rain.

But they weren't alone. Not for the rest of the morning. Trey spoke with overseers and examined products. He went everywhere. Through passageways behind innocuous doors and tunnels winding through the mountain behind the keep.

After each exchange, he became less himself.

Finally, he finished telling the miners they needed more nickel. It was the fifth time he'd changed a work order, and he never offered an explanation. He told them what to do, and they did it. But as far as Becca could tell, he never exerted his power. He didn't have to.

They responded with "For the Prophet," but some had anger in their eyes at his commands.

"Trey. Stop." This abrupt man wasn't the same as the one she'd known for the past week. He was slipping away. Maybe he'd never really existed.

He turned, rocking on his feet as if he couldn't stop moving.

"I wanted to talk about the dragons, and your egg." She grabbed his hand, hoping her power could guide her.

Fear. That wasn't what she'd expected.

"Quietly. Someone is always listening." His words set her heart thumping. Something was wrong.

"I have duties. I went away unexpectedly, and things got messy. Elizabeth has been scrambling. I must catch everyone up." The justification was completely at odds with his feelings, but she would play along and see where it led. Obviously, they couldn't talk about the dragons here.

"OK. But why you?" It seemed like a lot of responsibility.

He sighed, transmitting distress. "Because I'll take over when Elizabeth dies. No one else can do it."

He didn't want his grandmother to die. But he was also afraid of becoming her.

Becca had watched him interact with the villagers. Most liked him. He was clear and factual and didn't need to manipulate their thoughts.

"Don't you ever take a break?"

He scuffed the ground. "I used to. Things would run on their own. I used to collect data and assign the next tasks. But production dropped when I left."

"Why?"

His shock stunned her. "Valley Keep can't run itself."

Becca dropped his hand. That wasn't right. His fear was gone, subsumed by his need to make her understand.

"So, if you don't tell them what to do, they wouldn't do anything?" She couldn't keep the sarcasm from her voice.

He shrugged. "I don't like it. I wish people worked like they do in the caravan. But they don't. Not in the long term."

"You have to use your power for it all to work?" He must know that was wrong.

Trey ran his hand through his hair. "No. Maybe."

"Why do it if you think it's wrong?"

His conflict indicated he didn't want to use his power. He scuffed the dirt, avoiding her gaze. "Is it wrong? My grandmother took care of me when my parents died. She's been Valley Keep's leader longer than anyone in our history. She knows what works."

Becca pursed her lips. He sounded like her when she'd complain to Marcus about Mama. She'd known when Mama was being unreasonable, but she justified it, anyway. Now she understood Marcus's exasperation.

"She's your grandmother and the leader, but that doesn't mean she's right all the time. What would you do differently?" Becca's words echoed through her memories. No one had asked her that. Why hadn't she asked herself? She'd latched on to leaving as her solution and hadn't really looked any deeper.

He lifted his head, his brows furrowed. "Differently? Everything's for the good of the keep. She allocates jobs for people before they're even five years old. Everyone knows what they'll do.

"I don't know. I'd talk to them and test them. See what they like and guide them to the job that makes them happy." His face brightened as he worked out his own solution.

He didn't get it. Changing how he assigned duties didn't address the real problem. No one had a choice. No council or elders were in place to advocate for the people. Elizabeth controlled everything.

"Trey. Other villages don't have a leader who determines every aspect of their lives."

"I know that. I've read the history books. But they failed. That's what caused the Great Wars. Valley Keep has kept this tradition for decades. We live in peace and harmony."

That was too much for Becca. She'd break through Elizabeth's influence with logic.

"You question things. I felt it. And I bet others do too. What would happen if someone chose a different job? What if that girl married another boy? Would the village really fall into chaos? Deep down, you must know it wouldn't. That's why you feel off. Not because you weren't here. Elizabeth has brainwashed you into only seeing one way.

"You rode a ... You were adventurous. But now? I don't know what you are. A blind follower who does what his prophet says. Because she's no grandmother. A grandparent loves you for who you are when no one else does."

Becca stomped away, angry enough to punch something. Trey was infuriating. She blinked away her tears, annoyed that she couldn't stop them.

She'd fought her mother's control. She'd escaped. And now the boy who had captured her heart was more trapped than she'd been. For so long, pleasing her mother had consumed all her energy.

She stopped walking, her rage dissipating. Why?

Because she loved her mother. But she'd known that she would never succeed. Her mother's heart was broken. With the onset of her powers, Becca had felt the lack of love, and though she'd been shocked at first, she realized she wasn't really surprised.

That's why she'd hated her power so much. It confirmed what she already knew. Her mother *couldn't* love her in the way she needed.

Trey might have the same problem with his grandmother.

She shook her head. He didn't speak of love. He spoke of duty and legacy. She'd wanted to leave her village and start over. A new life. But really, changing locations wouldn't change her life. Leaving her mother had changed her life.

Yet Trey never spoke of leaving. From the moment he fell from Gregor, he'd wanted to go home.

And that was the key. He clung to duty and routine so he wouldn't be alone. Becca had Grandfa and her siblings, and even Peter had been kind. They all loved her, yet she spent all her energy trying to please her mother. Trey's grandmother was his only family, and she pushed duty on him so he could take over when she died. When she left him alone in the world.

Becca wrapped her arms around herself, and shame washed over her. She'd been too hard on him. Of course, he didn't want to be alone. He'd isolated himself, even in the caravan. She'd made friends, but he'd kept to himself. He needed to see that life existed without his grandmother and without the villagers.

She remembered his joy when she'd told him Grandfa's stories, and how he'd helped her with the eggs, even though he saw only rocks. Her steps lightened. She knew how to get to him.

Dragons.

They were the key that broke through her blindness. Her heart flooded with purpose. She could save him. He was worth it.

DISTRESS
BECCA

Early the next morning, Becca felt something missing, like the hole in her soul when her grandfather died. But this wasn't grief. She lay in her tiny bunk and lowered her mental shield.

Marie slept soundly, for once. Outside, the traders had started their day, despite the darkness. Nothing unusual. Their emotions were subdued and focused on tasks.

Frustrated, Becca reached under her pillow and rubbed her egg, sending comfort. But there was nothing from either egg. No glimmer. No flicker. No warmth.

Her breath caught in her throat, and fear squeezed her chest.

She sat up, cradling both eggs. The shells were softer, more like a leather saddle than a rock. She opened her heart, sending energy. Offering comfort. Begging for a response.

Trey's egg flickered, weak and insubstantial. Becca's breath caught in her throat. Her egg was silent.

She clambered into her clothing, stuffed the eggs into her satchel, and flew through the faint sunlight chasing away the night. The eggs needed water and friction. Then they'd be fine.

At the river, she lowered both eggs into the current, placing stones around them so they wouldn't escape. She squatted next to the river, rocking on her heels, but there was no glimmer of contentment.

Lullabies made Trish and Brandon feel better. Maybe that would work. The tiny dragons had to be healthy. She sang one of her favorite dragon songs from Grandfa's stories.

"There once was a lady so bold, who never did what she was told ..."

She tried another. And another.

Trey's egg flickered weakly. Becca plunged her hands into the freezing current and caressed the egg.

"I'm here. You're safe." She sent all her love to the tiny dragon encased within.

But there was no return warmth. No glow. No mental connection.

Becca stroked her egg. *"Please. Please, come back. I love you."*

Nothing.

The hole. The emptiness that woke her so early in the morning. It was her connection to the eggs. To the tiny dragons growing inside.

Her anguish filled the hole.

They couldn't be dead. Trey's had responded. She refused to believe her dragon was dead.

The sky turned pink and orange. People woke, had breakfast, and went about their day. She felt all their emotions, too afraid of missing anything from her tiny dragons to put up her shields.

Desire, happiness, and grumpiness washed over her.

"Becca, are you going to eat?" Marie's soft voice as she squatted beside Becca carried only concern. She couldn't see the eggs. To her, Becca was washing her hands forever, possibly lost in thought.

Becca nodded, still focused on the eggs. Nothing else mattered.

Marie handed her a buttered bun and a hard-boiled egg.

"Is something wrong?" She touched Becca's shoulder and her feelings rushed through Becca's mind.

Concern. Worry.

Becca groaned. Marie's feelings didn't bother her, but she didn't have any energy left to ease Marie's concerns. She needed help.

Lightning tingled through Becca's body.

She could figure this out. She knew enough healing. She could track and hunt as well as Marcus. She took care of the twins. Grandfa had taught her independence. And she'd needed it. Because Mama expected her to do everything. Even when she'd never done it before.

Mama's words were stamped into her soul. "You're the eldest. You should know how to do this."

It had always frustrated Becca. How could she know if she'd never been taught? Since when did age impart knowledge?

Becca carefully collected the dragon eggs and put them in her satchel. Marie gave her space and ate in silence.

She turned to Marie and bit her lip. It was harder than she'd expected. But the tiny dragons needed her to be strong.

"I need help. I think the dragons are dying." Pain squeezed her heart. Saying it out loud made it more real. She'd failed.

Marie didn't hesitate. "What do you need?"

Becca held up her palms in helpless entreaty. "I need a dragon."

Marie couldn't help. Becca shook her head. She was off-kilter, broken, disconnected from the real world.

Marie's eyes rolled back, and her face went slack. After no more than a minute, she blinked, confusion in her eyes.

"Was that a vision?"

Marie's visions had never been that brief. She rubbed her head. "Pack food and warm clothing. It was a voice in my head. I only saw you and Trey, waiting by a lake."

Her words unlocked Becca's brain. She needed Trey's help. Gregor could save the tiny dragons.

Becca pushed her horse all the way to the keep. Steam rose from his heaving sides as she tossed the reins to the stable boy.

"I'll be back shortly. Take care of him." Guilt chased her heels as she ran to Trey's room.

A tug pulled at her mind, from the mountains. She slammed up her mental shield. The keep wasn't a place to let her power free. The villagers' devotion to Elizabeth was unsettling.

Trey wasn't in his room. She ran to the kitchen, hoping it was early enough that he hadn't started his rounds. He was there, talking to the head woman. His eyes lit up when he saw her, but he continued his conversation.

She didn't have time for politeness. "I must speak with you immediately." Her voice came out louder than she intended, drawing the attention of everyone at the tables.

Trey frowned a warning, then turned to the head woman. "I'll speak with you later."

His face was blotchy when he glared at Becca. "What?"

She didn't care if she'd embarrassed him. Well, she cared a little. Becca pulled him to an alcove where they wouldn't be overheard.

"The baby dragons are dying. You have to contact Gregor now."

Since she was holding his hand, every emotion hit her as he processed her words.

Worry. Guilt. Pain.

His confusing feelings would have to wait for another time.

"Marie had a vision. You need to pack. Come on."

"I can't." He yanked his hand free, but not before she felt his sorrow.

"You have to."

He shook his head. "You don't need me. I can tell you where to go."

Pain rolled through him. He didn't want to see Gregor again. The dragon had abandoned him.

She brushed his hair off his forehead. "Trey. There must be an explanation for why he left you. He was shot, probably injured, and certainly terrified. Maybe his family wouldn't let him return. He's young for a dragon, right?"

Trey didn't look convinced.

"Please help me. Gregor knows you. I'm a stranger."

His emotions shifted. He would help her and get answers. Trey wrapped his arms around her, offering comfort. "Let's save your eggs. But I can't call Gregor. We met at Meadow Lake, but the caravan is there, and he won't land near people."

That was it, then. She couldn't save the eggs.

"There's another place. One of the abandoned mining tunnels. He'll have to fly right over it. We'll take the tunnels. I usually met him around ten in the morning. If he's coming, he might hear me and come to us."

He kissed her cheek. "But, Becca, he might not come at all." He was more worried about her disappointment than his own feelings now.

She was too overwhelmed to speak. Gregor had no reason to seek out Trey. She'd assumed Trey could contact him.

It was all going to be for nothing. Discovering the eggs. Rescuing them. Leaving home. Traveling all this way. And now the tiny dragons were going to die.

Trey squeezed her. "Don't give up. I've seen magical things happen. But we must hurry. We have only an hour to get to the cave."

His certainty that things would work out washed over her. And his warm chest helped too. He was right. There was magic, and if Gregor didn't show up, they'd try something else.

She wouldn't give up. Her tiny dragons had to live.

REUNION
GREGOR

Day 45 After the Long Sleep

As Gregor helped Ronin set the archive stone across from the Nightwood tree, he hoped this would be the last task. Fiona and some other dragons had decided to move to Sanctuary to prepare it for hatchlings. Between helping them set up and searching for a suitable stone, he hadn't had a chance to visit Trey.

This was important for the coven, so he hid his frustration deep within his mind. His desire to reconnect with a human boy was secondary to his duty.

"It's perfect. When the sun sets, the stone's shadow will stretch to the base of the tree. Symmetry in life and nature is important." Fiona rested her talon on the stone. *"Our survival will be recorded to guide future generations."* She winked at Gregor.

Finally, he could leave. She would thrive in Sanctuary. His presence had steadied her, even made her happy. Zanthor had noticed it and asked him to help Fiona prepare for the hatchlings. It wasn't the dragon way to bond with a mother figure, but times had changed. Their coven needed to strengthen their bonds any way they could.

Gregor sauntered up to Zanthor, giving him time to finish his private conversation. It was still early. Trey wouldn't be awake yet, but the flight from Sanctuary would take hours.

Zanthor turned and chuckled. *"Yes. You can see the boy now. Take Seri or Ronin. You're not to go anywhere alone. Not until you can control your power."*

It was a victory and a reminder that he needed supervision. Still, a protest escaped his tight control. Scents gave the coven what they needed. His power found the Source. It helped them find Sanctuary.

Seri bounded up, with her usual excess of energy. He didn't know how she did it, disguising her own doubts with enthusiasm. Dragons weren't supposed to be able to hide their emotions.

"I'll go with him. I need to stretch my wings." She'd spent the entire time at Sanctuary inside the caves with Renalia, ensuring the hatchlings had warm sleeping nooks and access to the hot springs.

"Let's go now, then." Gregor leapt into the sky. With a single flap of his wings, he rose over the Nightwood tree and circled the caldera.

If he didn't leave now, a dragon would claim Seri. The caves had given her some respite from the many who pounced any time she was alone, asking her about the future and begging her to save them. He could tell their adulation bothered her. It was disturbing. Even the greatest Seers of the past hadn't had all the answers.

"Thanks. Garianna was already on her way to find me." Seri's gratitude warmed his soul.

She had removed the illusion of snow that had hidden Sanctuary, so they flew directly into a brilliant blue sky.

"Let's go meet this boy of yours. And be careful. If he was injured, Elizabeth may still want revenge. You know how humans are. Changing allegiances over trifles. He may not be your friend anymore."

Gregor dipped in the current, enjoying the crisp air against his wings, as he considered her words. Humans didn't think like dragons. He'd left Trey to fend for himself against those gun-wielding villagers. There was no way of knowing how that might've changed him.

"I'll tread warily. Don't worry. Trey and I have a connection."

Warm sunlight on his wings and wind choosing his path soothed the last of his stress over the leadership change.

Dragons needed to fly.

Joy bubbled in his chest as soon as they crested the mountain peak. Fog rolled down, shrouding the valley and the keep, providing enough protective cover to fly directly to the lake. He'd missed his human friend, more than he'd realized. Even if their relationship changed, he was happy Trey had survived.

"Gregor, wait." Seri's warning reminded him to be cautious. Humans might see their shadows through the bare patches in the fog. But she wasn't concerned about visibility.

Human voices cut through the air. Horses snuffled as they ate. Chickens warbled at each other. The creak of leather and wagons. Sounds that indicated a human camp.

He rose into the higher current next to Seri. Disappointment dragged his wings. It wasn't safe. Either Trey had betrayed him, or he couldn't use the lake anymore. Either way, he wouldn't see the boy today.

It was an effort to turn back to Jason's Keep, but then nutmeg filled his nostrils, invoking his power.

"Seri. Nutmeg." The flame-haired girl from the village was near.

He swung his head, inhaling, trying to capture the direction. There. It was everywhere, but stronger up the valley. Closer to Valley Keep. He flew toward it, involuntarily lowering himself to keep the scent, each stroke of his wings strong and sure.

Nutmeg filled his mind.

He must find her.

Seri rammed into his side, her wings tucked tightly against her body as she spun under him.

He flailed to catch his balance. *Torin's breath.* What was she doing? He corrected his course, but she cut him off, her talons grazing his snout as he veered away. *"Seri!"*

"Oh, thank Torin. You're back. You can't disappear like that. I had no idea what you were thinking."

They were now too close to Valley Keep, but the scent was behind him. He turned.

"Gregor!" Seri screamed in his mind. Pain reverberated through his skull.

She didn't have to yell. Or maybe she did. He'd flown over the mountain range beyond the keep. The fog dissipated, exposing him in a cloudless sky.

Before he could flee, a voice entered his mind, crystal clear and feminine.

"Gregor, please help."

"Did you hear that?" His shock dislodged the compulsion from his power. The scent had controlled him again. But he had no time for shame.

The girl's desperation filled his mind now.

Seri nodded. *"I've never heard a human so clear. Usually it's images and emotions with a lot of babble. Her mind is focused. And that desperation. Why is she calling you?"*

He didn't know, but the scent urged him to find her.

"You must come. I need you."

He flew along the range, away from Valley Keep and that danger.

"Gregor, are you sure? No human can send that far. It might not be the girl."

No. It was. The girl from his dream. He felt it deep in his mind. A connection that had been there since the moment he woke in the Source. Her urgency lent strength to his wings. Halfway between the lake and the keep, he found her in a cave in the mountainside.

A girl with red hair stood next to Trey. His voice was feeble compared to hers, and trepidation filled his mind.

"There's no one else here. It's safe." Seri's assessment jolted him.

He'd failed again. If she hadn't been there, he would've blindly flown in. *"Should I land while you keep watch?"* Nutmeg clouded his logic.

"No. They've seen me, anyway. And I might need to break you from your power trance again."

He wondered how long she'd tried to connect before she'd rammed into him. Actually, that took a level of skill he didn't have. Seri was full of surprises.

As soon as he landed, the girl's worry attacked Gregor. Trey's thoughts were subdued and wary. Guilt rushed through Gregor. The boy no longer trusted him. Only the girl's need had brought them together.

Dragon Help

Becca

Trey had been calling out to Gregor for half an hour, but Becca could tell he was ready to give up.

"Please." She sent her own mental call, opening her mind to let him know she needed him, and she was safe.

She sensed the dragons before she saw them. Fog rolled down the mountain below her, shrouding the keep and the lake from view. The sky was the intense blue of a crisp winter morning. They appeared as specks over the fog and grew into two dragons flying side by side, one emerald and the other turquoise. Something shifted inside Becca. The sky was bluer, the air crisper, and she knew a female and a male dragon flew toward her.

"Trey, they're coming. Keep calling."

"How many?" Worry. Fear. He wasn't expecting anyone other than Gregor.

"Two. Don't worry. I sense only curiosity. They won't hurt us." She needed Trey to be calm and inviting. He mustn't frighten them away.

They flew faster than any bird, arriving in minutes. So much bigger in real life than she'd expected. Despite Grandfa's stories, she didn't know what to say.

Trey bowed low. Then tugged Becca's hand down. She bowed. Pleasure. Concern. Joy.

Becca straightened and stared into the emerald dragon's whirling eyes. Gregor. She could feel him. Darkness and sorrow, blue skies and pleasure, pain and comfort. She felt as if his entire soul was bared for her. She blinked, and the sensation ended.

"I was hoping you'd find us. This is Becca, my friend. There's a caravan at the lake." Trey's speech was awkward enough to make Becca cringe.

"Trey. I'm so happy you're alive. I thought you'd perished at the girl's village." Gregor's voice matched his eyes. There were so much meaning behind every word. He'd mourned Trey.

Becca couldn't help herself; she had to comfort him. *"He injured his shoulder when he fell, but that was all. He's alive, and he's missed you so."*

Both dragons turned their attention to Becca.

"She can hear your conversation with the boy?" Seri's voice was feminine, and energy wove through it like a musical accompaniment.

Happiness bubbled through Becca at being able to identify the turquoise dragon as Seri.

Gregor chuckled, and his delight flowed through Becca. *"Seems she can hear you too. And she can sense emotions."*

"Interesting. Get on with your conversation with the boy. I can feel his headache already. I'll speak with the girl. She sends like a rider."

Curiosity. Protection. And something Becca couldn't identify came from Seri.

Suddenly, it was like they were inside a bubble. She couldn't hear Trey or Gregor as they continued their conversation.

"Don't be afraid. This is how dragons speak privately." Seri sent a soothing scent through Becca's mind.

Becca inhaled, half expecting to find herself in a field of crushed mint.

"Who are you, youngling?"

Becca had imagined this moment her entire life. A dragon stood in front of her. Her mind went blank. Or she thought it did.

"Too fast. Concentrate on one thing. You indicated there was some urgency in meeting Gregor. Tell me about that. We can discuss the rest later."

Heat rose to Becca's cheeks at exposing so much of herself. She knew how to focus her thoughts. And Seri was right. She didn't have time to explain her whole life. The eggs were more important.

"I found some eggs. A lot, actually. But I have two with me, and something is wrong. I think they're dying." Her worry and pain crashed through her words. She didn't stifle them.

"I feel your love for these hatchlings. That's amazing. Show them to me."

Excitement and fear.

Seri's emotions were so clear and pure. They weren't cluttered with other sensations. But even more startling was how Seri responded. The dragon had the same power of sensing emotions.

Becca pulled the eggs from her satchel. She rubbed Trey's egg and felt the flicker of awareness, still too weak, but at least it was there. She held her egg against her chest, enveloping the tiny dragon inside with love.

Seri gasped, and the bubble broke.

"What?" Gregor's growl reminded Becca that these dragons were larger than any horse she'd seen.

Her hands trembled as she held out the eggs. Only her certainty that Seri wanted to help kept her legs locked.

Seri took the eggs and turned them carefully in her palm. *"These. They appear to be rocks. But Becca claims they're eggs."*

Becca's hope dwindled. The dragons couldn't see them.

"You have to put them in water to see them. They're protected with an illusion. I thought it was dragon magic." Becca forgot to speak mentally. If they couldn't even see the eggs, how could they help?

But the dragons ignored her.

"Can you see anything?" Gregor's question didn't make any sense. He expected Seri to see the eggs when he couldn't.

Seri shook her head, and disappointment crashed through Becca.

"She truly believes they're eggs. Won't hurt to check." Gregor still had hope.

"Trey. They can't see the eggs. I need water."

Trey ran back into the cave. He returned shortly with a bucket, making Becca wonder what other mysteries the caves hid.

She lowered Trey's egg into the water, and it transformed into a muted green orb. She rubbed it again, hoping to bring some radiance back, and it glowed, for a moment.

"Nothing. Maybe a hint of magic." When Seri spoke to Gregor, her voice was gentle and curious.

But when she spoke to Becca, it felt more like a command. *"Show me, child."*

"How?"

"Open your mind so I can see through your eyes."

Becca tried to imagine a dragon looking through her eyes. It must've worked, because Seri gasped.

"The other one. I must see it."

Becca put her egg into the bucket. It was almost translucent. The white crystal dulled to fog.

Seri's fear hit Becca like an omen of death. She shoved Becca aside and grabbed the egg in her long talons, then snatched Trey's egg from Becca's grasp. Before Becca could do anything, Seri leapt for the sky, her giant wings sending everything flying.

Gregor rumbled a deep vibration, which eased Becca's fear. He dipped his head until it filled her view. *"Thank you, Becca. We've searched for our eggs but couldn't find them. You have restored our hope that they survived. However, you were right to be concerned. The hatchlings are in distress. We will help them."*

His gratitude honored her.

"You've discovered more?" It wasn't as much a question as a fervent hope.

Becca looked at Trey, and he grinned. "This is what you wanted."

She sucked in a breath and exhaled. Wanting something and grabbing it were two different things.

"Yes. There's some in a cave, and I saw more in a river." Her heart soared. She would show him the dragon eggs and he would accept her.

But Trey grabbed her arm. His caution dampened her enthusiasm. Gregor had abandoned him. Trey didn't trust him. Not anymore.

They'd need a safe way to fly on the dragon and collect the eggs. She couldn't simply show him where to find them.

Gregor's excitement lifted her worry. *"We'll figure it out. We must save all the eggs we can, before they hatch."*

DAMAGED GREGOR

Gregor wanted to fly after Seri and see the eggs for himself. She'd been clever, using the girl's eyes to pierce the rocky illusion.

It didn't make sense that a girl could see them when dragons couldn't, but magic had changed and maybe illusions were different now. At least Becca could help him find the eggs, and the hatchlings would survive. She'd explained that some were in a cave and others were in the river along Pilgrim's Trail. Strange name. In his day, humans called it the Trail of Lost Hope. She was the only one who could pick out the rock eggs from the rocks.

"No. She can't go with you. Not by herself." Trey's feelings of betrayal were clear. He didn't trust Gregor with the girl.

"I'm sorry that I forgot you were on my back and dropped you. My wing was damaged, and fear took over. But I returned for you. There was only blood, too much. I thought you were dead." He let the boy feel his relief that he hadn't died. While it helped, he still felt the distance in Trey's mind. Their friendship needed time to heal.

So Gregor agreed to carry them both.

He left the younglings with plans for a double harness and flew to Jason's Keep. Seri had waited for him.

"What did you see?" Gregor wouldn't let her run off without an explanation again.

Distress made her eyes whirl. *"The hatchlings are dying. The male in the green egg is very weak, but I think we can save him. I don't know about the female in the white one. Magic connects the hatchling to the girl, so there must be hope."*

They'd finally found eggs, and now they might die. But soon he'd have more. He didn't understand Seri's concern.

"Why does this upset you? Hatchlings die. And Becca can find more."

"Magic connects her to our eggs. I don't understand why, but we must save these two."

"What can I do to help?" No scents guided him, but he had to do what he could.

"Find the other eggs. Hopefully the girl can find the hatchling we all heard too."

Seri thought magic had a plan. Her mind filled with threads of magic and connections. Her power was affecting her, and Gregor didn't know how to free her. She shouldn't be so frantic over two eggs. Dragons laid hundreds of eggs, and only one percent would hatch. Even then, half of the hatchlings survived the journey to a coven. Gregor had assumed the eggs that didn't break were empty or defective. It never occurred to him they had tiny dragons who died in the shell.

The helplessness of their plight weakened his belief that they'd survive. So many obstacles. If only humans had never meddled with magic and created the plague. If dragons had kept themselves apart from the Great Wars, none of this would've happened.

He chuffed. Now he was thinking like Sarcruze. Isolating themselves from humans. Maybe it was because he hurt over what happened with Trey. The boy didn't trust him anymore. Their friendship had shattered.

He'd made so many mistakes that day, but he'd been right. Nutmeg. The girl was important for their survival. Too bad it wasn't as straightforward as it sounded. He sighed.

Seri wrapped the eggs in grass to keep them from drying out more.

"Get the other eggs, Gregor, then cut all ties with both humans. Your power led you to them for this and this only. We don't need humans interfering with our survival."

It was harsh, especially for Seri. But her tone had the ring of prophecy. She was starting to believe she knew things. He was afraid her power was messing with her logic. Most likely, she was partially right. But now wasn't the time to correct her.

She was convinced Becca had damaged the eggs by taking them from the cave. He disagreed. If Becca hadn't taken them, they wouldn't have this chance to find more. Nothing was ever simple. The girl hadn't known she would harm the eggs.

But Seri had made up her mind. Becca was necessary to get the eggs, but the girl would not be allowed anywhere near the hatchlings.

Seri left, her mind already focused on her tasks once she reached Sanctuary.

"Fly swift and safe, Seri." Her power had enthralled her, but she was no danger to the coven, unlike when his power took over his mind.

Becca would help him find the eggs, and he'd bring them to Sanctuary. The coven would never consider banishing him again. His power and his decisions would be vindicated.

The girl was the key.

SANCTUARY MAGIC
SERI

DAY 45 AFTER THE LONG SLEEP

By the time Seri landed at Sanctuary, doubt had set in. The girl's vision of the eggs had been so clear, but she couldn't sense the dragons inside the rocks she carried.

Sanctuary had changed. Alcoves were carved along the walls of the caldera. Steam rose from the enlarged hot springs. More than one dragon could sit in the waters. Even the river had been groomed into a smooth circuit, with steps controlling the flow of water.

"You have news?" Fiona's mind was brighter, less distressed, though an air of melancholy clung to her.

Seri tightened her shields and projected excitement, letting Fiona and Brin experience the vision from Becca's eyes. *"We found eggs. The Source protected them with an illusion."*

Brin took one and hummed, invoking her power. *"I can't see anything."* She handed it to Fiona, who simply shook her head.

"We must put them in the river. I'm hoping Sanctuary can heal them. One of them might already be dead, because a human girl carried them in a satchel." Becca's interference with the development of the eggs still rankled, but Gregor was right. They wouldn't have found them if she hadn't.

Fiona took the eggs to the base of one of the three waterfalls and dropped them in. *"We organized each waterfall for different stages. This one has the most consistent flow and the deepest pool of water. It's perfect for the last stage of hatching, when the shell is no longer protecting the egg. Over there, the fiercest falls will be where we lay the eggs. The pools are shallow and will gently erode the outer shell as the hatchlings form. The middle falls will send the eggs into the river to circle and continue to mature."*

The eggs didn't transform. Even Sanctuary's magic couldn't reveal them. The Source must know they were safe.

"How can we care for eggs if we can't even see them?" Brin's frustration mirrored her own.

Both dragons looked to Seri for answers. Her feelings of inadequacy returned. All this hope laid at her feet. She sucked in her breath. How did seeing magic give her answers? She wasn't an Oracle, no matter how much they all wanted her to be. She turned away from them and accessed her power, wishing magic could soothe the maelstrom in her mind.

Within the branches of the Nightwood, the sphere of magic glowed, gold with strands of green, red, and blue, as if filled with answers just beyond her grasp.

There had to be a way to remove the illusion. Magic shouldn't be hidden from her.

Brin was right. They couldn't assess the eggs if they couldn't see them. Even laying in the waterfall wouldn't solve this problem. And they certainly couldn't monitor rocks for the outcomes of breeding pairs.

It was up to her. Green strands clung to the two rocks, swirling in the current. She'd seen that before, in the river when she'd held strands of magic. Maybe she could manipulate the strands somehow.

The sphere pulsed, encouraging her.

Ridiculous. Magic didn't have a conscience. It was an element of the world, like air and water. But water transformed. Why not magic?

She grabbed a green thread from the river. It wiggled and twisted, and her talon cut through the strand. She tried again. The strands were slippery and had the consistency of gel.

The sphere brightened.

A message she couldn't decipher. Frustrated, Seri strode up to the Nightwood and shoved the rock-that-was-an-egg into the ball of magic. There was some resistance, like shoving a talon into sand at the beach.

"Please. I need to do something. This egg is in distress." She wasn't sure why she spoke to the magic ball, but it worked.

The misshapen edges smoothed and thinned, until finally, a round green egg spun, suspended inside the magic sphere.

Hope bubbled in her throat.

But the egg was dim, lacking the glow of life. She wasn't done.

This had nothing to do with being the Oracle. This was magic. She'd studied it all her life. Humans tapped into magic with their spells and potions, combining it to create what they wanted. No reason she couldn't do the same.

The egg needed to be repaired, and healing magic filled Sanctuary.

Seri hummed deep in her throat, just like Brin had, feeling as though this would help her focus. She snagged a red strand. Unlike the threads in the river, this one felt more like sinew. It resisted as she pulled it from the pulsing ball. Then she looped the strand around the egg. A green strand glowed briefly. She grasped it and wrapped it next to the red strand. Both strands vibrated on the surface of the egg. Something was happening, but she wasn't sure which combination would do what she wanted.

The world around her fell away. The wind stilled, the flow of water settled to a whisper, and she could no longer sense Brin or

Fiona in her mind. As Seri pulled on a yellow strand, she felt a vibration through her skull bones.

Once the strand settled on the egg, magic sighed. She flew through the colors, selecting and discarding, tapping into the automatic part of her mind that formed harmonies and magical swirls of color.

Suddenly, the egg dropped from the magic ball.

She dove, catching it before it crashed into the roots of the Nightwood. But the egg was fine, glowing a brilliant green.

Brin gasped, her joy blasting through Seri's mind, reconnecting her to the world. *"Bless Torin. It's an egg. Seri, you did it."*

Seri handed the egg to Brin and grabbed the other one.

This one took more strands of magic, and Seri's shoulders ached with fatigue. But soon, the opalescent white orb glowed with health.

Brin clapped her talons. *"You did it."*

Seri couldn't move. *"I did. But it took a lot of energy. I'm as weak as a hatchling."*

She swayed, reaching out to the Nightwood for support. The golden sphere of magic seemed less substantial.

Fiona eased her to the ground. *"Rest. We'll care for the eggs now."*

Seri rubbed her head, so tired her thoughts couldn't form.

"Rest. You did enough." Fiona sent soothing mint to Seri's mind, and a lassitude came over her.

Seri closed her eyes. Gratitude fluttered in her chest for two beats before she fell into a deep sleep.

She was still weak when she woke, but not as much.

"Good. You've returned to us." Brin bounded up, full of too much energy and enthusiasm.

Seri sat and wobbled, her wings spread out like a new hatchling, supporting her weight.

"No. Stay still for a bit longer. Looks like using your power to make the eggs visible sucked all the energy from you."

Despair threatened to curl Seri into a ball. She couldn't go through that for hundreds of eggs. There had to be another way.

Brin laughed, a melody of too much happiness, considering Seri's state. *"Those eggs were in rough shape. It's no wonder they needed so much of your energy to heal."*

She leaned her head into Seri's. *"But we thought of another way."*

Seri shook her head, dislodging Brin. The older dragon wasn't making any sense.

"Stop teasing her and tell her what we did." Fiona's censure didn't diminish her own glee.

"We collected large rocks from the river where Garianna laid her clutch. And two were eggs!" Brin pulled Seri up and danced around her.

Seri's mind refused to figure it out. She'd never felt so sluggish in her entire life.

"Sorry." Brin's apology soothed Seri's confusion. *"You're not quite yourself yet. The magic ball removed the illusion from the eggs we found."*

"They stayed transformed?" It was like thinking through mud. The eggs were revealed without manipulating magic?

"Yes, and the eggs are healthy. You can check on them later, but rest for now, dear heart." Fiona sent another wave of mint, and Seri's eyes closed.

But she understood what to do. She didn't need to manipulate magic to see the eggs. They had a solution. If she weren't so tired, she'd be happy.

The next time she woke, her mind was clear. She lay in a hot spring, the heat and sulfur easing the last of the weakness from her limbs. Fiona must've moved her.

Shoving eggs into the magic ball to remove the illusion would be tedious. They needed a better way. Now that Seri's brain was working, the solution was obvious. She could direct the magic into the river. It would take a lot of energy, but she could do it.

That wouldn't work for the eggs already in the world. They'd all hatch soon, not only exposing that dragons had returned but also putting the hatchlings at risk from humans.

The white egg glowed with life now. A thin strand of magic connected the hatchling within to the girl. They had to use Becca to find as many as they could before they hatched.

Love fluttered from inside the egg, familiar.

Seri's heart stumbled. It should be impossible. This unformed hatchling had transmitted hope during Zanthor's battle. To have so much reach and magical power from inside an egg was unprecedented. They must nurture this hatchling.

Seri rubbed the egg's shell. *"There, there, little one. You're safe."*

The human girl had almost killed the tiny female hatchling, but she loved Becca.

Caravan Help

BECCA

With the dragons gone, Becca deflated. Saving her tiny dragon had driven her since she woke, but now the egg was gone, and she felt lost. The packed bags mocked her dreams.

"Marie's vision was wrong. We're not going anywhere today, and certainly not somewhere cold."

Trey grabbed her hand and pulled her through the cavern system. "Her timing was off, but we'll leave soon. Making a harness is going to be difficult without my grandmother finding out. She has spies everywhere. Fortunately, she specifically told me to spend time with you. So, we can use that to our advantage."

Heat flooded Becca's face. "She kept asking what happened to you. I didn't know what you'd told her, so I had to distract her. I might've exaggerated a little."

Drakelings danced in her stomach at Trey's laugh. With their hands entwined, his admiration and desire rushed through her.

"It worked." He stopped and pulled her in for a quick kiss, his lips soft as his delight tingled through her mind.

She melted into his arms, savoring his reaction, letting herself enjoy his solidness and his gentle caress. He made her feel beautiful.

He pulled away with a regretful sigh and a promise for later. "But we don't just need a harness. We need a vessel to carry the eggs. Your satchel barely held the two you had."

He was right. And the eggs would be bigger and heavier now.

"The traders should have what we need, and hopefully, none of Elizabeth's spies will bother us there."

They hurried back to the caravan and found John and Maggie fishing at the lake.

"What have you two been up to? You look ready to burst with excitement." Maggie's eyes darted between them, a warning about shenanigans emanating from her.

Becca brushed her hair behind her ear and averted her eyes. Her secret was so much more than a few sweet kisses with Trey, but it was better for Maggie to keep her assumptions.

A ripple of energy came from Trey. "We're looking for supplies to construct a large harness. I figured you might help."

He used his power without thinking. John would help without manipulation, but that conversation would have to wait.

John handed Maggie his rod. "You'll have to catch dinner on your own." He winked and strode off with Trey.

Maggie cackled, pulling up a line with a gaggle of fish. "He never catches anything. I caught enough for dinner an hour ago." She handed the line to Becca. "May's well put those hands of yours to good use."

It was something Mama used to say, but Becca knew Maggie didn't mean it as a disparaging comment about her idleness.

As Becca made her way through the camp, the excitement of meeting two dragons bubbled in her chest. It had been incredible. She'd heard their voices in her mind, and she knew how they felt. Not only had Seri believed her about the eggs, but Gregor wanted her to help him gather the rest. Two powerful dragons wanted her help. And once she collected the eggs, she hoped with all her heart she would see her tiny dragon.

She passed Trey at the supply caravan. He had various lengths of leather and rope laid out on the ground. He pointed at areas where the leather could break if stressed by sudden movements. She wondered what John thought he was making.

They didn't need her help. Trey had the harness in hand, so she went to find her friends.

Shelly, Marie, and Jane were washing by the river. Marie already knew about the eggs and dragons, but Becca wasn't sure she wanted the other two to know what was going on.

At her approach, Marie jumped up. "You're still here?"

"Yes. Our trip was delayed. Actually, I could use your help. We need a bag for large items. Something light but strong enough to support a lot of weight." It was hard to explain without stating the truth.

Shelly wrung out her clothing and plopped it into a basket. "Why not use a fishing net?"

"How much weight could a net hold?"

Shelly listed all the benefits of netting. Her experience was extensive, and soon Becca was more confused than before.

Marie interrupted. "That won't work. You need to carry water over long distances."

Jane and Shelly looked at her, and she dropped her head, focusing on her laundry. "Just a thought."

Marie was right. When Becca had told the dragons about dipping the eggs in the river, Seri had been shocked. A flash had shown Becca that eggs usually stayed in water until the dragons were ready to hatch. It had never occurred to her the eggs would need more water as the shell softened. Seri's anger before she took the eggs made sense now.

Pain shot through Becca. She'd killed her tiny dragon.

Marie touched her arm. "It'll be all right."

Her concern brought tears to Becca's eyes. No one since Grandfa had cared so much about her. She squeezed Marie's hand, drawing strength from her optimism. Marie was right. The dragons wouldn't have taken the eggs if her tiny dragon had perished. There was still hope.

Shelly had a solution. Fishers carried fresh water in waterproof leather satchels whenever they went out to sea. Fortunately, the yellow grass used to wax leather surrounded the lake. They scraped off the waxy surface of the grass and applied it to the leather. By the end of the day, they had ten waterproof satchels, each large enough to hold two small eggs or one large egg.

Now she had to figure out how to attach them to the harness and ensure they could support the eggs. The last thing she needed was for Gregor to decide the eggs were more important than his passengers and leave them stranded at the cave in her village.

DRAGON QUEST
BECCA

Before the sun turned the sky orange and pink, when only the animals were awake, Becca slid out of bed and grabbed her supplies. She couldn't sleep anymore.

It was too early to meet Gregor, too early to do anything. The sky was an endless indigo, broken by the occasional star bright enough to fight the encroaching dawn. She wasn't hungry, at least not for food.

Becca ached for her tiny dragon. Its presence had been with her even when she left it in the wagon. And now it was gone.

The river called her. As if she still needed to tend to the eggs. But she didn't have them anymore.

Becca kneeled and ran her fingers through the flowing water. It was freezing, fed by glaciers, but she didn't care. The river carried a soothing energy. The stillness of the caravan, the slight breeze tousling her hair, and the sounds of trees and grass reaching for the dawn seeped into her soul, offering comfort.

Life surrounded her. She didn't know if her dragon had survived, but she felt a whisper of hope and love. Not in her head. It wasn't an external emotion she sensed. It was in her heart.

She clung to the feeling. And for a moment, she felt as if her grandfather sat beside her, brushing his hand through her hair. "It will be all right, my fierce Becca."

Warmth spread through her fingertips and mist rose, swirling to form a shape. A dragon stretched across the river, its wings touching the trees.

Her ache over losing her tiny dragon eased.

Grandfa would've loved meeting Gregor and Seri. He'd believed when no one else had. When the world told him he was crazy. His stories had made her long for something inside herself. For courage. For adventure.

The misty dragon dissipated. Grandfa believed. Seri would save her tiny dragon, and they would be together again.

Becca was ready when Gregor landed next to the abandoned mine tunnel. She'd seen the dragon long before Trey, and Gregor's thoughts had filled her mind. Excited about finding eggs and bringing them home, he also yearned for acceptance, which she didn't understand.

"Excellent." Gregor's pleasure with their harness and carrying sacks made Becca glow with pride.

She stood back while Trey put on the harness and strapped their supplies to the sturdy clasps.

"Can I touch you?" She felt permission was needed. He wasn't a horse.

His chuckle vibrated in her head. *"Of course. And I know you think more of me than as a beast of burden."*

Becca sucked in a breath. She wasn't used to this level of mental connection.

"Don't worry, girl. Most humans are not as coherent as you. Your thoughts are clear. Focus on what you want me to hear, and keep the

rest in another part of your mind. "Gregor's voice was gentle, as if he understood her need for privacy.

It took effort, but adjusting her mental shield to protect her thoughts seemed the best option. She imagined a stage in front of the wall, where she could speak.

"There. You did it. That was quick." His surprise transmitted easily through her shields. Even though she couldn't sense Trey's emotions, she'd obviously need a stronger shield to block a dragon. But right now, this helped. Gregor couldn't injure them if she knew what he felt.

She laid her hand on Gregor's forehead. His eyes whirled, and she fell into their depths. Worlds and dreams resided in his gaze. She blinked, and the sensation faded.

His skin was supple and warmer than she'd expected. It looked like it would be rough but felt more like well-worn leather. Ridges and bumps covered his forehead in lines stretching from his nostrils to his horns. His eyes were larger than her fists. Intelligence shone from them. How could anyone consider this magnificent creature a beast?

Loneliness. Wariness.

"Thank you." She lifted her hand, shaken. His feelings were much deeper and richer than human emotions, and she felt as if they'd changed her.

Trey helped her onto Gregor's back, and they settled on his shoulders above his wings so he could fly unimpeded.

"Lean forward, into my neck." Gregor's warning didn't make sense, but Becca clutched the straps around his neck, and Trey leaned into her.

The powerful leap threw them both backward, but Gregor leveled out between one breath and the next, forcing them forward. If they'd sat upright, they would've knocked each other senseless. Riding a dragon was not at all like riding a horse.

Trey's warmth against her back was more intimate than she'd expected. Becca shifted to put more space between them, but Trey looped his arms around her midriff.

"Look." His breath in her ear sent shivers down her neck. They'd kissed, and even hugged, but this was different, and she felt tiny and helpless. If it had been anyone other than Trey, she would've been terrified. Instead, her body tingled.

She shifted her gaze from the comfort of Gregor's neck. Not ready to look down, despite the wind whipping her hair, she gazed past Gregor's head to an unimaginable world.

The sky curved over the land, a dome protecting it from the stars. Ragged mountains broke through the valley floor, reaching for the sky. Tiny turquoise lakes nestled in between unending, snow-covered peaks. Trees attempted to climb the rock peaks, but failed, tumbling down the slope, though a few hardy plants huddled here and there.

Gregor dove through the clouds, flying faster than she'd thought possible. Tears streamed from her eyes as the wind bit her cheeks and her hair whipped everywhere. She pulled a scarf over her mouth to protect her face.

"It's incredible." Wind snatched the words away.

But Trey squeezed her waist and spoke in her ear. "Don't talk. Just look." His warm breath on her neck was a stark contrast to the icy bite of the air.

"Do you feel safe, little one?" Gregor's voice was clear, his concern for her settling in her mind.

"Yes. We're good." She wondered if he'd asked Trey as well. Could a dragon talk to more than one person at a time?

Gregor's mirth shook his shoulders under her legs. *"We have two minds for talking. One public so all can hear, and one private. It's the same as when you converse in a crowd or only to Trey."*

Worried she was distracting him, she tried to stop from thinking of questions.

"Don't worry. You can walk and talk at the same time. I can fly and talk. It's no different."

There was so much she didn't know. Trey tapped her shoulder, drawing her attention to a herd of deer grazing below, and the view mesmerized her for the rest of the journey.

As they approached Chartsend, Gregor slowed, hiding within clouds.

"If you stay along the mountain, we can reach the cave without anyone in the village seeing us." She couldn't risk discovery either. Between Mama's control, Nathan's lust, and the villagers' fears, there would be no warm welcome. Even encountering Marcus would jeopardize their mission.

Gregor skimmed the trees as he descended, still far from the cave. He grunted and twisted, diving between the treetops.

Trey's grip on her waist tightened, his fear washing through her shields.

"Hold on." At Gregor's warning, she leaned against his neck, clutching the straps with all her strength.

He angled his wings at the last minute, so he landed on his feet with his head up high. Then Gregor crouched, and Trey jumped off. She followed, her legs trembling, unused to gripping anything as broad as a dragon's shoulders.

"I'm smaller than the other dragons, but I don't know if I can make it to your cave." Worry spun through his words. For the eggs. For them.

"The cave isn't far. Stay here. We'll get the eggs and return."

Trey grunted. "You two seem to have a lot to talk about."

His jealousy was clear, even with her shields in place.

"Sorry. I'm just reassuring Gregor that I'll stay in contact while we retrieve the eggs."

He turned away to remove the satchels, and it hit her. It wasn't just that she could communicate without the splitting headaches he experienced.

"Gregor's still your friend, Trey."

"I know. Here, take these. I'll carry the rest." He handed her three of the bags and strode away.

If he didn't believe her, there wasn't anything she could do. Gregor's feelings for Trey were strong, based on a genuine friendship. With a shrug, she dove into the shrubs to the right of his trajectory.

"This way to the cave." If he wanted to sulk, she'd leave him to it, but he had to listen to her to complete their task.

After an hour of climbing over logs and skirting huge rocks, they reached the cave. It seemed forever since she'd been there, yet it had only been three weeks. She'd changed so much. From a girl running from a life of misery with Nathan to a girl who rode a dragon to rescue eggs.

Fortunately, the cave looked exactly the same.

"Stay here. I'll get the eggs." She could sense their energy clearly, unlike the faint flutters from the past.

After wedging herself through the narrow opening, she strode to the pool. They were safely inside, rolling around in the depression, sparkling despite the lack of sunlight. So many colors. She wondered if they indicated the color of the hatchling inside. Seri and Gregor were shades of green, but in Grandfa's stories, Zanthor had been gray and Sarcruze a deep mahogany.

She tried to remember the dragons from the stories as she collected the eggs. This one was red, like the elegant Renalia. And that one was blue like lazy Ronin. It was unlikely any of the dragons in the stories still existed. Although, she vaguely recalled a story with a dragon named Seri. She wished she had her dragon book, but it was in the dresser at home, and she was never going back there.

The eggs were large and heavy. She carried two to Trey and went back for more until they had eight and the pool was empty. She couldn't remember how many there'd been, but some may have escaped into the underground waterway leading to the waterfall. They only had ten bags, so they'd have to come back to check.

Her heart fluttered like a drakeling's wings. As long as there were eggs to be found, she'd get to ride Gregor and spend time with Trey. She was on an adventure as exciting as Grandfa's stories.

COLLABORATION
GREGOR

Day 46 After the Long Sleep

Gregor flew over the river where Becca had seen eggs, now called Jade River. The humans had renamed the roads and landmarks along Pilgrim's Trail. From above, the river resembled the tail of a dragon with the Dragon Mountain Range forming the rest of the dragon, so it used to be called Dragon's Tail.

Humans worshipped Healers instead of the gods they prayed to during the Great Wars. At one point, dragons had filled that role. So much had changed for humans because of the plague, the war, and losing magic. The girl didn't know what it was like before, but she patiently described how things were now as they flew.

He swooped over the remains of a large camp, the stink from the firepit and human waste still pungent. Dragon excrement never smelled this bad, probably because they ate what nature provided instead of combining food to make a goopy mess.

"That's where I saw the eggs." Becca spoke so Trey could hear.

Gregor kept his thoughts private, annoyed at the boy's jealousy. He'd made his feelings clear. There was no reason for Trey to doubt them. It was insulting.

Trey had left all the communicating to Becca, even though Gregor had apologized for dropping him. It didn't seem to matter. Trey's thoughts churned as he focused on a memory that didn't make sense—something to do with his parents, loss, and Elizabeth as a younger version who smiled. Gregor couldn't figure out what any of it had to do with him.

So, he focused on the girl. He still got whiffs of nutmeg, as if his power was trying to tell him there was more to discover. But nothing could be more important than finding their eggs. A vision would help, but he couldn't invoke one.

"Gregor, can you fly closer and down the river?" Becca projected an image of him skimming the water.

"Not that low. I'd need space to adjust my flight. Flowing water has its own dynamics dependent on the depth and speed of the current, and it affects the wind." He probably should've just said yes. But he wanted to explain things to her. Becca's mind was so curious, and her ability to hear him bordered on draconic.

"As low as is safe is fine. I sensed the eggs before I saw them, but I was standing next to the river. I'm not sure how close I need to be." An image of energy rippling from a pool of eggs accompanied her explanation. She even thought like a dragon.

He dropped to the lowest current over the river. It was tricky, but most dragons mastered the technique before they could fly above the clouds. Daring hatchlings to perform the impossible was a rite of passage in a coven. Though Gregor had no hatchling mates, there'd been younglings who'd egged him on, probably earlier than they should have. He'd suffered many injuries in his youth.

He tilted his right wing and caught the vector five feet above the water. With a subtle turn, he followed the curves of the river winding through the forest. At least it was wide enough to accommodate his wingspan. Ronin wouldn't fit.

"Will this do?" He could go lower, but it wouldn't be safe. They didn't have the experience of dragon riders, and he'd never carried anyone else.

Becca replied with a mental shrug, and Gregor snorted. She wasn't like any of the soldiers he'd met in his time before the Long Sleep. Even Jason hadn't mastered the intricacies of transmitting physical gestures. Who was this girl?

Then he felt it. Becca's mind opened and her body shifted. She was doing something—maybe magic? He wished Seri were with them.

He couldn't help himself. Even though it was rude, he peeked into her mind. The river glowed, exposing the fish and tiny life-forms on the bottom.

She sensed energy. Gregor concentrated, trying to determine if she could sense the same things he could. His focus went to the wolf's den and the rabbits hiding in the bush as they passed.

Her focus was different, but the energy was the same. This girl had more than one dragon sense. Could magic change a human this much?

"There. In that eddy ahead on the left, where the river bends to the right."

He looked, but there were no bends in the river, not until much farther along where the river took a sharp turn around a hill. That couldn't be it. No human could see that far.

But her image in his head confirmed it. Gregor was losing track of all the differences. Trey was like all the other humans he'd known, but Becca was amazing. Unfortunately, the coven, especially Sarcruze, wouldn't agree. They'd be terrified. A human with enhanced senses would terrify them.

Gregor withdrew his mind from hers as he landed next to the river bend. He'd already imposed far longer than was decent, and he didn't want her to sense his fear.

Becca's excitement indicated she'd found eggs.

They spent the rest of the day searching the river. Becca found eighteen eggs in total. Since it was getting late, he left them to camp while he transported the eggs to Sanctuary.

It took three long trips, and he had no time to chat in between dropping them off and returning for the next batch. But finally, he could rest.

"Thirty eggs! You did well." Zanthor's excitement filled Gregor with pride.

He'd done it, found the eggs and shown his interpretation of his power had been right. But he had to tell Zanthor about Becca's unusual abilities. He'd learned his lesson. If the coven were to survive, they needed to have every piece of information they could. But he hoped the fact she could find eggs would counter any fear.

Zanthor was quick to pick up on the other dragon's emotional state. *"What is it? Has something happened?"*

Gregor looked around. The other dragons were too close. *"Privately."* If he could convince Zanthor, then he could use his power to convince the rest.

They flew away from Jason's Keep to a bare rock jutting from the mountainside.

"The girl, Becca, she has special abilities."

"Of course. She can see through the illusion protecting our eggs."

"It's more than that. She can communicate as easily as a dragon, not just words, but emotions and physical gestures."

Zanthor's eyes whirled. *"It's rare, but some humans are more receptive to our minds. They make excellent riders."*

Gregor had never heard of this. Maybe she wasn't a threat. *"She can see far, almost as far as I can. I'm certain she can hear better than any humans too."*

"Hmm. That is unusual."

"And ... she can sense energy like us."

"That's impossible." Zanthor's eyes whirled a warning. Humans could never be allowed to develop abilities that would threaten dragon superiority.

"She thinks she has magical powers. But from the way she segments her mind to protect herself, it feels more like a dragon ability. She claims Healers use energy to identify injuries."

"Strange. Healers didn't sense energy before. At least, not the same way we do."

Gregor couldn't help it. Zanthor wasn't getting it. *"Her powers started the same day we left the Source. I think she has dragon senses."*

Zanthor laughed. *"We can't breed with humans. They grow their hatchlings inside their bodies while we lay eggs. The physiology is different and frankly impossible for procreation. The very act would destroy a human. And I can't see any female dragon allowing a human to try. Don't be ridiculous."*

Gregor sagged with relief. She couldn't be part dragon. So many strange things were happening in this world. He'd worried others would jump to the same conclusion, and he didn't know what they'd do.

"But her abilities are extraordinary. Seri should have a look at the girl. It would benefit us to know how the Source has affected humans."

Zanthor released Gregor from the burden. *"Continue gathering our eggs. Her ability in that respect is useful. I'll send someone to help with transportation, so you can focus on finding them."*

Gregor trusted Zanthor's knowledge of humans and magic, but he still felt that Becca had actual dragon senses. Her abilities were too draconic to believe they were simply magic.

BECCA'S QUEST
GREGOR

DAY 47 AFTER THE LONG SLEEP

The next day, Ronin joined them in the search. It would be better for him to carry the humans since he was bigger and stronger. But Gregor found himself reluctant to suggest the change. He'd grown attached to their weight on his shoulders. Besides, the harness wouldn't fit Ronin.

Becca communicated as effortlessly with Ronin as she did with Gregor. *"Are you bigger because you're a different species from Gregor?"*

Ronin had more experience with humans and had even bonded with a rider. He answered her questions with patience. *"I'm larger because I'm older. Gregor is the youngest in our coven. Once these eggs hatch, he'll lose that honor."* His chuckle teased Gregor.

Gregor ignored him, swooping lower so Becca could feel the tug of an egg or see a flash of color. She'd explained how it worked, but he couldn't feel it.

They worked together. Becca located an egg, then Ronin collected it and flew to Trey, who put the egg in one of their leather baskets.

The rocks were getting bigger, which meant they were closer to hatching. It made sense. They'd traveled the farthest and would've endured the most erosion.

While Ronin took the eggs to Sanctuary, Gregor settled beside the humans as they ate their lunch. They chatted about humans and Valley Keep.

Suddenly, Becca gasped, whipping her head around to stare at the horizon. "Something's wrong. We have to go."

Trey stood and gathered their human lunch, following her without question.

Gregor didn't sense danger. No one lurked nearby.

"What do you sense?" He was curious about how her powers worked.

"Urgency and fear. And a tugging sensation. It's far. Farther than I thought my power could reach. But this feels as if many tiny dragons are calling me all at once. They must be in danger."

Interesting. She sensed the hatchlings inside the shell. No dragon could do that. He inhaled deeply, certain his power would flare if they were in danger. But there was nothing, only the faint odor of salt from the ocean ahead.

The humans climbed on, and he leapt into the sky. Becca's worry pushed him to fly swiftly, straight for the coastline.

"Stop. Land over there." Panic clouded her thoughts, and he wondered if her power frightened her.

As soon as he landed, she ran to the spot where the river diverted underground. She frantically tore at the grass and dirt around the opening.

"You can't dig through rock. And that's all you'll find."

Her distress triggered a tingling response on the tip of his tongue.

"We have to. They're in danger. So many eggs."

He really couldn't sense anything.

"Help her." Trey might not know what concerned Becca, but his demand had a push to it.

Gregor hadn't sensed magic from the boy before, but that push had felt like manipulation. It didn't matter. He'd worry about Trey's sudden ability later.

Her mind was focused, and he couldn't break through.

The eggs must be in the subterranean river. He flew along the ridge and dipped over the cliff, searching for the exit. Halfway down, the water cascaded to the ocean below, clear of debris.

The eggs were trapped inside the bluff.

When he returned, Becca was in the river, attempting to widen the sinkhole.

"No, Becks, you can't. You don't know how far it goes, or if you'll be able to breathe." Trey grabbed her arm, energy rippling from him. The boy definitely had powers.

"I have to." She didn't seem affected by his manipulation, although anger at the boy distracted her for a moment.

Ronin caught up to them, his flight back and forth to Sanctuary much faster than Gregor's would've been. He tilted his head at the two humans. *"What's going on?"*

"She's found eggs, but they're deep in the bluff. She's convinced they're in danger." Gregor kept it brief. He didn't know how to help, and her emotional state agitated him.

"Do you smell anything with your danger sniffer?" Ronin and his jokes.

Gregor shook his head.

"I'll check it out." Ronin walked the length of the bluff from the river to the overlook.

Meanwhile, Becca removed her outer clothing. Her intention to dive into the rushing current shocked Gregor. Trey was right. She wasn't rational.

Ronin returned. *"There's a cavern under the bedrock. The current is too strong where it flows out, so she can't access it that way."* He dipped his head at Becca. *"She's right. The only way is through the opening here. But ..."*

Gregor could see the problem. He had to free her from the magic compulsion. *"Becca, even if you swim to them, and the cavern isn't filled with water, you can't get the eggs out. We'll have to wait until they come out by themselves. They're fine where they are. If the eggs hatch, the hatchlings will stay near the water. Now that we know they're here, we'll watch for them."*

She continued digging, her thoughts frantic and focused on reaching the eggs. Her power had control. He'd have to pick her up and take her away. There was no other choice.

Then his nostrils filled with the acrid scent of smoke. Gregor lifted his head, attempting to discern the source, and the ground jolted beneath him, tumbling him like a rock.

Earthquake.

Gregor steadied himself with his wings. There'd been hundreds of earthquakes during the wars, but he hadn't felt one since they woke. He hadn't realized the vibrations were missing until that moment.

"It's merely an earthquake. No need to be afraid." Humans panicked when unbalanced. That's why sorcerers used quakes as a weapon during the wars.

But Becca wasn't panicking. She was excited. She jumped and ran past him. A crack had opened in the bedrock, the bluff tilting precariously over the ocean.

"Wait, youngling. It isn't safe." Ronin's warning did nothing to stop her from kneeling beside the crack.

The ground shook again, a longer shock, and trees tumbled across the river.

The crack widened as the bluff tilted more. Her desperation increased. Gregor had only a brief flash of warning from her before she jumped into the crevice.

He lunged and grabbed her with his talons. They ripped through her soft flesh as he snatched her up. Her pain shot through him, flooding him with regret, but he had no choice. She would've died. Trey's anger washed over him as he carefully laid Becca next to the river.

The bluff shifted, tilting skyward, and exposed the cavern beneath. Water rushed into the void, unable to escape. Another tremor shook the ground, loosening it even more. One more shake and it would slide into the ocean.

Becca's anguished cry drove an arrow into his heart. The scent of smoke filled his nostrils, stinging his eyes. Before he could clear his head, she dove into the muddy water.

Great Torin. She was as much enthralled by her abilities as Gregor. He sneezed to clear his nose. His power had already warned him of the quake. Now it was interfering with his ability to react. The scent skulked away, still present, as if warning him this wasn't over.

"Torin save us from impulsive younglings." Ronin impatiently shoved his head into the crevice, done with Becca's foolishness.

Images from Becca's mind bombarded Gregor. Eggs embedded in the cavern walls, sparkling even in the murky water. He understood her concern. There were a lot of eggs. But humans couldn't breathe underwater like dragons. Ronin had to pull her out.

"I'm trying. I don't want to rip her flesh like you did." He dunked his head and torso underwater, keeping his legs above ground.

Shame washed over Gregor. He knew humans were delicate. He'd been too hasty. Ronin was keeping his wits. He wouldn't kill their only hope of finding eggs.

"Get her out! Becca, come back!" Trey ran to the opening.

As if he could reach her with his puny arms.

Ronin yanked his head up, four rocks in his talons. *"Stop worrying. She found an air pocket and is grabbing as many eggs as she can. I can't reach her. She's shielded her mind from me."*

But she'd sent Gregor the images. *"Becca?"* He could see what she saw and feel her desperation, but she didn't respond to his call.

She sucked in a breath from a tiny air pocket and lowered herself to the next shimmering egg. Using her soft human hands, she dug at the wall until the egg was free. Then she popped back for another breath, placing the rock in Ronin's waiting talons.

After four eggs, her air pocket disappeared, and she swam up. She held up the egg, mud and water streaming off her face.

"Take it," she gasped.

"Stop it, Becca. You can't save them all." Energy rippled from Trey, stronger than before.

Unease tightened Gregor's shoulders. Trey's power was strong.

Becca erected a mental shield worthy of a dragon and dove back into the cavern.

So Trey changed his tactics. "Do something. She'll die rescuing your eggs." His anger amplified his power. But manipulators couldn't affect dragons. He was wasting his energy.

"I'll deal with him." Ronin's exasperation urged Gregor to put an end to this unnecessary risk. *"You're small enough to get her."*

Gregor dove after her, ashamed he hadn't thought of it. The cavern was exactly as Becca had projected, minus the sparkling eggs. This time, he tried to grab her gently around her torso. He'd already ripped her arms, and blood flowed from the cuts. She seemed unaware of her pain as she worked at freeing a large rock.

She shouldn't be able to hold her breath for so long. Yet another dragon sense.

He twisted his talons at an awkward angle so their sharp edges wouldn't do more damage.

As soon as the rock broke free, he yanked her back. Amazingly, she clung to the rock.

He felt her pain as her head hit the cavern, and then her mind disappeared.

Fear traveled through every cell in Gregor's body as he burst through the surface.

Smoke, more pungent than before, made him clutch her to his chest and fly up, away from danger.

The ground tilted below him. Slowly, it slid down and crashed into the rocks below, destroying any eggs still embedded in the bedrock.

Fortunately, Ronin grabbed Trey in time.

Gregor carefully lowered Becca to the ground. She didn't move. Blood dribbled from the cuts on her arms and pooled on her belly. Despite his caution, he'd punctured her stomach.

Dread made him want to weep. Soldiers perished from such wounds.

"No. Don't despair. Her heart beats, and she's breathing." Ronin's tone was soft, as if he didn't want any harshness to injure the girl more. *"But she's hurt badly and unconscious. I don't know if their Healers can save her in time."*

Trey said nothing. He examined Becca, manipulator energy pouring from him in waves.

Heal. Live.

If magic could save her, he was using everything he had.

Trey collapsed, his own expenditure of power stealing energy from his life force. Now they had two unconscious humans.

Spring. The scent that had revealed Sanctuary. Gregor inhaled deeply, recalling how his wing had healed immediately.

Sanctuary could heal Becca.

He gathered the girl in his arms, careful to hold her with the tough pads under his talons. Sanctuary was not for humans, but she would die otherwise. Because of his mistakes.

"Go. I'll follow. It's in Torin's talons now." Ronin gathered the eggs and the unconscious boy. His support filled Gregor with determination.

Gregor shot into the clouds, cuddling Becca against his chest and hoping his warmth would protect her from the icy winds as he flew north.

He'd finally found his nutmeg girl, but he'd forgotten how fragile humans were. If she died, they wouldn't find any more eggs, and the hatchlings would face the hostile world alone. If she died, the dragons would lose a part of themselves.

This girl was more than human. In his short time with her, Gregor felt the connection deep inside his soul. He had to save her.

RISK
SERI

Day 47 After the Long Sleep

The eggs were different sizes, confusing Seri. The largest should hatch in six days. A typical incubation period was forty-five days, sometimes longer, but never shorter. Even Renalia, with all her years of experience, wasn't sure the eggs would hatch according to the past schedule. The magic expended during the Great Wars had given hatchlings powers. It was possible it had changed incubation times too.

The two eggs the human girl had transported were the smallest. Despite recovering in the healing waters, Renalia wasn't certain they'd even hatch. Gregor's first batch of ten had been bigger, but still not the size they should be. The eggs retrieved from Jade River were larger, but varied as well, even though they'd eroded within the same waterways.

As far as Seri could tell, these were all from Garianna's clutch. They still hadn't searched the waterways in the coastal mountains where Hazley had laid her eggs.

"Seri. I need you." Gregor's desperation slipped into her mind, a distant call for help.

She sent a wave of support, unsure if it would reach him. His mind disappeared from hers as he concentrated on his flight.

Whatever it was, they'd deal with it.

As he flew closer, he ignored her requests for more information. He was blocking her, but guilt poured through.

Over the next hour, Seri and Brin gathered splints and healing plants, preparing for whatever injury he'd endured.

Gregor landed awkwardly and lowered a human to the ground. Tears streamed from his eyes. *"I flew as fast as I could, but it might be too late. Her life force is barely there."*

The girl's tunic was shredded and soaked in blood. Deep welts cut into her arms and blood oozed from her belly.

What had Gregor done? He'd been lucky when Trey survived. How could he put the coven at risk again?

Brin hummed, activating her power of echolocation. *"Two broken ribs. The puncture in her stomach is deep and may have ruptured a vital organ. We can clean the debris from her cuts and staunch the blood, and hope Sanctuary takes care of the rest. But her head feels wrong. Did she run out of oxygen or hit it?"*

"Both. She insisted on diving into the water to save the eggs, and there was an earthquake. I tried to save her, but my talons were too sharp." Gregor's anguish mollified Seri. He hadn't meant to kill the girl.

Brin sighed. *"You were right to bring her here. Let's get her in the hot spring and clean her wounds. Humans have tougher brains than you'd think. All we can do is give her time."*

Seri cradled the girl in the water as Brin cleaned her wounds. Dragons could be gentle when needed. Gregor must've panicked to have caused this much damage. Human hides were incredibly fragile.

It was one reason dragons had refused to fight in the wars. Killing a human took a single swipe. Fighting over human settlements made little sense, not when the world belonged to dragons. But some dragons wanted to help their riders protect their families. Those dragons flew archers over the war zone. But none would physically attack a human. It was something her coven had debated her entire life.

Threads of magic swirled around the girl, sinking into her chest and head. Her breathing deepened as she fell into a healing sleep, her life force pulsing now.

Seri sighed with relief and moved the girl to a sleeping alcove. They would line it with soft branches and heather to make it more comfortable, but the warmth of the rock would take the last of the chill from her body.

"Will she live?" Gregor's voice was soft in her head, his attachment to the girl clear.

"Yes. Magic will help. Sanctuary wants to heal this girl of yours."

Seri clutched his talons to her chest. *"I know why you did it. Human healers couldn't save her. But this will get you banished."* She leaned her forehead against his. *"You're pushing too hard. Retrieving the eggs with the help of a human is bad enough. Zanthor hasn't even told the others. Once the eggs hatch, the coven won't care how you found them. But you risk our safety by bringing her here. You risk everything."*

"I know. But we can't lose her. She's too important. I don't know how. And she'd never harm a hatchling. She has dragon senses."

His passion for this outrageous idea made her want to weep. His impulsiveness would get them all killed.

For once, her shields held, and Gregor continued, unaware of her fears. *"Zanthor doesn't believe me, but she shouldn't have been able to hold her breath underwater and save those eggs if she didn't have some ability. She's more than human. I can feel it."*

"Oh, Gregor." Her heart ached for him. He really believed in this girl.

This bond was deeper than his friendship with Trey. Was he destined to attach to every human he met? His willingness to see humans as worthy as dragons was something she admired, even though she didn't share it.

But their survival depended on hiding from humans. For now.

She didn't know how to help him, but she could solve the mystery of the girl's abilities. At least, enough to convince Gregor she was merely a human. Then his fascination would pass. They needed her to find the eggs encased in a rocky illusion, but that was it.

Magic clung to the girl, as if drawn to her energy. She might be a sorcerer, or at least have the abilities and not yet know it. But if she was, Seri would ensure the girl couldn't harm the coven.

She ground her teeth together, fighting an ancient instinct to eliminate a threat. But that wasn't the dragon way. They weren't violent beasts. Dragons had existed longer than any other thinking creature. Intelligence was key.

Once Becca recovered Garianna's and Hazley's eggs, they wouldn't need the troublesome girl anymore.

CHALLENGE

BECCA

Becca was colder than she thought possible, and then she was blissfully warm, enfolded in bubbling water. All she wanted to do was sleep.

Dragon speech spun through her head. Gregor's love. And guilt. Seri's admonishment. And another dragon. Brin. She was lovely, a mind of soothing mint and gentle humming. Becca drifted in and out of consciousness, vaguely aware something had gone wrong.

She'd been so focused on saving the eggs. Fear had driven her to find them long before the earthquake had ripped the ground apart. But no matter how hard she tried, she hadn't been able to save them all. Their final cries had pierced her soul, echoing her failure.

She'd been too weak, too slow, and now the tiny dragons were gone. Grandfa would hate her for what she'd done. So much for becoming a hero. Helpless sobs poured from her heart. She'd thought her ability to see eggs made her special, connected to the dragons. But she'd been wrong. They would hate her now.

She was the destroyer of baby dragons.

"Shh. The earthquake destroyed them. You saved enough." The rumble of Gregor's voice offered comfort, strength. *"Sleep and heal."*

She gave in to the lassitude seeping through her body.

It felt like only minutes later when she woke to pain. A pitiful cry filled her skull. A tiny dragon in agony. She whimpered as the hatchling's pain wracked her head and shoulder.

"These are the last of the eggs. The rest of the clutch was destroyed." Ronin's voice stabbed her mind.

"Quietly. The girl has regained consciousness and is incapable of keeping our mind-speech out of her head." Brin sent another wave of soothing mint, easing Becca's pain to a dull throb.

It was difficult to concentrate. She must've hit her head when Gregor pulled her from the cavern. Strips of cloth bandaged her arms, and black leaves wrapped around her stomach. She rubbed her hand over her skull but couldn't find a bump to explain her disorientation.

Gregor had taken her somewhere special. She could sense the life around her and everything was green, like spring.

Flickers of confusion, mixed with fear and pain, forced her upright. She had to find the source. But she couldn't go anywhere. She was in a shallow cave.

"You need rest." Gregor cautioned her with an image of the cliff above and below her.

Ronin cradled the large egg Becca had pried from the cavern wall.

"There's nothing to be done. The egg is crushed. It will hatch, or it won't." Seri's voice was soft, but pragmatic.

Becca couldn't believe their callousness. *"The tiny dragon is in pain. I can feel it."*

"Ridiculous. It's just an egg. Until hatching, there's nothing to sense." Seri's scorn made Becca's mind reel. She was certain the dragons had been desperate to find the eggs.

"I told you she was special. She senses the hatchling forming inside the egg. That's how she found this last batch before they were all destroyed." Gregor's pride didn't make sense, either, not when Seri's denial slammed through Becca's head.

"It's easy enough to check." Brin held the egg and hummed, causing Becca's entire body to tingle. *"She's right. A cracked skull and a broken wing. The hatchling won't survive."*

Becca swayed, more tired than before. Without Gregor's support, she'd fall over. But she had to do something. These dragons had already decided the tiny dragon's fate. *"She doesn't have to die. Break the shell and tend her injuries."*

Dragon shock rolled through her.

"Why would we do that, youngling?" Ronin tilted his head and turned the egg over.

"Sometimes, human babies need help, and a Healer takes it from the mother's womb early to save it." She felt their disgust at the human method of having babies. Animals grew their young inside their bellies. Not dragons.

"I know it's different. But the point is not how we have babies. It's that we can save some by speeding up their entry into the world."

Seri lowered her head, catching Becca's gaze. *"We don't do that."*

"But can't you try? Just this once?"

But they wouldn't. She felt their resistance. It didn't make sense to them. She clenched her fists. This egg was one among hundreds, and they expected most to die.

She'd risked her life for something they didn't even care about. Saving eggs wouldn't make the dragons accept her. All her efforts, her sacrifice, had been in vain. Just like with Mama. Becca couldn't make anyone love her. She was a tool, nothing more.

"Take the girl back to the village. She's no longer in danger of dying." A shiver ran between Becca's shoulders at Seri's tone. The turquoise dragon didn't want her around Gregor at all.

"Not yet." Guilt colored Gregor's words. *"Sanctuary will heal her wounds completely. We can't risk the villagers thinking a dragon attacked her."*

Becca wouldn't let that happen. But she couldn't guarantee that Trey would agree.

"You're making another mistake." There was a world of meaning behind Seri's words, but Gregor didn't back down.

"At least put her to sleep so she can heal faster. The sooner she leaves, the better for all of us." Seri's intent was crystal clear. Becca would never see the dragons again.

"I'll take care of her." Gregor's response eased her fears. They still needed help finding the eggs. Becca sighed. He valued her, but something else drove him—guilt at injuring her.

She couldn't let him blame himself. *"You were only trying to save me."*

"Sleep, youngling." A whiff of mint and the sensation of being cradled tumbled Becca into oblivion.

W hen she woke the next morning, her body tingled with energy. Her ribs ached and her arms itched, but her head was clear. She inhaled deeply, sensing the world around her before she opened her eyes. She was alone.

Becca sat up and discovered her shirt was missing. Long black leaves covered her modesty, but she was exposing more skin than a lady should. Mama would've been scandalized.

"Take it easy. You'll be as wobbly as a hatchling. Your body had a lot of healing to do." Brin's voice reminded her of warm summer days.

Becca was ready to explore this place the dragons called Sanctuary, but the ledge was higher than she remembered.

A gray dragon flew down to Becca, her eyes whirling blue and silver. Brin. The healer dragon who'd tended her injuries and hummed soothing mint.

"I'm not a healer." Brin's laughter sent bubbles of joy to Becca's limbs, making her feel like she could do anything.

Becca dangled her legs off the ledge, preparing to drop to the ground below.

"Great Torin. Don't do that, youngling." Brin gently scooped Becca between her claws as if she were a helpless puppy.

Becca held very still, remembering the agony as Gregor's claws had ripped through her skin. She'd been too consumed with saving the eggs to react. Now her heart pounded, attempting to leave her chest. There was no way to protect herself from a dragon's strength.

But Brin was careful. Once Becca was on the ground, she followed the dragon over a bridge composed of overlapping chunks of slate. A river flowed under and formed a circle around the lush green land. Three magnificent waterfalls filled the air with their roar as water cascaded over the towering rock walls surrounding the entire space.

"It's a caldera. After a volcano has shaped the land and settled into sleep, this is what's left. Though Sanctuary is a bit more."

That was an understatement. Steam from multiple hot springs rose through the air. Spring was everywhere. Deep green grass, vibrant flowers, pale saplings, and towering trees covered in brilliant leaves. Becca didn't know how long it had taken Gregor to fly there, but she remembered the freezing cold. This place shouldn't exist.

At the center stood a magnificent tree, as tall as a three-story building. The trunk was as big as her home, and moss-covered roots formed ridges and valleys as wide as the branches. The same long narrow leaves that covered her body fluttered in the warm breeze. Becca reached out to touch one leaf and stopped, stunned.

It was a Nightwood. Black as night. The tree of death.

She gasped, making the sign of the Healer for protection. And then realized the leaves were touching her skin. She tore at them, desperate to free herself from certain death.

"Stop, youngling. The Nightwood is life. Your Healers used these leaves as masks during the plague. Nightwood bark formed the basis for healing teas. The leaves won't kill you."

Becca stilled as heat flew to her face. Her heart still beat too fast, but Brin's amusement was enough to make her ashamed of her panic. She wasn't dying. The cuts under the leaves on her arms had healed.

In every story, the Nightwood was a death tree. None existed anymore. The first Becca had seen of its black wood had been the Prophet's terrifying door and chair.

Sanctuary was filled with life. She could sense the energy without having to concentrate. Obviously, the tree wasn't death. She needed to believe her eyes and her heart.

Everything she knew about history was wrong. Dragons existed. And they weren't beasts. They were intelligent creatures, just like in Grandfa's stories. Even the Dragon Plague was wrong. It couldn't affect humans. The past had been twisted into something it wasn't.

Comfort. Love.

The feelings didn't come from Brin, and they were achingly familiar. Joy coursed through Becca's heart, banishing the last of her fear. Her tiny dragon was here and alive.

"My egg. It's here." Becca had to find her.

The tug in her heart was as strong as it had been when she first found the eggs in the cave by her village. She lurched forward and stumbled.

Brin caught her, bending her immense body almost in half to offer her arm for support. *"You're weak. There's no rush. We healed the egg."*

"Let her go, Brin. I want to see what she does." Seri's voice was everywhere.

Becca stumbled over another stone bridge, drawn to one waterfall.

"Here."

So much love and relief, filling the emptiness. Becca didn't have to please the dragons to earn their respect. Her tiny dragon was enough.

She kneeled and plunged her hands into the freezing water, finding her egg with ease. The glowing white orb pulsed in her hands. She was home.

Seri landed beside her. *"Incredible. Magic flows between you and the egg. White and gold and blue. How do you do it?"*

Becca shook her head. *"It's not me. I can only sense emotion. That's my power."*

"Told you." Though he was far away, his feelings were clear. He didn't want to frighten her or hurt her again.

But she wasn't afraid. She should be. Her injuries had been severe, and Trey probably believed she was dead. But Gregor had saved her. If he hadn't pulled her free, she'd be as crushed as the eggs. Trey would realize that Gregor never meant to hurt him either.

"Where's Trey? Is he with his egg?"

Another wave of guilt flew from Gregor. *"Ronin left Trey at the mining cave. Humans aren't permitted here."*

Becca's heart went out to Trey. Gregor had abandoned him again. Even worse, Gregor had taken her to a special place. Trey had already been jealous of her effortless ability to speak with dragons. This would hurt him more.

Her tiny dragon sent a wave of hope, and Seri gasped. *"The hatchling comforts her."*

"Seri. What do you see? Is she using magic?" Gregor thought it was something else.

Becca couldn't imagine what. She couldn't use magic. Her powers were a part of her, like breathing.

Seri tilted her head, her eyes whirling and somehow frightening as they crossed. *"Not exactly. Magic surrounds her. She doesn't manipulate it. As far as I can tell, she doesn't use any magic at all, but it sure likes her."*

"So?" Expectation laced his question, and Becca realized he'd never thought she was using magic. He thought she was part dragon.

She laughed, unable to stop the waves of disbelief rolling off her as much as she couldn't stop the fear that wove into her chest. She was just a girl. Sure, she could sense emotions, and some of her abilities were stronger than before, but nothing like a dragon's.

"Ridiculous. She doesn't have dragon senses. It's magic and nothing more." Seri's tone warned Gregor to stop this dangerous line of inquiry.

Dragon thoughts were too intense, so Becca focused on the tiny dragon inside her egg. *"I missed you."*

"What's she doing?" Seri demanded.

Gregor laughed. *"Talking to the hatchling."*

"Impossible."

"Everything she does is impossible. Is it magic?"

Seri's mind disappeared, and Becca realized she was connected to all the dragons in Sanctuary.

"There's a thread of magic connecting her to the egg. That could be how she sees through the illusion."

Becca felt complete with Seri's thoughts back in her head.

Seri gasped. *"She's connected to every egg and to all of us."*

Seri's horror didn't match Becca's excitement at all.

BETRAYAL

BECCA

Becca laid her body against Gregor's warm neck, trusting he'd get her home before the sun set and she froze to death. The snowcapped mountains formed an endless landscape until they flew over the last peak and Valley Keep stretched below them.

Gregor tilted upright as he spread his wings and lowered his tail to land. She clenched onto the straps with her legs, the only part of her body that seemed to have any strength left. But he was careful and didn't drop her.

"Becca!" Marie's excited cry forced Becca's eyes fully open. But only for a moment. She could do nothing as they slowly closed again.

Strong hands pulled her from the riding straps, and then she was enfolded in the most delicious warmth. A blanket wrapped around her shoulders, and she sighed, nuzzling into Trey's chest. He smelled of hay and horse, but it was him. His heart beat erratically under her ear. So warm.

Becca wrapped her arms around Trey. She didn't care if he'd been manipulating her. He wasn't like Nathan. He'd never make her do something she didn't want. And right now, he was exactly what she needed. Who she needed. She loved dragons, but she didn't understand them. And Trey was there, waiting for her. Accepting.

"Great Healer, you're freezing, Becca." Anger thrust away the relief he'd been sending. "What did you do to her?"

"Be calm, Trey. We had no clothing for her. She'll be fine once she warms up." Gregor was offended that Trey would think he would harm Becca on purpose. Trey winced.

She giggled. It was funny knowing the intent behind his words, when Trey could only hear them. She knew so much.

She was half naked in Trey's arms. Such strong, capable arms. Those same arms tightened around her, pulling her closer to his heart. She never wanted to leave.

"She's back, Trey." Marie's voice was tight, but Becca was too tired to care. Although it was strange that both of them were there at all. Maybe Marie had a vision.

"What did you do?" Trey's fear fueled his anger.

Becca could sense it all, clearer than before. She frowned at the tension in his body. Trey was going to do something stupid if she didn't calm him down.

"I'm fine. Gregor took me to a safe place and healed me." She was reluctant to go into detail and wasn't ready to tell him about Sanctuary. If Trey realized she was covered in Nightwood leaves, he would panic even more. With a sigh of regret, she pushed herself away and covered herself with the blanket.

"How did you know I was coming back?" Focusing on Marie's vision might help.

"Trey asked us to keep watch after he returned. Shelly and Jane helped. You were gone two days, Becca." Marie kept giving Trey anxious looks, but all Becca sensed from her was concern.

"Then why are you angry at Gregor?" Becca was pretty sure she knew the reason, but did Trey?

He stroked her cheek. "I wasn't sure. Thank the Healer you're alive. Don't you ever do that to me again." The emotions coming from him were complicated. Affection. Fear. Desperation.

But she could put his fear to rest. "I won't. I was foolish to risk my life for dragon eggs." The dragons had made it very clear they only wanted to collect them and not save them.

"You don't understand." Gregor's voice was quiet. *"We need your help. But Trey's right. You should never do that again."*

His sincerity still held a little guilt, but he hadn't forced her to do anything. Her own desire to please had caused the accident. She didn't blame Gregor at all.

"You should go. I'll settle Trey and see you tomorrow. We have more eggs to find."

Trey hugged Becca tightly, reassuring himself she really was there. When he let go, she fell into his gaze. A world of love swirled behind his eyes, and she realized this was part of his power. She'd thought it was her feelings for him.

It didn't matter. Everything she'd ever wanted was in that look. She met his kiss with equal passion, and heat flowed through her veins with every heartbeat.

Everyone disappeared. There was only Trey and their connection.

Tingles flowed over her arms, across her shoulders, and down her back. She'd heard girls giggle about having wobbly legs, but she felt stronger than ever, as if she could do anything, as if she were invincible.

He held her lightly, giving her the chance to stop the kiss if she wanted. But she didn't. And his kiss deepened, sending drakelings to her stomach and speeding up her heart.

Marie's cough reminded Becca they weren't alone. Even Gregor still stood at the cave entrance, observing her.

Heat rushed to her face as she stepped away from Trey's embrace. Their relationship had changed. She could no longer pretend that he meant nothing to her. The look in his eyes made her feel as if she was the most beautiful woman in the world. But it was more. He admired her courage and her beliefs too.

She was home.

"You're safe, now." Trey's words sent flutters through her chest.

"I'll always keep her safe." Becca was surprised to hear Gregor's private promise to Trey as he left. He must've wanted her to hear.

Marie offered Becca a coat, warm from Marie's body heat, then wrapped the blanket around Becca's shoulders.

From now on, Becca would be more careful. There were still hundreds of eggs to find. That was her task. She could leave the rescuing to the dragons. They were more capable. There was no reason to kill herself for them. And, over time, the dragons would come to accept her and let her visit.

Gregor circled over them, then flapped into the night.

His outraged cry filled her mind. Then he fell from the sky.

GREGOR

Day 48 After the Long Sleep

The wind holding Gregor disappeared. He floundered, trying to catch the next air current. But there was nothing to push against. He was in a void.

He roared as he fell, and then his thoughts grew sluggish. Magic. He must warn the coven. He stretched his mind through his connection to Seri.

"Seri, I can't fly. There's no air." It had to be enough. He slammed to the ground, and the last of his breath whooshed out before his vision went black.

He opened his eyes, certain he'd only been unconscious for a short time, and sucked in a huge breath, filling his lungs. He must return to the sky. Back to safety.

Gregor leapt and pumped his wings to gain altitude, but a net blocked his escape. He roared, frustrated he'd allowed himself to be ambushed.

"We're coming," Becca breathlessly reassured him.

He wasn't alone. Becca was on her way, and he felt Seri approaching.

He wouldn't stay trapped for long. But then he realized what must've happened. Trey had betrayed him.

His chest hurt and not from the lack of oxygen. He'd believed in humans. But maybe Seri was right, and he shouldn't trust them. There'd been signs. The other girl had acted oddly, and Trey had been certain Gregor had hurt Becca. The accident had eroded Trey's trust completely. But he'd never imagined the boy would allow Elizabeth to capture him.

He was in a mining pit with grooves cut into the sides of the earth. A net stretched across the opening and humans scurried overhead, their thoughts filled with amazement. But mere ropes couldn't hold a dragon.

Elizabeth had made a mistake. As long as the air didn't disappear again, he could escape. But he was curious about her plans.

"I'm on my way. I thought I lost you. What happened?" Seri sounded closer than she should be.

"Stay away. The humans have captured me." He sent an image of his trap.

"Then why are you still there? Cut through and fly away." Her exasperation hurt. Ever since he brought Becca to Sanctuary, she'd been upset.

She was right. They shouldn't show any weakness, but she hadn't felt the lack of air. He must discover how they'd done it and prevent them from catching anyone else.

"Gregor, leave. We can find out later. Or just ask the boy."

A denial rose to his mind, and he realized he didn't believe Trey had betrayed him after all. Elizabeth was a Manipulator. She could use the boy without him realizing it.

Gregor inhaled deeply, hoping to capture a scent, but his power gave him no sign of what he should do, who he should trust.

He was tired of being afraid. Of the plague. Of banishment. Of humans. He was a dragon and shouldn't fear anything. The coven wanted to avoid humans, and he felt they needed to work with humans. Elizabeth couldn't hurt him, and if he found out what she wanted, they could bargain so he could interact with Becca and Trey more.

So he sat and curled his tail around his feet, waiting for Elizabeth's next move. He was in no danger. He could shred the net with one swipe of his sharp talons.

BECCA

Becca ran behind Trey as he twisted through the tunnels. He knew exactly where to go. Maybe he'd told his grandmother about Gregor. He hadn't known Becca was healing in Sanctuary. From his perspective, Gregor injured her, and then she disappeared. He must've been frantic with worry. After Gregor had abandoned him the first time, Trey had lost his trust. He had no reason to suspect Gregor would return with her.

But she could feel Trey's worry. He didn't know what had happened, and he didn't want Gregor to be hurt. At least Gregor had calmed down. His thoughts reflected curiosity now.

She burst from the last tunnel and ran across the top of a giant mining pit. Gregor's eyes reflected the setting sun as he lifted his head. Elizabeth stood on a platform with her acolytes around her.

Trey ran up to her. "What are you doing? Let him go."

Her smugness sent shivers of unease up Becca's back. "I knew you were sneaking away to meet a dragon. Now he's mine."

"You don't need all this. He isn't dangerous." Trey wasn't listening to his grandmother's words, so focused on freeing Gregor, he missed her tone.

Becca put a hand on Trey's shoulder, trying to stop him enough so he could think straight. Elizabeth had manipulated him, but he didn't know it.

"My dear boy, I'm doing what needs to be done. The world fears the Dragon Plague."

Trey stood still, energy pulsing from him. "What are you talking about? There's no plague."

Elizabeth leaned in, her eyes sparkling at her own wit. "Not yet."

The blood drained from Becca's head and flooded her thundering heart.

"Gregor, get out of there. She's going to make you sick."

Gregor jumped, ripping through the netting as if it were nothing more than leaves. He flew into the clouds and disappeared.

Elizabeth grinned, then turned to Becca. "I knew you were too smart for my boy. He's been a good trainee, but you have the mind of a true Manipulator."

Waves of energy buffeted Becca. Elizabeth's praise was false, a distraction. She wanted Gregor to escape.

"What have you done?" Trey grabbed his grandmother's shoulders and shook her. His anger overrode his sense. Fear for Gregor was making him desperate.

"I've given him the plague."

"Even you can't give someone a plague."

Satisfaction rolled off her. But she didn't influence Trey.

"I can and I did. And I know how much you care about the beast. Fortunately, for you, dear old Uncle Sid has been working on a cure." Her scorn didn't instill Becca with any confidence that the cure would work.

"You, my darling boy, will keep your uncle focused on his task. It will work out. You'll see. I'm doing this for your future."

Becca's hands curled into fists at the deprecating tone in her voice. She'd controlled Trey's life even more than Mama had her own. Helpless rage rolled through Becca.

They had to save Gregor. And if it was the last thing she did, she would pry Trey away from his grandmother's manipulative grasp.

But then Elizabeth's actual words filtered through, and icicles of dread spread to Becca's limbs. She'd already infected Gregor.

"Gregor, come back. You have the plague."

Denial and fear engulfed her, and then she couldn't sense Gregor at all. Not his mind or his energy.

"Becca. I lost contact with Gregor. What happened?" Seri's desperation cut through Becca's shock.

"Seri, you must find him. He has the plague."

The wave of horror from Seri was too much. Becca fell to her knees and covered her head, trying to erect her shields.

Energy pulsed from Trey as he confronted his grandmother. "My future? Infecting a dragon would endanger the entire keep. You'd never do that." His scorn held all the hurt of a child growing up, knowing the well-being of the keep was more important than he was.

Her abrupt laugh mocked him. "You should read our books more carefully. There were two plagues. One affected the people, and one affected the dragons. We recovered while the beasts perished. People tell stories, and gullible fools believe them. But I'll show the world a sick dragon and my healthy followers. I'll be known as the Savior."

"So you intend for Gregor to die?" Helpless anger emanated from him.

"Whether he dies is of no concern to me. But Sid lost his tenure at the university because of his theory about the Dragon Plague. He has a cure. Call your precious dragon back and find out if his theory is right."

Becca ground her teeth together. Elizabeth didn't care. She only needed the dragon back so people could see him. If Sid's cure worked, she would become a Savior. If the dragon died, and her people didn't get sick, she'd still be a Savior.

The acolytes pulled the torn netting from the walls. It didn't matter if Gregor returned. Enough people had seen the dragon. She could state he'd been sick all along.

Sid's experimental cure was Gregor's only chance.

"Gregor. There's a cure. Please tell me where you are?"

But there was only silence. *"Seri, can you find Gregor?"*

Her anguish gave Becca the answer she feared. *"I can't. He's cut me off. To protect the coven. There's nothing we can do."*

"We have a cure. Don't give up on him." Becca's heart hurt for Seri.

"Mere humans can't cure this plague. A powerful sorcerer created it. It'll take magic to cure it. And Gregor might even be immune. But the plague spreads through mind-speech, so he won't respond until he knows he's safe. He won't risk infecting any of us." Her hope was a desperate attempt to ward off the inevitable.

"Don't give up. We'll help him. But if Gregor doesn't return, then Elizabeth has already won. She can infect dragons. Even if the world believes she's the Savior, people will exterminate dragons to prevent the plague from spreading."

Seri flew too far for their conversation to continue, but Becca felt a whisper of determination from her. Seri wouldn't give up on Gregor.

Becca would help Uncle Sid with his cure, and then she'd deal with Elizabeth. The Dragon Prophet was a threat to Trey and to all dragons.

357

SACRIFICE

GREGOR

Becca's fear changed everything.

Ever since Gregor's first coven died from the plague, he'd used his power to help his new coven survive. His power meant survival.

Even though no scent guided him now, he would protect the coven. Without mind-speech, the disease couldn't spread.

He flew through the cloud cover and closed his eyes at what he must do. With his next breath, he broke his connection to the coven, to everyone he knew. The plague would end with him.

Losing Seri's presence was a hole in his soul, but she'd understand. As the Oracle, she knew the coven came first. She would discover how Elizabeth had infected him, and she'd prevent it from spreading.

The mountain cave overlooking Meadow Lake would be his home now. He wasn't the self-sacrificing type. Action was easier. But he could do this.

"Come back. There's a cure." Becca's anguished plea lodged in his throat. She was all heart. She almost died retrieving the eggs, and now she wanted to help him. But there was only so much a human could do, and she'd done enough.

Without his coven in his mind, he didn't want to block her too. Mind-speech couldn't harm her.

Time passed, and Gregor stopped congratulating himself. He didn't want to get sick and die. He inhaled deeply. No scent came to guide him. Maybe his power had left him. What use was it to a plague-stricken dragon?

He breathed out. There were no symptoms. Not yet.

When the plague killed his coven, an overwhelming smell of decay had driven him from his sleeping alcove and forced him to flee his home. He hadn't known about his magical ability. By the time he came to his senses and returned, it was too late.

If he'd warned them, he could've saved them. But if his power hadn't flared, he would've died too. It wasn't the only time he'd avoided infection. Secretly, he'd suspected he was immune.

Hope flickered in his chest. Maybe they'd made it to the Source because they were immune. They'd fled in fear, certain no one could stop the plague. But they'd survived.

Lavender wound its way into his thoughts. The scent had led him to the Source for a reason. His power had always directed him. The lavender faded, only a memory, not a guiding scent now.

For the fifth time, Gregor evaluated himself, but nothing had changed. He stood and flexed his wings, no longer sure that hiding in a cave and waiting to die was the right solution.

Manipulators had started the first human war. They craved power. When he'd first encountered Elizabeth, she'd twisted the truth to strengthen her position as Prophet. She could tell the world whatever she wanted, and they'd believe her.

Becca believed her. But what if Elizabeth knew dragons couldn't infect humans? Then infecting him was a test to determine if she could destroy the dragons. He had to stop her.

He leapt for the sky. Action was the right course now.

"I'll meet you at Meadow Lake. You may attempt your cure." His message to Becca was brief, so she couldn't read his thoughts.

"We'll save you." Becca's faith clenched his heart. She'd try her best, and so would he.

If he was sick, then finding a cure was critical. If he wasn't, then he'd deal with Elizabeth. He believed in protecting humans, but if it came down to his coven or a human, there was no choice. Once he knew if she had the plague or was manipulating them, he'd cut her to shreds, eliminating the threat.

This time, he would save his coven.

PLAGUE QUEST
BECCA

T rey dragged Becca back through the tunnels to his room. She yanked on the britches and shirt he flung from his dresser. Running around in a blanket hadn't removed the chill from her bones. At least she wasn't tired anymore, too infuriated with Elizabeth.

Becca peeled the Nightwood leaves off her arms, but left them on her torso. At least her wounds had healed. Otherwise she'd be unable to help.

"She's gone too far this time." Trey's voice shook with his anger.

Elizabeth didn't need to use her power on Trey. She simply applied emotional pressure to his weaknesses. Just like Mama. She'd known he would try to save Gregor. And that would keep him busy while she continued with her plans.

"Why is she doing this?"

"She always wants more, more respect, more everything. It's never enough. Our community is prosperous and self-sufficient. We have the best inventions and the largest crop yield of any village. But that isn't enough." His voice cracked, and waves of frustration buffeted Becca. Her shields were useless against strong emotions.

Trey pulled a journal from the chest at the foot of his bed and handed it to her.

"The family legacy. I've memorized it. Dragon riders built Valley Keep so they could live close to the dragons and have a community dedicated to raising riders. It's all in here. But dragons became a symbol for *our* strength and beliefs. Once I met Gregor, I understood the rules. Everything in here is about independence from traditional village politics and obligations. Valley Keep was never supposed to be a power center. It was supposed to be a safe place for dragons to interact with us. I've been so blind."

An embossed dragon and rider gleamed a rich brown on the leather binding. Becca's heart leapt. This was what she'd been looking for—instructions on how people and dragons could be together. But that meant ...

"There must be a cure for the plague in here." Otherwise there was no point in building a place for riders. Dragons would have to survive.

"No. Once Gregor told me there were two plagues, I searched through every word. There's nothing at all about the plague." He dashed her tendril of hope before it could take root.

"I should've known what she planned. A week after Gregor showed up, Uncle Sid came to live with us. She pushed me to spend time with him, even though I have no interest in the healing arts. He taught Healer methodology at the university, and every conversation was about the history of illnesses. I stopped paying attention when I learned they'd kicked him out for his radical experiments."

All his frustration melted away, and Trey rested his head against hers. "He's not a Healer, Becks. How can he cure Gregor?"

She didn't have an answer, but it didn't matter. As if his anguish didn't know where to settle, he strode to the door.

"Let's go. We'll talk to Sid first, then we can search the library. We have books older than this one. There must be something we can do."

Whook en Becca and Trey burst through the door of a small sitting area, a thin man with a bald spot shining through his salt-and-pepper hair looked up. Books and papers covered the table in front of him.

His smile was genuine. Sid liked Trey. For once, she was delighted her power could tell her the truth.

"Ah. She did it, then? Caught me a dragon?" Regret tinged his eagerness.

"Why would you release an incurable disease into the world? What did she promise you?" Trey exerted his power, inviting Sid to share a secret.

"I'll prove my theory that we can cure dragons the same way Healers cure people. Elizabeth is very supportive. My colleagues at the university said I couldn't prove anything. But she assured me she could get me a dragon." He grinned slyly at Trey. "Told me you've been hiding a dragon. I didn't believe her at first. So, where is it?"

"Not until you answer me. How did she infect the dragon?"

"I don't know that she did. Not yet. I must run some tests. But I found this book filled with strange symbols. And then about a month ago, I could read it. Turns out my ancestor was a magician. Isn't that incredible? It's a fascinating story. Did you know there were two plagues?"

Sid's fascination was genuine. On the table, opened books displayed animal anatomy diagrams. One had a dragon with strange symbols scrawled in the margin. Gregor was nothing more than a test subject to prove Sid's theories.

Trey couldn't sense any of this. "Give me the cure." His energy pulsed through Becca, but Sid remained set on his course.

"I must test the dragon's blood and use my See-er-inner. Unless it's infected, I can't prove anything."

She didn't know what tool he used, but she'd seen Healers examine blood to determine which medicine to give. Sid really believed he had a cure, but he wasn't about to hand it over without proving he was right. He was a Healer. Becca knew how to deal with them.

"Where's your equipment? How long before the dragon is symptomatic?"

Sid grinned. "You've had Healer training. Good. I could use an assistant." Then he frowned. "Not long. The book said anywhere from hours to days. But I gave Elizabeth only one drop of the solution. I must document all the stages."

He ran into his bedroom. Books were stacked to the ceiling, a microscope was wedged behind a chair, and small dishes of mold and unidentifiable smears sat precariously across the headboard. Sid pointed at items, and Trey stuffed them into a stiff leather pack that hadn't been waterproofed correctly.

Sid handed her the book with the dragon drawings, Bloodstar engraved on the spine. "Hold this and don't lose it." Then he pulled a large frame from behind his bed, scattering dishes and books across the floor.

Becca bent to pick them up and discovered a black orb under the bed. Even though it was small, only half the size of her palm, it was a dragon egg. But there was no energy, no pulse of life, heavy and incomplete. Chips and cracks marred the surface, revealing veins of blue.

"Where did you get this?"

"Ah. My dragonstone. Elizabeth gave it to me. Such a generous woman. That stone is referenced frequently in my ancestor's notes. I had to chip a few pieces off to create the solution to infect the dragon, but it's still mostly intact." His pride nauseated her.

The room faded, just like the time she'd taken the first egg to the jeweler. Somehow, Elizabeth had found an egg. The room spun as she realized what must've happened. Sid had used the dead egg to create the plague.

What if that meant all eggs carried the plague? She must warn them. Becca clutched the book against her chest. But wait. The egg was a sphere, not a lump of granite. No illusion hid it.

"Where did Elizabeth get this?"

"Oh. She's had it for generations, passed down from her great-great-aunt or something. Bring it, if you want, and grab those papers from the table. I must document everything. This is so exciting. I can finally test on a live specimen."

Her breath steadied. It was an old egg. There might not be any risk. But why would an egg have the plague? She had so many questions, yet Sid seemed confident. If his cure worked, all dragons would be safe. If only it didn't feel as if there was more to Elizabeth's plan. Whatever it was, Sid didn't know about it. For now, he was their best shot at saving Gregor.

RESOLVE

SERI

DAY 48 AFTER THE LONG SLEEP

Seri flew back to Jason's Keep, missing Gregor's presence in her mind. Becca claimed there was a cure, but if he hid from everyone, he'd die, anyway. Life without him would be empty.

She shouldn't feel more for Gregor than any other dragon in the coven, but she did. She always had.

Her mentor Crysta had said connecting more deeply with certain dragons made her special. But it was one more thing that set her apart, made her less of a dragon. She'd do anything to protect her coven, but she'd do more to save Gregor, Zanthor, Garianna, and even Brin and Ronin.

A dragon never put the well-being of individuals before the coven. Even Sarcruze hadn't protected Fiona, despite their relationship. The coven came first, always.

Logic and tradition didn't matter.

Gregor shouldn't be alone. He might not even be sick. They'd slept within the Source waters for over a hundred years. All that magic seeping into their bodies might have been the only way to protect them. She couldn't believe they'd lost so much time, only to die from the plague now. There had to be a reason.

The disease spread through mind-speech. But she didn't know how long it took to infect an entire coven, or if they could protect themselves and still help Gregor. If only she could access the archive stones of the covens who'd perished. They must've recorded the progress of the disease.

She was the Oracle, but she didn't know enough about the past to help them with their future. All she could do was see magic.

It was everywhere now, the same magic that had created the plague long ago.

If she could find it and manipulate it, she could save Gregor. Not the girl and her hopeful cure. Dragons didn't need humans.

New hope gave her strength. All she had to do was convince Zanthor to let her try.

Zanthor met her on the rim of the keep. *"What happened? I can't sense Gregor."*

She explained the situation as calmly as she could, proud when her shields held. Her doubts wouldn't convince him.

"I will see the difference. I've manipulated magic to reveal the eggs at Sanctuary. Once I know which magic causes the disease, I can modify it." Seri sensed his denial. *"Or we can take him to Sanctuary. Its healing capabilities are amazing. It even healed the human girl."*

"Gregor is lost to us now. Don't ruin his sacrifice by risking yourself."

She could feel the push of his own power, but she resisted. He didn't understand. She straightened her tail and stretched out her neck, prepared to stand her ground.

"I do." His pain echoed her own. *"The plague has returned. Brought back by humans. Sarcruze was right to avoid them. I know we can trust some. This girl who discovered our eggs, for one. But humans fear us, and they'll destroy us if we're not careful."*

Seri tried to explain the humans had a cure for Gregor.

"It doesn't matter. We must protect the coven. Come to Sanctuary, where we'll be safe. Build us a shield of magic, like the mirage that protects Sanctuary and the eggs from the world. No one will ever find us."

It was a solution. Dragons could rebuild in safety. She'd have time to work with magic and create a cure. But she couldn't abandon Gregor. Trey and Becca wouldn't give up, and they might actually have a cure that would keep all dragons safe.

Zanthor was a true dragon leader who put the coven first. Feelings wouldn't get in his way. But she wasn't a proper dragon.

She couldn't turn away or hide. His power reached for her, a pulsing purple thread of conviction. But she already knew he was right. She just couldn't accept it.

So she brushed the thread of magic away. She bowed deeply, acknowledging their bond and his leadership. Then she shielded her mind from his mind-speech, from the coven, and she leapt into the sky.

Gregor would not die. The answer was in the archives of the long-dead covens. She'd search every one and learn all she could about the plague. She was done living in ignorance. Done with fear and hiding. It was time to defeat this plague.

Even though he could stop her from leaving, Zanthor didn't. Maybe he believed in her after all.

DRAGON PLAGUE
BECCA

Becca and Trey encountered John, blocking their path. "It's best to avoid the lake for now. A beast has settled. Stick close to the caravan."

Before Becca could explain, Marie ran up and placed her hand on his shoulder. "Let them through. The dragon won't harm us."

If John knew everything, he could help them. He didn't trust Elizabeth and would keep the others away.

"His name is Gregor, and he's our friend. But Elizabeth infected him, and we have to help him." Becca pointed at Sid hovering behind them with his small wagon of equipment. "This man studied healing and says he has a cure."

John uncrossed his arms and waved them through. "I hope you're right. The last thing we need is another Dragon Plague."

The worry in her chest lifted. He believed her and would keep the others away. She ran down the trail. Gregor lay on the far side of the lake, trying to emit waves of calmness. Obviously, he'd frightened someone when he landed.

"We brought a Healer and a book with the plague spell."

"Bloodstar." Gregor's growl of hatred sent shivers of unease up Becca's neck. Maybe using the sorcerer's spell wasn't such a good idea. He'd infected the dragons long ago to destroy them. Would he really create a cure?

"Yes."

At least he'd confirmed they had the right sorcerer. Gregor sniffed loudly, then his eyes whirled, injecting her with hope. *"Read it to me."*

While Sid peered at his notes and had Trey take samples of Gregor's blood, Becca read the book.

There were detailed diagrams of a dragon heart and a human heart. Strange symbols covered the pages. In the next, two dragons faced each other. The one that made Becca gulp had a tall man standing over a dead dragon covered in spirals and death symbols. She was certain this was the plague spell, but she couldn't understand it.

The book contained hundreds of spells. As she read them out, Gregor would occasionally stop her and inhale deeply before asking her to repeat it or move on. She read until she couldn't focus anymore.

The moon had crossed over the horizon, but Gregor still seemed fine. His thoughts were clear, and he'd sat quietly while Trey crawled all over him, taking measurements. He wouldn't allow Sid near him at all.

Marie brought food and water throughout the night. Finally, Becca laid her head on the table. Even though she'd read every word, she couldn't figure out how Sid planned to cure Gregor.

"Sid, how did you recreate the disease?" Something was missing. Even if Sid read the spell, he'd need to be a magician to cast it. He didn't have any power that she could see.

"Oh, I didn't, m' dear. Elizabeth said the dragonstone contained it. I simply ground up a fragment and mixed a potion for her."

An egg, even one from a hundred years ago, couldn't make someone ill.

"So, Gregor isn't even sick?" Becca clenched her fists, resisting the urge to shred Sid's papers.

She'd been fooled. Elizabeth didn't need a cure. She only had to prove that people didn't get sick. Gregor should've stayed away. Calling him back had fallen right into Elizabeth's plans.

Gregor's sneeze echoed through the valley, and his fear shot through Becca.

"Is that normal?" She didn't know if dragons sneezed.

But he didn't answer. Decaying dragons filled his mind, and an incredibly disgusting smell of rot filled her nose. She threw up her mental shields. Something was wrong. Pain shot through her fingertips when she touched his forehead. He had a fever and was hallucinating.

Gregor had the first stage of the plague.

They spent the next hour trying to get him to drink water, but he was unresponsive. His skin sloughed off in translucent flakes, like fish scales. Slowly, his spicy body odor soured. They were losing him. She tried, but she couldn't reach him inside his chaotic mind.

Meanwhile, Sid sat at his table muttering and writing on his papers.

"Do something. He's obviously sick. What are you waiting for?"

Sid frowned and wrote a number in his ledger. "These quantities don't make any sense. Creating the disease only took a flake of dragonstone, a half a decanter of activation gel, and a sprig of lilac. Then I recited these words. But the cure isn't in the book. I devised it myself." His pride at his accomplishment overrode his confusion.

There wasn't time for Sid to bask in his brilliance. He needed to make the cure.

At her glare, Sid ducked his head.

"It's all theoretical, based on the cure for slipfoot. You inject the blood from an animal that is immune into the sick animal, and their own blood replicates the immunity. They cure themselves. I proved it with mice. And you can even do it before they get sick.

Quite amazing. But the quantities involved here are bigger than I expected. I must recalculate. Wouldn't want to make a mistake."

His confidence was underwhelming. It was all a game to him. Gregor meant nothing.

Becca left, not trusting herself to give him the space and time he obviously needed. Tears ran down her cheeks. Gregor was going to die, and it was all Elizabeth's fault.

She stared into the lake for a long time trying to think of a way to help Gregor. Eventually, Trey squeezed her shoulder, and she waved helplessly at Sid.

"He doesn't know what he's doing."

Despair rolled from Trey. He'd already given up.

Sid held up the See-er-inner. "Help me. I need to measure his heart."

Hoping this meant he had a plan, she returned to his side and held the frame over Gregor's heart.

"Keep it steady." Sid scribbled something in his notes.

Becca couldn't see anything. "What does this do?"

"It's supposed to show me a picture of his heart. I found it in our storage room. The book mentions it." As if that explained everything.

His focus was all on the science, but she was certain they needed magic for any cure to work. Magic created the plague, and symbols filled the book along with words she didn't recognize. But Seri could see magic, and she'd lived during the time when people cast spells.

"Seri! Gregor needs you." Becca flung her mental shout north, hoping Seri would hear her before Gregor worsened.

A horrible wet cough convulsed Gregor's body. His eyes filled with pus. Becca scrambled back as yellow sputum spewed from his mouth.

"I'm working on it. Stop shouting. Everyone will hear you, and they'll stop me." Seri's voice sounded far away, but Becca breathed a sigh of relief.

Humans didn't know dragons, but a dragon would know what to do. But then she remembered they'd hibernated for years instead of finding a cure.

QUEST FOR A CURE

SERI

DAY 49 AFTER THE LONG SLEEP

It was still dark when Becca's anguished plea confirmed Seri's worst fear had come true.

Gregor had the plague.

After everything they'd done, the coven would perish. She'd been so sure that the Source, so pure and abundant, would counteract any human magic.

But she'd been wrong.

Instead, it had transported them to a future of isolation. The coven would be safe at Sanctuary, but it wasn't the life they deserved. Dragons should be free to roam the world.

The plague had taken so much from her. From every dragon. She wouldn't let it take Gregor too.

Dragons had never quivered in fear. They met challenges head-on and fought for their right to this world. She was tired of hiding. It was time to fight.

Understanding the magic involved with the plague was key. She needed to find out what happened after her coven slipped into the Source lake. Once she knew how the disease progressed and what other covens had tried, she would save Gregor.

The first two keeps she found were empty, destroyed by humans. She flew to a keep nestled inside a dormant volcano in the Thoran

Sea. It was isolated enough no human could've found it. Their archive stone should be intact, and the coven may have survived until the end. Jason had visited them in the early days and invited them to join their coven. But Klaw had declined, confident his coven would escape the plague.

With four powerful flaps of her wings, Seri caught the highest and fastest current to the island keep. The girl's mental reach had been long, and Zanthor may have heard. Seri had to read the archives before Zanthor exerted his force as leader to stop her. She didn't care about banishment. She'd never wanted to be the Oracle.

Stopping the plague was all that mattered. If she failed, none of them would survive.

Humans and their magic were to blame. Once she figured out how to save Gregor, she would stop humans from using magic against dragons ever again.

The jagged outline of Klaw Keep rose through the clouds. She landed in the weather-worn keep and searched for the archive. Wind howled through the tunnels, a lonely call for something lost a long time ago.

Seri shivered. Would the world mourn the loss of dragons?

Magic coalesced over some alcoves, as if memories pooled in the rock. Yellow threads drew her through the tunnels, wrapping around her as she walked, their touch a warm breath of melancholy. She'd always wondered at the human desire to plant sticks to mark their dead. Soldier crosses and rock piles had covered the fallow fields during the wars, only to be trampled in the next wave of fighting. Then new graves were planted.

This felt like one of those graves. Nothing but wisps of magic to mark the dragons' deaths, but she felt it deep in her soul.

The island missed them.

She entered the cavern containing the coven's archive stone and found bones.

The skeleton of a dragon curled around the archive, ensuring its final thoughts were etched forever.

Time had long since worn away the skeletal integrity, and it collapsed as soon as she touched them. White magic swirled and settled on the pile, sinking into the cavern floor, etching a pattern of a young female dragon about Seri's size.

The archive pulsed beneath Seri's talon, and images flooded her mind in reverse time. Surprisingly, the final memory wasn't from the female youngling.

"I am the last dragon alive." The tone of finality and loss buckled Seri's knees.

Novak was the last living dragon of his coven. He was ready to die, but he didn't have the plague.

She didn't have Gregor's power, but she could smell the sweet green scent of new grass. Novak's power had been growth. Somehow, the texture of his thought reminded her of Sanctuary.

She skimmed through the archive. His story could wait. Right now, she needed to know when the coven became infected and how it progressed. Then she'd honor the dragon by hearing his final thoughts.

Magic swirled around the archive, forming images as Seri searched.

The coven had a meeting, trying to decide if they should completely isolate themselves from the rest of the world. There'd been much debate, and Seri's heart clenched in sympathy. They'd heard of her coven. The story of their sacrifice was the chief argument for waiting out the disease. They all believed Sarcruze's coven had perished. They already knew the plague spread through mind-speech, so everyone was careful to not contact the other covens.

But Sarcruze and Fiona hadn't been the only dragons to form a special bond. Through love and friendships, the disease spread from one coven to the next. Eventually, the disease faltered.

There was a push to send a dragon to check the nearest keep for survivors. The dragon returned, inconsolable. They were all dead, and he'd barely escaped the humans who were burning the corpses, convinced dragons had caused the plague.

One cough. That's all it took.

She scrolled through meetings and debates, but that's what did it. The plague had transformed, no longer requiring mind-speech to spread. The scout's return had sealed their demise. He unknowingly carried the plague from an infected keep.

It took three days to kill them all.

Black threads wove through the magic, showing Seri the spread of the disease from one dragon to the next. Many dragons fled, certain distance would save them. Those who stayed and used mind-speech died faster. Those who kept their minds locked survived longer. But the plague still won.

The youngest dragon, fifteen-year-old Tamin, cared for all she could, trying to ease their pain. The stages of the disease built on each other. First, yellow-brown fluid that lodged in the lungs. That's when the coughing started. Then fever brain. Once the hallucinations started, no dragon could protect themselves from the broadcasted mind-speech, not even the leader. The images haunted Tamin. It had been impossible to shield herself from them.

The final stage was the wasting, as if they were consumed from the inside. Hides sucked down to the bone, shallow breathing, and eyes white with blindness. This had been the worst for Tamin. Anguished moans had echoed through the caverns.

Strands of yellow magic whooshed around Seri, filling the cavern with the moans of dying dragons. A black cloud shrouded the stone.

She clutched the archive, terrified she'd invoked the plague from the cavern walls. Her breath faltered. She gasped for the next one. Her eyes watered. And fear consumed her. She couldn't breathe.

Tamin's death was a whisper of pink. Her power had been subtle, an enhancement to her own optimistic personality. She saw hope. She gave hope. And now it was gone.

Seri wanted to flee, but her talons were fused to the stone. The Source wanted her to see the rest. After Tamin's death, the black cloud dissipated, and Seri could breathe again. The moans faded to memories.

Years passed.

And then a black dragon came. Novak, a youngling only thirteen years old, the last dragon alive. His power was growth. Seri's heart raced as she made the connection.

Novak was the dragon under the Nightwood tree in Sanctuary.

He'd explored every keep with a small band of younglings, searching for survivors. He'd found two, but they'd perished the previous year. The plague lurked in every keep. They'd been careful, using small archive stones to communicate with each other. They'd surveyed each keep from the sky. Only Novak had flown down to access the archives. To honor those who died.

His guilt was a hundred times worse than Gregor's. Somehow, he'd carried the disease to his friends. They all died of the plague. He'd done what he could to ease their suffering, but his power was fading.

Magic was fading.

He hoped the plague would end when magic disappeared. But then he wouldn't heal anymore.

His last words stole her hope. *"I'm ready to die. The plague won't kill me, unless my power fades before the magic that supports the disease fades. But a world with only one dragon is not a world I can live in. I banish myself from this cruel existence."*

His pain and loneliness were too much to bear. Novak planned to fly deep into the Dragon Mountains until he couldn't fly anymore. He must've landed at Sanctuary, and as his power diminished the Nightwood grew. The Source had saved Seri's coven, but in doing so had sealed his fate. His healing energy had lain dormant until magic returned.

Green tendrils wove through the remaining threads of black and yellow until the cavern was clear of any magic. She'd reached the end of the stone's story.

Novak had given them Sanctuary. Not a cure, but it could slow the progress. Becca claimed humans had a cure. If only Seri had the original spell, then she could manipulate magic and reverse the sorcerer's curse.

She didn't know what to do. The coven had moved to Sanctuary. Only Zanthor and Ronin had remained at Jason's Keep. If she told them Gregor was sick, Zanthor would compel her to return.

With each stroke of her wings taking her farther from Klaw Keep, Seri knew she needed to decide. She could fly to Gregor and hope the humans had a cure, or join the coven and stay safe.

There was no vision from the Source, no guidance from a scent. She had only her knowledge and her heart.

Her wings tilted, and she flew south.

Gregor shouldn't die alone.

A wisp of pink magic flew ahead. Tamin's power held the answer.

Seri would cling to hope.

PLAGUE SPELL

SERI

There were too many people around Gregor. Seri tried to hide in the clouds, but they were disappearing. She'd have to land soon, but first she needed to understand how magic was interacting with those below her.

Shifting her vision came easily now. Yellow threads of magic crawled over Gregor, winding around his head and diving into his nose. Deadly black threads, thick with intent, roved over his body. His skin was flaking, and his rasping breath filled her with dread.

He was in worse shape than she'd expected. Tamin had slowed the progress of the disease by moving those infected to the cool caverns.

"He needs shade and something to cool him down." It was still early, but soon the midday sun would be hot with so few clouds.

Becca responded immediately, without the usual pesky human questions. A festival tent was erected over Gregor, and two girls ran back and forth to the lake to fill buckets with water.

Seri linked to Becca's mind and watched as the girl poured water over Gregor, soothing him. It was invasive to enter a human mind without permission, but the girl didn't resist. Seri's presence was a relief. Becca's fears matched her own. This girl would be her talons.

Waves of energy rocked Seri, and she yanked her focus from Becca's mind, scanning the tent for any change in the plague's magic. Outside the tent, Trey and Elizabeth fought. Seri heard the argument easily with her enhanced dragon hearing, but the words weren't important.

Red magic pulsed from Elizabeth, reaching for every human by the lake. Her confidence instilled the magic with strength, making the threads more substantial. Her control would've been complete, but blue shot from Trey, destroying every strand before it touched its target.

Gregor hadn't mentioned that Trey was a Manipulator too. The humans watched the argument, unaware of the magic battle over who would control them.

Manipulators like Elizabeth had driven the wars. But Trey's magic was different. He fought to protect Gregor and the humans from his grandmother's manipulation. He wasn't trying to control anyone.

An onslaught of red threads overwhelmed Trey and struck the man standing guard over the trader caravan. Elizabeth's magic hit an invisible shield and shot into the sky.

Seri dipped below the concealing clouds, unable to believe it was possible. But it was. She plucked his name from Becca's mind. John was a Shield. A rare power. She'd only heard of one in the past, and he'd turned the war away from his town. Two Manipulators and a Shield existed in this time. These magic abilities had taken humans centuries to master, and these younglings used them with no training or knowledge of what they were doing. She couldn't see any reason for the Source to grant these powers.

The red threads retracted as Elizabeth strode to her carriage, done with battle for now. Seri could discern the weakness in her energy, like an injured cougar, perfect for a dragon feast. Trey was affected, too, though not as much; only the slight tremble in his energy gave it away. He'd won this round. Elizabeth had removed her influence from the healer and left. Seri wasn't sure if she'd given up or if she'd merely been testing the boy.

Seri landed beside the lake on the other side of a tent.

"I'm here. Do we need so many humans watching?"

Becca's hope blasted her, as strong as the coven's faith in her as the Oracle. Seri cringed. Becca would realize soon enough that Seri wasn't an all-powerful savior. Why did everyone expect this of her?

Becca spoke quietly with John, and he led the traders away, leaving Becca, Trey, and a youngling named Marie surrounded by broken threads of magic. Seri huffed. The Source was up to something.

The human responsible for infecting Gregor sat at a table inside the tent. It took all her self-control to not slice the man in two.

Becca lay her hand on Seri's head. *"Oh, thank the Healer you've come."*

The girl's hope redirected Seri's rage at the horrid human. Barely.

"How was Gregor infected?" Gathering knowledge would help her focus. At least until he was no longer of use. Killing him might stop the plague from spreading to the coven. But she needed to prevent this from ever happening again.

Images flew through her mind, clear and in chronological order. Becca didn't send like a human. But the man's claims didn't make sense. A dead egg from the time of the plague shouldn't pose a threat. The shell would've protected the hatchling from mind-speech and from contact infection. Plus, it was dead. But Novak had contracted the disease from the remains at a keep. He'd never figured out how.

"Show me." Seri followed Becca into the tent.

The dead egg was small, its black shell pitted and worn, exposing the hardened blue leather casing inside. Black magic oozed from one crack. Definitely infected.

Seri backed away. Novak had been right. The disease had changed. What if she'd already breathed it in?

The man muttered over a table strewn with papers.

"It has a cure?" She couldn't bring herself to call him by name, and only the fact the black magic clung to the egg and didn't reach for her kept her from falling apart.

Becca grimaced. *"He says so, but he's spent over a day looking at numbers and doing nothing. And Gregor's getting worse."*

Seri found the book from the table and carefully turned the pages with her talon. She didn't need to say anything. Becca's memories of her last conversations with Gregor were all she thought about.

It was the original spell.

Seri's hope that knowing the spell would show her how to change the magic withered. She'd heard the stories. How the sorcerer Bloodstar had used magic to switched Karyn's perfectly healthy heart with Jason's plague-ridden heart. Jason's brother Charlie had recounted it many times. But he hadn't fully understood what it meant, or the power involved.

Even though the Source was handing out great powers, no human could cast this spell. It must've drained Bloodstar. He'd twisted nature. The symbols writhed with magic, even now. But saying the words and using the potions wouldn't be enough.

The sorcerer's spell called on time and the cycles of water. It was more convoluted than she'd ever imagined. To reverse it, they'd need to remove Gregor's heart and replace it with a human heart. It was impossible. No one could survive without a heart. Not a human, nor a dragon. They'd both die. But even if they could do it, the hearts had to be resized to work in their new bodies.

Seri's head dipped low as the last of her hope drained. The spell couldn't help.

The Source was cruel, giving this human the power to recreate the plague from the shell of a dead egg. A few words were all it took. She could even see which ones he must've used. They weren't simple, and he shouldn't have the power, but he did. No magic clung to him now. He couldn't reverse the spell.

There had to be something she could do.

The man had a cure, but it had nothing to do with magic. He kept mumbling about blood and immunization. Something about injecting the blood of a healthy human into a diseased human to help them fight the illness. It made sense to Becca, but they would need the blood to come from a dragon with an immunity to the plague.

The Source hadn't made the coven immune, despite their long sleep. Only Novak had survived the plague, and he now rested under the Nightwood in Sanctuary. But had he really? His magic was regrowth. Even if he caught it, his magic could heal him enough to offset the symptoms.

She had no other ideas.

Becca sat beside Seri and moaned. A thread of magic connected Becca to Gregor. The girl shouldn't be so open to his mind.

"I can't get him out of my head. Horrors fill his thoughts, and an awful stench of decay." Becca's revulsion wasn't enough to give up her connection to Gregor. She feared if she pulled away, she'd lose him. But keeping her link wouldn't help, not her or Gregor.

"You need to shield yourself from his mind. But not like the shields you use for emotions. Make a thick bubble between your mind and Gregor's. You can still hear him, but you won't experience everything else." It wasn't quite how it worked with dragons, but explaining multiple minds was complicated. Humans had only three—the conscious, the subconscious, and the autonomic. But the bubble would work without Becca knowing the specifics.

Her first attempt was successful, but she didn't use magic to do it. Seri frowned. There was something unusual about the girl she couldn't quite figure out. She'd never been this close to her. Gregor believed Becca had dragon senses, but she'd scoffed at his theory. Dragons and humans couldn't interbreed. But the plague spell had exchanged human and dragon hearts.

Karyn had died from the plague, and her mind-speech to her coven had infected them and every other coven who didn't know to protect their minds. Jason had survived the transfer, and he'd found Sarcruze and Zanthor and warned them. He'd spoken to Seri before her own coven had caught the plague and perished, leaving only herself and Garianna as survivors. Jason had saved all he could by being the spokesperson for the dragons, while Sarcruze had protected all who joined his coven by exerting his power as leader to prevent cross-coven mind-speech.

She'd never thought about what happened to Jason after they left for the Source. She'd assumed he'd died young, as humans do. But what if the dragon heart in his body had changed him?

Magic had transformed the heart to fit, but it was still a dragon heart, made of dragon blood and tissue. He could've passed dragon essence to his children. Humans didn't live long, but they procreated a lot. Jason's ancestors could have dragon blood and they might be immune to the Dragon Plague.

It was a tremendous leap, but Seri felt she was on the right track. The spell was irrelevant. Sid had the right idea. They needed to give Gregor blood from someone immune to the plague.

"Becca, do you know if you're related to Jason?"

Becca frowned. *"My father was Simon Kinsley, and my grandfather was Stephen Cheval."* Her family tree flashed through her mind as she tried to remember all their names.

"Stop. That one there." Seri focused on his name, so Becca would know who she meant. But she didn't have to. The girl's thoughts poured out. Her childhood of sitting with her grandfather and begging for stories of dragons. One of her favorites had been about Jason and Zanthor on a quest to save all the dragons. She knew about Jason's Keep, and Sarcruze, and their quest to isolate themselves from the plague.

But more startling were Becca's emotions. She loved dragons with an intensity Seri didn't think possible. Even riders didn't love their dragons as much as Becca loved them all. And it was intertwined with love for her grandfather and her own sense of capabilities.

And the pieces fell into place. Gregor had been right. Becca was Jason's descendant, and she'd do anything to save the dragons. Not because of her family or the stories she grew up on. Not because of her desire to bond with a dragon. It was more. Deeper. The same drive Seri felt to understand magic. It was her identity.

Still connected to the girl, Seri sensed other emotions she recognized. Everyone in Becca's life had pushed her to be someone else. It wasn't the same as the dragons' Oracle expectations, but it felt close enough. Dragons wanted Seri to rise into something impossible. Humans wanted Becca to conform, to stifle everything that made her unique.

"Zanthor. Is he here with you? Are you all at Jason's Keep? Was it all true?" Becca's hope whispered through Seri, clenching her own heart in sympathy for the youngling.

"Yes." It was enough. Becca's joy made her glow.

"And I think your blood might be the cure Sid is looking for. Jason had a dragon's heart, and it's possible you have dragon blood." She didn't want to rush Becca, but Gregor's breathing was deteriorating. Low rasps followed by periods of long silence. He wasn't getting the air he needed. Seri couldn't save him, but Sid's cure might work with Becca's help.

"I don't think it works that way, but I'm willing to try."

"Why don't you think it will work?"

Becca sighed. *"Healers use blood transfusions as a last resort. The blood must be compatible, the same type or something. I was young when my father tried it with a wee one in our village. He thought the mother's blood would help, but instead, they both died. My father said it was because their blood couldn't combine."*

Worry drilled a hole in Seri's gut. They had to try. If it failed, she could take Gregor to Sanctuary. But she couldn't carry him by herself. And Zanthor wouldn't risk the entire coven to save one dragon, no matter how much he cared for Gregor.

Dragon Blood

BECCA

Becca's heart pounded in her ears. Speaking with Seri made everything so clear. It was like she experienced her logic.

"Dr. Sid, I have what you need. I have dragon blood."

Shock. Excitement. Sid's reaction she'd expected, but Trey was terrified.

"No. How? Not you." Denial and fear garbled his question.

"During the spell, the sorcerer exchanged a dragon heart with a human heart. We've been focusing on the dragons. But the boy survived the plague because he had a dragon heart. Jason was my great-great-great … I don't know how many greats-grandfather. Seri thinks I could have some of that dragon essence in me."

"That's impossible. There's no way you have dragon blood." Trey's relief was overwhelming. He didn't want her to be a part of Sid's experiment.

But this might be the only way to save Gregor.

"Think about it. I have more than the ability to sense emotions. We don't know much about magic, but everyone we know, including you, only has one power."

"Sensing emotions probably makes it *seem* like you can hear and see better than average." He didn't believe her. When she'd told him that the rocks were actually eggs, he'd supported her. But this, when it mattered more than anything, he refused to see.

"It's more than that. I can feel the energy of life around me and identify it. Mind-speech comes easily to me, as natural as breathing. Even my sense of smell is strong. Gregor said I had dragon senses. It makes sense now."

Trey shook his head, and she sensed it was more than not believing her. She grabbed his hand so she could figure out what was going on. "You don't have to believe, but we have to try, or Gregor will die."

She felt his energy gather. He was going to influence her. Her heart sank. He wanted to control her for her own good, just like everyone else.

But he didn't. His energy pulsed against Sid. "Keep her alive."

Sid twitched and responded with abundant enthusiasm. "Of course. I have no intention of killing the girl."

Becca felt the wave of influence as a breeze against her face, and she realized he couldn't manipulate her. She knew when he exerted it, and she'd resisted Elizabeth easily. It didn't make sense, unless it was another dragon ability.

"No. I saw it. You sense their emotions the same way I do. It's not magic. But when Trey used his power, the energy wrapped around but didn't reach you. I could see it. A shield composed of hundreds of threads of clear magic protected you. It's there now. Your magic isn't sensing emotions. It's seeing the truth. Seeing through illusions and falseness." There was awe in Seri's voice.

Becca didn't know what to do with the feelings bubbling through her. Amazement, acceptance, and pride. Her magic was truth. Everything else, especially sensing emotions, came from her dragon blood. It felt right, and everything she'd gone through meant she wasn't cursed. She could control it, now that she understood.

"Is that why I can see the eggs?"

"Yes. You see through the illusion. You will probably be able to do more as you grow into your power. But for now, you can save Gregor. You see it." Seri's faith in Becca's ability was overwhelming. What if she was wrong, and it didn't work?

Trey grabbed her arm as she went to lie down on a cot that Sid had moved next to Gregor. "Don't do this. You don't have to do anything you don't want to do. Ever."

She knew that. She wasn't doing it to please anyone. She wanted to help Gregor, but it was more than that. Becca had loved dragons all her life, and now she knew why. Her ancestor had helped them survive. Jason didn't have to. He could've gone on living his life and left the dragons to their fate. Just like she could leave too.

But this was something she wanted to do for herself. Because she could. No one was forcing her. No one even expected it of her. Not even Seri. This was her choice.

"I know." She didn't owe him or anyone else an explanation, but he needed to accept her decision.

"If you change your mind or feel dizzy, I'll stop him." His concern made her strong. Even though this whole effort was to save Gregor, his entire focus was on her well-being. He would move mountains to keep her safe. But not because he thought she couldn't do it on her own. Because he loved her.

"I'll be fine. But you should monitor Sid. He's not a Healer. And he's so focused on his research and numbers, I don't trust he'd notice if anything went wrong."

Trey strode to the table, covered in calculations. "Exactly how much of her blood do you need?"

Marie scurried to Becca's side. "I'll watch her."

"I'll watch too." Seri's soothing mint flooded Becca's mind, and she knew Seri felt the same way about Gregor. Becca hadn't thought about dragons falling in love, but they were intelligent beings. Of course they would.

Seri's snort was part denial and part sadness. *"It's frowned upon. But it happens."* An image of a giant dragon and a smaller dragon avoiding each other flashed through Becca's head. Sarcruze and Fiona. They were alive too.

But her amazement was short-lived. The two dragons from Grandfa's story weren't together. Something drastic must've torn them apart.

Seri sighed. *"It's best to not form those attachments. So stop thinking about me and Gregor like that. We're family."*

Becca snorted. Love didn't obey rules.

After a lot of grunting and working out logistics, Sid inserted a needle into Becca's arm and attached a long tube to it. He did the same to Gregor. The tube looked minuscule poking from him. And there was a discussion on whether the large needle had reached a vein.

Marie swayed, gripping Becca's hand tightly, lost in one of her visions. Fortunately, it didn't last long, but the rush of sadness from Marie was disturbing.

"What was it?" Becca kept her voice low. Sid was too much under Elizabeth's control, and they didn't want him passing on information.

"Pain and loss are necessary. You must be strong." Her cryptic words didn't offer any comfort. If Marie knew what Becca should do, she had to tell her.

But Marie clamped her lips shut and shook her head. A tear rolled down her cheek, and she squeezed Becca's hand.

Sid bustled up, muttering to himself, and turned a lever on the tubing. Then he pulled on a syringe through the lever, and pain shot through Becca's arm.

Red, life-giving blood slowly wound its way through the tube to the needle stuck in Gregor. Minutes stretched and blurred together. The room swayed and lights burst behind her eyelids.

Marie murmured in her ear, "Are you all right?"

Becca didn't want to nod, certain she'd throw up. She didn't get motion sick, not even on a dragon. This had nothing to do with motion.

"Doesn't he have enough blood yet?" Even her voice faltered.

Marie left.

Everything sounded far away. The only thing she could hear clearly was Gregor's labored breathing. Her own breathing slowed to match, and she forgot about her protective bubble.

A maelstrom of clouds spun through her. Colors collided and burst. Scents vied for dominance. Lilac, nightberry, nutmeg, kelp, and rot. She landed in a lake of black water covered in rainbow ripples. Dragons struggled above, tossed this way and that by a malevolent tornado. A volcano blew up in the distance with a loud boom, and the wind screamed all around her, words torn apart before she could recognize them. Black water rushed into her throat and filled her lungs.

She was trapped in Gregor's fever brain with no way out.

DRAGON LOVE

SERI

As soon as she lost her connection to Becca, Seri sent a frantic command to Trey. *"Something's wrong. Check on her, boy."*

A sharp pain shot through his head, and she winced. But they didn't have time for finesse. She couldn't see what was happening inside the tent through his eyes. Without Becca's organized mind, she was blind.

After an agonizing wait, he answered. *"She's unconscious."*

He yelled at Sid. "We have to stop. She can't give any more blood."

"Not yet. The dragon needs more."

"Just look at the size of her. How much blood do you need? And how will you know if it worked?"

Sid didn't have an answer. Seri could see it in his mind. He thought they needed more than Becca could give, but he didn't want to alarm Trey.

Waiting outside wasn't working anymore. She had to see what magic was doing. With a single swipe, she ripped through the flimsy fabric and bent low to step inside. It didn't matter if she caught the plague, or that she'd never speak to Zanthor or her coven again.

The procedure looked like a grotesque human ceremony. Blood flowed through a tube from the girl to Gregor. Becca lay on a cot, white and listless, her energy almost depleted. She couldn't give any more blood without losing her own life force.

Seri spoke to Sid, not caring if she hurt his mind. *"Test him now."*

Sid yelped, but he ran to a large frame on wheels and fiddled with it. An image of Gregor's heart appeared, pumping Becca's blood through his veins. Black threads of magic wound around his heart, trying to get in. With every beat they squeezed, preventing the next beat from being as strong. A yellow haze spread from his heart, along his veins, and beyond the frame, shrouding his body.

She didn't know how long he could keep fighting. Seri turned her attention to the girl. She was weak, much weaker than should be possible, yet she still held on. The clear threads of magic surrounding her didn't flow in the blood leaving her body. No magic did.

They'd been wrong, or Becca's blood wasn't the right blood. Either way, they'd failed. Seri's tail drooped and her wings scraped the ground. It had all been for nothing.

Gregor would die. There was no cure. And now she'd be the next test subject. She wished she could warn Zanthor, but she couldn't. The coven would go on without her and Gregor. They would isolate themselves and live in Sanctuary. The humans had won.

"Stop the procedure. It's not working, and Becca will die." She sent her message to Trey as gently as she could. The boy wanted to help. He didn't need a headache for his efforts, and she knew he'd save Becca, at least.

She barely noticed as they removed the needle and tube from Gregor. She leaned against his hot skin and watched his scales flake in the cool tent.

So this was the end.

She felt Trey's power when he sent Sid away. It was stronger than Elizabeth's. His blue strands of magic were thicker, as if he'd accepted his magic. That was good. He might change Valley Keep for the better. If he could stand up to his grandmother.

Becca stirred. *"Did it work?"* She was too weak to speak to the others, but mind-speech required no effort.

"No. Your blood wasn't enough." Seri hated disappointing the girl. She'd given the dragons so much. But there was no avoiding the truth. Becca would see it, anyway. Her magic was truth.

The tent was quiet after Marie, Sid, and Trey left.

Seri reached out a talon for Becca to grasp as she slipped off the cot. Tears ran down Becca's face. But this wasn't the end for her. Zanthor may contact Becca to find the rest of the eggs. Their future depended on keeping all dragonkind away from humans.

It didn't matter. She wouldn't be around to see what happened.

Seri opened her mind completely, dropping all pretense. *"I'm here, dear heart."* She couldn't let him die alone, cut off from the coven he'd tried so hard to save.

His mind was chaos, but she recognized his vision from the Source. A rainbow of magic threads floating on the surface of the black waters. But his focus wasn't on the lake, or the coven trapped in a vortex of wind above it.

Gregor strained to reach the figure on the shore. The girl with a head of fire. Becca.

But it wasn't a normal fire. Threads of red, yellow, and orange magic danced with her hair. A blue strand spiraled around her body, forming a tube. It stretched from Becca's heart toward Gregor, but it couldn't get through the magical flames.

Seri pulled her mind from Gregor's and discovered Becca had nestled herself against her chest, her hand over Gregor's heart. Tears streamed down Becca's face.

"Don't die. I love you. Please don't die." All the pain, the yearning, the passion for the dragons from her grandfather's stories filled Becca's soul.

Strands of crimson, gold, and orange poured from her mind, and a deep blue thread of magic stretched from her chest. The strands combined and swirled around her arm, to her fingers, and dove into Gregor's heart.

Love, manifested as pure magic, flowed through his veins.

Becca was the truth. Seri could see it now.

Love was the magic that could burn the disease away. The plague was created out of war and hate, fear and desperation. Only love and acceptance, hope and joy, could undo it. The spell and Becca's blood weren't enough. Seri knew what they needed.

She curled around Becca, sharing her own love for Gregor, adding it to the magic flowing to him. She drew the strands between Gregor and the coven and wove them into her own strands. Magic connected them all. Not out of duty or obligation. Everyone in the coven loved each other. She pulled on the strands of magic flowing from Gregor to Trey. He loved the boy too.

She wove them together and wrapped them around Becca's steady connection.

Love pulsed along her creation.

The yellow magic swirled and joined the other strands, no longer consuming. Supporting.

The black strands resisted, but they weren't malevolent. They were merely magic that had been distorted, abused. She pulled each black strand off Gregor's chest and looped it into the other colors. Magic needed to be whole, not torn apart and twisted.

Slowly, Gregor's breathing cleared. Magic flowed from his lungs, his heart, and his head, to the rest of his body.

They'd done it. A dragon and a human had cured Gregor.

The room tilted, and Seri's ability to see the magic faded. Becca collapsed against her chest, and Seri's head fell into the crook of Gregor's shoulder.

She hoped it was enough.

BATTLE
GREGOR

No matter what he tried, Gregor couldn't escape this time. Once again, he was trapped in the Source, but the visions were terrifying. There was no getting away from them.

Suddenly, he felt Seri's presence.

She shouldn't be there, but he ached for her. He wasn't alone anymore. Once he found her light, he wrapped himself around her energy as it pulsed despair and love.

Clinging to her brought forth all his suppressed feelings. He didn't have to hide them. Not here. She was amazing. Her doubt was endearing and frustrating. She could do so much with her power and could do more if she only embraced it. Losing her was unbearable.

But he couldn't tell her. He couldn't speak. All he could do was cling to her energy and hope she knew how he felt.

Gregor sucked in a deep breath. He was ready, now, to face his demise like a dragon. With dignity and purpose. It was his choice. And then he took another breath.

A clear breath without the phlegm rattling in his throat. Hope shot through him.

He could fight this.

He didn't know how. There was nothing physical to fight inside the Source. But it wasn't his certainty that pulsed through his veins. It was Becca's.

Light surrounded him, and love filled his heart. More than he'd ever felt in his life. The light pushed the water away, and he inhaled again, feeling better from the inside out. Becca and Seri were both with him. They wanted him to fight. To live.

The ever-present scent of rot lifted, giving him relief, and a hint of lilac drifted past. He followed it. Lilac had led him to the Source. Maybe it would lead him to the center of this vision.

Horrific scenes tried to distract him from his path. His first coven writhing in pain as the fever consumed them. Dragons shedding scales, exposing their flesh, and falling through black waters, everyone he knew covered in yellow and black flames.

He followed his nose, even though it led him to a flame hotter than an erupting volcano. At the center of the flame stood Becca, tears streaming down her face. She was crying, for him. The white flame reached for him, pulsing with energy. It came from her chest.

What type of beast was she?

As if his question required an answer, she transformed. Scales covered her skin, tiny and translucent. The scales of a hatchling, barely discernible against her hide. And the flames changed into a white light that enfolded Gregor, pulling him closer.

He stood on a mountaintop, next to a shifting dragon girl. She wasn't a dragon, but she wasn't wholly human either.

And love surrounded him.

Seri appeared behind the girl, twisting Becca's magic around her talons and pulling black threads from him.

He wanted to cry out. To stop her. But his own power overwhelmed him.

Lilac, nutmeg, rotting kelp, and nightberry traveled up his nostrils and flooded his mind until he couldn't sense anything else.

Time passed. He didn't know how much, but the scents, the vision, and his friends disappeared.

Each breath felt clearer as he became aware of his surroundings. He was in a tent with Seri and Becca nestled against him. He could sleep.

The plague had been defeated. For now.

DAY 50 AFTER THE LONG SLEEP

The tent was quiet. Gregor opened his eyes, unsure how much time had passed. Seri and Becca still lay next to him, and Trey was outside. The boy had changed. There was strength in his mind.

Becca and Seri both slept, which was disturbing. It would take a lot to exhaust a dragon enough to sleep unprotected.

He shifted and nudged Seri's shoulder. *"Wake. The plague is gone."* He couldn't help the reverence in his whisper. She'd saved him. Somehow.

Seri stretched her wings and clasped his talons. *"I know. We healed magic."* Her cryptic response didn't matter. He'd find out the details later.

They had to return to the coven. Pine filled his nose, sharp and pungent. His legs wobbled as he stood.

"You should rest before we fly." Seri's concern sent a glow of something new through his chest. Her energy had shifted. Her emotions felt almost human, like Becca's love.

The girl still slept, curled into a ball at Seri's feet.

Nutmeg wound through the overwhelming scent of pine. *"We must go. It's not safe here. And collect the girl. I'm not strong enough."* Admitting weakness wasn't a dragon trait, but he didn't want to drop her. So Seri must do it.

"What? We can't take her to the coven. It will be difficult enough convincing them you're cured. There's no way they'd permit us to return with a human."

"She's not."

"Gregor. You're not making any sense. Sleep will clear the last of the magic from your thoughts." Her mind filled with images of his vision. She'd been there with him.

That she'd taken such risk filled him with terror and awe.

Dragon communication was so efficient. He knew everything that had happened during his illness and how difficult it had been for her. They were connected on a level much deeper than before. He could feel her inside his private mind. She knew what Becca was. They had to protect her from Elizabeth's influence.

He trusted his power. They had to show the coven that he was cured, and they had to bring Becca with them. But there was no way he could fly to Sanctuary. He was too weak.

The coven must come to him.

"We're flying to Jason's Keep. I'll rest while you go to Sanctuary and convince Zanthor to come." Gregor yearned for the healing energy of Sanctuary to give him back his vigor, but Seri couldn't support him.

Seri heard all his thoughts. He was too tired to keep them from her.

"I'll try." She cradled the exhausted girl in her talons and strode from the tent.

Gregor followed. They both departed as Trey ran toward them.

"Don't worry. I'll keep her safe. I promise you'll see her again." He hoped his words were true. He felt Trey's determination to recover Becca at any cost.

Dragon Girl

Becca

Gregor's voice rumbled in Becca's mind. He wasn't sick anymore. Relief opened her eyes briefly, but she was too tired to respond. Seri cradled her in her dragon hands as if she were a baby. Ironic, since dragons didn't carry hatchlings. Becca drifted in and out of consciousness during their journey. Oddly, she wasn't cold.

"I'm using magic." Becca wasn't sure what Seri meant, but she appreciated the warmth.

They landed in a hollow at the top of a mountain. The ice-covered edges protected Becca from the freezing wind. Jason's Keep wasn't how she'd imagined from Grandfa's stories. Dragons didn't need blankets or bedding or even cooking fires. It should've looked barren, but she sensed it was a home.

Seri sent her to the hot pools inside a cavern to keep warm. Hot, moist air flowed down her throat, easing the ache in her chest. She took off her clothing and slid into the healing waters, groaning as the heat and sulfur worked its magic on her body.

"Try to regain your strength." There was uncertainty in Gregor's voice. He'd brought her here because of her dragon blood. But her blood hadn't cured him. Seri had. With magic.

Gregor's denial was an image of Becca with translucent scales and wings.

She laughed weakly. The dragon blood enhanced her human senses. That she could believe, but there was no way she was a dragon. She was just a girl who'd dreamed of dragons her entire life.

"As much as I would love that, I'm not part dragon. You had fever brain. None of what you saw was real. I'm just a girl." His insistence hurt a little. She'd felt his acceptance of her from their mental connection. But it turned out he wanted her to be someone more. Just like everyone else.

She was the one who saw the truth. That was her magical power. And truth always hurt.

GREGOR

Exhaustion pulled at Gregor. Liquid rattled in his lungs, even though his head and snout were clear. Dragons didn't get sick, so he didn't know how long it would take for the symptoms to disappear.

Becca thought he was healing incredibly quickly. She kept checking on him, despite her own weakness. This concerned him more.

She'd given him so much energy, more than any human could hold. It defied physics.

He wanted to take her to Sanctuary where she could recover faster. She'd fallen asleep six times since they landed at Jason's Keep. If he hadn't been watching her, she would've drowned in the deep bathing pools.

But she wasn't concerned, and neither was Seri.

Once Becca got dressed, Gregor curled around her in a sleeping alcove next to the hot springs. Jason's Keep was too cold for humans. Her mind fogged as she drifted into a light slumber.

"This can't be normal." He hoped Seri knew if Becca would improve.

She sighed. *"Nothing about any of this is normal. But humans sleep to heal. Somehow, in curing you, she took on the fatigue of a human recovering from illness. The Source used her as a vessel to finish the cure. I don't know how that much magic affects humans. But her mind is clear and strong, and there are no signs of the plague around either of you."*

Gregor coughed, easing the rasp in his lungs.

"What about this residue?"

Seri strode into the cavern and the late-afternoon light reflected off the water, making her turquoise hide glimmer. *"Do you feel sick?"*

He shook his head.

"Well then, it will work its way out of your lungs, and you'll be fine."

He felt her own desperation for her words to be true.

"Maybe we shouldn't risk the coven yet." He'd been so sure, but now he couldn't smell anything.

"You don't have the plague. If you don't believe it, we'll never convince the coven." Seri stomped out. A burst of cold air indicated she'd departed for Sanctuary.

Her annoyance confused him. He sighed, too tired to figure out what he'd done this time. She should be happy. Becca had been the key to their survival. He'd been right to follow his power. Without Becca, Seri wouldn't have found a cure.

As he waited for her return, he searched through Becca's mind. She differed from other humans. It was obvious now. Her blood, her magic, and something else had cured him.

But what if Elizabeth used the egg again? Seri had cured the magic, but the egg still contained the plague.

"No. That won't happen again. Trey's hidden the egg." Anger at Elizabeth flowed through Becca's voice.

He'd thought she was sleeping, but each time she closed her eyes, her rest was shorter. She was getting stronger.

"Good. Seri healed the magic that created the plague, but we don't know if that egg could still infect us."

Becca leaned her head into Gregor's chest. She was so tiny, but she felt as intelligent as a dragon. *"If magic caused the plague in the egg to infect you, do you think pieces of dead eggs could infect humans?"*

He hadn't thought about the human side at all. *"The human plague didn't need magic to exist. I'm sure old eggs couldn't harm you, otherwise you'd be sick now."* He wasn't sure, but he wanted to reassure her.

Becca sighed. *"I hope so. Almost everyone I know has a dragonstone. At some point Healers collected dead eggs and cut them into disks. People wear them to ward off disease. I left my family, but I don't want them to die."*

Of course, humans would covet the colorful, hardened eggs. They'd adorned themselves with rocks. Gregor shrugged, and she shifted into the crook of his shoulder. He hoped her strength returned soon. If the coven allowed them to go to Sanctuary, her weakness wouldn't impress them. They needed to see her strength and passion. She was worthy.

They both dozed until Seri's voice woke him. *"We're coming. Get Becca ready."*

He'd barely pushed Becca upright and pulled her from the cavern before Zanthor, Brin, Ronin, Drekan, and Seri landed.

Gregor stood tall, his tail straight, his wings held away from his body. Becca stood beside him, and he felt her determination to appear strong too.

The other dragons conferred. He sensed the conversation but couldn't hear it.

Becca gasped, and he realized she could hear them. He dove into her mind and grasped the connection he craved.

The dragons combined their powers to scan them.

"See? There's nothing. His magic is clear." Seri kept her shields tight, transmitting confidence.

Ronin's energy shifted. *"He has congestion in his lung, but no more than when a youngling inhales water. It's clear."*

Brin's hum vibrated through Gregor's head. *"No fever brain. He hears us. How is that possible?"*

Their evaluations reassured him, but he needed Zanthor's approval.

Zanthor's focus was elsewhere. *"Step forward, girl."* His command was gentle. He'd dealt with humans far more than Gregor had.

Becca walked up to Zanthor and stopped a few feet from him. She wasn't afraid. Awe and joy radiated from her like a beacon.

"Hello, Zanthor." Her voice was clear as she broadcast to all of them. *"I've dreamed of meeting you."* And all the longing and sadness of her sixteen years poured into the words.

"Who are you?" Zanthor didn't expect an answer. The youngling wouldn't comprehend the impossibility behind his question. Or maybe she did. But not from a dragon perspective.

"I told you—"

Zanthor cut off Seri's words. *"She's connected to our coven. Not the same as the other dragons, but I feel it."* Bemusement was an unusual emotion for Zanthor.

Gregor held his breath. The coven couldn't handle more change.

"Told you she was special." Ronin's drawl broke the tension.

And between one breath and the next, Gregor was connected to the coven again. Their joy at his recovery restored his strength.

The dragons circled Becca, and wonder emanated from her. She wasn't afraid. She recognized them all from the stories she loved.

Gregor felt the shift a moment before Zanthor's acceptance sealed their coven bond with her.

Zanthor bowed. *"Thank you for saving Gregor and for your part in healing the magic that distorted the plague. We are honored."*

One by one, the dragons bowed, forming a circle around Becca and accepting her into the coven. Gregor was the last, but his bow was the deepest. He owed his life to this girl.

His thought triggered the others, and they said it together. *"Dragon girl."*

BECCA

B ecca felt as if she could float. Marie's vision had come true.

Nathan's taunt meant something completely different now. Dragon blood flowed through her, granting her dragon senses. The coven accepted her.

Soon, she'd return to Valley Keep, to Trey. They would deal with Elizabeth. Dragon riders had built Valley Keep to support their relationship with dragons, not as a place of worship. People couldn't live with dragons. They needed their own place, just like dragons needed Sanctuary.

Gregor would finish healing, and they would fly again. There were more eggs to rescue. And soon, her tiny dragon would hatch, and they would grow together. She would finally become a dragon rider, a hero in the sky.

For now, she basked in her true identity. One that didn't require her to change.

She was a dragon girl.

Thank you for reading Dreams of a Dragon Girl.

If you enjoyed this book please leave a review wherever you purchased the book or on Goodreads to help others discover this series.

To hear about the writing process, get sneak peeks into upcoming books, and read excerpts, sign up for my newsletter at https://www.bonniejacoby.com/subscribe/

For more information about other books in the series visit my website at https://www.bonniejacoby.com/books/

ACKNOWLEDGMENTS

When I started writing this story, I was alone with my characters and their world. But now I have a whole community of people to encourage me through the process.

Thank you Leslie Wibberley for reading every version of this story and being my cheerleader. Thank you Eileen Cook, my mentor and doubt monster slayer. You've believed in me when I struggled to believe in myself.

Many people supported me on my journey. Vale Amando, who read the earliest version. Jennifer Sommersby, my marvelous editor and friend. The members of The Creative Academy for Writers, especially Crystal Hunt, Jacqui Meyer Paul, Lisa Voisin, and Donna Barker, for all the support, resources, and friendship along the way. The members of the Ubergroup in Scribophile for feedback in the early days when I had so much to learn. My family, for listening to my struggles (despite the eye-rolls).

And thanks to my first super fan, Lori Hodgson, for loving my characters when I needed it most.